Ane radhas a'leguim oicheamna;
ainsagimn deo teuiccimn

WHITEMANTLE

Robert Carter was born exactly five hundred years after the first battle of the Wars of the Roses. He was brought up in the Midlands and later on the shores of the Irish Sea where his forebears hail from. He was variously educated in Britain, Australia and the United States, then worked for some years in the Middle East and remote parts of Africa. He travelled widely in the East before joining the BBC in London in 1982. His interests have included astronomy, pole-arm fighting, canals, collecting armour, steam engines, composing music and enjoying the English countryside, and he has always maintained a keen interest in history. Today he lives in a 'village' that only sounds rural - Shepherd's Bush.

Visit Robert Carter's website at:
www.languageofstones.com

By Robert Carter

The Language of Stones
The Giants' Dance
Whitemantle

WHITEMANTLE

BOOK THREE OF
THE LANGUAGE OF STONES

ROBERT CARTER

HARPER

This novel is entirely a work of fiction.
The names, characters and incidents portrayed in it are
the work of the author's imagination. Any resemblance to
actual persons, living or dead, events or localities is
entirely coincidental.

Harper
An imprint of HarperCollins*Publishers*
77–85 Fulham Palace Road,
Hammersmith, London W6 8JB

www.harpercollins.co.uk

This paperback edition 2006
1

First published in Great Britain by HarperCollins*Publishers* 2006

A catalogue record for this book
is available from the British Library

ISBN-13 978 0 00 716927 6
ISBN-10 0 00 716927 2

Typeset in Plantin Light by Palimpsest Book Production Limited,
Grangemouth, Stirlingshire

Printed and bound in Great Britain by
Clays Limited, St Ives plc

For Andrew Ritchie – the Brompton man –
who gave me back my fitness.

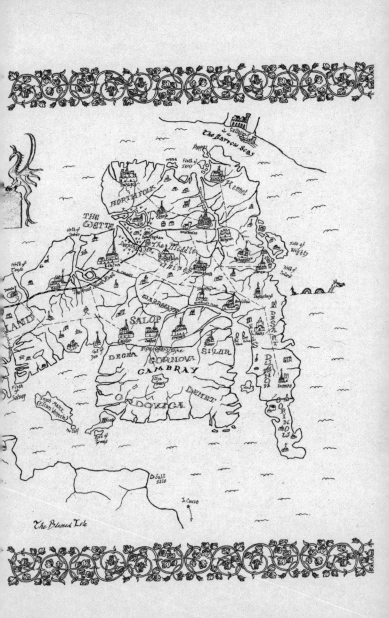

CONTENTS

PART THREE: ON THE SEVENTH DAY

PART FOUR: THE END OF ALL THINGS

(N.B. In the novels of the 'Stones' cycle there is never a chapter thirteen)

'I think we ought to have as great a regard
for religion as we can, in order to keep
it out of as many things as possible.'

Sean O'Casey
The Plough and the Stars

PROLOGUE

THE STORY SO FAR

Whitemantle is the third novel in the Language of Stones cycle. The first two, called *The Language of Stones*, and *The Giants' Dance*, recount the story of Willand, an ordinary boy who stands on the threshold of manhood. On the day that Will turns thirteen, the wizard Gwydion takes him away from home and explains certain extraordinary prophecies that concern the third and final coming of an ancient hero-king called Arthur. Gwydion suggests that Will himself is that predicted incarnation, but Will does not want to believe it.

However, as Will's adventures progress dark forces are seen to be at work, chiefly embodied in the person of Maskull, a ruthless sorcerer and Gwydion's arch-enemy, and the Sightless Ones, a sinister order of tax collectors who squeeze the common people and try to persuade them to believe in the mind-enslaving 'Great Lie'. Gwydion is at pains to hide Will's true identity from the world, and so the boy is lodged in secret, first with the fearsome hog-headed Lord Strange, then with the family of Duke Richard of Ebor, where he is educated in lordly ways. Will also comes to learn 'the redes' – the rules that govern magic – and he meets a girl named Willow who becomes his friend.

He is also befriended by the House of Ebor's venerable herbalist, Wortmaster Gort, and he stands up to Edward, the Duke of Ebor's wilful heir, eventually winning his respect.

But while Will is learning, the Realm is slipping into war, for the present king is descended from a usurper, and there are many who believe he is not the *rightful* king. In fact, King Hal is being controlled by his beautiful but greedy queen, Mag, and her violent ally, Duke Edgar of Mells. Set against their party is the House of Ebor and its allies, who believe that Duke Richard must be recognized as sovereign. Duke Richard himself is content to wait until the sickly Hal dies, for the latter has no heir, but when the queen falls unexpectedly pregnant, rumours begin to circulate that the child has been fathered by the Duke of Mells as part of a scheme to keep Richard from his just deserts. The gauntlet of conflict is thrown down.

Meanwhile Will, who is now fifteen, has begun to see that, whatever dukes and earls may think, the world is actually maintained by magic, and the *real* reason the Realm is sliding into war is a magical one. Gwydion tells him of something called 'the lorc', an ancient network of nine 'ligns', or earth streams, extending throughout the Isles, which carries power to an array of standing stones. Each of these 'battlestones' contains great harm and has the power, when awoken, to draw men to battle. Gwydion also explains that he and Maskull are the last remaining members of a wizardly council of nine whose task it once was to direct the progress of the world along the true path. But as Age succeeded Age and magic gradually left the world their numbers shrank, until there are now only two wizards left. At last, Maskull has revealed himself as 'the betrayer'. He has turned to sorcery and is now directing the future along a path of his own choosing – but it is a path that will lead to a final Age of slavery and war.

Will and Gwydion set out to thwart Maskull by finding and uprooting the deadly battlestones. Will shows an extraordinary sensitivity to the lorc, and after many heroic struggles he locates the controlling 'Doomstone' in the town of Verlamion. There a bloody battle is halted when Will uses a talisman, a green stone fish he has had since birth, to crack the stone, while Gwydion fights a magical duel against Maskull. When Will confronts Maskull the sorcerer tells him, 'I made you, I can unmake you just as easily,' but then disappears as Gwydion lands a vanishing spell on him and transports him down into the Realm Below. In the end, the king and Duke Richard are reconciled. Will is rewarded and returns home with the greatest prize of all – Willow. But his origins, and his ultimate destiny, remain shrouded in mystery.

The second novel, *The Giants' Dance*, takes up the tale more than four years later. Will and Willow are now nineteen and living at Nether Norton, Will's home village, with their baby daughter, Bethe. One summer's night Will sees the skies begin to blaze with a lurid purple light. Immediately he summons the wizard.

Will has recognized the purple light as that of Maskull's magic, and when they investigate they find the village of Little Slaughter has been smashed to powder. In the ruins Will finds a little fish carved in red stone, the counterpart to his own talisman. Gwydion says that Maskull, who has escaped from the Realm Below, has directed a shooting star down onto the village. He asks for Will's help once again.

Soon they meet with loremaster Morann who reports a rumour that the Doomstone Will once cracked has now repaired itself. But as they struggle to discover the where-abouts of the other battlestones and so hold back the tides of war, Will becomes the target of a killer, and realizes that Willow and Bethe have been brought into jeopardy also. After the battle they have all been dreading takes place at Blow Heath, Will finds himself in Ludford Castle, where Willow brings him his green talisman. Meanwhile, the political situation has continued to bend to the lorc. Edgar, Duke of Mells, who died at Verlamion, has passed his title to his son, Henry. The latter now schemes with Queen Mag to end the agreement that saw King Hal rule with the Duke of Ebor as his 'Lord Protector'. While the queen's forces besiege Duke Richard at Ludford, Will becomes greatly affected by the lorc. He tries to find the battlestone that is located there, but is afflicted by madness, and a second attempt is made on his life by the dark-robed assassin who visited him once before. When Will admits to Gwydion that the red fish talisman he found at Little Slaughter has gone, the wizard says that the village was destroyed because Will's would-be killer once lived there. He is called Chlu, 'the Dark Child', and the village was obliterated to make Gwydion believe Chlu was no more, whereas in reality he had become Maskull's agent.

Will tries to understand the significance of Chlu and what he desires, but answers concerning him are few. Now Ludford is overrun and the Ebor forces flee over the seas. Gwydion magically disguises both Will and Willow so that they may masquerade as an emissary of the Blessed Isle and his wife. They attach themselves to the royal court, but they are ensnared by the wiles of Lord Dudlea who wants Will to arrange the murder of Richard of Ebor before he too can return into the Realm. Maskull is behind this demand and when his plan fails he punishes Lord Dudlea by turning his wife and son to stone.

Nothing is seen of Gwydion for many months and Will fears for him. Then news comes that an army loyal to the House of Ebor, and commanded by Edward, Duke Richard's heir, has landed and is marching north. As *The Giants' Dance* reaches its conclusion, Will battles Chlu face to face and drives him off from one of the battlestones, but in doing so he loses his main weapon against the battlestones – the red and green fish talismans fuse together and become a real, live fish, which escapes. However, there is better news when Will finds that Gwydion is being held in the queen's dungeon at Delamprey. He works hard to free him, and also to redeem himself by thwarting the battlestone that lies buried there. He discovers that one reason Maskull has been so keen to see the war proceed is because he knows a way to tap malign power from the battlestones and use it for his own ends. He has even employed some of this power to make sorcerous manacles which have impaired Gwydion's ability to do magic.

Seeing no other way, Will promises Lord Dudlea that if his forces will betray the queen and allow Edward an easy victory, then Gwydion will undo the spell that has made statues of Dudlea's wife and son. Dudlea agrees, and in consequence the battle of Delamprey is soon over. Unfortunately, though King Hal falls into Duke Richard's hands, the queen makes good her escape: this means that the war will go on.

Once Gwydion has the manacles stricken from his wrists, he tells Will all he knows about the Dark Child – Chlu and Will are twins. Chlu's name is, in the old tongue of the west, 'Llyw', and according to prophecy Will must never pronounce that name in a spell or he will be no more. Gwydion goes on to reveal that almost twenty years ago, he surprised Maskull while he was conducting magical experiments on two baby boys. He rescued them and took them in secret to two separate villages, to lessen the chances of them being found. These places Gwydion then magically hid from prying eyes. Since discovering Chlu's whereabouts, Maskull has been using him as a means of locating Will. The sorcerer knows he must destroy Will because Will stands between him and the future he is

Robert Carter

trying to bring about. Will is to become the third incarnation of Arthur, and once that is allowed to happen,
Maskull will fail.

Will is angry that Gwydion has delayed telling all that he
knows for so long for fear of affecting the outcome of the
prophecies and appalled at the responsibility that now faces
him. It is up to him to act, and to act heroically, but how
can he become King Arthur, as Gwydion says he must? In
addition, the wizard warns that the harm they have been
drawing out from the battlestones in an attempt to prevent
the fighting has not been destroyed, merely dispersed. Like
a poisonous smoke, it is filling the world and bringing down
the very future that Maskull so desires. And so, as the second
book of the Language of Stones cycle ends, Will sees that
he must solve the riddle of his own nature, the riddle that
will rescue his world.

6

PART ONE

THE ENCHANTED
CHAIR

CHAPTER ONE

DOUBLE DEPETRIFICATION

It was a mild summer night in July and the sun's dying beams cast shadows from the elms. To the wise man the trees told of storm and strife and contentions in the upper airs, but down here in the evening glade neither breath of wind nor drop of rain threatened, for a strange peace enfolded all.

Four men dressed in the livery colours of Lord Dudlea sat quietly in the clearing – a waggoner, the waggoner's lad, and two servants. They were warming themselves and spooning down chicken stew, but although they enjoyed the gentle cheer of their master's camp fire, still a dull foreboding shadowed their minds. The sleeping infant that had been left among them was the only one untroubled by the magic that lay heavy on the air, and each of the four knew that before the night was done weird deeds would be accomplished in the lordly tent that stood nearby. They knew it because the great wizard, Gwydion, had told them it would be so.

Only one of them had any idea of what was in the wooden crates they had brought with them, or why a wizard should be here with their lord in a forest clearing at dead of night. Inside the tent that stood thirty paces away the mood had now become brittle. Lord Dudlea waited impatiently as Gwydion refreshed himself, drawing power from the meadow. Candlelight flickered as Willand carefully lifted the lid from one of the wooden caskets and began to tease out the straw packing and bare the stone cold flesh within. When Gwydion returned he asked Dudlea to sit alongside Willow on the far side of the tent then turned to look with close interest upon the fine-veined marble of the lady's cheek.

'This spell has been well worked,' Gwydion said at last. 'I have never seen detail like it.'

Will saw how stone eyelashes and other wisps of hair had been shattered under the first and least careful of the handlings that had brought her here. A sprinkling of fine-spun stone was to be seen in the folds of the statue's wrappings as the last coverings came off.

It was an incredible transformation, a perfect statue of Lord Dudlea's wife, but no mortal sculptor had made it. This was malicious work, that of a potent sorcerer.

As Gwydion reached a hand under the figure's head, Dudlea stood up and said, 'Please, let me—'

'Sit down,' the wizard told him shortly.

'But if you're going to lift her, I'll call my—'

'It's not necessary,' Will said, looking up.

Gwydion's tone became compassionate. 'Leave your men be. They are keeping true to their word, and on that much hangs. I asked them not to spy on us, come what may.'

'*Come what may?*' Dudlea blinked in alarm, and Gwydion laid a calming hand on his shoulder that made him draw in a long draught of air.

'Take courage, John Sefton! You must be strong, for hope is one of our most important magical resources.'

Dudlea nodded and backed away. At Gwydion's signal, Willow tied the tent's flap firmly closed. Her daughter, Bethe, was sleeping by the camp fire, wrapped tight in a blanket. She and Will had been reunited with her only yesterday after a torturous separation. She had fared well in the care of the Duchess of Ebor, and as soon as Duchess Cicely had set foot in the Realm following her husband's victory she had made every effort to return the child to her mother as quickly as possible. Still, Willow's feelings had not yet fully settled. Will knew that was a concern to the wizard. He had tried to smooth their worries before the spell-working was begun. Any source of disturbance was best anticipated and dealt with ahead of time, for emotional auras would spark and fizz in bright display during magical transformations.

Will leaned over the nest of straw, checking the lady's perfect visionless eyes informed by a glint of surprise, the knuckles, the fingers, so expressive in their attitude, gripping the stiffened folds of her robe.

'She's quite undamaged,' he told Dudlea, touching the man's spirit. 'The delicacy of her face is scarcely blemished. Look how its waxy shine remains unscuffed. Nothing so much as a fingernail has been broken.'

John Sefton, Lord Dudlea, King's Commissioner of Array and sometime commander of ten thousand men, broke down and wept. At Gwydion's summons he came forward and his jaw flexed and his knuckles turned as white as his wife's on the edge of what he feared might yet become her coffin. His tears fell upon her, but if he had imagined that tears alone would wake her, then he now discovered otherwise.

'Open the second,' Gwydion murmured.

The face of the lord remained bloodless as Will prised open the crate that contained the boy. The waggoner had been well paid and charged with two duties. But speed and care did not ride easily together over the Realm's badly rutted roads, and the cart had bumped and bounced over thirty leagues to bring it to this place of particularly good aspect. The boy, too, was perfectly captured in stone. He lay mute in the finest alabaster, ten years old and innocent. Just like his mother, he was covered in fine spicules of stone. A little detail had eroded here and there, but he seemed to be undamaged.

At Will's prompting, Dudlea came to gaze upon his son, and again he wept with relief. How different the man was now to the Lord Dudlea who had bare weeks ago tried to force Will into carrying out a murder. It was a satisfying change, a true redemption perhaps.

Gwydion's voice rose, at once soft and sonorous, and gave the command, 'Come to me, John Sefton.'

At that the lord went meekly. Without being asked, he knelt before Gwydion as an earl might kneel before his sovereign. Gwydion laid a hand on his shoulder, saying, 'I want you to understand what I am attempting. It is done neither for your sake nor out of charity towards your kin. No offer that you could make would ever be sufficient to pay for this service, and it is to your credit that you did not sink to the proffering of silver or gold to me. This is to be a corrective. It is a private matter between wizard and sorcerer, and also the rescuing of a promise made by another to restore your wife and son to you.' His eyes flickered to Will and back. 'Fortunately for you, I happen to owe that person a favour. It is wise to power some spells on gratitude whenever possible.'

'Thank you, thank you. I'm as grateful as any man could be,' Lord Dudlea babbled, and it was plain to Will that he considered himself fortunate indeed. He had clearly remembered Will's warning to him not to offer payment or reward and not to disrespect the wizard.

Gwydion's face darkened. 'However, when the promise was made, the promiser did not know whether there was a spell to reverse what had been done to your kin. He did not know if it was even possible. And in that falseness of promise resides my present difficulty, for lies do poison magic. They weaken it.'

'I understand,' Lord Dudlea said eagerly. Though he did not understand much at all, and his eyes were fever bright. 'I can vouch that Master Willand's word was given in true hope, at least – hope that a greater good would be born of it.'

'That, alas, is not nearly enough. For magic springs from moral strength. In the true tongue the name of magic means 'keeping the word'. Such stuff may not be coldly traded, for in that case the results will not be as expected. And those whose hopes are pinned upon debased magic are doomed to be disappointed.'

'Then, if only for pity's sake . . .'

'Pity, you say? How that word has been warped over the years! Pity is properly what we feel for those who have given themselves over to weakness and so harmed others. What you mean is not pity, but fellow feeling. Do I have fellow feeling for you, John Sefton? Do I have enough? That is what you want to know.'

The lord stared back as if already stricken. 'Do you?'

'The question you are asking now is: have you merited it?' He shook his head, apparently amused, and turned back to the crate. 'I must not try to remove the spell directly, for that is now all but impossible. However, I may attempt the laying on of a counter-spell.'

Dudlea swallowed hard. 'Do whatever you think, Master Gwydion. Only, I beg you, please do not fail them. I love my wife. I cannot live without her. And my boy is both son and heir to me.'

The wizard inclined his head. 'You have a quick mind, John Sefton, and how uplifting it is to hear a squalid politicker such as you speak from the heart at last. Is it not time that you put on the mantle of statesman and set aside your childish plots? You are not yet become another Lord Strange. You may still choose dignity. So cease your peddling of lies and threats, keep the promise of your ancestors, even as I shall keep Willand's promise tonight. And remember that men of privilege are but stewards of this Realm. You should not fail it in its hour of need.'

The lord had hung his head but as Gwydion finished he looked up boldly and met the wizard's eye. 'I've behaved like a fool, Crowmaster. I told myself that desperate times called for desperate measures, but I see now that I was only being weak. I will take your advice as my watchword.'

'See that you do. What passes here tonight is not to be spoken about. And, since true magic depends upon truth of spirit, what you pledge to me here and now will take effect in the flesh of your wife and son. If you break your bonden word to me, the counter-spell will be undone and your kin will slowly – painfully – return to stone. Do you understand this warning that I give to you?'

Dudlea closed his eyes. 'I do.'

'Then return to me your solemn word that what you witness here tonight will remain with you alone unto death.'

'I do so promise.'

Gwydion gathered himself. He stood gaunt and twisted as a winter oak as he drew the earth power inside him for a long moment. Words of the true tongue issued from his mouth. Cunning words coiled like ivy, blossomed like honeysuckle, gave fruit like the vine. Then he stepped around the crates, gathering up a charm of woven paces and waving hands, dancing out in gestures and speaking a spell of great magic that began to fall upon the two effigies.

A crackle of blue light passed over woman and child as they lay side by side. Will seized Lord Dudlea's arm when he started forward, knowing he must not let the lord interfere once that blue glow had enveloped them.

A noise that was not a noise grew loud in their heads. And slowly, as Gwydion danced and drew down the power, shadows flew and the tent filled with the tang of lightning-struck air. Their skins prickled and their hair stood up, and slowly in those two strange beds of straw the cold white-ness of marble became tinted as living flesh is tinted, and the wax of death began to give way to the bloom of life.

Will felt the unbearable tension of great magic. He closed his mind against it, but it tore at him as a storm tears at a hovel. Willow, tougher by far, hung onto the lord's flailing arms, holding him back as his wife and son rose up from their coffins like spectres. Lord Dudlea called out. His eyes bulged in helpless horror as a weird light played blue in his wife's eyes. Something moved the boy's lips, then jolted them again as the figures floated free above the ground. But just as Will began to think they could not hold the lord any longer, a shuddering racked both woman and boy and they fell down as if in a faint. Yet now they were moist and soft and alive, and as the noise and light vanished away they began to breathe again.

'Oh, joy!' Lord Dudlea called out as he attended his kin. He reached up to touch the wizard's robe. 'Thank you, Master Gwydion! With all my heart I thank you!'

Will opened the tent and stepped out as soon as he could. Willow went with the wizard to join those by the fire whom Gwydion said must now have their minds set at ease. They left Lord Dudlea to his family, and Will stood alone under the moon and stars, trembling, a mass of glorious emotions coursing through him. The power that flowed at Gwydion's direction was truly awesome, and Will reminded himself that it was not every day the dead came to life again.

They parted company in the early morning.

Lord Dudlea took Gwydion's hand. With bowed head, he pledged himself. 'I shall keep my word, Crowmaster. I shall wait for the army that now marches south towards Trinovant, and I shall offer service to Duke Richard of Ebor.'

'Is that wise?' Will asked. 'You were his captive before you escaped. Then you joined the queen against him.'

'It was the king's court to which I fled, not the queen's.'

'Oh, indeed? Rumour has it that you tried to arrange the murder of Richard while he was still in the Blessed Isle.'

The lord's eyes opened wide and his wife looked to him as if she had been betrayed by a foolish act carried out in her absence. 'That rumour is a lie.'

Gwydion looked upon the lord pityingly and spread his hands. 'A lie, John Sefton? We have not even taken our leave of this clearing and already you have betrayed your promise to me. Is it so hard to be true to your word?'

'Forgive him, Master Gwydion,' Lady Dudlea begged. 'I have been his staff. Without a wife to oversee his policies things naturally go awry with him.'

The wizard smiled. 'It would be better if you let him be, lady. Grown men must learn to rely on their own consciences. It seems to me that the main question you now have before you is this: how will Lord Warrewyk receive you when next you meet? He murdered a great many of the queen's friends after the battle.'

Lord Dudlea met Gwydion's eye. 'However he looks upon us, I shall lay myself upon the king's mercy. If that means pleading for the Duke of Ebor's mercy too, then that I shall do also.'

'Do you think he has the strength to do the right thing?' Willow asked when they were out of sight.

But Gwydion only smiled.

The wizard took them south on unfrequented roads, ones that went the longer way around but avoided the great chapter house at Verlamion. For that Will was grateful. He disliked and feared the Sightless Ones – or 'red hands' as the common folk privately called them – and he knew that at Verlamion they would be as thick as wasps about a honey pot.

The company spent the morning journeying through fruitful farm land. Will knew that if the weather kept dry for a month this part of the Realm would see a good harvest. But then, when the reaping and threshing was all done and the nights began to close in and leaves began spreading red-gold in the hedges, then out would come the Sightless Ones with their tally sticks and counting frames to take away the best portion of the bounty from the churls who had grown it.

At Aubrey End Will announced that he could feel the presence of a green lane. The flow of earth power was strong in the soil and Gwydion marked the place with his sigil in the bole of a tree. The lign tasted, Will said, like that of the elder, and Gwydion said that, unless he was very much mistaken, they would soon cross the lign of the rowan too, and this they did before they had gone another league.

Will looked along the lign and knew it for the same stream of dark power that flowed through Ludford, many leagues to the west. And when he looked eastward he knew they could be no more than a couple of leagues west of Verlamion. A shiver passed through him. Gwydion had said that the Elders of the great chapter house there would stop at nothing to bring to book the defiler who had cracked their Doomstone. Will had not cared that it had turned out to be none other than the lid that sealed the tomb of their revered Founder. He had only wanted to break the lorc's stony heart that day, and he had saved many a life by his actions.

They came to the banks of the River Gadden well before noon. It was here that Will felt yet another lign prickle his skin. This one was fainter and harder to follow, but it seemed to trend a little south of east, much as the rowan lign had. There was no doubt in Will's mind that it was the yew lign, the same that passed close by the Vale.

'Keep up!' Gwydion called back, flicking the reins of his horse.

'Master Gwydion, I can feel the Eburos lign.'

'What of it?'

'Nothing – except I thought it was our task to find more battlestones.'

'There is no time to tarry at present. We must reach Trinovant before nightfall!'

'Then ride on ahead of us!' Will told him. 'We've a young child to consider. And this old nag's already tired out.'

The wizard waited for them to draw abreast. 'I would rather you came along with me,' he said with exaggerated patience. 'This is not a safe time for anyone to be on the road. News of the battle has yet to reach these parts and there will be much uncertainty in men's hearts.'

Will saw that Gwydion's impatience was unsettling his horse. It had soon taken him fifty paces ahead and was champing to get on further still.

Willow watched the wizard with concern. 'He's getting grumpier by the hour,' she whispered. 'I hope he's all right.'

'He's worried. And is it any wonder, when things have gone so far astray?'

He partly meant their quest to rid the Realm of battlestones, but he was also thinking of the unspeakable bloodshed that had followed the fight at Delamprey. While a greater battle had been narrowly prevented, the murder of so many noble prisoners at Lord Warrewyk's hands had blighted the victory. Will was sure that act had sown the seeds of revenge – seeds that must eventually be reaped as a yet bloodier harvest.

So far as the battlestones were concerned, the loss of Will's talisman had been an even greater blow, for it was the only real weapon they had ever possessed. The more he thought about it, the more it seemed that Gwydion was right – Maskull *had* finally gained the upper hand.

'And you can cheer up, too!' Willow said. 'Things might have gone a lot worse for us. That loathsome woman – I won't dignify her with the title of queen – is running away into the north with what's left of her friends. Things look set for a change at last, and probably a change for the better.'

'Maybe. But Master Gwydion once told me to remember that we're peacemakers – we shouldn't be feeling pleased that Duke Richard's forces won at Delamprey, even though he's been a better friend to us than his enemies ever have. The balance has been shifted again, and that's the important thing.'

Willow settled Bethe in a more comfortable position in front of her. 'I don't see why we shouldn't feel happy for the duke. We lived among his household. You were even schooled with his sons. Duchess Cicely helped my father and me when she might have sent us back to face Lord Strange's displeasure. And she looked after Bethe as if she was one of her own.'

He sighed, trying to see how best to put it. 'I'm not saying Duke Richard isn't a good man at heart. He's probably better than most, but he's human like us all, and—'

Willow grunted. 'And *what*? When fighting against him is that she-wolf who cares nothing for nobody. Tell me where's our loyalty supposed to lie?'

'You just have to try to see things more broadly. That's what Master Gwydion means.'

'Oh, is *that* it?'

Will sucked his teeth. He saw the way his infant daughter's eyes swept across the land, drinking in everything they noticed, delighting in every bird and squirrel she saw. Her expressions were so much like her mother's, and yet Willow said they were exactly like his own.

'It's got something to do with the way the past gets made out of the future,' he said. 'There's the future where all is uncertain and yet to be fixed, and there's the past, where all is done and cannot be undone. But where the future *touches* the past, there's a thin line. That's what we call the present. That's where we live.'

'I see,' she said unconvincingly.

'And the present's the only part we can affect with our free will, don't you see? Because what we choose to do in the present affects the way the future is turned into the past.'

'Well, I know *that*,' Willow said, unimpressed. 'That much even Bethe knows, don't you, sweet baby?'

'But . . . but the point is, Master Gwydion says there's only one "true path", one track through time that's the best of all possible destinies. If everybody did what was right by everybody else then the best possible world would come about as soon as blink.'

'You mean like it does in the Vale when everyone argues and we all somehow come to a compromise in the end?'

'Exactly! But you see not everybody can do right because there are powerful people out here and they've multiplied their strength so that now most people just take orders and don't even think about what they're doing. And then there's Maskull, who's done that more than anyone. And because he's a sorcerer that means he *understands* the harm he's doing, which is even worse.'

Willow let it all sink in. She shook her head. 'Then why is he doing it?'

Will shrugged. 'He's a renegade, a cock who thinks the sun has risen to hear him crow. He's broken his vows of guardianship and forgotten all about humility and kindness and all the things he always said he cared about. He wants to live forever and go on and on in charge of the world, and he thinks he might have found a way to make that happen.'

'So that's the path he's leading us all towards.'

'Yes. It's one that will reward him alone. He's started behaving as if he's found a way to live forever and enjoy power forever. But to do that he needs to turn the future of the world far away from the true path. And Master Gwydion says that if we get pushed too far from the true path, then we'll never be able to get back to it. Maskull will have won, and the world won't ever be the same again.'

Her eyes narrowed. 'We won't *ever* be able to get it back?'

'No. If Maskull steers history along that terrible, false path, he'll take us towards a world without magic – it'll mean five hundred years of ceaseless war, and the end of the world that we know. Now you see what Master Gwydion's really fighting for: he wants us to have the best of all possible worlds, or for us to come as close as we can to getting that. That's why he wants us to follow the true path. It's not all that complicated an idea in the end, but it's hard to make it happen.'

Willow offered no reply. There was just the sound of horses' hooves clopping along the dusty track, the buzz of flies in the hot July air and a baby gurgling to herself at all that she saw and heard.

After a while, Will said unhappily, 'You know what? The battlestones are Maskull's big chance. I've begun to see it all quite clearly now. Master Gwydion had everything going along nicely, but then the lorc awakened and the stones started the very war that Maskull needs to turn the destiny of the world to dust. While the stones stay in place they're like rotten teeth in a jaw – there'll be a lot of pain and suffering up and down the Realm, and that's what Maskull needs if he's going to work his designs. That's why we have to root the stones out.'

Once more Will felt a pang of guilt at the way he had lost his talisman. It seemed suddenly to be a gigantic setback. He thought again of the moment when he had broken the malice of the Blood Stone at Ludford, and he was more certain than ever that he could not have done it without the green fish.

'You told me you thought Master Gwydion was losing his powers,' Willow said, as if reading his thoughts. 'But it didn't look like he was weakening last night. Lady Dudlea and her son woke up like nothing heavier than a troubled night's sleep had lain upon them.'

Will's gaze was fixed on the road ahead. 'That's true, but depetrification isn't so difficult, and I helped him somewhat. Did you see how he milked it for all it was worth?'

'Milked it? What do you mean?'

'You must have noticed how he went as close as he could to trading without crossing the line. Trading magic for favours is against the redes. But he asked Lord Dudlea to change his ways while the fates of his wife and son were still in the balance. I'd call that pretty close to coercion.'

'Oh, you're reading too much into it.'

Will grunted. 'Am I? Master Gwydion's not above a little chess playing, you know. Look how he works on you and me to get his bidding done – tempting us out here, making us follow him all over the place. You shouldn't underestimate him, you know.'

'He's done no such thing, Will. It was you who summoned him. And it was my choice to come with you.'

'Oh, he makes it seem that way, but the truth is he's a dozen times wilier than any fox.'

'Master Gwydion can't help it if the Vale's become too dangerous for us to go home to. I'm just happy we've got somewhere else.' She paused. 'We *have* got somewhere else . . . haven't we?'

Will sighed. 'He told me he's taking us to the royal palace – you can call that a home if you like, but I wouldn't.'

'The royal palace of the White Hall . . .' Willow's voice softened as she fussed with Bethe. 'Just the place for King Arthur.'

He looked sideways at her and blew out his breath, somewhere between a laugh and a sigh. 'Master Gwydion said that in the days of the First Men Arthur was an adventurer-chieftain, but at his second coming he was a hero-king. I wonder what the third incarnation is destined to be?'

'Gort told me that the legend of Arthur's return speaks of his return as a crow . . .'

He laughed. 'A crow! He probably meant I'm to become a bird.'

She resisted his amusement. 'I think Gort meant you're to become a wizard of sorts. He said the natural talent was strong in you – and getting stronger – whereas in all the rest of the world the magic is leaking away. He says your magic feels ancient.'

He grunted. 'Sometimes it makes me feel very old, I know that much.'

'Is it so hard to accept, Will? Arthur's third and final appearance as wizard-king?' She smiled privately, then abruptly changed the subject. 'I wonder what it's going to be like, living in the big city.'

'Well, I'd guess the royal palace is no better than all the other lordly houses we've seen – a forbidding fortress and a boast when seen from without, yet a hive of treachery within.'

'No place to bring a baby to, then?'

That focussed him. 'No.'

As he settled into a morose silence he thought of the battle they had succeeded in spoiling at Delamprey. Though it would be remembered as a victory for the Duke of Ebor, the duke had not even been there. The fight had been won by his son, Edward, and by his fearsome ally, Lord Warrewyk, the greatest and richest man in the Realm. In truth, though, the entire result had been secured through Will's own efforts.

Now Duke Richard had joined his son, and the victorious army was slowly marching south towards Trinovant where it was certain to be happily received by the towns-folk in a day or two's time.

'Please! Try to keep up!' the wizard chided them.

'We can't go any faster, Master Gwydion!' Will called back.

The wizard turned away, equally irritated. 'We must reach the capital before Richard of Ebor does. You know that.'

'But we'll do that easily.'

'And do you think Maskull has left no magic there? The White Tower and the White Hall will both be webbed about with all manner of mischief. I must find it and deal with it before it can bear on events. And I must find clues to the whereabouts of the secret place where he has done all his dirty work. That will be no easy task.'

Will lapsed into silence again. He had more than enough on his mind without troubling himself about Gwydion's problems. Chlu lay heaviest upon his thoughts. It was strange to think that he had always had a brother, stranger still to know that brother was his twin, but strangest of all to find that it was Chlu who all along had been trying to kill him.

'I must find out why, and make my peace with him if I can,' he told Willow.

'Some chance of that when all he wants to do is murder you. And mind what Master Gwydion said about speaking his true name. He said that if you did that you'd be destroyed.'

He shook his head. 'He said that would happen only if I spoke Chlu's true name as part of a spell. Don't worry, the pronunciation is difficult, for it's a Cambray name and the men of Cambray have their own tradition in both magic and words that is hard to approach and even harder to master. And anyway, Master Gwydion says that knowing a person's true name always gives a measure of power over them.'

'Well, I wouldn't take the risk if I were you. Promise me you'll keep away from Chlu if you can.'

'I can't promise that. I need to know what Maskull has done to him. Perhaps I can heal him. And perhaps in return he'll be able to tell me what I most want to know.'

□ □ □

CHAPTER TWO

TRINOVANT

As they rode south, shadowing the last league of the Great North Road, they crested a heath dotted with elm trees and Trinovant began to rise up out of the afternoon haze. Will saw the dark needle of the Spire, which rose up like a crack in the sky, and the blue-grey sprawl that lay below it, sunk in summer haze.

'The Spire contains the shrine of Ercowald,' Gwydion said, 'to which many pilgrims make journeys on the days when its precincts are thrown open to the ill and the dying, the lovelorn and despairing. They are given to wash in the troughs that surround the building, and perhaps make bargains of the heart with the hidden agents who speak to them persuasively from behind the iron grilles. Pilgrims come here even in freezing weather, when the ice on the troughs must be broken. On two great days in November and February there is a special 'Day of Whipping' in which the most committed of the Fellows go in procession through the City, beating themselves with scourges, for these are the ones that are mad beyond repair and have come to revere, and even to love, the suffering of their own flesh.'

Will felt a shiver of revulsion go through him. He looked to his wife and daughter, anxious now about the ordeal that was soon to come. It was said that at each of the City's seven great gates there was kept a pair of dragonets, silvery wyrms whose task it was to guard the capital. Gwydion said that in olden times they had been bred to smell out treachery, and would pick clean the ribs of anyone whom they thought unworthy to enter.

Gwydion had spoken many times of the great city of Trinovant. Often he had likened its size and power to that of Tibor, the Slaver capital of old.

'Over the centuries this place has grown into a vast, walled capital, a city of spires and towers and palaces, of the Guild Hall and the White Tower and Corfe Gate. A sprawling, rollicking morass of people live here, huddling inside for warmth in the cold midwinter, sweltering in the sweats of high summer. It is a city of high and low, from the bright, castellated battlements of royal palaces to the crowded hovels of the poor. It is quite unlike anywhere else.'

Now, as the shadows of the elms stretched more and more, the wizard turned, pointing ahead. 'And do you see the white heart weather vanes of the Sightless Ones? Look how they rise above the walls. Those walls that will soon pass on our right are not the walls of the City, but those of the House of Silence. Beyond it lies the College of Benedix and the glass-makers' yards, which is another rich establishment of the Fellows . . .'

Will listened as Gwydion pointed out the various marvels that were to be seen as they approached the City wall proper. So much of Trinovant seemed to have burst out and overspilled into the land beyond. But these unprotected buildings were not all mean houses and trade stalls as he had thought. His eye passed along many a row of tall merchants' houses, some of three and even four floors built right on top of each other. In the street there were all manner of people – such a flow of traffic coming in and out of the

City that Will could hardly believe there was not some special reason for it.

As they came past the great chapter house to their right, Will got his first sight of Eldersgate. It was like the gate of a great castle, all decorated with the rough likenesses of several great wyrms – the five great dragons of Umberland, Gwydion said. Their heads snarled down at them stonily.

'What you will never see of this city are the cellars down below,' Gwydion told them. 'The whole place is greatly under-mined. There are the secret passageways of the Guilds and many a sunless dungeon that lies beneath every lordly mansion flanking the river. There are tunnels too, linking together the many places of secret power – places like Bayard's Castle and the Fitchet's Den. The lords dwell there and the streets around them are wide and throng with sellers of costly wares. You will see, but first we shall pass by more humble ways, for we must go by Fish Street, Salters Ride and the Cloth Market, and so by unstraight ways to our destination, for today I must speak with Magog and Gogmagog.'

'Magog and Gogmagog . . .' Willow mused. 'Weren't those two the last of the giants? The ones that were put to flight by King Brea in the olden days?'

'Put to flight? Not at all. Do you not know your own history? They were taken captive by Brea. Chained by him, then brought to his oaken palace, which was from that time onward called the White Hall.'

Will said, remembering his lordly schooling, 'I was told by Tutor Aspall that Magog and Gogmagog were sent to the White Hall to do service as porters. Perhaps they serve King Hal still, for I don't know how long giants live.'

Gwydion grunted. 'Long, but not *that* long. Today's Magog and Gogmagog are not the same as those giants of yore, yet they serve the present king after their own fashion, for today they are two great statues which stand in niches on each side of the throne. They look down upon the king's proceedings and call out to give warning whenever his throne is in danger.'

'They must be crying themselves hoarse at present,' Will muttered.

'And so it may be for the next few months, unless I am allowed to set to work to prevent the catastrophe.'

'What will you do?' Willow asked.

'Do? I must do many things. But first there is a far greater work of un-doing. As I have already told you, I must pull down the grey skeins of sorcery that festoon the White Hall. Maskull has dwelt here for many a month, and in that time he has crept over every wall and tower like a long-legged spider, spinning webs of deceit about the royal house. Those spells must be swept away before the king and his captor come to town. I must find the workshop of Maskull's wickedness.' He sighed and glanced to his left. 'What say we slake our thirsts at The Bell Without?'

'Bell without what?' Willow asked.

'Without its clapper, I guess,' Will said. 'The Fellows of the Charterhouse yonder are of the White Order, and they keep a ritual of silence.'

'A creditable surmise, but you guess wrongly. The inn is called The Bell Without, because it is without the walls. There is another alehouse inside the City called The Bell Within.'

Will smiled at that. 'They seem to like their drink here. That's a good sign, at least, for those who can drink and be merry are good men indeed!'

He was pleased they were taking a rest, for his throat was dry. As he dismounted and looked around the inn yard his thoughts lingered on the captive King Hal. The queen had wrought her easy-melting king like wax, but since the fight at Delamprey, she and her allies had fled into the north to find succour and no doubt try to regroup their forces. The captured king had been invited to ride in Duke

Richard's company. The plain truth was that the king was now as much in the duke's power as he had once been in his wife's.

'What do you think Duke Richard intends?' Will asked as they sat down. 'Do you think he'll play fair, or does he mean to keep the king under his thumb?'

The wizard drew a deep breath. 'That is a most pertinent question. In truth, I am no longer able to read Friend Richard's heart in matters of state. As for Hal, he wants little more than to be allowed to return to a scholarly cell and to peruse the parchments and papers that are his delight. But still he knows he is the king, and he may not prove as pliable to Friend Richard's plan as the latter might wish.'

Willow frowned. 'Do you remember what Mother Brig once told Duke Richard at the Ewle revel at Ludford all those years ago? She warned him that he'd die if ever he dared lay his hand upon the enchanted chair. Could she have meant the throne of the Realm do you think?'

The wizard became circumspect. 'We all die – eventually.'

'But she said more than that,' Willow insisted. 'She said that Duke Richard would die in his first fight after he touched the chair.'

'You have a surpassing excellent memory, my dear.'

'It was a surpassing memorable night, Master Gwydion. But tell us – did Mother Brig really mean the throne of the Realm? And is what she foretells bound to come to pass?'

Gwydion looked down the passageway towards the stables. 'Brighid makes many a claim regarding future happenings. Some are important, while others are not. It is the way with seers.'

'But all she says *does* come to pass, one way or another,' Will said, not letting Gwydion off the hook. 'I believe she swore a destiny upon the duke.'

But the wizard was not to be drawn further on the matter

of great prophecies. Instead he said, 'You know, one thing has already come to pass as you foretold – Duke Richard has given the Delamprey battlestone to Edward.'

'A gift of thanks to recognize his victory, I suppose.'

'Indeed.'

Since the fight, the battlestone had shrunk down twice. The first time was just after pouring forth its stream of malice, when it had transformed itself into a nondescript plinth of brown ironstone incised with words that even Gwydion could not read. Later it had shrunk again, once Will had used the remaining powers of the stump to burn away the manacles from Gwydion's wrists. That time, it had been as if the very substance of the stone had collapsed, and it had faded to grey.

'What can Edward want with it, I wonder?' Gwydion mused.

Willow said, 'I suppose he's fetching it to Trinovant in hopes that it'll be a touchstone to his ambitions. But isn't it now drained of the power even to confer boons?'

Will nodded. 'If I know Edward, he'll delight in it mostly because his father has given it to him. He'll value it because his father values the stumps of Blow Heath and Ludford, and he'll tell himself it has virtues even when it does not.'

'In that, then, he will be like most men,' Gwydion said regretfully.

'But aren't you going to claim it from him, Master Gwydion?' Willow asked.

The wizard shrugged. 'I might have to.' Then he took a draught of ale.

'Have you had any fresh thoughts on the inscription?' Will asked. 'Or are you still, ah – stumped?'

Gwydion raised an eyebrow. 'If that was meant to be a joke it was not very funny. But since you ask, I am no further forward. The verse is not written in any tongue that I have ever met with.'

'At Delamprey you said that that was Maskull's doing.'

'It is one of his nasty little snares. His arrogance shines through in all that he attempts.'

'And he knows you well enough to be able to pose a problem that you cannot solve,' Will said. 'But that in itself could be a clue, don't you think?'

The wizard gave him a look that told Will it was a mistake to teach grandmothers to suck eggs. 'Maskull has done enough dirty work – I could not read the marks I found in the stone.'

'Well perhaps it's only the script that's unknown to you,' Will said, hoping his optimism would infect the wizard. 'The language itself may be one that you know.'

Gwydion stroked his beard. 'True. It might only be a cipher that I have to crack . . .' He fell silent, but it was a silence unlike the dark ones that had overtaken him lately.

Willow had taken out a heavy bronze coin and she had begun spinning it on the table top. Will watched it whirl faster and faster as it settled down. He picked the coin up and spun it again, fascinated for the moment by its odd behaviour, at the rising sound it made before it came to a sudden dead stop. Is that what's happening to us, to the war? he thought oddly. Getting faster and faster until suddenly everything stops on doomsday?

Knives and trenchers were laid before them, and with more ale came pie and cheese and warm bread. As they ate and drank, they talked of lesser matters, and when Willow excused herself and Bethe briefly from their company, Will took the opportunity to ask a rather more pressing question.

'Chlu's true name, Master Gwydion – pronounce it again for me.'

Gwydion flashed a glance at Willow's departing figure. 'And give you a knife to fall on?'

'I think I must have that knife, whether it is safe or not.'

'Very well then – Llyw.'

'Thloo.'

'That will not do at all. It is a difficult sound for those unused to the language of Cambray. But see – put the tip of your tongue against the roof of your mouth as if you are making a luh sound, then breath past it.'

'Dzzllll . . .'

'Do not voice the sound! Just breathe.'

'Shlllew.'

'Almost. Again.'

'Llyw.'

The wizard smiled. 'You see? The rede is correct: practice does make perfect. But take care how you use your new-found knowledge, for there is danger in it.'

By now Willow was coming back, so they made ready to go. Gwydion steered them away from the stables, out of the inn and then onto the high road, saying that he had arranged for their horses to be left at The Bell Without and now they must walk.

They had almost reached the moated bastions that flanked the triple arch of Eldersgate. The soaring stone structure, deftly wrought and set with dragons, seemed dour and unwelcoming. A group of travellers waited gloomily beside a barrier.

Will waved a hand in front of his face as he caught his first clue that this was no ordinary gateway – the smell took him back to the wyvern's cage he had seen at Aston Oddingley. He now understood why Gwydion had left their horses at the inn. All travellers wishing to enter the City were made to dismount fifty paces before the Eldersgate. Stolid Midshires cart horses stamped their shaggy hooves as they approached the drawbridge. Even brave warhorses were unharnessed and led aside to be specially blinkered and let in by a side arch so they would catch no sight of the dragonets.

Will saw that this brought good trade to the gate-keepers and porters who dealt with the animals or worked in gangs to pull carts and wains in through the main arch. It gave them the opportunity to charge twopence a time for their labours, and Will smelled more than the stink of wyrm about it.

Once they were nodded through the barrier he glimpsed the two dragonets that were chained inside the middle arch. They were not great dragons, being only about the size of bulls, yet they seemed to be more dangerous than lions. They were flightless wyrms, specially bred to their task, small-winged but powerfully clawed, with barbed tails and flickering red forked tongues. Their hides shone like quicksilver as the muscles beneath rippled. They snarled and trod back and forth fearsomely.

Willow clutched Bethe to her as she approached the gate. Gwydion walked beside her. 'It is best not to look the wyrms in the eye,' he said. 'Such beasts as these have attended the gates since the time of King Ludd. They are supposed to safeguard the City against the entry of people of ill purpose, for it is said they can smell guilt in the sweat of a man like dogs can smell fear. But over the centuries their keepers have fallen into sorry disrepute. For a silver coin they will give an easy passage to any wayfarer who happens to rouse the guardian beasts to wrath – which you will see happens most often whenever a wealthy person arrives. Do you see that merchant in the blue hat? Watch how they winch the chains back so there is a wider way for him to pass. They drive the animals back with those white shields quartered in red.'

The keepers set up a loud banging on their shields, hitting them with red-painted truncheons shaped like short swords until the dragonets turned their heads aside.

'The keepers seem careless of the danger,' Willow said.

Gwydion surveyed the goings on in the gatehouse. 'The

colour red and the number four are held to be worrisome to the beasts. They are said to shy away from the good-hearted, but it is just the loud noise and how these rogues have trained them, for they are also the ones who give them their feed.'

Then, all of a sudden, Gwydion cast up the wing of his travelling cloak and ushered Willow and Bethe past the beasts. The nearer of the two dragonets was momentarily quieted, and Will saw in his black eyes a spirit more touched by sadness than rage. On an impulse, he put out his hand to the creature and felt its moist red tongue flicker with interest over his palm.

'It wants for salt,' he said, pitying it its life trapped in this acrid stall. 'And it wishes for a run in the fields.'

'Get on by!' one of the keepers shouted. 'No lingering! No loitering!' He shoved Will through the door and spat insultingly when he saw he was not going to be offered any coin for his assistance.

'Beggars coming through!' the head keeper shouted. 'Get you gone out of the City quickly again. We already have too much vagrancy here!'

'And too little respect!' Gwydion told him. 'This outrageous preying upon travellers goes too far. I shall speak to the king about it!'

But seeing no staff in his hand, the keeper said, 'Oh, my lord, so sorry! Come here and I'll give you a kick, and you can pass that on with my compliments to his grace the king when next you see him!' And he laughed them away with the usual welcome he kept for customers who made no donation.

'Is everyone so rude and ruffianly here?' Willow asked.

'It is a game they play hereabouts.' Gwydion gestured up at the tall dwellings that made a deep gorge of the street. 'And is it any wonder they keep rough manners, when they must live piled one atop the other like bees in a hive? The lives of too many here are ruled by greed and false ideas about the getting of gold. You will soon see how it is.'

He hurried them on until they had passed inside the gates, and Will began to savour the curious character of the City. He reacted to it with an odd mixture of disgust and delight. The place was filled with people, yet it seemed dirty and dangerous. There seemed to be countless shining possibilities to be found at every turn, but no easy way for him to get at those possibilities without a purse full of silver. The great heap of buildings stretched as far as his eye could see in every direction. There were throngs of people, but not a tree or any splash of green. A tumbled roofscape blocked the view of the River Thamesis, which Gwydion said was also called Iesis. There was one landmark that could be plainly seen – a huge black steeple of sinister aspect that rose high above more humble rooftops and made Will's spirits dip. The sight of the great Black Spire of Trinovant struck him with an immovable dread.

Gwydion followed his gaze. 'No taller tower was ever made in the Realm. It stands six-score times the height of a man, and is guarded by special Fellows who dress in robes of grey and yellow. They are called Vigilants. You will see them, for we must go by that place. But first, we must go another way – not a pleasant way, for it is now the junction of two vile sewers. I knew them long ago as pretty brooks lined with willow trees. The Wall Brook drains the Moor Field. It meets with the Lang Bourne, and goes thence down into the Iesis and so carries with it all the refuse and offal and filth that the population of a city such as this cares to throw into it.'

As they walked on through the hot, close afternoon Gwydion remarked on the uneven and filthy state of the streets. 'But you will see little of this unpleasantness about the mansions of the wealthy, for those whose task it should be to care for the City even-handedly have long since given themselves over to the far more agreeable business of supping at lordly tables, or else wrangling with one another for the privilege of doing so.'

'I can see how the lords and those who serve them might live well here. But what of the rest? How do the poor live?'

'As the poor always live. But here there is also a middle ground – every trade still has its guild, though their power is not as it was, and whenever things become too oppressive a great mob takes to the streets and there is a riot. Burning and looting happens more often than you might imagine. Why do you think there are no thatched roofs allowed here in Trinovant?'

Will was almost sorry he had asked. As they got deeper into the commercial heart of the City, the streets began to teem. He saw great flocks of sheep in the road, and stockmen herding cattle to the pens that stood near the shambles. He followed on in silence, watching as Gwydion stopped here and there at corners to search out strange marks that had been left chalked on posts or scratched into beams. They seemed to guide him like secret clues. Often he tasted the air for spell-working tell-tales and magical resonances. And when he found them he quietly danced, undoing the dismal tokens of bone and blood that his rival had hidden in so many nooks about the City.

'They do much mischief,' Gwydion said, holding up his latest find. It was a severed finger and a cockerel's claw that had been bound together with a silken thread and put high up on a ledge. 'This and others like it overlook many of the City's crossroads. They power the spells that Maskull has trussed about the commerce of the streets. Six or seven of them will have to be rooted out if the stock market here is to flourish again!'

A pack of Fellows watched from a little way off. They slunk away from the wizard's eye as he turned to face them, then dissolved among the crowds. Will was amazed to see so many

Sightless Ones walking openly and almost at liberty within the City. They were always in groups of at least three, sometimes led by a sighted guide. Fellows from different chapter houses dressed in different coloured robes, and there seemed to be a certain coolness, or perhaps even rivalry, between them. Will was reminded that although called 'Sightless Ones', they possessed a strange, groping sense that served in place of vision, and the more he walked the City streets, the more he began to fear there were those among them who had already identified him as the defiler of Verlamion and were passing the news to a higher authority.

'Come!' Gwydion whispered sharply. 'You do right to beware the Sightless Ones, Willand, for they do not forgive and they are surely hunting for you. But do not gawp so plainly at them. See how they tilt their heads at you! Mind you do not give your thoughts away so easily.'

Will did as he was told and guarded his face as the wizard took them past narrow alleys that stank ripely in the heat. There were many beggars and peddlers and barrow-men here. Gwydion said they would do well to get quickly across the Wartling, the main Slaver road that cut diagonally through the City. They passed down thronging lanes, and in time came to another market. There was much that Will had never seen before, and more for which he saw no good reason. The street sellers offered too many wares that were unneedful – dubious foods, badly made flutes, sweetmeats, vain hats, posies of wilting flowers, false charms, and little songbirds confined in tiny cages, too distraught to do anything but hop back and forth and chirrup warnings to one another.

Nor could Will's own talent find silent rest. Threat and malign intent bubbled among the press of bodies, and there was such a cacophony of human weakness in the air that it pained him to feel it all. He was relieved when the wizard steered him away from the Cheap and down a lane towards the wide river where the brown-grey waters sparkled in the sun. Ships from beyond the seas rode at anchor, loading and unloading their cargoes at Queenhythe. There were the smells of faraway places here – salt and spice and spiritous liquors. Oddly, it made him feel homesick, though he could not say why.

'In the days of the First Men a great burgh stood here,' Gwydion told them. 'It was known as Ludnaborg by the seafarers, and was the greatest and most famous of all the burghs in the Land of Albion. Then came the Desolation, when giants and dragons ruled here, but afterwards came Brea, out of a far land. A descendant of Abaris and son of Frey, he built the Wooden City after the style of Trihan, which was the place of his birth. And he called it "New Trihan" or in his own speech "Trinh Niobhan" and that was eleven hundred years before the founding of the Fellowship of the Sightless Ones.'

Will looked up at the unfinished buildings, and at the men who climbed over them like squirrels. New warehouses were being thrust ever higher, packed tight against one another. 'When will this city be finished?' he asked.

'Finished?' Gwydion laughed. 'Never! Here they do not think about reaching perfection, only of staggering greedily onward, for in this city bigger is always held to be better, despite what the redes have to say on the topic.'

Will could not but marvel at the monstrous bridge of twenty-one piers that had been flung across the Iesis. A traffic of small boats and wherries shot under it where the water flowed rapidly in shadow, while above many houses stood crowded upon the span. There were fortified gates at each end that could be closed to prevent entry into the City, though Gwydion spoke of the many times that the bridge gates had been forced, such as when Jack the Carter had led fifty thousand Kennetmen in revolt against the king and then given the order to kill all the lawyers.

'Not all revolts are to be discouraged, then,' Willow said wryly.

And Gwydion laughed. 'Sometimes a good bonfire serves to cleanse the body politic.'

Beyond the bridge to the east a great castle brooded on the northern shore, revealed now by the sweep of the river. Soaring lime-white walls stood out bold and square above the waters, and Will knew that this must be the White Tower, the main fortress which the Conqueror had built to control the City almost four hundred years before.

A strange feeling began to course through Will's body, making him feel faint.

'Will you take us to Tower Hill?' he asked, pointing to the great keep.

Gwydion's eyebrows lifted. 'Do you think I should?'

'I . . .' He shrugged. 'I don't know.'

'We cannot go there, for the White Tower remains under siege both by land and by water.'

'Under siege?' Willow said, surprised. 'Who's attacking it?'

'Men wearing the Earl of Sarum's livery. A body of them stayed while the rest of his host marched north to Delamprey. Friend Sarum has begun calling himself the military governor of Trinovant if you please!'

Willow sniffed. 'But I thought Duke Richard's allies were welcomed into the City by the Lord Mayor and his Aldermen.'

'They were. And the White Tower was the bolt-hole into which all the king's supporters jumped for safety. They're still there and dare not come out.'

'They'll have to when the king himself orders it.' Willow resettled Bethe on her hip. 'Don't they know that he's coming here?'

Gwydion offered a vinegary smile. 'I expect they do. My own best guess is that Richard and Hal will arrive in three days' time, which is why I must get on with my work—'

'What does the mystical head of Bran say about the matter?' Will asked suddenly.

The question came out of the blue. Gwydion halted and squinted at Will. 'Again?'

'I asked you about Bran, Master Merlyn!' Will's voice was deep and otherworldly. 'Or does his head lie elsewhere these days?'

Gwydion continued to look hard at Will as he made his reply. 'Bran's head remains buried within the grounds of the White Tower. It is still attended by thirteen ravens, just as I promised you, Sire.'

Will, pale-faced and uncertain now, put a hand to his head. 'I . . . I don't feel . . .'

And it seemed suddenly that he was falling.

When he opened his eyes again he found it hard to breathe. He struggled, but quickly realized that Willow was holding a cloth to his nose, which was bleeding.

'Are you all right?' she asked. 'You banged your head.'

'I must have . . . fainted.'

'What do you remember about Bran?' Gwydion asked as Will stood up.

'Who?'

'Bran. He was the twenty-eighth king of the blood of Brea, a great king who with his brother, Beli, took armies across the Narrow Seas and led them against the rising power of sorcery in the East. The brothers sacked the great city of Tibor, and later Bran took his men under the earth. That was the last time any mortal king ever attempted to journey into the Realm Below. It is a place from which few have ever returned. The feat was achieved only once – by a far greater adventurer than King Bran. That man's name was—'

'Arthur . . .'

'Indeed. Arthur.'

Will felt as if he had been reminded of things that he had once known but had later forgotten. 'Bran's name signifies "raven". He was . . . the son of Dunval the Lawmaker . . . who was himself the first king to wear a golden diadem as the sign of kingship in these Isles. Dunval's two sons were Beli and Bran, and his daughter was Branwen the Fair. And Bran married the daughter of Isinglas – but I can't recall her name.'

'Esmer.'

'Yes! Esmer. *Esmer* . . .' Will looked up. 'Gwydion, did I know these folk in my former life?'

Gwydion laid a hand on his shoulder. 'You did not. They lived in a time that lay between your first and second comings. Perhaps you know their names for another reason – for they are part of the histories that I taught to young Wart.'

Will closed his eyes, and put his face in his hands for a moment. When he took them away again he began to sing.

> *'Then made Great Dunval his sacred laws,*
> *Which some men say*
> *Were unto him revealed in vision—'*

He paused. 'But why should I bring King Bran to mind now, Master Gwydion? Of all the histories you must have taught me in a previous life, why this one?'

'I cannot say for certain. Do you not remember what happened at Bran's last battle at Gerlshome when he was wounded by a poisoned spear? That wound caused him such great agony that his head was cut off by his brother as an act of mercy. Bran's bodyguards bore his head to the White Tower, and all the way it spoke to them, telling where it must be buried—'

'It was to protect the Realm against invasion,' Will

continued. 'The head was set to face the Narrow Seas. But after many years Great Arthur dug it up again, so that *he* would henceforth be the sole guardian of the Realm.'

Gwydion nodded. 'I found the head shut up in a golden box after Arthur's death. It was I who re-interred it at a place then called the White Mound. Oh, the head was quite clear about where it wanted to rest, and enough of its protective power lingered on for the Conqueror to fear it considerably five hundred years after. He built the White Tower over the very place where I buried it.'

Will looked suddenly to the wizard. 'Gwydion, the White Tower lies upon a lign! I'll wager my life on it. Bran's head became a part of the lorc! That's how it spoke to Arthur during his second coming.'

'Well, we cannot go to the White Tower now. Nor can we go across the river. Over the bridge lies the Cittie Bastion of Warke. There the Grand High Warden, Isnar, keeps his winter hearth. It is a main counting house wherein the Elders of the Fellowship keep a great stock of gold. They have many rituals concerning the accounting of it. Come along, Will – a thousand hollow eyes stare out from that place. It is best not to spend too long looking back at it, for its golden glimmer ensnares many.'

But Will did not take his gaze away from those blank walls across the water until the morbid feelings that emanated from the place made him turn about – and then he saw the Spire again. Its gigantic presence shocked him now. It seemed to have followed him and grown huger in the hazy sky. Its dark surface was a mass of strange ornament, pillared and fluted, with arches and niches and buttresses and every kind of conceit carved in stone.

The whole weight of it seemed to be falling upon him, and as he looked away he thought that the character of the City had changed. Hereabouts the streets were narrower, and the aspect of the ground felt dull and blighted. They were now so close to the Spire that he could see dark motes in the air, circling its top. Ill-begotten things were fighting and disputing, or so it seemed, about some high platform.

'*Birds?*' Willow said, following his gaze.

'They are not birds,' Gwydion muttered darkly. 'Do you not realize the size of them? They are bone demons, come to feed on human remains.'

'Bone demons?'

'Ugh!' Will grimaced. 'You mean, there are dead bodies left up there? Exposed?'

'They call it the Bier of Eternity. When a High Warden dies, his remains are not hidden within a chapter house like those of lesser Fellows.'

'That's horrible.'

Gwydion's grunt was dismissive. 'The Sightless Ones make singular claims about what happens when a man ends his days, dangerous claims that play upon the weakness of fear, and one form in particular: the fear of death. They intensify it greatly, for they know that in the end they can make a profit from it. What do you think they sell to make such stores of gold? Have I not already told you what is meant by the Great Lie?'

Will did not care to hear more. He fell back and walked a pace or two behind his wife, watching to see that nothing unpleasant happened. She would not let go of Bethe for a moment, nor did she pay any heed to the ragged men who reached out to tug at the hems of her skirts. Yet Will did pause, touched, despite his fears, to see a press of beggars crowding expectantly on the other side of a barred portal. It was the begging hole of a hospice or lazar house, one of the morbid lodgings that Gwydion had once mentioned. The Sightless Ones maintained such houses to draw in the sick, though those who were admitted were expected to feed themselves by imploring passers-by to give them alms. Deformed men whose auras burned dim thrust hands and stumps up through the bars, crying pitifully. Skull-like faces pressed together into the light and the stench of unwashed bodies gusted from the hole. The spectacle was horrifying and made Will take a step back. But he could not look away. The beggar who most caught Will's eye was heavily mantled in grey. A deep hood hid his face, but it did little to disguise him.

Suddenly, Will's belly clenched – his feelings flashed dangerously, and he thought of Chlu – but it was not Chlu. Chlu could not be here, surely, for the queen and Maskull had gone into the north and the Dark Child must have gone with them . . .

Will continued to stare at the beggar, unsure why he had been so affected by him. What had marked him out, packed as he was among so many other beggars? He was certainly large. Will looked at his outstretched forearm. It was solidly muscular, though his hand was swathed in filthy rags. He seemed troubled, and, for all his strength, less adept at beggary than the rest, though hardly a man on the point of losing his will to live.

Will understood from the way the beggar inclined his head as he thrust his bowl through the iron bars that he was blind. Then with a shock he realized that the rags the man wore were the tattered remains of a Fellow's garb. He was no beggar, but their warder . . .

Will recoiled, but then he steadied himself and some strange impulse of charity came over him, for this man, though he was a Fellow, seemed somehow more needy even than the beggars who surrounded him.

When Will brought out an apple from his pack it was quickly seized and jostled away before the Fellow could take it, so he brought out another and deliberately guided the man's bandaged hand to it. This time it was taken and Will turned away, driven back in part by the foul stink of the place.

'Why did you do that?' Gwydion asked as Will caught them up.

'Even their warden was hungry. He was begging too. Don't they feed their own inside the Fellowship in Trinovant?'

Gwydion brushed the matter off. 'They are drinkers of blood. Why did you give him an apple?'

'Because he wanted it. And because giving is getting.' Will's solemnity melted away and he smiled. 'That's something I once learned from feeding ducks.'

When they came to the end of the street the way opened out into a space dominated by the massive structure of the Spire. The foundation storeys and the monument that stood opposite its entrance were wholly faced in black stone. The Spire itself was railed off and the area around it paved in a complicated pattern of black and white stone across which Fellows in yellow garb patrolled. Surrounding the Spire beyond the spiked rail was what looked at first like a market, but Will soon saw there were no buyers at these craftsmen's stalls. Each booth had its own canvas awning. Each was occupied by a different kind of worker. There were butchers and bakers, metalsmiths and wood-turners, coiners and token-makers, bodgers and cobblers, tinkers and money-changers. Smoke was rising from many of the stalls, and there was the smell of charcoal and the ringing of hammers upon anvils.

'See how the Fellowship draws in so many of the useful trades and binds folk unto itself,' Gwydion said. 'But these craftsmen are not serving the commerce of the City. None of what they make is used beyond the Fellowship.'

'Then, is the rest of it set in store?' Will asked, seeing the quantity of goods that was made here.

The wizard grunted. 'That question shows that you little appreciate the scale of wealth that the Fellowship commands.

What you see here is power, for through it the Grand High Warden exercises a torturesome control.'

Will frowned. 'Torturesome, you say?'

'Surely. For on the other side of the Spire is a yard such as this, except that there the artisans' business is the breaking apart of whatever is made on this side.'

Will balked. 'What on earth is the point of that?'

'By this means Grand High Warden Isnar regulates every key trade in the City. He can quickly destroy any cooper or candle-maker or any other producer of wares who dares to displease him. He has succeeded in stran- gling this city and many another, for what could be more torturesome to a man than the prospect of having his livelihood taken away?'

'But what about the famous Trinovant Guilds?' Willow asked. 'The mercers and drapers? The grocers and vint- ners and ironmongers and all the rest? Don't they fight back?'

'They cannot. Their power is now all but broken by the Fellowship.'

As they drew closer to the Spire grounds, Will saw rows of money-changers' booths and beyond them the block-like monument. Such an edifice stood outside every Chapter House, no matter how small, but no other in the land was like this. It was as big as a house, and its top was decked with statues of monstrous animals and its sides cut with mottoes in the Tiborean tongue. The words were mostly obscured by spills of wax from ten thousand red candles that forever burned among the bronze or basalt legs of the beasts, but the letters were carved deeply and Will made out the legend.

SEIUQ OLEAC NI ALOS

When he asked Gwydion what it said, the wizard told him, 'The Sightless Ones cherish many strange utterances, though their meanings are more often than not meant to be mysterious to outsiders. That one says, "There is rest only in the sky."'

'What does it mean?' Willow asked.

But Gwydion only shrugged and said, 'Who can say? They call it "a mystery". They call by that name every piece of nonsense they choose to spout, for they hope in that way to pinch off all reasoned thought about it. Remember: it is ever their aim to convince others of that which is not. That is how they gather power to themselves.'

Will heard coughs and the clink of mason's steel on stone. A row of skinny prisoners were chained in a line, white as millers with the dust of their task. They were rough-fashioning stone blocks into balls of the sort that were shot from great guns, and Will grieved to think that such a destructive trade must now be profitable. He wondered if these products were likewise broken up on the far side of the Spire, or if they had already been sold to an arsenal of war.

Next to the shot-carvers was a row of decaying tents that served as stable and fodder store for half a dozen chestnut horses. A large brown and black dog sniffed suspiciously at the air, while men with cruel faces lounged at their ease nearby. All were dressed in well-used riding suits of red leather.

'Are they messengers?' Will whispered doubtfully as they came almost to the monument.

Gwydion grunted and lowered his voice. 'The Fellowship has no need of messengers. The vanes of their spires and towers do all their talking for them.'

'Then what do these men do?'

'They are the enforcers of the Iron Rule.'

'You mean these are the men who take children away from villages that cannot pay the tithe?' Will's eyes narrowed as he met their stares. Two or three of them were looking towards Willow now, showing frank interest in the child in her arms.

A flash of anger burst in Will's heart, but just then the dog came roaring forward, teeth bared, barking ferociously, until it was yanked back by its chain. The sight made Willow flinch away, and as Bethe's cry pierced the air, Will turned towards her. Then something brushed his cheek and struck the ground a pace or two away.

It was a crossbow bolt.

CHAPTER THREE

THE BIER OF ETERNITY

Those enforcers of the Iron Rule who saw what had happened rose to their feet and a shout went up. Daggers were drawn, cover taken. The enforcers were men well used to coming under attack. They moved to cover, alert as weasels, looking high up on the monument to the place from which the crossbow bolt must have been shot, but they lacked the means to reply and so their caution was all the greater.

Will saw that the shaft of the bolt was short and set with two triangular leather flights. So powerfully had it been flung into the earth that its iron head had been wholly buried. He knew with utter certainty who had shot at him and why, and when a black-swathed man moved from behind the rump of a great stone griffin Willow knew it too.

'So Chlu didn't go north after all!' she cried as Will bundled her between the tents and pressed her hard up against the monument's base. Then she saw the look on his face and knew what was in his mind. 'Will, no!'

But he was already climbing. His hands thrust against the pole that held the nearest awning taut. His feet found purchase on the letters graven into the plinth. When he reached to grip a bronze griffin's claw and haul himself up, a red waterfall of molten wax cascaded over him and froze in his hair and on his skin.

He gasped at the sudden burning on face, neck and hands, but as the pain passed he saw that above him the crossbow's string was being drawn two-handedly upwards. Chlu straightened his back, fingers straining as he pulled on the cord. A second bolt was clamped between his teeth.

Time stood still in Will's head, blotted out by a certainty as strong as any rage. The wax slid under his feet and fingers, but in another moment he had pulled himself upright and was facing his twin. When Chlu saw there was not enough time to cock and raise his weapon, he stood up straight, ready to face him.

Their eyes met. Will felt a tremor pass through him, a moment of horror to be looking into eyes so like his own, yet so informed by hatred.

'Tell me what I've done to make you want to kill me,' he demanded. 'If you bear a grievance, tell me what it is or, by the moon and stars, I'll stamp your face into the mud here and now!'

The other's malicious stare wavered as a laugh gurgled from him, but he made no reply.

'I know who you are. Master Gwydion told me everything. I don't blame you for what you've done. I just want us to talk out our differences.' Will held out open hands. 'Listen to me! Don't you know that we're *brothers*?'

But Chlu's growling laugh cut him off. It was a deep, barely controlled, animal noise that seemed to catch in the back of his throat. 'I'm not your brother – *I am your doom!*' He swung the weapon in his hand at Will's head.

Will raised an arm and fended off the blow, but he was not fast enough. One of the steel prods caught in his face, tearing open his left cheek, and as the crossbow clattered to the ground Will was knocked backwards across the plinth and tangled among bronze limbs. By the time he had recovered his feet Chlu had fled.

There were cries below as the men in red tried to shadow Chlu along the monument, but he had already found a way down where they could not follow him. A stone yale, a horned, tusked animal, rearing up on its hind legs, stood at one end of the monument. Chlu had threaded his way between its legs and leapt down into the maze of black and white paving that formed the closed precinct beyond the iron fence. Now he ran unmolested towards the base of the Spire itself.

The Vigilants who guarded the gate were ill-prepared for their swift-moving trespasser. Chlu dodged them easily and disappeared inside the Spire's vast, ornamented gates. Will felt a warning turn over his guts, but a great surge of desire thrust him onward. This was not a simple wish to corner Chlu, but an overwhelming need to find the answer. He knew he must not let his twin get away.

'Who comes?' came the cry from the Fellows. 'Who comes?'

They lifted their heads, turning like beasts testing the air, and Will saw how difficult it would be to follow Chlu now that the guardians of the Spire had been stirred up.

Blood dripped from his cheek. He wiped his hand on the waxy shoulder of his jerkin, then he leapt down from the monument and ran straight to where the knot of gate guards were standing. More were hurrying in from all quarters now, groping towards the great iron doors. They moved slowly, no match for Will's own fleetness of foot, but they were armed: cudgels had been drawn, and whips snaked from sleeves and cracked out towards him, but only four Vigilants directly barred the way.

He put his shoulder down and charged, knocking them aside like so many skittles. Ahead the vast doors were closing. Three Fellows pushed on each, heaving them round on massive hinges. He threw himself forward, dived head-long through the gap into a darkness that was suddenly filled with echoes as the great slabs slammed shut.

He felt himself skidding along an ice-smooth floor, then he lay for a moment trying not to breathe. He was in total blackness. Whatever sense had given him warning before he entered the Spire, it screamed at him now. He stared hard, willing his eyes to pierce the gloom, then he began to see dim shapes in the vast cavern that soared above him. Brown light was seeping in from somewhere, and as his eyes adjusted so the thought began to harden that he had been deliberately drawn into a trap.

He was at the bottom of a curving stair that rose up to an immense height. As the echoes died away, there came the sound of footfalls from above, mounting higher and higher. Again Will strained to hear, but the more he tried the more the sounds faded and the less sure he was.

If he opened his mind he would know instantly where Chlu had gone, but he dared not do it in this place. The air was rank and thick and quiet as a blanket, but he was sure there were Fellows groping silently in the darkness, and still more coming from hidden holes to left and right.

When he drew breath the stink of burnt grease laced the air. That and some oversweet fumigant seemed to rob his breath of vigour. And there was something else too, a musty note that he could not quite recognize. He crawled towards the stair, then began to feel his way up. The surfaces were cold here, solid and unmoving, made of dense basalt that drank in what little light there was. But he could feel the intricate decoration that was carved into every part of this curious ceremonial staircase as it carried him up in a spiral. Beneath his fingers the steps were dished, worn down by use, and in the middle the stone was smooth, whereas every-where else the surfaces were sticky, as if years of accumu-lated grease had varnished them. Feeling his way forward on all fours kept him away from the place he most feared, the stair's unguarded edge, but after a while going blindly forward he was hit by a sudden terror and halted. In the dark corner of the stair he saw guards.

That frozen moment spun out longer and longer, then the stinging in his cheek pushed itself back into his consciousness. He flung himself into a corner, not knowing whether to go on or turn back. They can smell blood, he reminded himself, but then shouts came from below, words ringing in the air.

'Follow the defilers . . .'

By now the pursuit had gathered in strength in the concourse far below. Fifty of them at least, a hundred maybe. Too many to burst through, too many to escape – and if those massive entrance doors were the only way out . . .?

It seemed his decision had been made for him. When he turned again, he had resolved to fight his way past the motionless guardians above no matter what. He approached the first of them stealthily. It made no sound, nor any move towards him. He had almost crept past it when the dam that held back his fear broke. He lashed out with all his strength and almost broke his arm against the unyielding breast. It was only then that he realized that what had checked him was a statue – a row of Grand High Wardens, standing there on the landing, eternally guarding their dark niches.

A mixture of relief and anger flooded him. His heart hammered as he climbed ever upward, until his breath heaved in the bad air and he had to halt again. But not for long. Maybe, after all, there was an undercurrent of meaning in the mysterious message inscribed on the monument far below: 'There is rest only in the sky.'

Up it must be! he thought, pushing himself onward. It's the only way. And if there's no escape, what does it matter? That's not the reason I came here.

But what *had* decided him? Had it really been his choice to wildly follow Chlu? He doubted it now, for it felt like the insistent power that sometimes showed itself within him. The power that Gwydion called Arthur. That power had flowed before, and always at crucial moments. It was a mighty power – ancient, courageous and strong – but it was a flower that had not yet fully bloomed. Its mark was a sure and certain impulse, so that when it lay upon him he did not think of consequences but behaved as if he was doing exactly what was needed to urge the world towards the true path. Whatever that power was, it had sent him to corner Chlu, so corner him he must, and what better place could there be than a dead-end way up in the sky?

But what then? a less certain voice inside him asked. *What will you do when you have him at your mercy? Will you have the strength to do what must be done?*

It seemed when he looked up that the gloom within the Spire had lifted a little. And so it had – the walls here were pierced by narrow shafts of light. They revealed tiers of ever-narrowing, ever steepening steps circling the column of stale black air. Will's foot skidded off a broken tread. A sudden fear of falling into the pit stabbed his groin and he gasped and threw himself hard against the wall. Here, far above the hubbub below, sound carried with greater clarity. Again he drew breath, a cold sweat spangling his face. Blood was still dripping freely from his left cheek, leaving a trail that would unerringly lead his pursuers to him.

But at least the Vigilants had satisfied him on one point. The voice below had said 'defilers', which meant not only that Chlu was still at large, but that he was not working with the Fellowship to spring a trap on him.

It was scant comfort, as the sound of clicking footfalls came from above. Will's eyes tracked a faint shape stepping ever upward on the far side of the darkness. He wanted to call out, but knew he had better not give himself away to those eyeless men scanning the darkness below. He pressed on, grimly determined, climbing until the steps gave out. The great spiral had many turns, but here, at a mouth-like portal in the wall, it abruptly ended.

He passed through the arch, glad to be off the stair and away from the void, but he saw that much lay between the inner and outer skins of the Spire. To left and right there were doorways and stairs, landings and passages, many of them numbered, but bafflingly so. Some ways were sealed behind iron doors, while others stood open. All directions led off into darkness, but near the stairs thin lancets admitted spears of daylight. Better still, the ground was dusty and there were scuff marks. He followed the trail to the foot of a stair and climbed higher, pausing occasionally to make sure he was still closing on his quarry. When he had mounted to the forty-ninth stair, the Spire suddenly grew meaner in its decoration and he halted again, oppressed by a mighty warning from within.

Was Chlu now in his trap . . . *or was it the other way around*?

The idea still troubled him that Chlu had led him into the Spire on purpose. Why? Why should he think that? This was certainly a place where he would be stripped of Gwydion's help. And if Chlu had not gone north with the fleeing queen, then maybe Maskull hadn't either . . .

The air was rank here. The musty smell had grown worse. Will tried to swallow his burgeoning fear, but tasted the taint of death. He took stock. Each flight of stairs was plainly made now, every one a little narrower and steeper than the last. He had come to unfrequented heights, and whereas the floor had been greasy with spots of old candle wax, now the stonework was bare. Stark landings opened onto the great void within the Spire, and the stairwells through which he climbed looked down dizzyingly past dozens of floors. Flimsy iron rails were set around the edges, low enough that Will imagined himself crashing through. But at least the mute statues had disappeared along with all the carved and patterned marble. Here was only dust and pigeon droppings on the grey flags, and around him plain arches and slender pillars of iron, so that his journey seemed to him shadowed by the shedding away of earthly power. He saw that an ascent of the Spire was meant to parallel the life of a Fellow, from his entry into the Fellowship up through the various grades and degrees, losing his sense of self, until finally he came to death. And here, written in stone, were the austere last stages of the journey that an Elder made into the darkness as he departed his sour life.

A shriek shocked him out of his thoughts. He heard groaning and grinding in the bowels of the building. The nearest of the pursuing Fellows was still many floors below. It would be some time before they arrived. Yet Will was forced to search each landing before moving on, listening warily now so as to be certain that no ambush awaited him and to make sure that Chlu could not double back and slip past him.

Will could not easily tell how high he had climbed. All he knew was it was a long way. His breath came in gasps and his legs ached. And there was that foetid smell again, something vile that carried down on the draughts lacing these dismal corridors.

As the Spire narrowed, so the fear of Maskull weighed more heavily on Will's mind. He cast about for ways to encourage himself. 'Chlu thinks I fear the Sightless Ones,' he muttered through gritted teeth. 'He chose this as his refuge because he thought I wouldn't come here. I bet he hasn't counted on being hunted down. He hasn't bargained for this!'

He clenched his fists. No fear, not even the fear of Maskull, would undermine him. This time Chlu was going to have to turn at bay. This time he would be brought to account.

Something heavy lashed out at him from the gloom. Will ducked and it glanced off the top of his head. A length of chain clanged then pulled taut, wrapping itself in a spiral grip around the nearest pillar. He saw his chance and slammed his fist into Chlu's face, but Chlu put his head down and Will felt the bones of his hand jar in pain as his punch connected instead with the bow of Chlu's skull. Chlu roared and charged him down onto the filthy floor, then reached out again for his weapon. But Will kicked out with his foot and the force of the blow threw him back. They both watched as, between them, the chain unwound itself from the pillar, snaked slackly over the side of the staircase and vanished.

It was as if a spell had been broken. They roared at one another and came to grips again, falling down, rolling over and over. Dust swirled up, stinging throat and eyes and blurring everything that Will saw. His knuckles were soon skinned raw, but every punch he landed drew a reply and every kick a counter. Thoughts of the aid that magic might give in the moment of last resort were no comfort to Will, for he knew that powers taken for granted were powers that betrayed. And when Chlu put a deadly hold on his neck, he found he could not summon the power. Try as he might he could not ask in the right way and his escape was made only through the explosive strength that desperation put in him.

They slid across the floor in opposite directions. Chlu fell against the steps, winded and dazed, but he was up first. He drew something from the back of his belt and held it before him like a dagger in the shaft of light.

Will struggled on heels and elbows. He was gasping for breath and half-blind in a haze of dust and dry bird-lime, but he had seen the deadly spike clearly enough – it was Chlu's unused crossbow bolt.

He put out a hand behind him and found – clear space – no rails, no banister, nothing but a thin current of foul air falling from above into which his fingers grasped emptily. He froze, suddenly knowing his peril, for he saw that he was lying on the edge of the precipice. It would take barely a touch to send him over. If Chlu were only to toe-poke him he would go spinning down into the dark, and that would be the end. A powerful fear surged up inside him. How quickly the tables had turned, and how faulty had been the inner feelings that Gwydion had so often recommended. Where Chlu was concerned, it seemed, such warnings were no help.

Terror filled his mind as Chlu came forward and rose over him menacingly. The weird light from above enfolded them. Will gasped.

'Llyw, no!'

The Dark Child froze. He flinched back as echoes died on the air like a faint detonation – the noise of the chain hitting the bottom far below. It was followed by distant voices calling out in confusion. Will's dust-filled eyes stung, but he could see that Chlu had begun to back away from the stairwell. A groan escaped him, and then he turned and fled.

Will rolled away from the edge. He coughed, tried to wave away the dust, got to his feet and sought the safety of the wall. He found that he was shaking as he drank in the relief that flooded through him. What had driven Chlu off? The effect had been almost magical, as if some bogeyman of the Fellowship had appeared and frightened him away.

But there was nothing to be seen. The Vigilants were far below, and there was no monster here, nothing save dust and the shafts of light cutting the scene at crazy angles. And then he realized what it must have been – he had pronounced Chlu's name in the old tongue of the west. The name had worked the trick, for had not Gwydion warned him never to speak Chlu's true name? If he ever did so as part of a spell, then his own doom would be sealed also.

He spat and laughed thinly. Blood soaked his sleeve. He was cut and bruised, but no serious damage had been done.

I have Chlu's true name, he told himself, thinking out the consequences. And now he knows that, he'll believe he's in my power. He'll think that I've already won. How desperate he'll be – and how dangerous! I mustn't underestimate him again, and I mustn't forget that he's a match for me in head and hand, however much our hearts may differ.

He gathered himself ready to press on up the stair, then saw there was blood in the dust. Big drops, red as rubies. He smeared fingers across his own wounded cheek. But, no – this blood was not his own.

And there were new sounds now – scuffling sounds – this time from above. Then a muffled screeching set Will's teeth on edge. What was Chlu doing? Moving something heavy to the edge, ready to pitch it down the stair?

No . . .

When he rounded the next corner a flood of daylight came from above. This was no tiny brown-glazed pore opening on the outside world, no mean-spirited lancet pierced through the fabric of the building. This was direct light – full sunshine. The hairs were lifting on Will's neck. He screwed up his eyes and half turned away from the gust of warm, filthy air that assailed his senses as the landing opened onto a scene of horror.

Here were a dozen hunchbacked figures, part-man, part-bird, creatures that might have been made long ago by vile sorcery out of some vain desire to fly. The beasts stood no taller than children. They wore coats of quills, and their heads were wrinkled and pink. So cruel and quarrelsome were their manners that they took Will's breath away. They danced excitedly, snapping at one another and ripping at the open ribcage of a corpse that lay between them. The creatures were fighting over what was inside. Mottled brown wings opened and flapped as they strove to drive one another away from the carrion. But despite their preoccupation with the ghastly feast they nevertheless took notice of Will as he mounted the final stair.

They did not bear the interruption well, hissing and spitting at him, their pink-and-grey snouts sneering up to reveal long yellow eye-teeth. Will stared, horrified by the scene. If this was the Bier of Eternity, Will knew, then these must be the bone demons who came here to strip the bodies of flesh. The mortal remains of some high officer of the Fellowship had been stretched out upon a grey granite funerary bed and elaborately chained there. The Bier was low, its edge no higher than Will's knee. It was carved with token-words and with locks and skulls and other symbols of death, and Will saw that the decayed corpse had been presented like an offering upon a grim altar. Over it all a pale canopy was spread, splashed now with the liquor of death and tattered by violence.

As Will's eyes took in the scene, the creatures began to make menacing advances. They bounded towards him, testing him by darting in and out. Then, as if at a signal, they rushed him all at once, leaping forward in a flurry of clawing and ripping.

Will threw them off, then took up the only weapon that lay to hand – a thigh bone. He slashed back and forth, seeing that he must drive them back, that an all-out attack was his only hope.

He realized with horror that the weapon he had snatched up was slimy with rotting meat, but this was no time to scruple. He struck the nearest creature on the head as if with a mace, and it fell down. But the second tore at him furiously until he grabbed its tail and whirled it away out into empty space. By then, a third had used its hind claws to slash the sleeve of his jerkin open. He knocked it against a pillar, but now a fourth fastened its jaws on his calf and a fifth took him painfully by the forearm. Before he could shake them off others came to menace him, crowding upon his head like so many hornets. He threw down the bone, put everything out of his mind and, among the scatter of brown ribs, danced out two steps of a spell of magic.

This time the power ran through him strongly. When it blasted forth it flung the creatures off in a burst of pale green light and sent them tumbling. Those that were tangled in the canopy tore it down in their panic. The rest gathered themselves in rage and fear and scuttled back towards the open air. When Will approached them closer, the least fierce of them threw itself into panicked flight and the others soon followed.

The whole pack screamed at him impotently as he stepped over the Bier of Eternity. The stinking, part-dismantled body entangled his ankles and the rusty chains with which it had been ceremonially shackled threatened to trip him. Disgust overcame him, but as he tore down the rest of the canopy, he wiped his hands, then moved out into the light, where the yellow rays of the afternoon sun seemed to wash him clean.

Out on the parapet there was some respite from the stench, but he dared not step any closer to the edge than this – the fall was unfenced and the bone demons swooped and wheeled in the air beyond. They were looking for their chance to return, hesitating only when Will came fully out into the open to throw a magical gesture of satiety at them.

'Go on, you bloody-snouted curs! You'll feast no more today! Away with you!'

Then his eyes widened. How high he had come! All of Trinovant was laid out for him, its sprawl of roofs, its rich palaces and prickle of lesser spires all encompassed by that many-gated wall. There, the White Tower, and yonder, the bridge, tiny now, with the great shining river Iesis also made small, a twisting, turning ribbon of light . . .

But where was Chlu?

When Will looked up he saw there was still a great deal more of the Spire rising above his head. Its summit cone went up dizzyingly for a dozen more levels and came to a point that was topped by a large iron vane. This carried the device of the bloodless heart, the letters A, E, E and F standing out starkly, and a great gold-headed, gold-fletched arrow that acted as a pointer. Will knew the letters stood for a phrase in the language of the Slavers that meant 'to and from the Fellowship'. Unlike ordinary weather vanes, this pointer was not pushed around by the wind. It was swung by some ingenious means so as to send out messages.

Seeing the moving sky made Will feel as if the Spire were toppling. A sudden fear of the immense height gripped his belly again and made him step away from the edge. As he did so, he saw Chlu. The latter was standing astride the Bier, and it appeared that he was ready to parlay.

'Why have you stopped running?' Will asked.

Chlu stared back. 'I flee who chases me, and chase who flees me.'

Will faced him warily. 'What did Maskull tell you? What spells did he place upon your head to make you want to hurt me?'

Chlu's face was as bloodied as Will's own, laid open beneath his right eye where Will had kicked him, but there remained an ember of arrogance in his expression, a hidden glow that would easily re-kindle.

'I'm not bound to Maskull,' Chlu said. 'My will is as free as your own. It always has been.'

'You don't even realize how he's using you!'

A humourless half-smile passed over Chlu's face, and he prepared to take a step forward. 'Oh, I am the sorcerer's stooge while you're the wizard's favoured accomplice. I am the blind man, but your hawk eyes see forever. Is that the way it is? I'll tell you plain, Willand: Maskull uses me no more than the enchanter, Gwydion Crowmaster, uses you!'

'That's enough!' Will raised a hand to stay Chlu's sly approach. 'Maskull said he made me, and that he could just as easily unmake me. For years I thought that meant he must be my father. Master Gwydion told me not to believe it, but I couldn't help myself. And now I've learned the truth, and so must you – we were twins, Chlu, two babies stolen away from our natural parents. By Maskull.'

Chlu shook his head, spread his hands in an open gesture that nevertheless showed he did not accept Will's words. 'So you were told, and so you believe . . .'

'Hear me, Chlu! Maskull worked a spell upon us in a secret workshop. Neither of us are natural men. He's altered us. He didn't make us, but his tampering caused us to be as we are. Now don't you see why we must work together?'

Chlu's eyes were slitted against the glare. He threw up a hand against the golden light that haloed Will's head. The shape of his fingers echoed Will's own half-formed magical gesture, but there was a wounded quality about him that seemed too much like self-pity. He began slowly shaking his head. 'Why should I believe a word you say?'

'Because it's the truth.'

'Truth?' Chlu spat out the word. 'What? That you are the Deliverer, and I the Destroyer? Why should I choose to believe a truth like that, when it so clearly does not serve me?'

'The truth is not there to serve you, Chlu. It simply *is*.'

Chlu rapped out his words mockingly. 'Truth! You can put that name to anything you please!'

'No! No, you can't! Do you think you can just choose to believe whatever pleases you? You can't do that! You have a duty to respect what is. It's the nature of our world!'

'I would rather believe what Lord Maskull tells me. He

has shown me *wonders*. And he's promised that as soon as I've rid our world of you I shall have my desire.'

Will stared, incredulous. 'Your . . . *desire?*'

Chlu's gaze was unfaltering. 'I am to join Lord Maskull in the future that he's going to make. He'll be the king and I the prince, and we'll rule a whole world between us!'

'Do you really believe that? Chlu, he'll use you for his present purpose and afterwards discard you without a second thought.'

'Oh, no, little brother. A new world is coming.'

'But it's not coming, is it? Because I'm here to prevent it.'

'You have it in a nutshell.' Chlu's eyes became murderous and hard. 'And that's why you have to die!'

'Listen to me!' Again Will's hands rose up in a spell-maker's gesture and kept Chlu from taking another dangerous step forward. 'You should know that Maskull was labouring at the very limit of his art when he made us. Something went wrong. Master Gwydion saw it all: a great, spinning ray, then a burst of violence that tore a tower to pieces. And that blast tasted of fae magic, a magic from the olden times that was once mighty but now is all lost, except in the stones of the lorc – *and in you and me.*'

'Gwydion is a deceiver. He lies to you.'

'Why should he lie? Whatever separates us, Chlu, comes of the same power that fills the battlestones. Maskull tampered with that power so he could alter us. Can't you feel it? The power that runs in the lorc – it's the same magic that was used to change us. It binds our destinies to the stones, and to one another.'

'Very neat. Only Lord Maskull tells quite a different story.'

Will let his hand fall. 'Of course he does.'

'You were chosen by the deceiver as his favourite. It was Gwydion Crowmaster who stole us away and then hid us in two ready-prepared places. They were shrouded in magic, kept secret so that no one else could find us. And there, as the years went by, that meddler worked his spells upon our minds. He grew us like barnyard animals, all the while twisting us to his scheme. And when he found which child was the most compliant to his magic, that was the one he chose to further at the expense of the other.'

'It wasn't like that.'

Chlu's voice rose and he jumped from the Bier. 'Oh, but it *was*. While I was sent to tend pigs among filthy villagers, you were taken to be schooled alongside the sons of a duke! But Lord Maskull found me and pulled me from my torment! He took me out of the prison village of Little Slaughter, withdrew me before the evil enchanter could shatter it and murder me! Lord Maskull rescued me! He set me free!'

Will was aware that the bone demons had gathered once more, and were spitting and cackling. 'You've got it the wrong way round. It was Maskull who broke Little Slaughter. Maskull found you, Chlu, on that we agree, but he removed you from Little Slaughter not to help you or to set you free. He doesn't want to share overlordship of the future with anyone. He's using you as his instrument. He needs to have you as his lodestone to seek me out. That's been his purpose all along.'

'That's a view that puts you at the centre of all things, and makes me the villain!' Again that bitter, unbelieving laugh. 'Lord Maskull wants to find you all right. He wants more than that. He's sent me to kill you. And so I shall.'

Chlu threw wide his hands and the bone demons flocked as if at his command. A purplish-red glow like an angry wound pulsed from him. 'You see how I make them obey me?'

The creatures jostled forward, encircling Will, pulled by Chlu's hatred, pushed by their own fear. They dared not close on the green-blue aura that rippled around Will's form. But then Chlu bent down, scooped up the dripping skull of the dead Elder and flung it with all his strength. As Will blocked it filth, stinking and foul, blinded him, and he spat the vileness from his lips. Then, without warning, his aura exploded in all directions, filling the world with an immensely bright green light.

All Will could hear were the shrieks of the bone demons as they took to the air, and then came the rattling of chains. When Will regained his sight he saw that Chlu had vanished once more.

CHAPTER FOUR

THE VANE

There was no doubt where Chlu had gone. A chain dangled from a hole in the vaulting. It hung over the Bier, and was swinging. Chlu must have hauled himself up through the hole, and Will knew that he must follow.

But as he pulled himself up on the chain he felt Chlu's struggles cease and knew that his twin had found a ledge higher up. Once through the hole, Will saw that the space that formed the tip of the Spire was hollow. The sharp cone rose up a dozen times the height of a man, its interior lit by four great vents.

The light was dim and diffuse – dust had been kicked into the air, but Will saw that six huge chains depended from a platform at the top. The structure was trussed internally with huge beams and straps of iron that held the stonework together. Chlu had swung up into these rafters and had begun to climb along them and up a series of ladders.

'Come on, little brother!' Chlu howled. 'Catch me if you can!'

Will heard the undertones of his own spirit in the challenge, and, undaunted, he climbed onward. But the way was treacherous. *Always go first through a thicket, but second through a mire* – that was something Wortmaster Gort used to say while out on his long walks. Going second here definitely put the follower at a disadvantage.

The ladders were crumbling – many rungs were wormy. They cracked under Will's feet. Even the lashings that held them to the beams were dry and brittle. No stonemason or carpenter had come into the summit in many a long year, so that nothing had been done by way of repair or renewal. Now that Chlu had climbed some distance ahead he began to unrope the ladder tops and kick them away. He laughed as he tore up whatever was at hand to throw down, but he could not halt Will's progress up into what, for one of them, would be a dead end.

Will fended off the missiles and pressed on doggedly, coming at last to a place about two ladder-lengths below the top platform. Here his daring faced a sterner test. The walkway had been almost wholly smashed by Chlu. In the middle all that remained was a single balk of timber. Will knew that one false step would mean falling to his death. He stopped and raised his arms to Chlu in a last appeal to see sense, but his twin's reply was to fling at him the iron he had been using to tear up the planks.

Will took a step forward, but was immediately thrown off balance, and when he put out a hand he found one of the giant chains. Each link was as long as a man was tall and all six chains came out of a line of holes pierced in the upper platform. They disappeared far below, somewhere near the Bier, but what their purpose was, Will could not see.

He hugged the nearest link to save himself. It shivered as it came under tension and began to move downwards. Having grasped it, Will dared not let go, and so he was pulled to his knees then dragged down off the beam. For a moment he swung out wide over the drop, all his weight held on one twisted forearm. His legs dangled and his guts filled with a paralysing terror that snatched away all power over his body.

Don't look down, he told himself in a silent scream. Keep your head up and hang on!

Distant grinding noises rose up from the space below when the chains jerked into motion. Will felt terror engulf him. His breath came in short gasps. The imperative to keep his grip consumed him as the pain in his wrist peaked. The struggle locked his muscles in a death-like cramp. He cried out, thrashed, managed to turn himself, then captured the link gratefully between his thighs. He squeezed his chest against the link and knew that he had bought enough time until the pain subsided and he could regain his courage. It had not been elegant, but he had avoided the fall.

Of course! he thought as he clung on. It's the vane! These chains are how they work the mechanism. They must be sending out a message.

He forced himself to recall what was up above. On the very top of the Spire the great vane would be swinging and dancing this way and that, its various parts clacking and clanging as it sent the news of an unthinkable defilement to every chapter house in Trinovant.

'What's the matter?' Chlu shouted in delight. 'Are you finding it hard to get close to me?'

Will hung on, both in body and mind. He was shaking with shock, but the pain was ebbing and it was clear from the fingers he could still flex that his wrist had not been broken. Cramp complained in every muscle, sweat streamed down his back. It was hot up here, and he realized how much closer he must have come to the sun by now, way up in the middle airs of the sky, where Gwydion said the air lost its virtue and a man's breathing came hard.

He calmed himself, then he began to think out his best

chance. He could fit his foot into the eye at the end of the link and so let one of his legs bear his weight. The chains were within reach of one another and as one stopped moving down another began moving up. So he jammed his other foot into a link on the next chain, which fortunately soon jolted into motion. When that chain stopped, he moved on to a third, which disappointed him by going down again. But still it was clear how he might be carried up and up by making correct guesses. With luck he might get as far as the platform with its six holes.

He clambered from chain to chain, feeling for advantage, but as his mind opened he felt Chlu's malice interfering with his judgment, willing him to fall. He overshot and saw with horror that just one more upward movement of the chain would carry him up through one of the holes. He would be stripped off the chain like a beetle from a corn stalk.

Fortunately, the next movement took him lower, but his relief lasted only a moment because now he came level with Chlu.

Having kicked away the ladder and guard rail to fling down on Will's head, Chlu had trapped himself on a narrow ledge. Had they chosen to touch hands they could have done so, but Will's twin crouched against the wall in that hot, dark space. He snarled, repelled by a consuming hatred, and struggled with something that protruded from the wall.

Will could see no way down, but then Chlu's hunched shoulder moved, a catch gave way and a bar of brightness pierced the gloom as Chlu threw open a heavy wooden shutter and let in a flood of sunlight. Will saw with amazement that the builders of the Spire had seen fit to place a hatch here.

The grumbling sounds that issued from the chain holes were now complemented by the squeaking and squealing of iron joints. For a moment, Chlu's body blocked the light, but then he climbed through the hole and once more Will was left alone.

The square of blue sky beckoned urgently. He leapt towards it and his fingers scrabbled for purchase, but he managed to get one hand on the sill and launch the other at Chlu's ankle. The latter kicked him off, and when Will looked out he saw above him the final ladder – a series of iron staples, maybe a couple of dozen in all – leading to the uttermost tip of the Spire.

Chlu was already halfway up that deadly route by the time Will emerged and started after him. The rake of the Spire's summit cap was severe. The ascent, which was almost vertical, became an overhang as the stone bellied out just below the vane. Brilliant sunshine burned the outline of Will's shadow onto the weathered sandstone as he forced feet and hands to follow one another. Despite the danger he felt vastly alive. The sun's heat burned his back, and had filled the rusty iron rungs with heat. The air up here was clean, sweet and he could taste blood in his mouth. It was as if the danger itself had sharpened all his senses, made him aware of every detail . . .

He looked to himself suspiciously, testing for evidence of magical attack. Was Maskull watching from somewhere? Was that the plan? Had the sorcerer been waiting all along on some rooftop down below, ready to cast a burst of violet fire skyward and sear both his troublesome creations into flaming brands?

Will blocked out the thought and put all of himself into the climb. He also tried to put out of his mind what he had glimpsed from the corner of his eye, but that was more difficult. It seemed as though the wide world below curved away from the Spire in every direction, the drab roofs of the City and then a green land, losing itself in a bright haze of blue which was neither earth nor sky. And against that background he had seen a speckling of dark shapes – bone demons, gathering again.

Will's certainties told him that a reckoning was at hand. He tried to pull the shreds of his spirit together and scramble faster up the iron staples. The thinking part of him stood aghast at the course he had taken. Why had he done this? He was no murderer. What did he hope to gain by chasing Chlu to this lonely, lofty place? Now he had arrived his actions seemed bizarre and inexplicable. No one could climb such an overhang with a foe like Chlu guarding its top. Only a fool would throw himself at death without surer knowledge that his leaving the world would make a crucial difference.

Even so, there had been no mistaking his inner promptings, the ones he had promised Gwydion he would always try to take account of. The desire was unquestionable: *Find him! Get to him! You must!*

But what had driven Will on had not been determination, nor any righteous plan. It was not fear or hope of gain that made Chlu attack him. It was a force as elemental as day and night.

Soon, he thought grimly, one or both of us is going to have to die. I feel that, and he feels it too.

A raucous croak awoke Will's fears. Black wings fluttered, dappling the brightness with shadows. He gritted his teeth then he looked up to see that it was Chlu who had attracted the wrath of the creatures. He had hauled himself up the double rows of ornamental carvings that lay just below the vane, and there he was being swooped upon by black shapes that wheeled and dived at him. But they were not bone demons.

Ravens! he told himself with sudden relief. They're Bran's ravens, come from the White Tower!

He took his chance. Hand over hand, he pulled himself up through the overhang, jamming his toes behind the rungs until he had hauled his upper body round to where the capstones were sheathed in lead.

Chlu was struggling on the leaden base of the vane, fighting off the birds that mobbed him. Above, the mechanism's ribs were grinding and squealing as they turned, a heavy iron pointer wheeling this way and that. Seen this close, the letters were huge, each taller than a man, and the ribs on which they were mounted swept shudderingly around a huge white heart – a heart bled dry of all desire. Like the letters, the fearsome token was no more than a peeling sheet of thin, white-painted copper thrown into motion by levers and sprocket wheels turning below. The haphazardly rotating ribs threatened to cut Will off at the ankles, while the heart turned crazy somersaults in its cradle as it spelled out its arcane message.

Without another word, Will leapt at Chlu and seized him. The ravens scattered as he slammed Chlu up against a stanchion. He tried to hold him there, but Chlu's fists beat him back with hammer blows. Will threw off the onslaught, knowing he must not use magic to overcome his twin. They traded punch for punch, kick for kick, dodging the flailing vane, somehow avoiding the randomly moving ironwork, and little by little Will forced Chlu back. At last he was pushed out onto the rib that supported the letter E.

Will told him, 'There's nowhere left for you to go.'

'Nowhere' Chlu gasped, 'but Hell!'

Arms outstretched for balance, Chlu turned and teetered along the rib in an insanely risky dance. He reached the safety of the giant letter before the support could move and throw him off. There he turned again – not at bay, but triumphantly. He banged the copper sheeting that made up the letter with the flat of his hand, sending out a sound that rolled like thunder.

'So what's it to be? Do you have the guts to come for

me? Or shall we sit here looking at one another until the Fellows come for you?'

Will shook his head and shot out an accusing finger. 'You think you can find a way to live forever? You can't!'

'It's the end of this Age. Your old world is finished! Only Lord Maskull has seen what's coming next. He's shown me there is a way!'

Will spoke the words that Gwydion had first taught him long ago.

> *First there were nine,*
> *Then nine became seven,*
> *And seven became five.*
> *Now, as sure as the Ages decline,*
> *Three are no more,*
> *But one is alive.'*

Chlu showed his teeth. 'You see? All was prophesied! The *one* is Lord Maskull!'

'But what if it's not like that? What if Master Gwydion is the last phantarch? What then, Chlu?'

Chlu laughed. 'You're an ignorant fool, little brother. Your mind is too busy with small things to understand the greatness of the change that's now upon us. Lord Maskull does not claim to be a phantarch. He never wanted to be that.'

'Then what?'

'It's as I told you. You know nothing of the wonders that were shown to me! This is not just the ending of another Age, not just the passing over of one phantarch for another. This is the end of the world!'

'The end of the world? What do you mean?'

'Magic has always been draining away, right from the beginning of the world, and now it's almost gone. This is the end-time, and when the last Age closes our world will become subject to a new power. Another world is coming for us, little brother, and it's going to swallow us up!'

The ravens cawed and circled, but kept their distance. Down below, the whole beautiful world seemed to have been laid out beneath them. Will held on to the ornamental iron that supported the rib. He was jolted as it revolved, stopped, then revolved again, but nothing could tear his gaze from Chlu's own. It did not matter what nonsense Chlu talked. It was the strangest of fascinations just to look at him.

Will let Chlu's words wash over him, barely aware when they broke off. He knew he had no choice but to go out along the rib and see his labour through to the end. He let his eyes fall, tried to judge the best moment to start out along the rib, but its shifts were capricious. They lacked all pattern, so the direction it would next move in was impossible to foresee, and even if he did choose correctly and even if he did reach the end, Chlu would just be able to push him off.

He watched the golden-headed arrow of the pointer as it swept under the ribs, then he put a hand to his left cheek. When he opened it there was blood in his palm: the cut was bleeding again. Chlu's right cheek was cut in exactly the same place. Out on the rib, Chlu's every move mirrored his own. When Will wiped his hand clean against his breast, Chlu did the same. They both looked up and then away, and in that moment Will saw the hideous connection operating.

A confusion of fear and pain reached up to enmesh his thoughts. There was only one way forward. He must clear his mind of all clouding images. His inner promptings had brought him here, they must be allowed to guide him now. He closed his eyes until his mind became ice clear, then he jumped from the rib and ran forward into empty air.

As he reached the edge, the arm of the pointer swung

neatly under his foot. One step – two, three – each footfall landed miraculously square on the iron strut. The fourth step brought him crashing hard up against the side of the giant white letter E and there he hung as the pointer swung away again.

The impact shivered the sheet of copper and clattered Chlu hard. Only a knee hooked around the lowest horizontal of the letter saved Chlu from falling, but the copper was flimsy and the rivets corroded, and it began to come away from its support. The next time the rib kicked into motion, the letter tore like dry parchment. Chlu pitched suddenly forward. Will, clinging like an insect to the top of the letter, reached a hand down and grabbed Chlu by the shoulder. But in reaching out, he too lost his balance and they were flung from the vane in opposite directions.

CHAPTER FIVE

'KILL! KILL!'

They fell at hurtling speed, but the copper sheet worked briefly like the wing of a bird. The air rushed against it and pushed them clear of the Spire. Then they tumbled and the world began to spin faster and faster. The metal's edge was caught by a billow of air and ripped from Will's grasp. He tried to call out, but the gale that tore his jerkin open also forced its way into his mouth and nose and stopped his breath.

The ground was roaring up to meet him, threatening to slam him into the patterned precinct below. But while a part of him recognized that he was no more than a count of three away from oblivion, another part of his mind froze. Time drifted, then crawled. His headlong dive slowed more and more the closer he came to the ground. The fall would take forever, and the crowds gathered below with horror and disbelief captured on their faces would look up at him until Doomsday before they would see him land. He felt his body become as light as a hawk's pinion. There was time enough to minutely examine the smooth black and white stones below, the patchwork of artisans' booths and the enforcers in their red leather gear. He saw the way that unwelcome sunlight bathed the Vigilants in their yellow and grey robes, hampering them as they turned their empty eye sockets to scan the sky.

Will studied without concern the spiked rail that was rushing up to impale him. In that strange, pliable moment he noticed that the green glow had lit once more around his body. He stretched out his arms and legs, steering his dive, then turned over onto his back and threw his limbs wide.

But the glow was already burning away like the light of a shooting star, and then time came back with a bang.

Suddenly he was tearing through old canvas and into a mass of hay as the fodder tent exploded around him. All the air in his chest was blasted out and everything went dark. He struggled to draw breath, trapped now in a form-less chaos, dazed, numbed and drained by so sudden a calling up of magical effort. He blacked out and came to again in what seemed like a single moment. He was still unable to draw breath, choking on dry grass, aware only that horses were bucking and bolting dangerously nearby. His hand made contact with something hard and dry, and it seemed he had never felt anything so solid before. It was the hard-baked ground. He burrowed and twisted along it, pushing forward through the loose hay like a mole, until a spangling of sunlight showed him where holes in the collapsed awning lit a possible way out.

When he poked his head from under the corded canvas edge what he saw amazed him. The entire row of tents which the enforcers had used as a stable had come tumbling down. Their horses had stampeded through the row of money-changers' booths that stood nearby, carrying several of them down and scattering piles of coin into the street.

The crowd that had gathered to watch the drama unfolding on the Spire top saw their chance and fell on the silver. Men, women and children were filling fists, aprons, hats, fighting one another for what they could get. When Will turned his head he saw the enforcers' fierce dog. It was roused up, but undecided about what to bark at next. Geese and ducks fluttered all around him. A column of Vigilants, led along by their sighted helpers, men in belted black shirts who had thrown open the precinct gates, were crowding purposefully into the space before the monument.

Their masters were giving them orders, calling out at the sacrilege, shouting up a hue and cry. Already some were beating at the fallen tents with their rods of office, aware that they had come close to the place where one of the defilers had landed. They were whipping the crowd into a ferment with their shouts.

'It's a bone demon!'

'Seize it! Kill it!'

Seeing the whips of the Vigilants, those of the crowd who had not been quick enough to get at the coins turned to this new sport. It was terrifying to see, and worse still for Will to know he was its target. As the Vigilants' shouts turned into a chant, individual will dissolved, and what was left was a thirst for blood. Will saw the unreasoning frenzy that entered men's faces, the raised fists that began to pump the air. The mob became a single, many-legged monster.

Will was still dazed from his fall and drained by the involuntary magic that had saved him. He knew he could not fight or outrun a mob. He doubted he could summon any kind of defence now. And the Vigilants were drawing ever closer, using their uncanny sightless sense to close on him.

By the moon and stars, he thought. I'm a dead man!

He cast about, looking for Gwydion or Willow, but they were nowhere to be seen. He twisted and turned, untangling himself from the fallen awning. He ducked under a horse's belly and dived through a tattered curtain that screened off the back of one of the few remaining money-changers' booths. Then he burst out into a space that was piled high with sacks of charcoal and set about with three or four small ironworker's forges, all of which had been abandoned in the excitement.

His head was spinning – at least his knees had not given way yet – but he had not made his escape unnoticed. A new shout went up behind him.

'There he goes!'

Will was no bone demon, but a mob sees only what it wants to see, and the hunt was on. Men thundered after him. He stumbled, then crashed on through the forges, throwing down a bellows and a hearth of hot embers in his wake. He emerged into an aisle between two rows of booths. The lane was almost empty, and those who were in it had not yet been caught up in the riot. He ran along it towards the nearest buildings, swaying past a woman carrying a yoke and pails, almost colliding with a bullock cart. He side-stepped neatly round a corner and swung into the open road.

But when he looked back he saw the pursuit surging into sight once again. Ahead, and coming west from another part of the City, were more Fellows, this time wearing brown robes. He had only one option, and that was to take to his heels again. He turned back and saw a huge Fellow in grey rags blocking his path. There was a side alley no more than twenty paces away, and Will made for it, but as soon as he entered he decided he had made a mistake.

The grey-robed Fellow moved into view and scanned the air sightlessly. Will ran on, for now this place reeked of danger – narrow ways such as these were likely dead ends, and he felt as if he was already caught in a trap. He shook his head to clear it, tried to open his mind, to drive out the hubbub of thoughts and fears.

There were dozens of people in the alley. It led to a

small square surrounded by badly kept houses with a stinking dunghill at its centre. It was deep in shade, with only a meagre patch of sky above. The noise of over-crowded life came from the dwellings. Too many people lived here – women looking out from jutting upper floors, dirt-nosed children playing in the filth, men watching what passed.

Goats foraged and dogs ran out to snap at him as he sprinted by. Two men looked up from their work at the tail of a water cart. Beyond the square, several narrower ways branched off. He dared not take any of them, but ran on down the main alley until it forked and he was faced with a choice.

The noise of the pursuit grew louder. He noticed cart ruts underfoot running to the right. He chose the same fork, hoping they would lead him out of the maze. By now he was breathing hard, his heart pounding fit to burst, and he flattened himself against a wall, filling his lungs, needing to listen out. If only he could get away, then he would head for the royal palace of the White Hall. Gwydion would be bound to take Willow and Bethe there, no matter what they thought had happened at the Spire.

But just as he began to think he had foxed his pursuers he heard cries and a clatter of footsteps. Men in black shirts were running across the junction ahead of him. When they turned, they saw him.

'That way!'

'He's there! Spread out!'

Will cursed and dodged back the way he had come. As soon as he reached the corner and moved out of sight, he jinked into one of the narrower ways, fervently hoping that this was no blind alley.

It was certainly deserted, running for thirty paces or so until it reached a dog-leg. Beyond that was only a small yard, hemmed in by house ends and walls that would be impossible to climb. The building that dominated the yard sent Will's hopes plummeting. It was different to the others, built of expensive dressed stone, heavy and dark, and set back beyond a dry moat that was half choked with rubbish.

Could this be the back of some large, lordly house? he wondered. But he knew he was grasping at straws. A wide flight of steps bridged the moat and ran up to an arched door that was flanked by ornamental carvings. At the centre of the door there hung a brazen fist.

His heart sank. This was the sure sign of a chapter house. Will halted, angry at his false choice, fearful that his other options had disappeared. There were shouts and yelps echoing from the walls – no way out forward or back, and by the sound of it the mob had already decided correctly which way he had gone. They would be here very soon.

He planted his feet with deliberate care, and opened his mind, to invite what powers might be here to emerge from the dry, compacted earth underfoot. He felt the flows, but they were feeble, as if they had been pinched off by the tumble of mean hovels. Barely a tingle ran through his toes, and the aura that usually sheathed him like a cool, blue flame hardly flickered into life. Yet when his eyes rolled back in his head, he was able to give himself over to the ecstasy for a brief moment. A spangle ran over his ribs and launched an upwelling along his spine that drove fatigue before it and refreshed him.

But the joy did not last long and the light of forgetfulness soon faded. When he stepped out of his rhapsody he began straight away to spin and dance out a spell of alteration upon himself. Having assisted Gwydion with the restoring of Lord Dudlea's wife and son, the appropriate formulas of the true tongue came readily to his lips. He had been the subject of magical disguises before, and so his flesh did not resist the changes that came over him. When he emerged from the alteration he had assumed the form of an old man, a beggar. He was filled with hope that this would be a sufficient armour in which to hide.

He could feel the wrath of the mob. A weird pressure on the nape of his neck made the hairs there stand up and caused him to turn. Picking his way among the filth that clogged the dry moat was the Fellow in tattered grey garb. His head was cowled within a deep hood, and it was tilted in the manner that Will had seen each time he had come under the sightless scrutiny of a Fellow.

A shout came from behind. 'This way!'

Will turned to see the first forerunners of the mob coming into the yard. They stopped in their tracks. Bigger men joined them, sweating and breathless. They would not approach their prey, though they were roused for blood, for an Elder was coming.

'Kill! Kill!' some fool shouted, hoping that a chant would be taken up, but it failed: there was no one to kill, save an old beggarman and a brooding Fellow who was now rising up menacingly out of the moat.

They stared at the Fellow as he came forward. He was a huge man. By now a dozen helpers had closed off the yard and three Vigilants were led forward. The men in belted black shirts who carried cudgels and clubs deferred to the Elder as if he had the power of life and death over them. But still they looked with unavoidable respect upon the tattered Fellow who came to meet them.

'Who comes?' the Fellow boomed.

His way of speaking was strange, his voice somewhat lisping, though deep and laced with a quiet kind of menace. When he gathered himself he was a figure to behold, the rends in his robes showing glimpses of a frame of tremendous power.

Unseen now, Will backed up the steps of the chapter

house. Above him, the brass fist came to life on the door and splayed grasping fingers from which he was forced to draw away.

One of the Vigilants was ushered forward, but the big Fellow raised a denying hand to him.

'Who comes?' he repeated. 'Who comes to disturb the peace of this House?'

One of the black-clad men spat. 'Yaaah, Hell-damned Grey Robes!'

'There!' shouted another of the Vigilants' sighted helpers. He pointed towards Will, whose bewilderment at the various competing orders within the Fellowship was not helping him make sense of his danger. 'That's what we've come for. Him. That's a bone demon, sitting on your stair! A bone demon from the Spire!'

The Vigilants tilted their heads, their attention focussing now on Will. The big Fellow took a short step forward, which made the others draw back. 'There is no bone demon here. Only an old man whom I hope will yet be persuaded to our purpose.'

The leader of the Yellow Robes sniffed the air then threw up his hands. 'Magic!' he said. 'Foul magic has been done here! The demon has taken on new form!'

They all looked towards Will.

'Let us fall upon the beggar!' one of the mob shouted. 'Aye!'

They began to surge forward, but the ragged Fellow did not move aside. Instead, he stood four-square and let slip from inside his sleeve a heavy chain. Raising it on high he swept an arc clear before him. Then he said in a stolid but commanding voice, 'It may be that this old man already belongs! You may believe that approaching him is *forbidden*!'

The Vigilants drew back from the death-dealing chain that circled and swung over their heads. It filled all the yard with the soughing of stirred air, and no one dared come within its compass for fear that it too was touched by the magic the Vigilant had smelled. It was plain to the stupidest that, in so narrow a space, a chain in the hands of a man like this might easily murder a dozen of them if they tried to take the recruit away from him.

'You may imagine that we are angry with you,' the Vigilant Elder said in a high, wheedling voice. 'One might ask: who is this Fellow? And where does he belong?'

The hooded head turned to face the questioner. 'And some may hear that he is Fellow Eudas, and that he belongs to the Black House. But certain exalted ones may choose to take care! For perhaps the lowly Fellow was a soldier before he begged admission to the Happy Family.'

Will marvelled at the oddly indirect language of the Fellowship. He had heard Gwydion use it when they had visited Clifton Grange disguised as mendicant Fellows. Now the curious but deadly exchanges sent a shiver down his spine.

'How then if the lowly one might be commanded to stand aside? How then?'

'All respect to the exalted! But he may suppose that this Fellow, lowly or not, might decide to send the first man to take another step towards him down to see for himself the fires of Hell.'

A different Fellow pushed his way to the front. He too was an Elder, but one of the senior Brown Robes whose order dwelt in the House-by-Cripplegate. When he drew back his hood, painted eye sockets seemed to stare out from his skull like the eyes of a madman.

'Why, oh why, should a lowly Fellow be believed, if Fellow he really is? Perhaps it is only an impostor who speaks in such a rude and obstinate way to Elders. Proof may be required! Else one may say that he himself is an incarnation of the very demon which fell to earth!'

'Aye!' the helpers cried, taking up the idea with enthusiasm. 'Let him throw back his hood and show himself!'

The crowd that now filled the alley was fifty or sixty strong. As those at the back began to chant, 'Show! Show! Show!' the brown-robed senior gathered himself as if for a fight, and spoke as directly as his station would allow. 'Can it be this lowly servant has not heard our friends a-calling? Let him show himself! Or must these same friends force him to uncover?'

'Force?' There was scorn in the reply. 'Such an ugly word. Shall it be said that these friends are going to force a lowly Fellow who is doing his duty by the Iron Rule, who moves in zeal and commits nothing contrary to the holy principle that binds all members of the Happy Family? Force, is it?'

The Elder trembled with fury. He was not used to backing down. He cried, 'How best to put an order such as this? Come now, friends: the lowly Fellow cannot kill us all! Now let him prove himself. Show, show, show!'

The chant started again, but Eudas stood unmoving in the face of it, until it died away. Then he said, 'The lowly Fellow has stated his case: the beggar belongs to *him*. However—'

A moment passed. The chain continued to circle overhead, but then Eudas snapped his wrist and brought it snaking down into a dead heap beside him. With the next movement he put his hands to his hood and pulled it back onto his shoulders.

Those who stared gasped at what they saw. From where Will crouched he could not see what had caused the reaction, but there were many in the crowd who turned away, while the rest goggled in frank horror.

The Elder's fingers reached out briefly, then he nodded, disappointed that the orbits of Fellow Eudas' eyes were indeed vacant. The realization struck a dull note of fear in

Will's belly as he huddled lower against the foot of the chapter house door. Above him the brazen arm reached down as far as it could in a vain attempt to seize him.

'Is it not wholly as the lowly one said?' the big man asked in his quiet, deep voice. 'Now, if the exalted ones please . . . he may be left to his work, and may peace attend all.'

'There is peace only in Heaven,' the brown-garbed one cried, making a sign in the air. 'Perhaps this is something the lowly Fellow forgets!'

'One may say he knows which of those gathered here upholds the Iron Rule, and which is trying to break it. How if someone should take report of what has passed to the Council of High Wardens? How if due consideration was made upon the facts?'

Will watched as heads were bowed in fear, but then a voice at the mouth of the alley shouted, 'This way, everybody! The bone demon went down Fish Street!'

When the last of the crowd had bled away, the big man quickly pulled up his hood and hid the face that had so horrified the crowd. He stooped and picked up the chain, feeding it artfully inside his sleeve and across his shoulders. Will watched him, his mind still crawling with fears, certain that his best hope was to remain an old beggar for the time being.

But there was another danger to be handled now.

'I thank you, sir. I thank you for my life,' Will muttered, rising. He made humble nods, gathered his tattered coat about him, and began to make away, but the Fellow moved across his path.

'If you really do want to thank me for your life,' he said simply, 'there is only one way to do it.'

'No, no,' Will said, trying again to slide past. 'I'm truly grateful that you've helped me, but I've no wish to spend my latter days inside a chapter house. Kind though your offer undoubtedly is, I—'

'Hear me out, friend.'

Will shivered with revulsion. 'Oh, but the life would be hateful to me. In fact, it would be worse than the death from which you've just saved me.'

But Eudas placed a staying hand on Will's breast. 'I also have made that choice.'

That brought Will up sharp. 'What did you say?'

'I am trying to tell you that I have escaped the Fellowship.'

Astonishment made Will stare. 'But how can that be? *Once a Fellow, always a Fellow* – isn't that part of the Iron Rule? No one ever leaves the embrace of the Sightless Ones.'

'I did.'

Will began to feel the integrity of his disguise running thin. Very slightly, the mottling of age on his hands had started to lighten . . .

Hands! Of course!

'Let me see your hands,' he told the Fellow.

'You don't believe me.'

'Do you blame me for that?'

Straight away, Eudas unwrapped the dirty cloth strips that were bound over his hands. Will's fast-improving eyesight could see that the knuckles were not as cracked and red as those of other Fellows, and the nails, always horn-hard and yellow, had begun to grow out normally.

Will dropped the hands, amazed. 'You've stopped washing.'

The dark hood gave a single nod. 'I have.'

'You've abandoned the ritual!'

'I have not washed in a month.'

'But that's impossible! The strength of mind that would be required to break free from such coils as the Fellowship winds around a man's spirit . . .'

'It has not been easy.'

Will knew it was time to put aside his astonishment and ask the crucial question. 'But tell me, ex-Fellow Eudas, if you are not recruiting lost souls to your house, why did you risk yourself to help a worthless beggar?'

There came a growl from deep inside the big man's chest, and his strangely accented words gave Will even more to think about. 'There was little risk. If they had not gone away I would have killed them all. And if there is justice in the world, it will be you who helps the worthless beggar.'

CHAPTER SIX

ONCE A FELLOW . . .

By now, Will's suspicions were fully aroused. He peered hard at the hooded Fellow, trying with all his mind to penetrate the disguise. There was more to this man than met the eye.

'You must forgive an old man,' he said, sticking to his story. 'I'm in no position to help anyone. Now, if you don't mind—'

The big man seized him by the shoulders. 'The worthless beggar I want you to help is . . . *me.*'

Will imagined that in a moment he would slap the Fellow playfully on the shoulder and say, 'Come now, Master Gwydion, without your staff you are not so nimble in magic as once you were. Don't you think I can see through your disguises as well as you see through mine?' But that moment was not to be, for it seemed there was something even stranger than magic about this man.

'Who *are* you?'

'If you would know that, then listen and I will tell you.'

The big man sat down on the steps and began to lay out his life's tale, and Will, unable to do otherwise, sat down beside him and listened.

'I have always been lucky. My given name was Lotan,

which in my native tongue means "the fortunate one". I was born seven-times-seven years ago in a land far beyond the Narrow Seas, in a country that you call the Tortured Lands. One day, when I was still a child, all my family was murdered. It was my good fortune to be the only one who escaped alive.'

'Good fortune indeed,' Will murmured, though the irony of his remark went unappreciated.

'Since then, I have roamed upon land and roved upon the sea. I have carried myself to all corners of the world. I have lived in many strange places, and in a few of them my luck has been sorely tested, but never was I bested in fight, and never was I made a slave. This does not mean that I have not done dark deeds, but sometimes a man is given no choice.

'At last I tired of travel. I came into the port of Callas, and being somewhat skilled in the arts of war I decided to make my fortune as a mercenary soldier. I was accepted into the garrison by the captain there.'

Heavy chain links clinked inside Lotan's robe as he finished.

'It would have been a fool of a captain who turned you down,' Will said, aware of the man's powerful frame.

Lotan shrugged. 'I am what I am.'

'Lord Warrewyk. Is it not he who has been Captain of Callas these five years?' Will said, unable to resist probing after loyalties.

The hood turned. 'The time about which I speak was long before Earl Warrewyk's day. I served three dukes who were captains before he – the Dukes of Gloustre then Southfolk, and latterly Duke Edgar of Mells, who was my last commander. That was six years ago.'

Will showed no reaction, but the information was sound. Duke Edgar had been killed at Verlamion – hacked to death by Lord Warrewyk's men. Edgar had been a staunch supporter of the queen, and his cruel son was her chief supporter now.

The big man continued speaking, and soon Will heard a burr in his voice that spoke of fond recollections. 'Strife and easy living were mine in equal measure during my time in Callas. I ate two good meals every day. I lived a manly life. I fought alongside men I trusted, men who trusted me. But the life of a man-at-arms is, at its end, always hard to bear, for a soldier feels more sharply than others the passing of his prime. As the first grey hairs grow he feels the aches begin in his flesh. There came a day when I began to think of retirement, of using what little gold I had gleaned to open an alehouse. I wanted no more than to pass my remaining days in quiet kind, but my plans were overtaken by greater events.

'Five summers ago, in the last month of my service, war threatened, and I was sent with the bodyguard of my Lord of Mells to a new place. We took ship across the Narrow Seas and came into this Realm to prosecute war.'

'Did you go to Verlamion?'

The hood stirred again. 'You know of that place?'

'I went there . . . once.'

'It has a rich chapter house. But it was in the streets of the town that spreads around the chapter house that the battle was fought. In truth it was not much of a battle, but it was the one fight in which my luck failed me. Duke Edgar became trapped. His bodyguard were slain around him, and though I tried to protect him, I took for my troubles an axe blow – here. It cut through the steel brow-strap of my helm and robbed me of half my face. The blow was given to me by one of Lord Warrewyk's men. It has been my ruination.'

Will winced, echoing the reaction of those who not long before had stared at Lotan and screwed up their faces at the sight of him.

'When the battle at Verlamion was over, I was left for dead. But then a Wise Woman found me and bound up my head and stayed with me, thinking that I would soon die. She could not heal me beyond the laying on of gentle herbs, but even so I did not die for there was something about her ministering that lifted me up. Instead I lived on for three years, begging in the streets of Trinovant in a red cloud of torment. At last I could bear the suffering no more. I gave myself into the keeping of the Sightless Ones who, to have me, plucked out my eyes.'

Will heard the rumble of Lotan's regret, and looked up at the blank walls of the chapter house, which for all their impressive size and strength seemed also inhuman and cold-hearted in their proportions.

'At first, the losing of my eyes felt like a mercy, for all pain leaves a man who surrenders himself. Forgetfulness enfolds him like a blanket and for some that is a powerful comfort. But not for me. The longer I remained within the chapter house, the more doubts came to plague me. I was sure I had made the biggest mistake by going there, for though my head had been deeply cloven and now I was blinded also, still I remained whole in spirit. I have never been one who runs with a flock. My thoughts are my own. How could I surrender myself to that which I did not truly believe?'

Will's brow creased as he tried to understand. 'Surrender yourself? To what? To the service of the Fellowship?'

The big man seemed to struggle with the idea. 'Not to the Fellowship exactly, but to that power which they would make all men bow down before.'

'What's that?' Will asked, horrified. 'A monster?'

'It is an invisible power, one that all other Fellows swear they can feel in the world. But try as I might, I could never feel it. That is why I could not progress.'

'What is it?'

'I don't know. They have a name for it, but that name may not be spoken.'

'I've often wondered what could be at the heart of the Fellowship,' Will said, still unable to grasp what he was being told. 'Do they mean a power of magic? I know the Sightless Ones use a form of sorcery, and I can tell you for a certainty that natural magic is real, but—'

'Oh, it is not natural magic they revere, but something else. An ancient invention, a great piece of wickedness . . . it did not originate with the Fellowship – they have come about because of it. But they have used it ruthlessly.'

'But what *is* it?'

A gurgling laugh escaped the big man. 'Only an idea. But one so powerful that it has made slaves of all those who were rash enough to open their minds to it.'

And Will suddenly recalled what Gwydion had said about the Great Lie. That too was only an idea, but the wizard had said that it was immensely dangerous – an idea that, in a manner of speaking, had the power to turn other ideas to stone. It worked upon men, women and children, not by shackling their bodies as the Slavers had done, but by imprisoning their minds.

Lotan turned. 'The axe that made me so terrible to look upon has left me good for little beyond the terrifying of mobs, or perhaps the begging of pennies from those who desire to buy a glimpse of horror, but I remain my own man. I can do no other.'

Will heard no self-pity in Lotan's voice, rather a wry humour that spoke of inner strength. 'Friend Lotan,' he said, 'you still haven't told me why you chose to save an old beggarman from the mob.'

'Because you decided to be kind to me.'

'I?' Will peered hard at the dark shadow that lay beneath Lotan's hood. 'How was I kind?'

'You gave me an apple.'

Will froze. 'That . . . was you?'

'I sensed your magic, even then, and so I followed you.

I have no eyes, but in consequence I can feel much that was once hidden from me. I was drawn towards the Spire when you went there. And when I heard the hue and cry, I came here to make your acquaintance. I have hunted down many a man before, though few throw off the sparks that you do. It was not difficult to direct you here.'

Will was astonished. 'You knew about me all the time?'

'I was here when you entered this yard. I witnessed your change of form. I knew what you were, and—' he grasped Will's wrist, '—I chose to help you.'

'But . . . what do you want from me?'

'I want you to help me.'

Lotan suddenly threw back his hood and showed his ruined face. Empty sockets yawned, and Will saw what work the axe-blade had done – livid flesh ran from ear to chin and his cheek was sunken where an entire upper row of teeth had been smashed away. 'Please, I beg you, sorcerer – give me back my sight!'

The word sorcerer made Will recoil, but a spasm of sympathetic pain flashed through him.

'I am no sorcerer,' he said. 'It's true that I'm somewhat versed in magic, but—'

'But you will not help me.'

'I cannot. The restoring of your sight is a task far beyond any magic that I can work. Even the healing powers of a king could not—'

Lotan's grip tightened on Will's arm. 'You transformed yourself! I felt you do it. I sensed it all from where I stood in the shadows. Nor was that any spell of seeming. You have powerful magic in you, powerful enough to shift shape, powerful enough to give me back my eyesight – if only you would decide to use it!'

'You're right—' Will said, pulling away, overawed by the bodily presence of the man.

'I knew it!'

Will's disguise was quickly reverting now, and he felt uncomfortably exposed. 'What I mean is, you're right that it's no simple thing to make transformations. It takes powerful magic, but it's a thousand times harder to unpick the spells of another – especially when the original change is one that was agreed upon freely. For that very reason, such magic as I am able to call upon cannot so much as remove a tattoo – not unless it was printed in the flesh by force.'

'Please help me!'

'Listen to me, Lotan! You gave yourself under oath to the Sightless Ones. That was your given word. Such an oath is binding. It is not within the scope of my powers to reverse that change.'

The other slumped, like a great brazen statue being melted down in a crucible. 'The gold I saved while I was a soldier, I buried it in a meadow near Verlamion before the battle. Even after all this time I could help you to find it—'

As Will shook his head more grey vanished into thin air. 'Magic does not work through payment. The rede says, "Magic may be neither boughten nor sold."'

'Then I am going down into the fires of Hell . . .'

Lotan's head collapsed into his hands and he rocked back and forth in silence. For a moment he seemed to be sobbing soundlessly, and Will considered the full misery into which this man had sunk. It was frightful.

What he had said to Lotan had hurt because, as the rede said, 'Refusals disappoint, and great refusals disappoint greatly.' And Will knew he would have to hurt Lotan even more.

Unable to wait any longer, Will stood up and began to unravel the transformation that had disguised him. He stepped out the gestures that helped the magic to unwind and restore him to his true condition and at last grew still.

'You move with elegance,' Lotan said emptily. 'I could feel it. I think you must be a very handsome young man.'

Will knew he must check himself. In too short a space of time he had been placed under a tremendous obligation. His feelings had been slammed from pillar to post, and now he felt an overwhelming desire to do something that he might regret.

I can't so easily walk away from a man who has just saved my skin, he thought. I can't leave him in this alley and tell him there is no hope, when I know a man who might just be able to set everything to rights.

He tried not to think of Gwydion, but it was no good. The part of him that wanted to see the world become what it ought to be overflowed like a fountain. Of course, it was horribly wrong to presume upon a wizard's powers – he had learned that lesson only too well at Delamprey. And it would be cruel to offer false hope to Lotan. But how could he just cut a man's hopes adrift?

What shall I do? he asked himself. It would compromise Gwydion greatly if I were to tell any stranger that an Ogdoad wizard had entered Trinovant recently.

He scratched his head, but no better idea came into it. 'There is a man I know who is far wiser than I. He may have some advice for you. Only advice, I say. But I will ask.'

'I *knew* you would help me!'

Will felt a wave of gratitude break over him. 'I make no promises,' he cautioned. 'And now I must go. Shall I look for you again in this place?'

'Yes!' Lotan's empty eye sockets gazed towards the narrow patch of sky that opened above the alley. He threw himself to his knees and clasped his hands together in an attitude of such rapture that Will was embarrassed. 'Have I your word of honour that you will come back?'

'You may count that as a promise.'

'I do not know why, young sorcerer,' Lotan said fervently, 'but I believe you.'

Will looked sharply around as Lotan seized his hand again. 'You must not call me "sorcerer", "enchanter", "warlock" or "magician" – these words are easily mis-understood and lead to trouble. I'll look for you again here about midnight, though I can't say which midnight it will be.'

'Then I will wait for you here *every* night.'

Will turned and looked down the alley. 'Which way should I go if I'm to find the White Hall?'

Lotan drew back. 'You have business at the royal palace?'

'If I do, it's my own business.'

'Then you should avoid the Spire and go out of the City by the Luddsgate and along the roads they call the Fleete and the West Strande.'

'You mean the White Hall lies *outside* the City?'

'Didn't you know? It's on the north bank of the river, maybe half a league from here. To find it keep the warmth of the setting sun on your face, but always follow the stink of the river as it bends south. You will not mistake the place for the walls are high and the echoes carry there like the ghosts of the past.'

As Will emerged from the alley he found the small street deserted. The overhangs of the houses closed in above him, and in the quiet he was aware of cooking smells and the distant sounds of commerce on a busy street. The way out of the maze was easier to find than he expected.

On the main street there were crowds of people hurrying this way and that, occupied, but seldom speaking to one another. A few, Will saw, were born to indulgence, rich merchants who rode upon horses and had men to clear a way for them and their well-adorned ladies. But there were many others aimless and rat-like: cut-throats, pick-pockets, dirty-faced women, some wanton, some carrying babes-in-arms the better to further their trade in pity. He melted into the crowds, meeting very few inquiring looks but following his feelings as best he could. He took bearings from glimpses of the Spire and noted the colours of the robes the Fellows wore. Grey signified the chapter house of Farring-without-the-Wall, the Black Robes were Fellows of Hollbourne-by-the-Spire, but others robed in white were heading westward in large numbers, as if they were required to leave the City before the curfew bells tolled.

By following the White Robes Will soon came in sight of a gate and found it was the one they called the Luddsgate. There he supposed he would meet with more unhappy drag-onets, but there was a paupers' footway that led out, just a simple passage for those carrying no goods. It stank in the heat, but a different smell assailed him once outside, for the road ran across a stout bridge, and below it stretched brown mud banks between which the waters of a tributary ran. When Will looked down it towards the Iesis he was amazed to see that the level of the river had dropped right down. He hurried on, and soon he saw serjeants-at-law by the dozen sitting around the Inns at Linton Greene. They all wore gowns of dark green, and they had long, green-dyed feathers in their caps, which Will knew showed the number of their successes. Gwydion had told him how all lawyers had been compelled by a king of old to dress in this fashion in order that common men might know the greatest of villains on sight.

Will went on again, leaving behind the steeples of the Inns, then past the lordly houses of Arandel, Mells and Southfolk, until an almost unseen figure passed close by and crossed his path, pulling him suddenly into a doorway.

His aura flared green and he threw up a self-protective hand, but immediately he felt it seized and bent down hard in a grasp that forced him to his knees.

'Agh!'

'You fool!'

'Master Gwydion!'

'Shhh!' The wizard's eyes accused him. 'Now that was a fool's errand was it not?'

Will understood but was unrepentant. He shook himself out of the wizard's now-relaxing grip. 'You have your errands and I have mine. Were you watching when we fell? Did you see what happened to Chlu?'

'I saw the pair of you lighting up the entire City with your rude magic.'

'I didn't do it on purpose. I was falling to my death.'

'And every Fellow within a dozen leagues must have turned his head upward when you leapt off that vane.'

'I didn't leap, I fell.'

'You should not have been up there in the first place.'

Will felt anger churning inside and stabbed a finger at the wizard. 'Don't you tell me what I should and should not be doing! I was following my feelings.'

'Oh, *dangerous* man! It would be better for you if you got far away from the City now. The Fellows are very greatly roused up and most unhappy with you!'

'I don't care about them. And I'm not running away.' He reached out and prevented Gwydion from turning aside. 'I asked you if you saw Chlu fall. Did you?'

Gwydion's face was granite as he looked down at the presumptuous hand on his sleeve. 'Chlu came down on the far side of the Spire. I cannot say what happened to him.'

Despite his anger, Will wanted to tell the wizard all that had passed, but he could see Gwydion was in no mood to receive complicated news. Instead he demanded, 'Where are Willow and Bethe?'

'Safe.'

'I said "where?" Answer me fully now, Master Gwydion, or I swear—'

'At the palace. Do you remember Jackhald, who helped us raise the Blood Stone from the well at Ludford? He's been made captain of the guard here. He's agreed to find you lodging.'

'Well, that's something at least.'

'But no thanks to you. Follow me, for we have work to do.'

Will pulled up short again, his hotness cooling. 'Master Gwydion, that's not the way to the White Hall.'

'Indeed it is not.'

'Then I'm not going that way. I know the importance of your work as well as anyone, but it's as I've told you, I have one or two errands of my own, and the first of them is to see my wife and child!'

⊡ ⊡ ⊡

CHAPTER SEVEN

LEIR'S LEGACY

Three days later, on the day of Duke Richard's arrival, Will announced his intention to go down to Luddsgate to see the duke's army make its triumphal entry into Trinovant. Willow said she wanted to come and insisted that she would bring Bethe too.

Will agreed only reluctantly. He was worried that another attack might be mounted. In the time since their encounter on the Spire nothing more had been seen or heard of Chlu, but in quiet moments when Will turned his mind towards the City he could feel an ache in his bones. It told him that his twin was alive and nursing malice somewhere within the walls.

Willow had already told Gwydion of Will's plan to go down to see the arrival. Now she went further, suggesting that the wizard should break off his single-minded search for Maskull's magic tower and come along also. 'Surely,' she said, 'it'll be helpful to take note of which nobles are riding alongside Duke Richard in the parade. Shouldn't you see what order of precedence they come in?'

The wizard was about to say something in reply, but then he stared at her hard, as if reading another intent in her request.

'Willand's drawn,' Gwydion said. 'And you feel that in him, don't you?'

'*Drawn?* What on earth do you mean, Master Gwydion?'

'Drawn towards the City, or more precisely someone at present biding his time out there. Does it not worry you, the prospect of another quarrel? Another bolt from the blue? I think it should. Though it will be something else next time.'

'Will's already thought about that,' she said, shutting the idea out and replacing it with another notion – that perhaps not all of the harm that had flowed from the magic bracelets and into the wizard's wrists had been emptied from him, for he seemed darker and wearier than ever before. 'Now, are you staying or coming?'

Now that the last moment had come, Gwydion decided he would indeed accompany them into the City. They took a small river boat which rowed them to the Saltwharf Steps. After landing, they went up the slope towards Luddsgate, just managing to avoid the Spire precincts, and pressed in with everyone else who had lined the route.

Thousands of people had come from all parts of the City. They filled the streets, crowding upon balconies and even climbing up to roof-ridges and chimney stacks to see the great Duke of Ebor admitted through the Luddsgate.

The gate itself, Will saw, was a broad tower of limestone banded with Slaver brick and carved with the achievements of the kings of old, just as the Eldersgate was carved with northern dragons. Gwydion explained, 'The duke has chosen to enter Trinovant by its grandest gate as a reminder to all the inhabitants where their loyalties ought to lie. It was upon the timbers of this great portal that the burgesses of the City, bare months ago, nailed a daring proclamation.'

'What did it proclaim?' Will asked.

'They bravely declared all the gates of Trinovant barred against the return of their own king – until "redress and remedy" might be found for the duke concerning the king's actions in besieging him at Ludford Castle.'

'Good for them,' Will said.

But Willow was not so sure. 'It doesn't seem all that brave of the townsfolk in hindsight. They must have been thinking about their own skins, and what Lord Sarum and Lord Warrewyk would do to the City if its people sided with the queen.'

Gwydion examined the gate expectantly. 'It looks like the City's gamble has been good. Queen Mag and her friends were up to their necks in debt with every merchant in Trinovant. That is a matter that would take some settling before she could be welcomed back.'

Willow's head craned forward with the rest of the crowd as the first beating of drums and blowing of shawms was heard on the west wind.

Will lifted Bethe and sat her astride his neck, and she rode there agog at everything she saw.

'Why doesn't the duke go straight to the White Hall?' Will asked. 'That's the place where all royal business is done, isn't it?'

The wizard waved a dismissive hand. 'First, Friend Richard must be at pains to show how much the people love him. The governance of Trinovant depends on shows of respect as much as it does on force.'

'Then he's going to the Guild Hall?'

'To be received by the City's notables – the Lord Mayor, his Bailiff, the Sheriff, and the Aldermen of the twenty-six wards. All of these tom-fools he will shower with promises and praise, and they will do him a show of honour in return before he sets himself to the real work of the day.'

'Do you think he's testing the water?' Willow asked.

'Certainly he will be watching how the people regard him. And showing them what force he has at his command, in case there's a riot in the offing.'

'A riot?' Willow asked in alarm. 'Is that likely?'

'He has already made the king call a Great Council.'

Will snapped round. 'Well, thank you for telling me! When?'

'Every lord in the land is ordered to present himself in three days' time.'

'To bend the knee before King Hal?' Will asked.

Gwydion nodded. 'Richard wants those who can be persuaded to stay – where he can keep an eye on them.'

'Yes,' Willow agreed. 'And all those who will not come will be forced to declare as much.'

'Three days . . .' A vivid memory of Lord Warrewyk's bloody handiwork came into Will's mind. 'Well, apart from the noblemen who were done to death following the battle at Delamprey, I imagine there are quite a few others who won't be turning up.'

The wizard paused, considering carefully. 'Perhaps more lords will heed the call than you imagine. Of course, there will be diehards, men like Henry, Duke of Mells, who have gone into the north with the queen, but there are many more who, in truth, want only to tend their own flocks. They will pay lip service to whichever camp is the stronger. If I am any judge, most of the lords who attended the Council at Corben Castle will attend here also.'

Will dropped his voice to a murmur. 'Then they must be sweating rivers just now – a few days ago half of them swore they would see Duke Richard's head chopped off for treason. Some of them would even have done it themselves if it meant getting a share of his lands.'

'But do not forget in whose interest lies the peace now, Willand. Friend Richard wants to maintain the comfortable fiction that Hal is back on his throne and that all is now right with the Realm. Richard will be graciously pleased to forgive all who come to Trinovant to kneel before the king.'

'Do you really think so?' Will looked hard at the gate. 'Will Richard settle for that? For myself, I wonder what he's really up to.'

Gwydion tapped his nose and winked. 'Soon we will know how it is going to be.'

Will saw a band of men appear under the great arch. City waits, they were, musicians in motley garb who played merrily upon sackbuts and shawms and beat upon tabrets with long sticks to herald the coming of the king. Each of the Guilds had sent liverymen, and they lined the road. Near them were arrayed the serjeants-at-law in their green finery, and walking at their centre the King's Serjeant, carrying a golden mace upon his shoulder. Behind him came the Recorders and Justices – the judges of the law, and regulators of the people.

'I'm surprised Duke Richard trusts to his safety at all,' Will murmured, 'with so many kinds of lawyer gathered in the road to greet him.'

'Ha!' Gwydion sniffed. 'Our falcon does not mind a few toads strewing his path when he has the king himself in his talons. But if you are asking about the niceties of the deal, I will tell you that all the legalities have already been tidied up. Several edicts have been issued in the name of the king. These are writs that overturn those given out at the Great Council that was held under the Corben Tree – the ones that attainted Friend Richard. None of it was ever ratified, and so says the king: "All that was Ebor's, is Ebor's once again." You see how much has been done in preparation for Duke Richard's arrival? Not least all the counter-magic that I have expended!'

Despite the heat, Will felt a frostiness issuing from the wizard that seemed to confirm what Willow had said. He wondered, and not for the first time, what exactly happened when a wizard began to fail. Gwydion himself had said that the end of the present Age was nigh. What would become of Gwydion before he went into the Far North in search of his philosopher's stone?

Will shut his eyes, feeling a familiar nausea move into the pit of his stomach. His heart began to thump faster. Chlu was somewhere in the crowd, searching, coming ever closer . . .

He closed his mind, guarding his talent, doing the equivalent in magical terms of hanging back quietly in the shadows. He was not sure whether that would be enough to hide him from his twin's murderous awareness, but when Chlu appeared again he would meet him face to face. Beads of sweat stood out on Will's forehead, but the feeling of danger passed away and his heart slowed again. He wiped his face and scanned the crowd, but there was no one familiar to be seen there.

'Are you expecting anyone in particular?' Gwydion asked from the side of his mouth.

'Hmm?'

'You seem pensive. Scared perhaps. Are you expecting Chlu?'

Will grimaced at the wizard's imputation, and said uncomfortably, 'The only reason I escaped from the Spire is that Chlu fled his true name.'

'You should have told me that sooner.'

'Should I?'

'Do you feel him now in the crowd?'

'He dare not attack me here.'

'I agree. But only because there is no clear shot of you. He will not keep away for long.'

'I hardly need you to tell me that.'

'Nor will the fact that you know his true name afford you even a meagre measure of protection for long, for sooner or later Chlu will speak with Maskull about the matter and Maskull will tell him the truth.'

'Which is?'

'That you can only use his true name to destroy him by destroying yourself. He will gamble that you have not the skill, or more likely the courage, to use a power like that.'

'Then he'll be wrong!' Will said, but he instantly regretted his unconsidered reply.

'Is that so?' Gwydion nodded judiciously, absorbing the remark and weighing it carefully. 'Is that truly so, Willand? For, if it is, then you are as great a fool as any that I have ever met.'

But now the music had grown louder and the iron-collared dragonets were roused to groaning and flapping their stubby wings. The keepers at the capstans heaved on the bars to make the silver beasts draw back into the depths of the gatehouse and the stalls where they were out of sight.

High up between the towers of the Luddsgate itself stood a great, weathered statue of the ancient Brean king, Ludd. Men had climbed perilously to bedeck it with garlands and oak branches, and now sweepers were rushing to clear the way below. Fellows from nearby chapter houses came with incense burners and sprinklers of rose-water to disguise the air so the horses would not bolt at the stink. And then, almost too suddenly, the waiting was over. Three heralds in royal tabards came in sight. Then Duke Richard of Ebor appeared, bare-headed, sitting astride his famous white warhorse. Save for his helmet, he rode in full battle armour.

Through that tremendous portal Duke Richard passed in splendour, but it was not his own sword that he raised aloft, but rather King Hal's. He lifted it up like a sign – or perhaps a boast – while a few paces behind, on a little bay horse, rode the quiet, plainly dressed figure of the king himself.

Duke Richard's intention, Will knew, was to show himself to the people – this was Richard of Ebor, the king's great saviour and Lord Protector once more. He must be seen to be the hero who had saved the sacred sovereign from the grip of greedy friends and a wicked wife. But Will read another message, for in the middle of it all the humble, pale-faced figure of the king seemed hemmed in by gaolers – Sir Thomas Cyrel and Lord Bonavelle, square-chinned men who sat upon massive chargers, and who else but the iron-handed seneschal, Sir Hugh Morte, loyalest of Ebor retainers, bringing up the rear?

Yet, imprisoned though the king was by these huge forces, a moment came when, to Will's mind at least, everything was stood upon its head and Hal appeared to be the serene embodiment of kingship. The whiff of dragonet made the larger destriers skittish, and though they were blinkered and under short rein it was only with difficulty that their ill-tempered riders were able to control them. Yet through the commotion the little bay walked on at ease, as if enfolded by the mystic aura that only a true king possessed.

And then clarions called – the sound of silver trumpets recognizing the return of the king to the City, and Will tried to gauge how much of the cheering proclaimed the arrival of the king and how much his captor. There were many in the crowd who waved wreaths of victory, or pinned on their breasts the badge of the fetterlock and falcon. They called out loudly, 'A Ebor! A Ebor!' But despite their raucous shouts, Will still detected King Hal's subtle empowerment, for many more of the people were glad to have their monarch back than cared how his deliverance had been accomplished. And Will shook his head in amazement because although Duke Richard knew it not, the truth was that he had placed himself wholly in the king's power.

As the leading columns of the duke's formidable army entered the City, drums were beaten at their head and the penetrating buzz of crumhorns and the drone of bladder pipes waxed suddenly loud. Pans of sorcerer's powder flared up in shows of light and smoke, and petals scattered down from the arch upon the helmeted heads of the soldiery.

Suddenly, the whole scene became a riot of flags bearing the colours of the victors. Helmets and bright armour glittered as ranks of mounted knights came on steadily, five abreast. There was a clattering of hooves on flagstones. A great cheer was raised and all the ghastly, glorious panoply of war came surging through the gate, edged weapons displayed to awe the minds of those who gazed on.

Will frowned as he saw the train of great guns. The three greatest of them were named 'Toune', 'Tom o' Linton' and – perhaps worryingly – 'Trinovant'. They had been named for three cities by way of a warning, for these three had the strongest circuits of walls, and the names were a boast that nothing could withstand the might of these engines of war.

Close after the guns came Lords Sarum and Warrewyk, and riding between them Edward, Earl of the Marches and heir of the House of Ebor. Will saw his wife's eyes as her head turned to follow the duke's son. Edward was handsome, a manly figure, made even more attractive – or so it had once seemed – by a cultivated air of superiority that was copied from his father. It had been a youthful jealousy of Will's that Willow must have been in love with Edward.

How easy it was now to see that the lorc had exploited in him one of the three human weaknesses. But back at Ludford Castle he had been ready to kill the heir of Ebor. Despite their boyhood friendship he had been ready to run his heart through with a dagger. Though the murderous impulse appeared ludicrous in hindsight, still he had been scarred by the incident. He had been left with a feeling of shame that was unearthed each time he thought of it.

In response to the burn of embarrassment, Will opened his mind to draw an inner breath and so quench it. Now that Willow had seen the results of Edward's headstrong, even merciless, nature, the notion that she might ever have harboured desire for him seemed doubly absurd. Before the battle at Delamprey Edward had promised to give common quarter. Yet he had regarded that undertaking so lightly that an unthinkable crime had been allowed to pass. Willow had seen the freshly stained grass, the bloody beheading block, and Will had noted the disgust written in her face. So many captive noblemen had died at Warrewyk's hands in that hour of madness that a continuation of the war had been virtually guaranteed.

But that's how ill-wielded magic breaks back, Will thought ruefully. In truth, it was all my fault, and not Edward's or Warrewyk's. That's how the Delamprey stone succeeded against me in the end; though I managed to curtail the fight, I continued the war.

'There's Edward,' Willow said, squeezing Will's hand. 'And to think you two were schooled together. Little good it did him, the oathbreaker.'

'Don't blame him so easily,' Will said. 'It was his bad fortune to have tangled his destiny with the battlestones. The lorc lays out many pitfalls to swallow the unwary.'

She scowled. 'I suppose Warrewyk and Sarum are bound to be bad influences on anybody.'

'That's right enough.'

'How d'you think Lord Dudlea has fared?' she asked, scanning the knightly host. 'Has he kept to his word and thrown himself on Duke Richard's mercy?'

'I doubt it. I expect Master Gwydion's warnings will all have washed off him along with the first shower of summer rain. And even if he does as he promised, Warrewyk will probably take him aside and talk him into some other kind of skulduggery.' Will's eye followed Warrewyk and Sarum. 'Look at them in their finery – they think they're so important and grand. Yet for all their vanity they're as driven by the lorc as straws are before the wind – and the joke is they don't even know it's happening to them.'

Will looked around at the crowd, then raised a hand to his temple and winced as if afflicted by a sudden pain.

'What is it?' Gwydion asked, concerned.

'Nothing.'

'Your manner belies your word, my friend. Have you seen some stir among the red hands?' he asked, looking around. 'Tell me quickly now!'

'No, no . . .'

Gwydion looked beyond him at the crowd. 'Then is it Chlu? Did you feel him?'

Will gave no answer except a scowl which was meant to tell the wizard that he had again shot wide of the mark. But the truth was that he had indeed felt Chlu.

Gwydion clapped a hand on his shoulder. 'I think it is time we were gone from here.'

'Gwydion, no!'

But this time the wizard was adamant. They slipped away, following Gwydion along the City wall and down beside the Luddsgate. As they went out through the paupers' passage, a new concern overtook Will. He remembered his so-far unfulfilled promise to Lotan.

Master Gwydion must have laid a powerful spell on himself, he thought, *one that turns aside seekers after unwelcome favours . . .*

But Will knew he was making excuses. Gwydion was four paces ahead and striding out. Will could easily catch him up and tell him about Lotan right away, but he made no effort. Instead he half convinced himself that he would make a better job of it once they had a little privacy.

The wizard strode on ahead as they made haste across the Hollbourne and along the West Strande towards the main road junction at the Charing Crossroads. There stood the infamous monument, a miniature spire, before which was a place of ashes. From time to time, unfortunates were dragged here in chains by the Fellowship and slowly roasted to death, a punishment reserved for those suspected of being warlocks, though sometimes visited upon the heads of those who voiced open criticism of the Fellowship and were then found to have intractable natures.

Happily no such grim entertainment was in progress now. All along the way there were men-at-arms in steel bonnets, leaning on their pole-arms as they waited to march into the City. Will noted that the soldiers were all wearing either red and white or red and black, and upon their breasts were the devices of the white bear of Warrewyk or the green eagle upon yellow of Sarum.

'What's the matter with you?' Willow asked, seeing his face.

'I have the strongest feeling that I ought to tell Master Gwydion something.'

'Then you must, and right away.' She stared at him. 'What is it?'

'Something that might seem unimportant now, but which might just turn out to be otherwise. Come on.'

As they went, a rambling assemblage of buildings grew up around them, sprawling royal mansions, all of different sizes and styles and apparently put up at quite different times. Ahead, Gwydion had already turned off the common highway. He came now to an arched gate where they were given access by the palace guard, but only after Will showed Captain Jackhald's men the warrant that carried the seals of the royal household.

'Gone are the days when such as I could come and go without let or hindrance,' Gwydion muttered.

'So you've noticed the way our liberties have been boiling away?' Will said, half jocularly.

The wizard scowled at him. 'It is no laughing matter. What is to become of this city? We need a king, Willand, one who has the courage to set things to rights!'

Will made no reply, for he knew the barb with which the remark was set.

Within the walls lay smooth-scythed lawns, a little brown

in patches now, and two large oak trees. There were tiny, neat hedges. Beds of roses and cobbled quads were surrounded by turrets of red brick and stone that rose up in some places four floors high. In one of the two towers a statue of King Dunval stood in a niche, holding, Will presumed, a scroll of law in his hand, and in the other tower, facing the royal lawmaker of old, was the great dial of an engine of time.

This clock was the latest thing, Gwydion said, sent as a present to the king a few years ago by Duke Richard. 'To remind Hal that time was passing, but perhaps not passing swiftly enough.' It had come from near the town of Awakenfield in the north, in lands where the Ebor writ ran more strongly than the king's. It had been made in the workshops of the famous Castle of Sundials, and its chime was loud and commanding.

Will drew a deep breath and looked around. Many centuries were piled up here, the newer parts scrambling over the old like ivy in the place where Brea had first raised his halls and houses of carved oak so long ago.

But the chief splendour of the present palace was the White Hall. This huge oblong of pale limestone carried mock battlements at roof level and a series of pinnacled buttresses along each side. Its most arresting aspect was its lights. Each panel was artfully made to be both tall and wide, and was gorgeously decorated with what must have been an acre of coloured glass. All was ingeniously supported by traceries of lead and narrowly cut stone, and each panel told in pictures a history of a different Brean king. Will recognized in the first of them King Bladud the Leper in conversation with his unforgiving father Hudibrax. The next carried a portrait of the long-beard, Old King Coel, with night to his left and day to his right to show the passing of his one hundred and twelve years. Then came Gurgast, being eaten by the dragon, and after that a grave depiction of King Sisil leaving Queen Meribel and his infant son to sail off into the Western Deeps to search for the land of Hy Brasil. But what caught Will's eye most were the bright greens and yellows shining from the last panel, for it showed Leir and his three daughters, two of them undoubtedly wicked, and a third who could do no wrong.

Perhaps it was just a trick of the light or the position of the sun, but Will had the impression that the king winked at him. And it was easy to imagine that a dozen gargoyles made faces and rude gestures as they passed below, showing that even here the traditional humour of the masons' guild had not been forgotten. And though Gwydion insisted there was much dark magic still waiting to be swept away, there was much here also that seemed benign.

They went straight up to the small, comfortable apartments that the royal chamberlain had grudgingly afforded them – through an arch, up some stone stairs and along a cool passageway onto which three doors opened. By the time they came to their own door, Will had decided he must speak urgently to Gwydion of the strange Fellow who had stepped forward to save his life.

But no sooner was Will's decision made than it was dashed aside, for as their own door opened they found a surprise waiting for them.

'Now then! Ha-har! And look who's here to greet you!'

'Oh!' Willow cried out. 'It can't be!'

'Wortmaster?' Will said, equally delighted. 'What are you doing here?'

'Where else should I be? Hey? Answer me that! I'm come down with the rest of my Lord of Ebor's people. And just lately I have been as busy as a bee in June! Ha-har! Look at you!'

Gort opened his arms in a wide embrace and hugged them left and right, until Bethe started up such a howling at being pressed into the face of so bewhiskered a monster that Gort was driven into retreat.

'There, there, kitten! Oh, she doesn't know me . . .' Gort said, dabbing a fond finger at Bethe's nose. 'Do you, hey, little poppy-kin?'

'Aye, and maybe she knows you too well, Wartmonster,' Will said, grinning.

'Oh, Will! How can you say such a thing?' Willow patted Bethe's back until she drew breath. Then Willow began to grin and coo in the way that mothers do to disconcerted babes everywhere.

'That child has lusty lungs,' Gort said, poking a finger in his ear.

'She's tired.'

'Maybe she'd like a nice piece of cheese. I've fetched down a fine Cordewan Crumbly for you.'

'Not for Bethe, I don't think. But I'll take some of it gladly. Here, have a chair, and tell us your latest news.'

They all sat down. Bethe's storm of tears dried up and soon she was at Gort's knee and smiling up at him as he cut pieces of Cordewan Crumbly.

'Did I tell you the young victor of Delamprey has brought the stump away with him?' the Wortmaster said.

'The battlestone?' Will asked with sudden interest. 'We thought he might do that.'

'Hmmm, well he has. It came south in Edward's own baggage train. It's being heavily guarded.'

Will got up and began to walk about. 'You're going to have to speak to Edward, Master Gwydion. How will we ever be able to decipher the stone if we can't get to see it?'

Gort waved a hand towards the window. 'It's sitting down there in Albanay Yard, Master Gwydion, but they won't let me near. Me, or anyone.'

'Edward will quickly tire of it.' The wizard tossed his

head in dismissal. 'But Wortmaster, surely you have news of greater import than this?'

'Oh, I've been much abroad since last we met, Master Gwydion, and busier still since the king was taken – going here and there, sowing appleseeds and bringing to mind things once said by Semias.' He grinned and looked out from under the overgrowth of his eyebrows. He cast a meaningful glance at the wizard. 'I did as you wanted.'

'Then you *have* brought it . . .' the wizard said, as if hardly daring to believe. His eyes roamed to every corner of the room, but evidently did not find what they were searching for. 'Well? Where is it?'

'I have it. I have it indeed. It is here somewhere,' Gort said distractedly. 'And I have something else too!'

Gwydion's expression grew suddenly suspicious. 'What else? Wortmaster Gort, what *else*?' He wagged a finger. 'I hope you have not gone beyond my request and made a tomb robber of yourself.'

'Pooh!' Gort took the comment like a slap, and said to no one in particular, 'Did you ever hear such a charge? And me a right stout and dependable spirit when it comes to the doing of favours for people, hey?'

Gwydion closed his eyes, and a look of sorely-tried patience came over him. 'Wortmaster, what have you done with the *staff*?'

'Have no fear. It's been well looked after. There now! You can't see it because it's packed up small in your old crane bag! Appleseeds, appleseeds, appleseeds . . .'

Will and Willow exchanged uncertain glances as Gort bent down and began to rummage in a small bag that suddenly appeared from under the skirts of his robe. Will recognized it from his first days travelling with the wizard. When the Wortmaster straightened up he had in his hand a gnarled stick of wood. It was a full fathom in length and it gleamed and sparkled. Under ordinary circumstances it could not possibly have come out of a bag so small, but Will knew the crane bag was no ordinary scrip.

'Master Gwydion, is that your staff?' Will asked doubtfully. Then he turned to the Wortmaster. 'Have you remade it, Gort? It seems different.'

Gort shuffled and shrugged. 'Not I. Making staffs? I'm not suited to that kind of work. Oh, not me!'

'No one is these days,' Gwydion said, taking the staff and looking it over closely. 'This is not mine, Willand. Mine was broken, and no power in the world can remake it.'

'Then whose is this?'

Gwydion's eyes looked far away and he seemed to be seeing the ghosts of a distant time when the world was yet young. 'This is quite a piece of work. It once belonged to Maglin whose self-sacrifice is famous – he who was Phantarch after Celenost failed and went into the Far North.'

'Maglin?' Will said uncertainly, hardly knowing why he felt dismay at the name. 'The second phantarch? Wasn't it Maglin who presided over the Ogdoad during . . . the Age of Giants?'

'Maglin's rule was sorely troubled,' Gwydion said, 'for it was his lot to steer the Isle of Albion through turbulent waters. In Maglin's time we of the Ogdoad were much taken up with the healing of the world after a great mishap befell. We repaired the fabric – plugged a hole you might say, through which all the magic had been draining. We seven guardians stood our ground, and Maglin was our champion. There was a furious fight, and though in the end we succeeded, it was a costly victory. Maglin himself closed up the hole, but he had to give too much of himself. You may judge the bitterness of his fate for yourself, for though he was phantarch for a thousand years, yet in all that time no men dared come into these Isles.'

Gort shook his head at the memory. 'During Maglin's

phantarchship the last of the First Men died, you see? Only wyrms and giants thrived here after that.'

'Until King Brea came?' Willow asked.

'Until King Brea came.'

Will looked at the staff with new eyes. 'So is this the Staff of Justice, then?' he asked in amazement. 'The third of the Four Hallows of the Realm?'

Gwydion was quick to undo that idea. 'Oh, this is not the hallowed staff. This is just an old wizard's helpmeet. But well-fashioned and supple enough still, I hope, to do daring deeds when put into the right hands. I asked the Wortmaster to bring it out from a place that you know well, Willand.'

'A place that *I* know well?'

'You mean the Vale?' Willow asked.

'Not the Vale!' Gort laughed.

Puzzled, Will turned to Gort, but the Wortmaster merely stooped and reached into the crane bag to lift out another article, this time a cloak of white feathers. 'Appleseeds, appleseeds, appleseeds . . . ha-har!'

And Will instantly knew the cloak for what it was. 'That's the kind that wizards once used to wear. It's a swan cloak. Maglin's staff must have come from the tomb of King Leir!'

'Ah-ha . . . Right you are!' Gort danced the cloak by the shoulders so that the sheen on the feathers became otherworldly. 'This is the White Mantle, the cloak that was once draped over that great king's dead body by Semias.'

'Leir's cloak,' Will breathed, recalling the moment he had discovered the lost tomb. Wonderful things had been arrayed around that vault, but they all belonged to a dead man. He turned to Gwydion. 'You told me that the cloak was brought out of the Realm Below long ago by Arthur, and whoso-ever wore it would become invisible.'

Gwydion shook his head. 'These, I believe, were my

words. "He who wears Leir's mantle *shall remain unseen by mortal eye.*"'

'Well, isn't that the same thing?'

'My meaning at the time was that Leir's tomb was fated to remain undisturbed by lesser men, until such time as it should be found by one who is greater than Leir. However, you are right that a swan cloak will cause anyone who wears it to fade from view unless that person is a true king.'

Will slowly understood the implications and he began to redden in the face. Then Gort threw the cloak neatly about Will's shoulders and stood back. 'It fits! It fits!'

Will tried to shrug it off. 'Oh, Wortmaster, what are you doing? Of course it fits – it's a cloak.'

'Fit for a king, I'd say,' Gort insisted.

'Master Gwydion, you've put him up to this nonsense.'

But the wizard merely drifted into the shadows as the shimmering feathers settled around Will, sheathing him in glory.

'Please, Wortmaster,' he said unhappily. 'Take it off me. I daren't wear such a fine thing.'

But Gort would not take it off him. Will looked down at the empty clasp of gold and silver, the setting that had once held a great blue-white diamond called the Star of Annuin, and he could not help but think that the world was rushing headlong towards an unthinkable chasm, and that a great weight would soon fall upon his inadequate shoulders.

CHAPTER EIGHT

MAGOG AND GOGMAGOG

Three days passed, and the wizard came and went, busying himself in the seeking out of tokens. Much had been hidden away in the palace by Maskull. Three dried toads were found nailed to the rafters of the royal bedchamber. Maskull's magical traps still tied up parts of Trinovant in a spider web, nor could Gwydion's dancing unweave it all. He had made many libations at key points, shaping counter-spells at crossroads and leaving sigils under stairs. Yet too often the working required the moon to be at the full, or a vial of royal blood that was hardly to be had. Still, the wizard erected a cordon around the palace in the form of a single flaxen thread, and within its circuit he made scatterings of ash. Various woods were needed to cleanse and restore the White Hall, and so he had hung swags of holly and twisted dried mistletoe over door lintels, and sent Gort out to the royal forests beyond Hammersmyth to fetch back a boatload of oak, ash and elm.

One thunderstruck evening he had ranged up and down like a demon, flinging open shutters to light and air to admit the purifying blast of the west wind. That cool messenger of the middle airs had swept out the stink of incense and guttered the votive candles placed in so many corners by

the Sightless Ones. Gwydion had found slips of paper
containing malign formulae, seed pods, withered berries,
dead flowers, knots of hair and knuckle bones, old cod-
heads, the mummified body of a black cat with the halter
still tight about its neck. But nothing had worked to remove
the last lingering stench of dismal fortune that hung about
the palace.

In cellars as dank as dungeons he had found the carefully arranged shards of a broken mirror, things stolen, things
lost, things entombed under stone flags. Equerries and under-
chamberlains were disturbed from their beds at midnight.
High palace officials were roused up in the misty dawn as
the wizard came in bearing in his hands the bones of a long-
dead prince, to mutter and dance and run his new-found
wand over chest and chimney-breast alike. And finally, in a
tower occupied by no one at all, Gwydion had felt his way
forward with remorseless care, for in a solitary cell at the top
of a stair Maskull had kept his workshop of vile creation.

The sorcerer's chamber was not without subtle defences.
Magic was set, ready to snare the unwary. Walls that were
not walls, seemingly thin air that was. And so Gwydion
halted his attack. He let his investigation flow around the
problem, then proceeded crabwise. At last, he went at it
like the village worthy who goes to the local well, draws out
on the end of long tongs the wriggling, spitting young of
a water drake and dashes out its brains against a rock. A
huge wasps' nest was smoked out and taken down from
the roof space, and when the wizard broke it open he found
it to contain a human skull. Inside that was a dripping
honeycomb that Gwydion sealed in a great jar.

'But surely wasps don't make honey,' Will objected.

'They do not, for this is a magical manifestation,' the
wizard told him. 'And such honey as this may not be prized
for its sweetness.'

It might, he said, turn out to be a powerful ingredient

in spellbinding one day, but when Gort saw it he removed it to a rubbish heap and ritually destroyed it with vinegar and salt, while phantasms of light danced angrily about his head.

Many more dolorous items were taken from around the dismal portal, things mainly plastered into the cracks of the walls outside the sorcerer's stubbornly locked cell. But by his patient arts Gwydion drew these thorns, one by one, from the flesh of the body politic.

'That's better,' Will said, as the sun set on the second day. 'It feels much cleaner now.'

The wizard shook his head grimly. 'I have lifted not one seventh part of all the filth that was installed here by malicious sorcery. Eheu! . . . but I must rest my weary bones, for I have more to do tomorrow. I warn you all: the matter is not yet settled – do not attempt to climb those steps.'

But Gwydion's greatest worry remained the further outrage that Maskull must be planning. The sorcerer had pushed them into a corner, for what could they do now but wait? And waiting was not good for Will's peace of mind.

He began to fret over which of the battlestones would next come to life. His sleep was haunted by unrestful shadows as the brown river tides rose and fell. Summer nights spent so close to the stinking mud banks of the Thamesis were humid and sweaty. Tiny, fragile flies, grey and lighter than down, came from the marshes of the far bank. They came singing through the open windows to raise red lumps on him at knuckle and elbow and foot, annoyances that made him scratch until blood came. Only the cool dawns were a relief, and the peace that came after thunderstorms. Tomorrow, he knew, would be far worse, for it was the day appointed for the Great Council to convene.

The afternoon grew hotter, and all the establishment of the palace of the White Hall waited on tenterhooks for the great men of the Realm to arrive. As when the queen had called the Great Council at Castle Corben, all the lords of the Realm had been called. Most had heeded the order, though many seemed less than pleased to be here.

Will went up with Willow and Gwydion to a dusty wooden gallery, a choir stall that had not been opened in years. A plank of wormy wood served as a seat and the panelling of the stall had been carved and chipped and smothered in lettering by bored scholars who had waited out their tedium by figuring memorials to themselves. Will squeezed into the space between his wife and the wizard and moved forward to the rail. Bethe had been left with Gort. Gwydion had said that the child's unwitting contributions to the day's oratory should not be encouraged, and Gort said he would look after her for he had always had a hearty dislike of ceremony.

'Do you see Magog and Gogmagog?' Gwydion said, jogging Will's arm. 'They will be as pleased as anyone to see the king, I dare say.'

Will looked up at the guardian statues which stood in niches above the middle part of the White Hall. They were giants, but giants of a coarse and oafish kind. Big-handed but slow-brained. If the effigies were supposed to be life-sized, Will thought, then those giants of old must have been far bigger than the wood ogres and moorland trolls who still lived in the mountain fastnesses of the north, though not as large as the giant Alba. These heavy-boned guards were twice as tall as men and dressed after the fashion of Brea's ancient court, or perhaps in mockery of its warriors, for they wore beards and wreaths twined in their locks, and were armed – one with a sort of halberd, the other with a pole that carried a spiked ball upon a chain.

'A tale tells that these ancient effigies were wrought in the Kingdom of Corinow, made from oaks cut from a druids' grove. Another tale maintains that it was a sorcerer who gave them their present form.

'And which tale is true?' Willow asked.

'I cannot say. But these two have guarded the throne of the Realm for a long time.'

Will smiled, but then he saw something that made him start, for as he looked up at Magog the nearer giant's eyes swivelled until they bored down into him.

'It's looking at me,' he hissed, feeling naked under that simmering stare. 'They're alive!'

Gwydion grunted. 'Oh, they are certainly that. How else do you think they protect the throne?'

Will's own eyes flickered as he looked around. The interior of the White Hall was a riot of dazzling ornament. Carved wood and white marble below, fluted stone and coloured glass above. The air had the resinous, beeswax smell of ancient chambers, and was so far unspoiled by the incense burners of the Fellowship. There was a lot of air to perfume in this hall, and all of it uninterrupted: no pillars held up the roof, only slender pilasters set against a wall of shining glass. These supports launched themselves upward like great, stone plant stems, branching at the last possible moment into rayed patterns that criss-crossed the plaster-white ceiling. A colourful shield, one for each of the lordly houses, showed on every roof boss, while down below statues and carvings decorated the walls. The finest statues, Will noticed, were mostly of the kings of former times, with an occasional hero and an even more occasional queen. Borders and screens contained the lordly benches, carrying the likenesses of every flower and animal in the land. But here in the middle of the White Hall, the decoration ran out of hand. Everything was gilded and bright, and the reason was easy to see – white marble steps ran up to a dais upon which there was a single golden seat.

Will knew without being told that this was the throne

of the Realm. It was not like the other royal chairs that he had seen before, makeshift thrones used by the monarch on his travels about the Realm. This was the seat on which kings were crowned, a chair guarded by giants.

Under it rested a solid block, one that Gwydion had once called the 'Stone of Scions'. He had told how it had been stolen away many years ago from Albanay, and had come long before that from Tara in the Blessed Isle. Now Will's attention was captured by it.

'What lies under the throne looks to me like the stump of a battlestone,' he said, pointing.

'And to me,' Gwydion said. 'Indeed I have long thought that its origins may be connected with the fae. Certainly, it has magical powers that lend themselves to the good governance of the Realm. The stone sings a single high note when the rightful king first sits there, but these days only the rightful king may hear it sing.'

'That's not much use,' Willow said. 'To the rest of us, I mean.'

'It is, alas, all that this jaded world now affords us by way of royal magic.'

'The rightful king . . .' Will muttered, reminding himself how he and Edward of Ebor had once huddled around a flickering candle flame in Foderingham Castle. The duke's son had explained exactly how much those words meant to his father.

Just who is the rightful king? Will wondered. It was a perplexing question, a matter of blood and complicated lines of descent. But this family quarrel had seen competing cousins arm themselves to the teeth and ready themselves to murder or die in order to assert the right to rule. What place in such a quarrel was there for an outsider, one who was not family and not of the blood? What place was there for a King Arthur?

Hundreds of nobles had by now gathered in the two

wings of the hall. Edward was sitting with Lords Sarum and Warrewyk and others of the Ebor clan. Will saw Edmund, Edward's younger brother, placed less prominently. He was dressed in velvets of sombre black and brown, as if trying to hide the deformity that had twisted his arm and leg. That illness – caused, Will knew, by tragic contact with the Dragon Stone – made his mouth foam at the corner and his eyes wander skyward at times, though his wits were quite intact.

On the far side Will saw Jasper and his father, Owain, who had moved as close to the neutral camp as they dared. Certain luke-warm supporters of the queen, like Lord Dudlea and the Earl of Ormerod and Willet, clustered near them. All the great northern magnates were absent, as Will had known they would be, for the rumour was that even now the queen and Duke Henry of Mells had found a refuge in Albanay and from there were sending promises and favours to the famous Pierce clan of Umberland.

No summons from Trinovant could yet have reached the Earl of Umber and the other lords of the Albanay Marches. And if it had, no reply should be expected from the third earl, for his father had died at Verlamion, choking on his own blood, with a Warrewyk arrow lodged in his throat. Certainly, Henry of Mells and Harry of Umber had common cause against Ebor. And if those whose sires had died in battle found it impossible to attend the latest Council, how much more did the heirs of the lordly houses of Rockingham and Shroppesburgh, Bowmonde and Egremonde? Their kin had been murdered in cold blood.

Not every lord, however, had been infected by the wish for personal revenge. According to Gwydion's advice, the two sides had been invited to seat themselves strictly in order of precedence, but old habits held sway, and the earls and barons grouped themselves on the benches of their allies, seeking strength in numbers against the

liberties of the new regime. The mood of the gathered
lords was surprisingly calm, Will thought. Flintily watchful
rather than fearful, coolly disdainful rather than burning
with bile. The humour of the hall was sober and subdued,
as if the nobility were unable to breach the smothering
blanket of peace that had been thrown over them. The
lofty white ceiling threw back a soft, pale light, and Will
knew without having to open his mind that, here at least,
the wizard had done a thorough job of cleansing the air
of vile spells, and perhaps he had laid on a few vital influences of his own.

But the restful air of the White Hall did not stay unsullied
for long, for now the representatives of the Fellowship began
to issue into the north and south aisles. Two lines of Elders
were led forward by sighted helpers. These gnarled princes
of the Fellowship were caped in heavy cloth of gold. Each
wore a tall, glittering hat that swayed this way and that as
their heads turned from side to side. The High Wardens
were announced by criers and men swinging incense
burners, and followed by hooded standard bearers who
raised on high flags showing the white heart, the slaugh-
tered lamb and the bloodied thorn. Will's dislike of their
shameless flaunting hardened further, for he knew that every
last thread of that shiny apparel had cost some common
fieldsman a month of bread and cheese. Will felt the cold-
ness pass along his veins each time the strange scanning
movements of the Elders' heads turned his way. Then he
saw that at their head was none other than Grand High
Warden Isnar.

He looked away lest his hard stare was latched onto. As
the sickly smoke of their silver thuribles and golden fuma-
tories reached the gallery, he guarded his mind against the
persuasive odour and against the probings of the strange
sense that the red hands had in place of their sight. Will
would have liked nothing better than to stand up and

announce himself boldly to Isnar, but this was not the time to give in to such an urge.

After the Elders had taken their places there followed another dirge, and when that was complete, a fanfare rang out. The Lord High Admiral and the Earl Marshal of the Realm walked up the aisles, then came the two Constables and the Keeper of the Tower, followed by an array of Stewards, Chancellors and Chamberlains, men whose titles Will had long ago been tutored to commit to memory. One thing was striking: these were not the same men he had seen holding those titles during the meeting at Castle Corben.

Once they had all taken their seats, the King's Champion came clattering in. Resplendent in full armour and sitting on a white horse, he issued a ringing challenge, raising his voice – and his sword – to east and west. Then he threw down his right gauntlet and waited to hear if there was anyone present who would deny the king his throne.

In the echoing silence that stretched out after the Champion's intimidating words, Will wondered what would happen if the doors were suddenly flung wide and some fearsome fighter in black armour walked in. But the moment disappointed him. Instead there followed more miserable music, then a coughing and a shuffling of feet before a serjeant-at-law in a green gown bustled in and banged the foot of his ceremonial rod into a specially placed wooden plate on the floor to declare the proceedings lawful. Then the Four Pages of the Hallows fetched in the symbols of kingship – a golden sceptre, a sheathed sword, a chalice and a crown. As soon as they were set down on their cushions at the four corners of the dais, Will knew that all was in place for the king's arrival. Throughout his long reign, King Hal had always been attended in ceremony by others – at first by his regents and later by his wife. While Queen Mag's star rode high, two thrones had stood side by side on the dais of the White Hall. But now, as Will had already noted, there was just one.

Everyone waited patiently for the king. An uncomfortably long time passed and still Hal did not appear. Fidgeting began, then a murmuring spread among those at the back. The lords sweated in their velvet coats. Slanting sunlight shattered into a thousand shards of colour as it played across the scene. Images of ancient kings swept imperceptibly across the assembly. Half an hour went by, marked by the clanging strike of the time engine in the palace tower. No one dared to move.

'A change has come over Duke Richard while he has been in the Blessed Isle,' Gwydion whispered at last. He tapped his hand on the elm-wood railing in front of him like a man coming to some unhappy conclusion.

'A change?' Willow asked, turning. 'Why do you say that?'

She gave the wizard a worried glance and Will saw that her concern was for Bethe, that any 'change' the duke might have met with in the Blessed Isle might also have affected their daughter while she was there.

Willow stiffened when Gwydion said, 'I fear that perhaps he may have fallen under some malefic influence. I should like to ask Morann about it.' She raised her voice in question. 'Malefic influence?'

'Yes, Master Gwydion,' Will whispered, taking his wife's hand. 'What do you mean?'

'Only that power may have finally corrupted the good duke, just as I warned it would.'

Willow sat back. Will also subsided. He offered his wife a brief smile of reassurance, but the wizard's grim words continued to resound with him. Duke Richard had always been bent on restoring his blood-line to what he regarded as its proper place, and there was nothing like a win upon the battlefield to spur on lordly ambitions.

Will's hands gripped one another as he turned the matter over in his mind. His contemplation of the lonely seat below recalled to his mind the time when Mother Brig the seer had held a Great Council of her own. Her dire warning to the duke was that Death would take him in the very next battle he fought. Will now believed he could see the circumstance against which the message warned.

'He can't be . . .' he murmured to himself. 'No, he can't be thinking of *that*.'

But then, all of a sudden, the waiting was over, and instead of King Hal making the loneliest journey of his life, it was Duke Richard of Ebor who came striding along the north aisle.

In all respects Richard seemed to be exactly the man for such an occasion – tall, confident and in the flush of victory. He had impressed Will from the first moment, and now he looked every inch the warrior-king. But despite everything, Will's fingers laced one another tightly against the disappointment that was now waiting to pounce.

'Oh, no . . .' he breathed. 'Oh, no, don't do it . . .'

In Duke Richard's hand was a twisted ivory rod. It might have been the staff of office of the Lord Protector, but Will knew better. It was a unicorn's horn. Long ago he had sensed the magic in it. Now he felt a deep certainty that it had been a mistake for Duke Richard to bring it here.

As the duke mounted the dais and approached the high throne, he stopped and turned to look down at the lords gathered below. Despite the silence, he seemed caught by the glamour of the moment and unable to resist the temptation to linger upon the royal dais in full view of the house.

Will drew breath, staring at the serried ranks of lords, watching them turn their heads, ready to receive their king – yet seeing only Richard. Richard of Ebor – not *with* the king, but *in place* of him.

As Will watched, Richard seemed to struggle with

himself. Will swallowed hard, hoping against hope that the duke would turn away, but he did not. He approached the throne. And in his mind's burning eye Will saw Death sitting in that golden chair. Death beckoning. Death, grinning a welcome.

Will rose up from his own seat, leaned forward across the rail, hands gripping it tight as talons. It was like watching a sleepwalker reaching the edge of a cliff. Unable to do otherwise, Will shouted out.

'*No!*'

The word echoed in the still air. But it did not stop the duke. He put out his arm and dared to lay a familiar hand upon the throne.

He turned, waiting for a rising tide of calls that must surely come, calls for him to seat himself – the rightful king coming back after three generations of usurpers, returning to claim his own again! But Will's shout had roused others to call out. There came no approving tide to urge Duke Richard on. Instead there were shouts of, 'No! No! No!'

Noblemen got to their feet and turned to one another aghast. This could not be happening. Could it? Surely, Richard of Ebor had declared many times that it was *not* his intention to claim the throne from Hal. If that had been his aim, then he should have done so at Verlamion.

But Will saw how easily Richard had been deceived. He had spent too great a time among his own people. For too long he had spoken only with those who would not gainsay him, and he had lost his sense of the general feeling. Had he, Will wondered, fallen prey to his own secret ambitions?

Will watched him now as he attempted to seize the dangerous moment, to jog the elbow of fate in one brilliant move. There would be a glorious turnabout, as he swung the affairs of men about at the pivot. He would do it. He, Richard of Ebor, the rightful king!

But the brilliant moment turned to dust in his hands. He had failed. And what was more, he *knew* he had failed.

All Richard of Ebor's personal charm ran to earth in that instant. He spread his hands in appeal, hesitated, tried to rally. But his face had paled and everyone saw then that he had brought them to the brink of disaster.

Sly Isnar was quickly on his feet, calling on Ebor to stand away, to acknowledge Hal as his rightful king. Will looked on in astonishment now, for Richard's too-rapid reply was madness.

'My noble lords, why should I do that when, by the laws of blood, I have a better right to the throne than the grandson of a usurper?'

'Why don't you do something, Master Gwydion?' Will whispered, horrified.

'I must not interfere!'

'But, look at him . . . he's dying! How could he have so misjudged the spirit of the hour? How could he have disregarded Mother Brig's plain warnings?'

Down below, Richard turned defiant now, adamant that he would not leave the king's dais. Doubtless he was telling himself that should he do so now all would be lost. Maybe he was asking: whose army controls the City? Who do the common people of Trinovant love? Who has the king in his power?

This gathering could still be cowed! He would make a declaration! He would speak from the throne!

But though the lords were mindful of their safety, they were not cowards. The closest of Ebor allies took Duke Richard's words stonily. Many others rose to their feet. They called out that they had fought for him in good faith as a deliverer. They had sworn only to divest weak, holy Hal of his queen and her rapacious friends. Such men now remembered that they had sworn allegiance to Hal as their king. They had certainly not fought at Verlamion or Cordewan or anywhere else, to unseat the king and put Richard of Ebor in his place.

As Richard made to lower himself onto the throne, Will saw the Stone of Scions flare green. As those emerald rays touched the guardian statues above, they stirred. Weapons trembled in giant hands. They began grinding their teeth and tearing the air with thunderous warnings.

'Pride!' shouted Magog.

'Ambition!' shouted Gogmagog.

Ebor looked up and grimaced at the stamping, raging giants. A fit of dizziness seemed to seize him, as if he felt the ground opening beneath him. He staggered, reached out again to steady himself against the arm of the throne, and dropped the unicorn horn which he had been so tightly grasping.

Then Richard fell to his knees, and the White Hall burst into uproar.

Edward bolted forward onto the dais and lifted his father. Edmund struggled forward as best he could to lend a hand. But Richard shrugged off the help of his sons. He straightened proudly, and walked away from the throne. At the foot of the steps he was enveloped by his personal bodyguard, who pushed a way through the commotion all the way along the north aisle and out of the White Hall.

PART TWO

THE MAN WHO WOULD
NOT BE KING

CHAPTER NINE

THE LAMB HYTHE YALE

Dawn struggled through cold mists as the last of the summer died. There was now moss greening the faces of the gargoyles and grotesques that stood along the roofline of the White Hall. The boatman stamped and patted his arms against his coat and at first gave Will scant respect for having bribed him from his bed to go out looking for yales.

Oars squeaked dryly in their thole pins as they went out across the river. Breath steamed in the half light. Across the river the towers of Isnar's own chapter house rose leaden grey behind its wall.

'Going to be a hard winter, I think,' the boatman muttered.

'Do you think we'll see a yale?' Gort asked, and Will thought he heard in Gort's question another – and if we do see a yale, what will that presage?

'You can always hope, sir. Here was always a good place before sun-up, back in the old days.'

'Have you seen many?' Will asked, doubting the man.

'They used to come all along the south bank at this time of year,' the boatman said. 'Why, as a child I remember my grandad saying they could be seen all the way from the Shad right up to Wandle Brook.'

Will was tempted to point out that that was not what he had asked, but he let it go and said instead, 'They're not so rare, then?'

'Rare? Myself, I seen only thirteen in as many years.'

'Rare and getting rarer . . .' Gort murmured.

The boatman rested on his oars. 'Begging your pardon, sir, but the yale's an animal that don't come and go according to your desire or anyone's. He'll let you see him – or not – according to his own mind. And that's how it should be.'

This was the top of the tide. The boat glided ever closer to the muddy shore opposite the White Hall. Over here it was like another world – the rotten smell of Lamb Hythe marshes, the sun heaving itself up over a festering terrain of reeds and rushes. And among it all the private walls and towers of Lamb Hythe Cloister, and the wooden ways where twice a year the flocks were unloaded from boats and driven into the red hands' slaughter yard.

Movement caught Will's eye. A light skiff was going the other way, crossing from Lamb Hythe to the Palace Steps. It carried a hooded figure fast through the early morning, and Will's curiosity alighted briefly on him.

They're everywhere, he thought dismally. Clustering here especially, always ready to drink at the fount of power. There's no doubt which way they're trying to steer the world. The question is – *why*? And I wonder what Maskull thinks of them. I guess he'd do a deal with them in a moment if he thought it would nudge the world a little further towards his own embrace. But why would they want to make an ally of Maskull when they get so rich peddling lies of their own devising?

They were coming to shore now. Water birds watched them approach, kept their distance. 'I'd just as soon not see a yale,' Gort said miserably. 'An animal as grand as that should be left to go about its affairs unseen.'

Will took his eyes off the solitary boat. He felt urgency

gnaw at him again. 'Wortmaster, I think you've guessed the real reason I asked you to come out here.'

Gort nestled deeper into his rug-like coat. 'What's that, then? Planning an intrigue, are we, hey?'

'No intrigue. I'm worried. We should be up with events, not following them like, like . . .'

'Latecomers at a funeral?' A large dew drop had formed on the tip of Gort's nose, and he wiped it away. 'You're right, Willand. But we can't get any closer to the centre of events than we already are. We're stuck with our situation, don't you see? "Bereft of ideas" as Master Gwydion calls it.'

'He might be, Gort. But I'm not. And I've heard his arguments a hundred times – we must be careful of Maskull, we must act at the fulcrum of events, more haste means less speed – I appreciate all that. But while we sit here the queen is being given hospitality by the Regent of Albanay, and we ought to have more concern about her intentions.'

'I expect we ought.' Gort's eyes fixed on him. 'But whose back are you talking behind right now? Is it the queen's, or Master Gwydion's, hey?'

Will looked away and sighed, then he let his mouth run away with him. 'Gort, I can feel the pressure inside me. It's building. Everything's getting tighter, like the Realm is a great bow and something's drawing it back and back still further, drawing it until it's about ready to snap! One day it *will* snap, or else an arrow will be let fly with such power that—' He stopped suddenly.

'That what?'

'That everything we know will be pierced through the heart.'

Gort made no reply at first, only looked back dourly, but then he said, 'And amid all this plummeting of the whole world into disaster the thing you wanted most was to take me out in the early morning and show me a yale. Ah, well.'

Will let out a hopeless sigh. 'You must think me a weak-ling and a very great coward, not to move, not to do some-thing myself. I should be like King Arthur of old and seize the world by the scruff of its neck. Gwydion expects it of me, but I don't know how.'

The mists ahead flickered as if with the light of King Elmond's fire. The hairs on Will's neck rippled, and he shuddered. After a while he said, 'Tell me what happens when a phantarch fades, Wortmaster.'

Now it was Gort's turn to set his eyes wandering among the mistbanks. Moisture frosted his beard. 'Oh, well . . . you stop seeing him for what he is and start disregarding him. You stop hearing the sense in what he's saying. The magic leaves him and the glamour goes, you see. After that, he takes himself off and is soon forgotten by mortal minds. Like all magic is.'

They sat in silence for a while, Will digesting the Wortmaster's words. He was thinking what a world without magic could be like. It seemed inescapably horrible. The boatman had shipped his dripping oars and was sitting quietly, but Will knew he would stir soon. They would have to leave before the ebb tide got going and made it impos-sible to land at the White Hall steps.

The boatman stiffened. Then he grasped Will by the shoulder and held up a finger for silence before pointing into the reeds.

The beast was beautiful, a presence that came out of the vapours to blend with the uncertain light. It was a creature somewhat like a great, white deer, though lion strong and perhaps more like a he-goat in the shape of its head. Thick-necked and powerful it seemed, and its horns and tusks gave it an air of majesty. The pale golden discs of its mark-ings rippled against white as it sank into the mud on each step. Proudly it came, not acknowledging them, down to the water's edge to drink. A big, bull yale that threw back its head, looked at last towards Will, then swivelled its long, twisted horns and gave a throaty call before vanishing again like a silver shadow into the mists.

'Well . . .' the boatman said smiling. Then he turned the boat, ready to row them back across the Iesis. 'A rare old sight, that.'

As the oars creaked and the grey waters parted, Will looked to the Wortmaster and said, 'I had the strangest feeling just then.'

'Oh?'

'I could have sworn the beast spoke to me in the true tongue.'

Gort looked back with an unreadable face. 'They say that yales have something of the power about them. I didn't hear anything, but then my ears are full of bristles and old wax.'

'They weren't words that people could hear. They were the kind that just seem to arrive inside your head.'

'Oh, that sort.' Gort snuffled and sneezed. 'What was the message?'

'It made no sense. It just said, "Save me."'

Memories of that astonishing moment in the White Hall when Duke Richard had made his lethal choice ran through Will's mind. It was hard to make sense of it all. Immediately afterwards, he had followed Gwydion down from their dusty little gallery, arriving just in time to see the duke emerge white-faced and tight-lipped into the brightness. He had refused to hear Gwydion, and then he had lost his temper with Sir John Morte, his seneschal's son and his own kinsman. 'Do not strew objections in my path, cousin. If this nest of vipers will not leave my hall then you must drive them out at bill-point, do you hear me?'

And so it had been. Richard had sent the lords out of the City to think again. Then the great doors of the White Hall had been slammed shut and locked, and the statues that had stamped and thundered against the duke had been looped with ropes and pulled down. Teams of frightened men had hauled them out through a back way, lashed by the strained shouts of their overseers. And Will had seen them, ancient Magog and Gogmagog, broken with hammers, their trunks and limbs shoved into a corner of Albanay Yard, stacked there like so much lumber, ready to be burned.

But somehow the burning had been overlooked, for no one had the stomach for that kind of sacrilege. Perhaps it was natural respect, perhaps it was what some liked to call superstition, or perhaps the men had a disinclination to burn anything that could stare back at them. But the fate of the guardians soon faded from the duke's mind, and the oak wood lay warping under sun and rain. The pile became the haunt of spiders and wood lice, and as autumn came and the west wind drifted russet oak leaves around them, the ancient guardians were forgotten.

By the time the gusts of the equinox gave way to the first frosts, Richard's manner had become icy too. He had withdrawn, keeping mainly to his apartments, and was now seldom seen about the palace. Duchess Cicely asked Gort to offer him healing. She wanted Gwydion to talk with him. But all they found in the duke's heart were immoveable regrets and a morbid desire for power that he would not relinquish.

One day Will saw him stride across Albanay Yard with his guards and go alone into the White Hall. From their small, high window he watched him walking up and down the aisles, looking at the empty benches. The next day Richard sent out a demand to the lords that his right of succession was to be recognized for he was, as his great army proved, the *actual* ruler of the Realm. The next Great Council – which he would announce at his pleasure – surely *would* see an abdication.

Now, as Will looked out over the same windswept precinct, he saw the wizard hurrying purposefully towards the royal apartments. There was something about Gwydion's demeanour that made Will take notice.

'Hoy!' he cried, and dashed down the stairs in pursuit. 'Master Gwydion! Wait!'

But the wizard would not wait, and his destination did not bode well.

'This is the red hands' doing!' Gwydion cried, bursting in on Edward while he was at his papers.

Will had not been able to stop him, and Edward, who had not asked for Gwydion's visit and clearly thought it an intrusion, looked annoyed. Nevertheless he maintained his poise under the wizard's blast, waving back his people, and nodded a brief understanding towards Will. He even went so far as to set aside his dignity as Earl of the Marches by offering an indulgent smile to the wizard. 'Really, Crowmaster, you mustn't upset yourself so. You're seeing the Fellowship behind everything these days.'

'They *are* behind everything!' Gwydion shook his staff wrathfully. 'These are dark days. But mark this! I shall have their spies crawling on their bellies through Albanay Yard before this day is done!'

Edward showed himself to be mildly amused, though Will knew he was not. 'I'd ask my father's leave before doing anything as exciting as that,' he said, and then added, 'though it would be marvellous fun to watch, I suppose.'

'Smirking scullion! I should strike you to your knees!'

Edward rolled his eyes, half in innocence, half in vain show. 'Old man, what have *I* done to deserve this?'

Will tried to calm the wizard, fearing for him now. 'Master Gwydion, come along! Let's not be angry with our friends.'

Edward looked askance at Will. 'The Fellowship is the

Fellowship. He should know what they're like by now. Why does he hate them so?'

Will answered with a tight smile. 'He gets a little . . . *upset* sometimes.'

Gwydion looked sharply to him. 'Do not manage me, boy! And I do not hate the Fellowship. We are opponents. We want different things for the world.'

'Oh, leave them be. They're charitable enough,' Edward said.

It was like tossing kindling on a bonfire. 'What acts of *charity* have you seen them perform? Answer me!'

'Many. They maintain poor houses. They feed the starving. They, they . . .'

'That is not *giving*. It is *buying*! In the days of the First Men, there were no poor! Do you not see the difference?'

'Crowmaster, those ancient days are gone. You cannot hope to set the clock back.'

'Imbeciles!' Gwydion threw off Will's restraining hands and marched away, trailed by Captain Jackhald and two hapless guards.

Seeing now that they were alone, Edward said, 'Can't you keep a tighter grip on him? He frightened the life out of me, bursting in like that.'

'It won't happen again.' Will spread his arms. 'But you realize . . . he's right.'

'Oh, not you too!' Edward looked witheringly at him. 'My father's not in league with the Fellowship. Isnar called for King Hal to be recognized, or have you forgotten?'

Will saw an opportunity. 'Perhaps Master Gwydion spoke more deeply than you allow. What he meant was that folk are drawn to the Fellowship through the deepest of fears. I've thought much upon what the Great Lie means and I see now why Master Gwydion was loath to tell me about it. It was not so much because he feared I would be deceived by it, just that everyone must come to his or her own understanding of the world, and of people, before the enormity can be truly understood.'

'Be that as it may—'

'Edward, the Great Lie persuades folk that they can avoid the meeting which, in truth, all mortals must make.'

Edward sat back, serious now, trying to see the meaning of Will's change of tack. 'You speak of . . . Death.'

'Yes, I do. The Sightless Ones promise an invisible life beyond the grave, a life that stretches out in endless comfort wherein every initiate will be reunited with those he has loved in life. But this is an *invention*, a dangerous infection of the mind that must be stopped from spreading!'

Edward's face clouded, and he snapped, 'What do you know about it?'

'Enough to know when it's got its grips on someone.'

'Meaning?'

'I think you know my meaning right enough.'

Now Edward tried to laugh off the remark. 'So? What of it? Many people, high and low, are coming to *believe* just lately. We can't all be wrong.'

Will held his glance. 'There are many ways to foster beliefs such as you are coming to, Edward. The Fellowship works especially hard on the easy clay of young minds. And later, they make it easier to believe than not to believe, for they know that given two ways, most folk will choose the easier. They seek to catch the unwary: people who are in torment, or youthful idealists – those who aren't yet too old to see all the faults in the world, but who can put forward no remedy themselves. These are the easiest of prey—'

Edward grunted. 'I'm no wide-eyed idealist!'

'True. But be warned: the glib answers offered by the Sightless Ones seem to make a lot of sense, but they are in truth quite hollow.'

'While you're always right about everything, I suppose?'

'No, Edward. I'm not always right about everything. But

I'm right about this. The Sightless Ones devour people who have been unaccustomed to think for themselves. They go after those whose thoughts run as a maze – those, perhaps, who are feeling *guilt* for what they've done.'

Edward seized on that as Will had known he would. 'Guilt? I feel no guilt.'

'Don't you? Not even after you lied to me at Delamprey?'

'When did I lie to you?'

'You said you would call for common quarter, yet there were murders. Cold-blooded, planned butchery. And you planned it. After the battle was done, unarmed men, bound, then beheaded—'

'Warrewyk's doing, not mine!'

Will drew back. 'Well . . . it's good to see that, despite your protests, you have some small, lingering sense of shame about it. Enough at least to want to pass the blame.'

'I'm not ashamed!'

He laughed. 'I can smell shame, and it coils about you as thick as chimney smoke.'

Anger welled up visibly inside Edward. 'Get out! You're not my confessor!'

'Oh – it's gone that far, has it?'

'What do you mean?'

'Edward, I know they send their Elder across the river every day. I've seen him in his little boat. He comes from the cloister at Lamb Hythe to hear your private thoughts. And I wonder what you've been telling him.'

'That's none of your concern!' Edward's self-control failed wholly now. 'You've never understood rank, have you? You think you can speak to whomsoever you please? Say whatever you want, whenever you want? Well, you can't! Not in this world. You're nothing, Willand. A jumped-up peasant who thinks he's important because he hides behind the skirts of an old magician. I could have your head struck off on a whim. And I might just do that.'

'For once, Edward, consider the truth! We're men, the same flesh and blood, you and I, and worthy of the same respect. I proved as much to you long ago. And while magic exists in the world you should not discount it.'

'Magic? Oh, those days are over! The magic is rushing from the world like blood from a stuck pig, or haven't you noticed? That's why your greybeard of a crow is fading away. He's all used up. And when the magic's gone, what will he be then? And what will *you* be? Eh?'

Will took none of the bait. He raised an admonishing finger. 'I warn you, Edward. You're drifting. The red hands have caught you up in their net, just like they caught your father.'

Edward leapt at him, shoved him hard up against the wall. His teeth gritted. '*What* about my father?'

Will returned his fury stonily. 'Do I really have to tell you? Before this year's out, he's going to *die*.'

The struggle to bring the casket upstairs depended largely on Will's strength. It weighed almost as much as he did, though it felt heavier now that he had Gort and Gwydion to hinder him.

'Put your back into it!'

'Hnnng!'

'Careful of the door!'

They manhandled the casket onto the table. It was like a cupboard; wooden but lantern-shaped, and with scarlet panels and gilding. And it was locked.

Gort asked, 'How did you get Edward to release it?'

Will gasped and wiped the sweat from his face. He took off his heavy coat. 'Never mind how I got it, Wortmaster. It's here now, isn't it?'

'Boxed up like a sacred relic,' Gort said, fingering the doors. 'Edward must have had high hopes for this to give it such a pretty little house.'

'What persuaded him?' Gwydion asked.

Will clapped grey dust off his hands and looked at the trail of it that had followed them across the room. 'I told him he could put on a show for friend or foe, for his family and those bound to him as servants, but he could not fool the Crowmaster.'

'You do me honour,' the wizard said flatly. 'But I would prefer it if you did not try to humour me. That is always a mistake.'

'I simply told Edward that I was not interested in debate. I said I was asking him about what he most truly and sincerely believed in. "Do not forget, my friend," I said, "the world eventually becomes what the sum of men believe it to be. Be careful therefore what you believe."'

'That was well said, at any rate . . .' The wizard's words tailed off and he wandered away. When he stood in the light by the window he seemed thin and colourless, as if some transparent quality had settled on him.

Gort, still thrivingly substantial, ran a hand over the treasure chest and smiled up at Will impishly. 'But have you got the key, hey?'

'Oh, I forgot to ask,' he said, pulling it out of his pouch and returning a sly smile to the Wortmaster.

'Irony monger,' Gort said and sniffed. 'There's a rede about speaking plainly, you know.'

'Then I'll speak plainly: get out of the way.' Will thrust the big key into the lock and turned it, then he and the Wortmaster looked inside the casket.

After a moment's shocked silence, Will said, 'Master Gwydion, where are you? Come and look at this.'

The wizard was still staring out of the window, his back to them. 'I believe I know what you wish to tell me,' he said.

'You mean you knew the Delamprey stump would be like this?' Will picked up a handful of grey dust and let it filter down. It felt like nothing at all. 'Ashes?'

'Less than ashes. And I suspected it would be so.'

'Then this is Maskull's doing?' Will offered, aghast.

'Oh, hardly.'

'Then who?'

'You, Willand.' The wizard gave a little laugh. 'You.'

'Me? But . . . *how*?'

'It was you who dissolved the fetters from my wrists, was it not? Remove both the spirits of harm *and* kindness from a stone and what is there of substance to remain? Unable to sustain itself in the world, it has quite reasonably fallen into dust.'

Gort looked up. 'But then how shall we work upon it, Master Gwydion?'

'Yes,' Will echoed. 'What are we going to do?'

'I think, my friends,' the wizard said, smiling, 'you are both missing the point.'

CHAPTER TEN

THE WINDOWLESS CHAMBER

Two nights later the black flashes came again. Will closed his eyes and forced himself to lie still on the bed. The room was pitch black. The sky beyond the window ranged moonless and starless under a snow-heavy overcast. When he opened his mind again he did it cautiously; all he could feel was the blood coursing in his skull and a rare tingling in his hands and feet. But the flashes had been real enough, and the ache they left in their wake made him feel hollow.

There were three ligns passing near Trinovant – Collen, Mulart and Celin. Collen, the lign of the hazel, crossed the river by the White Tower less than a league away. Mulart, the elder tree lign, crossed a couple of leagues further to the east. And Celin, the holly lign, met the river near Harper's Cottage, a wooded place below Hammersmyth and only about a league to the west of where Will now lay.

But it was not the lorc that rumbled and flickered on the edges of Will's mind like a distant summer thunder-storm. The flashes reminded him of a time not so long ago when he had looked out from a lakeside hovel and scanned the night for Chlu.

He's dancing out magic, Will thought. But he's not doing it in any well-considered way. He's doing what Maskull has taught him, making selfish moves that will serve him and him alone. He'll think that better than begging for his bread and ale.

The dark flashes rippled through Will's head like pain, like light turned upside-down. There was no adequate way to describe these echoes of sorcery.

And Chlu must feel an equivalent pain whenever I gather magic to me, he thought. That's part of the way he finds me, though there's a more permanent bond. Maybe he's decided there's no reason to hide himself from me, maybe he's in a tight situation and using his talents to fight his way out . . .

He imagined his twin inhabiting the shadow world of the City, slipping easily among the careless lives that swilled in and out with the river tides. Chlu would haunt dark, stinking alleys. He would terrify and prey upon whoever he could, until silver and gold were his in good store. His lodgings would be comfortable, but he would know no peace of mind for he had only one mission.

And right now he's tired and angry and drunk.

Does he know I'm here?

Yes. He knows.

Does he know I can feel him twisting out his dirty magic, misusing it to cheat, to waylay and to rob?

He knows that too. It's like a taunt. A signal he's putting out. A reminder that he's still waiting for me . . .

People like him have no place in the world. None.

He sat up.

Willow turned over. 'Can't you sleep?' There was a measure of irritation in her voice.

'I'm sorry. Did I wake you?'

She yawned. 'I have to be up early. I'm going to see her grace again tomorrow morning.'

That brought his spinning mind down to ground with a bump. 'Duchess Cicely? Why?'

'She's asked me to wait on her.'

'You're to be one of her ladies?'

'It's all arranged. I ought to agree after she looked after Bethe for so long in the Blessed Isle.' She sighed. 'Don't worry, I'll take Bethe along with me.'

But Will grunted at her. 'The duchess is becoming too attached to our daughter for my liking.'

'Oh, what do you mean? She likes children, and hers have all grown up. She's trying to honour me.'

She felt for his hand and squeezed it. 'It's *him*; you've been thinking about him again, haven't you?'

'Yes.'

'In the middle of the night everything always seems to be at its worst.'

He drew encouragement from her tone: she knew very well that she couldn't help him directly, but that didn't stop her trying to unburden him in other ways. That was true love, and it melted him inside like butter.

After a moment he said, 'Shall I go out of the palace? Shall I find him? Do battle with him? Shall I do that?'

Another moment passed while she considered, or at least bit her tongue. Then she said, 'No, don't seek him out.'

He turned on her. 'Why not? I'll have to meet with him again in the end. Why should I let *him* choose the time and the place?'

'Ask Master Gwydion in the morning. Let him be your guide. But for now . . . get some sleep.'

'Oh, Willow. We're losing the fight.'

'No, we're not. Things will seem a lot rosier in the morning.'

She could not understand, and it was unfair to expect her to. His thoughts drifted to the worthless casket of grey dust he had obtained so artfully from Edward. Edward must have known the stone had crumbled away, of course. He had been secretly laughing at him.

'Maybe it does serve me right,' he murmured, 'when everything I do seems to take us further from a solution. Since the stump that bore the unreadable inscription turned into dust we can't find out where the next stone lies. And if we can't get to it before it begins calling men to battle, we can't drain it. And even if we could get to it we still couldn't drain it because it would only make things worse . . .'

She made no answer and he closed his mind firmly shut and decided that, for the moment, his main concern must be to protect himself and his family from Chlu's next attack. But one last nagging doubt lay at the back of his mind like a worm in an apple. As his thoughts cleared, he understood that it was about Chlu, but it was also about a piece of unfinished business.

The toothed wheels inside the time engine in the tower shifted one last notch, a lever moved and clicked and the bell clanged out the first hour. He sat up and swung his legs out of bed.

'What are you doing?'

'Going out.'

'Out where?'

Struggling, he put an undeserved measure of scorn into his answer. 'Where do you think?'

Cold steamed in the air, a cold that soon became pain wherever it bit into exposed flesh. Will twisted a knee painfully and stifled a curse: here was ice where a puddle had frozen solid. In the morning the palace servants would diligently attend to the slippery patches with their shovels and scatter pink grate-ash onto them, but for the moment they were treacherous.

He went through the private arch that led up past Edward's apartments. It was by far the shortest way to where he was going, but it meant passing along a dark passageway and then through the door beyond. There he surprised one of Jackhald's hidden guard who came forward too late to challenge him. He thrust a palm at the man's face and muttered, 'Sleep!' The man collapsed with a thud.

A big ring of iron turned the latch. Heavy and cold, it drew the heat from his fingers and made a dead sound. The bolts needed heavy force to move them, but they yielded under hammering from the heel of his hand. Then the door swept open in an arc.

The inner yard was black, but he could see a shape rising up in the darkness. He knew the place well enough from memory. It was a tower, set apart from the rest of the palace and not of its fabric. It was older and built of stone and Slaver brick. He found another arch, another door, then a dark passageway that began at the tower's foot but soon became a stair.

This was the place from which the wasp's nest had been removed. He felt sickness rise in the pit of his stomach. The walls shimmered like reflections in a stilly pool. He groped towards the immoveable door, touched cold steel, ran his hands over band and rivet, hinge and lock. Then he whispered up a frosting of magelight and stood back, shoulders hunched, elbow in palm, thinking. A movement. He turned. A pang of fear. The air here was thick and suddenly hard to breathe. He cast a panicked spell at arm's-length into the shadows. 'Sleep!'

'Oh, not I, villain!'

Will's skin bristled as the magic broke back on him. He shut his eyes, but it almost made him pass out. When he resisted, iron force clamped around his ribs and blew the air out of him. He tried to fight it off, steadied himself against the wall. 'I see no villainy here . . . unless it be your own . . . Master Gwydion.'

The pain went away instantly. Blue magelight alighted on the wizard as he stepped out of the shadows. He let Will breathe again.

'Why have you come here? I told you to beware this place and not to climb that stair.'

'I came to find you.'

'In the middle of the night?'

'I couldn't sleep.'

In reply Will heard only the loud cracking of knuckles, then, 'How did you know I was here?'

'Where else would you be? You've been here for the last three days.'

'Is that so?' The wizard let his hands fall to his sides. He managed a mirthless chuckle. 'It might be true to say that this chamber is getting to be something of an obsession with me.'

'Whatever it is, you're too close to it.'

The wizard's eyes rolled up like a seer's and he muttered distractedly, attempting, or so it seemed, a portentous speech. 'I see two ships sailing across a night sea. One is large the other small. Soon the Sightless Ones shall vomit up blood and ashes! Go away, Willand. I feel I am . . . just about to make a great discovery.'

Will suppressed a sigh. 'That's sorcery. These defences are Maskull's and, as you've so often said, he knows you very well. Now, please—'

Will's unimpressed tone prickled the wizard. 'What do you *suggest*? That I back away, when this is our only path forward? Whatever Maskull has left here will furnish us our best clue as to where he has gone and what he might be doing.'

'That sounds like your pride talking to me.'

'Oh, indeed . . .' Gwydion took the point wearily, condescendingly, as if Will could know nothing about a wizard's pride. It was a card he often played.

'Don't patronize me.'

'Willand, I have a job of work to do here. I would that you had not come, but since you have . . .'

'Why do you say that? What do you think is in there?' Will's doubts crowded in on him. 'You wouldn't be trying to use Maskull's own weapons against him, would you?'

For a moment the wizard's outline showed stark against a flare of magelight. His voice was thin and barely audible. 'Willand, Willand, Willand. Could you think that of me? Even in this desperate strait?'

He felt ashamed. He had gone too far. 'No. Of course not. Forgive me, Master Gwydion. I shouldn't have said that. Neither of us is quite himself at the moment, I don't suppose.'

'I know very well what has happened to me. And I know what is happening to you. That is why I continue to counsel patience.'

'You always counsel patience.'

'Then why not expect it of me and be easy in your mind? O, that I could be as easy in my own. Perhaps I should show you my problem and burden you like a beast.'

Will rubbed at his arms. 'I wish you would. Standing here bandying words is doing neither of us any good.'

As the wizard wafted his magelight higher, Will looked up at the stout door. It was clad in bands of iron and held together by a hundred rivets. And it seemed as impenetrably sealed against magic as it was against the striking of brute strength.

Will felt an intense jag of frustration. 'Master Gwydion, I beg you to forget about this door! You are playing with trifles while our real difficulties go unaddressed.'

'Am I? Am I so?' the wizard cried. 'And perhaps you are the wizard and I the fool?'

His own attitude hardened. 'Fool? Is that what I'm called for my loyalty?'

Gwydion looked at him long and with penetrating eyes. 'Hmmm.' Then he raised his staff and drew back the solid door with no more effort than if it had been a curtain.

Will shrank back. 'By the moon and stars! How did you do that?'

'You see, despite what you may have decided, there is life in the old dog yet. I have had the way in here for three days. It is that which lies inside that has me in a quandary. Now tell me what you *really* came here for and we shall speak more amicably.'

Will showed weary innocence. 'It was as I said: I came to look for you.'

'Are you sure it was not for any *other* reason?'

'Do you think so? If you do, then you really are losing your edge.'

'The magic that closed this room against me for so long was not an ordinary spell. There was a meticulous record written through it of breaches made past, present and future. When I interrogated the spell I read of no breach before my own, but it implied there would be another entering here after me. Someone entering to steal. That is why I chose to lie in wait.'

Will put his hands on his hips. 'And so you thought *I* had come to steal?'

'You came. I know not why.'

'I've *told* you why!'

'But you are not being perfectly honest with me.'

'I am!'

'You're keeping something from me. I know that too.' The wizard tutted, then twisted away and danced briefly, showered blue sparks around, after which he gestured peremptorily. 'Well, don't just stand there with your mouth agape. Come into my parlour, as the spider said to the fly.'

As Will walked into the sorcerer's lair he felt a drenching cold fall over him from head to foot. The chamber was lit only by shafts of light that came from slits high above. Dark shapes were trussed up in the rafters, hanging still or slowly twisting. The place stank of sorcery. Charts and writings in an unreadable script adorned the walls. There was a mortar and pestle, with powders of green, yellow and red scattered about. Lines were deeply graven in the stones of the floor with letters incised at numerous points. There were cages in which small animals and birds had died, their water pots dry, their small bones mouldering among their own droppings.

'What a nasty little den this is,' Will said.

'But be assured there is beauty here too,' replied Gwydion, leavening his disgust. He pointed to a single black rose turning round and round endlessly in a ghostly silver vase. Suspended jewels seemed to communicate as they twisted and turned, sending back and forth scintillas of light in red and green. 'There are wonders here. Great wonders.'

He picked up a wand and watched with detached interest as it changed into a green-eyed serpent and back again. 'He has tampered with harm and kindness both. It seems the fetters he put on me were not his only triumph.'

'Are these things all of his making?' Will looked around and his eyes lighted on another fetter. This one was crude, black and heavy but not so unlike those that had been clapped on Gwydion's wrists. Beside it lay an iron bracket from which the lamplight glinted dully. He hefted it and found, as he expected, that it too was heavy. But beyond his expectations he also felt a curious sense of empowerment simply by lifting it up. It was a mechanism attached to a handle made for a man's hand to grip. 'Is it a weapon, do you think?'

The wizard took it from him and laid it aside. 'Maybe. Do you feel harm in it? Some kind of arquebus, it seems to me. Many of the things Maskull has fashioned are weapons, but not all. See here – this is a medicine chest in which he has bottled a hundred flavours of kindness. Each of them is able to ease a specific illness or wound. I can guess what Gort will say when he sees these vials – that such cures are null and void, for Maskull created them in pursuit of a selfish end. But when damaged flesh is knit up again, who but Gort these days will bother to consider the spiritual ailments that come of using corrupt magic?'

Will opened the chest and looked at the little bottles. Marvelling, he shook his head. 'The magic in these vials heals, yet no one should dare to use it . . . now there's a paradox, and a dilemma. Is there such a thing as tainted knowledge?'

'It is the same as dirty silver – coin is coin, some say, while others will not stoop to the spending of money made by crime. Everyone must decide for himself what he will and will not employ in magic . . .' Gwydion's voice tailed off. 'You will see all manner of half-stable mixtures of kindness and harm here, things that are by turns a wonderful delight and unspeakably foul. Give me your hand, and I'll have my revenge of you.'

A gobbet of fear invaded Will's belly when the wizard took his fingers and thrust them into a sparkling jar. But he need not have worried, for his heart was filled with a sudden blast of joy.

'Well?'

'A jar of . . . *happiness*?' Will said in wonderment as Gwydion pulled his hand out again. 'Who would have thought Maskull would make such a thing as this?'

'I would not.' The wizard grunted and nodded his head towards another, similar jar. 'However, I will not ask you to put your hand into that one.'

'What does it do?'

'Try it and see.'

He savoured the last, fading rays of pure joy and his eyes slid back to the first jar. 'I'd much rather try this one again.'

But this time the wizard caught him firmly by the wrist. 'Oh, I think not, Willand.'

He felt an almost overwhelming urge to shrug off the wizard's grip and gratify himself once again. But then the urge slowly withdrew and the truth stood revealed.

'Ah . . .'

Gwydion nodded. 'Ah, indeed. A second time and you would have been lost. Now you see that the jar is not one of pure kindness, but a kind of trap.'

Will thought of the ked then, and understood how Maskull's slave-creature must have felt after it had been ensnared. 'I see.'

'I think you begin to.' The wizard's smile was flat. 'But, regarding Maskull – what are we to do about him? How are we to make progress?'

Will bent his mind to the problem. 'Well . . . we knew he was keen to find the battlestone at Delamprey and help it into action. We knew he was tapping harm from it. And now we know what he was making. That's a kind of progress I suppose.'

'But it does not solve our problem, which is that we have all along been playing into Maskull's hands. For the past three days I have been here, searching out a remedy, a solution to the biggest question: why, despite all our best efforts, is the world still tending towards that dreadful condition that we have been fighting to prevent?'

Will drew a deep breath. 'But I thought all that was down to the harm released from the stones. You said we'd been draining them, thinking we were doing ever so well, but if there's no battle then the evil we release isn't used up. If it's dispersed it works to the detriment of the world in another way.'

'Despite all that I have said to you about "good" and "evil", Willand, still you have no difficulty in treating Maskull as if evil was his aim. Why do you suppose he does what he does?'

Will took the remark sturdily. 'He does it because he's weak. He's selfish and he's greedy. He has his ambitions for the world just like you do, Master Gwydion, but the difference is that he wants to fit the world to his vision, instead of letting it be the other way around. And he doesn't have much patience with anyone who opposes him.'

'But Maskull does believe that he is doing right by the world,' the wizard said. 'We must never forget that. And we must expect him to fight to his last breath to bring about what he considers to be the correct end. Now tell me: what is that end that he's steering the world towards?'

Will could not grasp the meaning of the wizard's question and he floundered. 'You once told me it would lead to five hundred years of war and untold suffering. Is that what you mean? A future wholly without magic? Centuries of strife and terror? The crushing down of people until everyone is yoked to one great vision – Maskull's vision?'

'But did I not tell you that Maskull wanted another world? A place not unlike our own, yet quite separate from it?'

'You might have said that, but if you did I had no clear understanding of what you meant. I just thought you were talking about his vision of the future.'

'Then look at this!' The wizard gestured at the wall where a painted chart hung. 'I can now show you exactly what is in Maskull's mind, for he is not planning to invent the world that he wishes to bring us to – *it already exists.*'

Will looked at the chart, and saw that it contained a picture he had seen many times, a picture he had been shown by Tutor Aspall in his youth. It showed the scheme of the world in its three parts – the known world, round and flat, with many lands to the east and a great sea to the west from which the waters endlessly fell. In the centre of the world where sea and land met, were the isles of Albion and the Blessed Isle, and on Albion's three parts were written 'Albanay', 'Cambray', and 'The Realm'. Above it all was painted the great perforated dome of the sky, complete with sun and moon and a suggestion of the brightness that lay beyond, while underneath was the Realm Below where the fae had taken refuge, and below that the stilly waters of the abyssal ocean . . .

'Yes, but I don't see how this—'

'You will!'

The wizard peeled the chart away from a wooden board on which it had been held, seemingly by magic. Daylight filtered around the board's edges and through the cracks, as if it was a window shutter. He heard the soughing of air, but felt nothing because no air was coming into the room. It was leaving it.

Ah, he thought, suction was holding the chart up.

Now that the cracks were unobstructed, he saw a thread of smoke rising up from one of the oil lamps. It was being sucked towards the window like water in a mill race. When Gwydion undid the catch, the shutters threw themselves open and light streamed in. Will saw that behind the shutters was a strange little window not much further across than his shoulders.

The wizard opened his palm at the scene. 'Behold!'

A significant draught had started to blow through the room. It pulled at Will's hair as he approached and peered out. There was a faint red-yellow halo just beyond the window, as if the air that was leaving the room was feeding some kind of magical flame. But if it was a flame it was transparent enough to see through.

The palace yards were down below. But they were not quite as Will remembered them. Great white buttresses rose up all around and there was in the air a cacophony of bells. And over there was the river, and many people loping along, horses gliding and provision carts in great number all moving with a strange and unaccustomed slowness. But beyond Albanay Yard there was no Thomas Quad, and all was rose-tinged grey as if the light of early dawn was upon them.

He craned his head, put his face right out, then looked back at Gwydion in astonishment as the rushing air ceased to tug at his hair. 'But . . . it's *daylight* out there,' he said. 'And all the trees are in leaf!'

Gwydion's face was intense. 'That's because it's a summer's day. Out there even time itself elapses at a different rate; it runs slower. Do you see how slowly the birds are flying? How the clouds seem to hang motionless? And look at the people. Do you recall what once I told you in the Blessed Isle? Change place and you must also change time.'

'There are no colours there!'

'None. All is in shades of grey.'

'But where *is* it?' Will's heart beat faster. He could not take in all the strangeness. 'That's not another place. It's *here*. I can see a spire in the distance and the City walls. And that's the Iesis – no other river curves just like that.' He stared again, shaded his eyes. '*What kind of sorcery is this, Master Gwydion?*'

The wizard grew suddenly grim. 'What you are seeing is Maskull's great hope. This is what lies at the end of his long collision course. You are looking out upon his other world.'

CHAPTER ELEVEN

PROMISES AND PIECRUSTS

The next day Will could not prevent a dark cloud descending over him as he recalled the view from that window and thought over what Gwydion had told him. If that really was Maskull's other world, then everything had arrived at a new level of urgency.

Willow was watching their daughter as she played near the hearth. The infant was chewing wooden animals that Gort had made for her, and Will's heart squeezed as he looked on mother and daughter together. He knew the day was fast approaching when he would have to leave them again, but this time it felt as if it would be forever.

'I have something I want to tell you,' he said. 'Something important.'

He told her about what he had seen in the tower, and what Gwydion had said. He was hoping, by talking it out, to make better sense of it himself, but although he could see all the parts there was no clear pattern to the whole.

Willow shook her head uncertainly. 'Another world? I can't imagine that.'

'Gwydion explained it to me. He says we're like two vessels making our way across the sea at night, each unaware of the other. We're just a tiny boat, but they're a great big ship.

All the time we're sailing along, turning a little bit this way and a little bit that way just as the winds and waves allow, but all the time—'

'—we're getting ever closer to being run down by the big ship. Is that it?'

He nodded. 'And one day we'll get so close that it hits us.'

'Is that what Maskull's trying for? He wants to steer us into collision with this other world?' She tried to puzzle her way through the idea. 'So the more harm Maskull can release into this world, the closer we get to that other, grey world?'

'That's it. And because of the stones, it's happening faster and faster.'

She looked sourly at the prospect. 'And what happens when we collide?'

'Master Gwydion says the big, grey world will just suck us in and gobble us up. It will hardly notice us in its path, and after we've become a part of it, it'll just carry on more or less as before. But we'll notice it all right, because the closer we approach it the more we'll have to become like it. It's so much bigger than us that we're the ones who'll have to do all the changing.'

'I don't much like the sound of that.' Bethe began to cry, and Willow picked her up. 'There, there, poppet. Take that out of your mouth. Can't we stop it happening? Steer ourselves away?'

'I don't know if we can.' Will saw that he had swum way out of his depth. He also realized that he had succeeded in sinking Willow in his gloom.

'Just think of Maskull sitting at his window, spying on that other world. What do you suppose he was looking for?' She shivered and after a while when she received no answer, she said, 'What's it like out there?'

He told her what he had seen through the strange

window. 'It looked like an odd sort of a place. Master Gwydion says the other world has no magic of its own, so that whatever magic's left in ours will vanish away as we get closer to the collision. He says that's why the Ages are getting shorter. It's the fundamental reason that magic has been leaving our world, though he has not seen that reason clearly until now.'

He thought of a piece of Gwydion's wisdom, which he had heard after the battle at Delamprey. 'Men's memories fade, Willand, and memories of magical things fade the fastest. Already men have forgotten the beams of blue and purple fire that played over the skies of Verlamion. Eventually they will forget that they ever saw a wyvern in flight above Delamprey. What will be recorded in the chronicles of later times will be little more than a dull roll of horses and men, and only noble men at that.'

Willow looked up at him. 'I think I see what Maskull wants. It's to rule in that other world as well as this. He's bound to think that a bigger world is a more fitting target for his ambitions.'

'But it looks as if Maskull may have found a way to take some magical weapons through the collision. He's been making preparations to carry forward whatever he needs. Can you imagine a world without magic, except that wielded by Maskull?'

She looked shocked. 'So that's how he plans to live forever and become master of us all . . .'

'What Master Gwydion says about the other place is very puzzling.' He paced, turned, paced some more. 'In our world things become as most folk believe them to be, but not in that other world. There the world just is, and folk must find out its nature or remain in ignorance. Here there's magic, but out there the redes don't apply. In our world the ideas of "good" and "evil" are just that – ideas, and false ideas, lies dreamed up by the Sightless Ones for their own twisted ends – but in their world they *really exist*. And they have something called . . . God.'

Her eyes flickered. 'What's that?'

'It's something to do with the Great Lie. But over there everyone is forced to believe in it. It's a sort of invisible force that tortures their world horribly, yet must be praised and obeyed. But it's also something they can blame their own shortcomings on. It's as if the Great Lie were actually true. I don't understand it fully, but I do know that thinking about it makes folk very sick in the head.'

'Oh!' She looked at her daughter, then up at him, and was as worried as he had ever seen her. 'How terrible!'

He looked out of the window and saw a line of Sightless Ones, hooded heads bowed, each with a red hand on the shoulder of the one in front, each turning this way and that. More of them had been seen about the palace in the past week, conducting their strange ceremonies. Will had thought the ritual observances were just an excuse to bring their agents closer to Duke Richard, the man at the very centre of power. But now Will began to see what the Fellowship was really about. They were the means by which the God-monster would enter the world. They were trying to make everyone believe, and so push the world closer to its day of reckoning. '*Soon the Sightless Ones shall vomit up blood and ashes . . .*'

'What was that?'

'It's just something Master Gwydion said when I found him last night.' Will felt for the answer. 'He told me I wasn't being honest with him. I know why now. It was because I was going there to tell him something, but I still haven't done it.'

'But what is it, Will? You must tell me.'

As always she had gone to the heart of his problem. 'I've . . . I've made another stupid promise on Gwydion's behalf. I wanted to explain myself, but for some reason I wasn't able to tell him about it.'

'A promise to whom?'

He told her about Lotan, about the way the huge blind man had saved his life and had thereby set up an obligation. The admission felt like a tun being lifted off his shoulders. 'What else could I do?'

'Your promise was only to bring him hope – that there might be help for him?'

'I went no further than that.'

She considered. 'I suppose it seemed like a good idea at the time, to make friends with the Fellowship? Oh, Will, you're forever telling me how dangerous they are.'

'There's almost a rede in that: every stupid action seems like a good idea at the time. Do you really think it's a trap?'

'It might be.' She studied him. 'But maybe you're not being so stupid after all. Maybe it's the wiser part of your mind telling that stubborn know-it-all part what you ought to be doing.'

'Hmm.'

'But you're not taking any notice of it. Gort says you're resisting becoming King Arthur. Maybe that's why you can't tell Gwydion about Lotan.'

He laughed in frustration. 'Gort's right about that. I don't know how to become a king.'

She reached up and touched him. 'You've always been a king to me.'

He pressed his lips to hers, then came and sat down beside her. For a long time he looked into the fire that burned in the hearth, wondering if there might not after all have been some unsuspected subtlety, some spell of procrastination, put upon him.

He checked himself, turning inward as he knew he must to examine his perceptions. True, the fire seemed oddly unnatural to his eye. But that was because instead of wood it burned upon a kind of stone, black 'wyrmstone' sent down from the city of Toune by boats that plied the east coast. Merchants brought it in special ships, their holds steaming as they unloaded at the Dowe and the Queenhythe. Gwydion had told how all along the banks of the Black River in Umberland there were seams and outcrops of the filthy stuff. Men laboured in dark holes and pits to dig it out. Wyrmstone – shiny as obsidian but light as jet, easily crushed, yet imbued with the power of *fire* . . .

He stirred and went to the table to find the piece of wyrmstone he had put aside that morning.

He said to Willow, 'Gort told me that whenever a great dragon was slain and slit to the gizzard, quantities of this would fall out of its gut. There were always ash heaps around their dens. I wonder how he explains this, though.'

He showed her what he had discovered by chance when he had cracked open the wyrmstone.

'That's pretty,' she said, looking at the perfect imprint of a fern in the black stone.

'But, Willow, how did it get in there?'

She scratched her chin, not quite seeing his point. 'Magic, I suppose. What else could it be?'

'Yes. What else could it be? And if it is magic, then what does it signify?'

And that, Will thought, was the most difficult question, not least because the Age was drawing to a close and according to Gwydion all kinds of strangenesses appeared to plague the world at the end of an Age – signs and omens in plenty, gross rarities and now perhaps even the unseating of magical meaning.

He hefted the rock thoughtfully. 'I must show this to Gort.'

'The Wortmaster's not here.'

'Oh?'

'He got a bee in his bonnet this morning – he dragged that big medicine chest out into the passage and started going on about not wanting to have it in his room. He said he was going to have the matter out with Master Gwydion.'

Will decided not to mention where the chest had come from. 'And where is Master Gwydion?'

'He went down to Queenhythe to check on the ship rumours.'

He looked blankly back at her. 'Ship rumours?'

'Haven't you heard yet? It's all over the palace. Everyone's been talking about it this morning.'

'I haven't spoken to anyone.'

'Then it's just as well that I get out and about more than you do. It seems that a big Bristowe ship came in last night. The crew have been spreading stories around the City about having found Hy Brasil at last.'

'Hy Brasil?' He screwed up his face. 'You mean the land that was meant to be out in the Western Deeps? But it doesn't exist.'

She seemed balked. 'Isn't that the land that King Sisil sailed to in the olden days? I'm sure it was.'

'Who knows where King Sisil went? He was never seen again. Master Gwydion always told me there was nothing out there in the west. Nothing except a great waterfall at the Rim of the World.'

'How does he know?'

'Because he's been there. He told me all about it. The sky roars past quicker than anything you ever saw or heard and the waters are clear and sugar sweet and pour out over a great lip of pale stone . . .' He sat back in his chair, watching yellow-grey smoke escaping up the chimney. A quantity of it belched back into the room. Wyrmstone stank as it burned, and he suddenly thought the fireside was intolerably stuffy. Though rain was beating on the leaded panes he got up and flung open the window.

'Oh, Willand, no!' Willow said. 'It's freezing out there. Think of Bethe, would you?'

He poked his head out. The ghastly quality of the light

came not so much from the tint of the glass; the clouds themselves were leaden and yellow bellied. Instead of the tonic cold of rain on his face, the bite of fresh air in his lungs as he expected, there was only the smell of chimney smoke. But it was still the world he knew out there, and that was something.

'Master Gwydion's failing. I'm sure of it,' he said, shutting the window again.

'That's not so.' Willow turned, unwilling to believe. 'His powers were cruelly damaged by those fetters, I'll grant you, but they're returning.'

'Too slowly,' he said. 'Too slowly. And no one can foresee how far they'll come back.'

'He has a fine old staff to lean on.'

'That relic of Maglin's? Bringing it here was originally Gort's idea. He wanted to set my mind at rest. They both did. You think I don't know that?'

'Master Gwydion's as sharp in the mind as ever, and that's what matters,' Willow said, unflagging in her support. 'This morning he pinned a parchment to the back of his door on which he'd written out the whole of the Delamprey stone's inscription stroke by stroke all from memory. And when you thought it must be lost forever. Now what about that?'

'All right, I was wrong to assume that,' Will admitted, adding with heavy irony, 'so, he has the words. Now all he has to do is work out the meaning. But it doesn't matter if he works it out or not. We can't actually do anything about it.'

'Maybe things aren't as bad as you suppose.'

He breathed a heavy sigh. 'I'm suffocating, Willow. We've got to get out of this stalemate. We've just got to!'

She said nothing, but the knock on the door that came almost immediately made her jump. When Will opened it he saw a palace messenger who said nothing and would not meet his eye, but who handed him a letter. On it was a bright red seal that he could not fail to recognize. It was the king's cipher.

As Will emerged into the freezing passageway a white shape streaked by on the stair. Golden eyes looked at him with feline calculation. It was his friend, Pangur Ban, and the cat was smiling.

Will carefully sat down on Maskull's medicine chest, to see if the cat would come. He twisted around Will's ankles before jumping up onto his lap where he began to knead and pluck.

'Are you coming with me to see the king?' Will asked, lifting the cat off. But a miaow in the tiniest of voices was the only response he got. Once put down, Pangur Ban would not be picked up again and he would not follow. Whatever his message was Will could not grasp it.

A single servant showed Will to a guarded door. Hal sat in a shaft of light cast from a narrow window as he worked alone in his stone-cold cell. Yet he seemed content enough at his little desk, quill dipping and scratching, dipping and scratching. It was common knowledge that the king sat like this for hours at a time, seeing no one.

Will waited until the figure, who was wrapped up in a long black coat and black cap, eventually looked to him.

'Your grace asked to see me.'

'Ah . . .'

The quality of the king's grace was unlike that of other men's. Will was instantly aware of it, just as he had been on their only other meeting. Something inside him seemed to resonate with an aura of royalty, and Will suddenly knew why the common people loved Hal as a sacred figure. Despite his grandfather's terrible crime, he had become their king. It was as the rede said: 'It taketh three generations for great events to repair themselves.' And now that time was up it was almost as if the usurpation had never been. Almost . . .

'Approach us closely,' the king said. 'Ah, now we remember you.'

'Your grace.' Will stepped up to the desk and saw that it was strewn with ancient documents, dozens of cracking parchments all annotated in the king's regular, formal hand.

'We should apologize for the sparse surroundings in which we are obliged to receive you, but the Ebors are a large family and they are presently occupying the greater part of our palace.' He gave a smile as pale as the winter sun. 'They have asked poor Hal to make do with a small apartment, and he has consented, for he can do no other.'

It was odd, in private, to hear a man refer to himself as if he was more than one person, and even odder to hear him speak as if he was someone else. Will had expected Hal to take easily to captivity, for he had been a prisoner of one kind or another all his life, yet somehow, despite it all, he still retained the personal dignity of a monarch.

'Your grace,' Will offered, 'I can make it my business to speak with the duke, so that if you are uncomfortable . . .'

Again there came that penetrating look from eyes that were as dark and liquid as an old dog's. 'You are kind. But we do not take our lodgings amiss. This is as much as we have ever been accustomed to. And if now we might enjoy a life of quiet study and the freedom of the palace cellars, then so much the better.'

Will reminded himself that Hal's best received acts of kingship had been the endowing of schools and other places of learning, and that the cellars that ran beneath the White Hall were where the record rolls were kept. These ancient documents were the king's only delight.

Will waited respectfully for the king to speak again, but saw Hal's eyes flicker to the guard who waited at the door.

Will turned suddenly and danced with a nimble step, so that even before the guard had shifted his weight from his halberd he had been struck on the forehead by the weight of Will's spellcast.

'Sleep!'

The guard's expression of surprise changed to one of bliss, and he slid slowly down to the floor.

Will looked at the man mistrustfully and muttered to the king, 'Your grace, I have a strong dislike of spies and eavesdroppers.'

Hal took the magic in his stride. 'So I see. But that was well done, perhaps, for we have asked you here to discuss our predicament.'

Will's fears grew. 'Did you say predicament, your grace? Then would it not be more fitting for you to discuss it with Master Gwydion, whose skill in difficult matters is very much greater than my own?'

'We think not. If we wished to speak with Master Gwydion we could have asked for him by name. This time we are minded to go another way, for we think that a lad such as you came to our aid once before and may do so again.'

'Your grace speaks in riddles.'

'Do you not recall what you once did for us? It was after the battle in our good town of Verlamion.' The king's inky hands began to knead one another, revealing something of the anxiety he had been keeping in. 'Had Lord Warrewyk's men found poor Hal's hiding place, then he would not be speaking to you today. Will you help us in our plight?'

Will knew he was being gently – but expertly – drawn into a position that would put him in conflict with Gwydion, and he wondered how to refuse without giving offence. 'I'm no advisor of kings, your grace.'

The king's unblinking eyes looked through him. 'Then you must advise us in a personal capacity, man to man.'

Will felt a distracting pressure along his left side, a glow where the sleep spell had broken back against him too weakly. Something was amiss.

He took the king's quill knife and stepped over to the felled guard. 'But first, what's to be done with Sleeping Beauty here?' He lifted the man up by the buckle straps of his jerkin, and felt a weight that seemed deliberately limp. 'Now, if he was awake and listening then all I'd have to do would be to kick his behind and send him away for his impudence. But since I've laid him down with a spell, I'll have to test that he's truly asleep. Look away, your grace – I'm going to cut off one of his ears. If he wakes then I shall have to take his tongue also.'

The moment Will took hold of the man's head he opened his eyes and tried to struggle to his feet. 'Get your bloody hands off of me!'

'Fortunately for you, they're not bloody yet.' Will cuffed him down and tore open his shirt. 'Oh! And what do we have *here*?'

The soldier tried to grab the medallion back. 'That's mine!'

But Will had the man by the throat and the medallion by its leather thong. He cut it away and then examined it. It was a disc of pewter with a hole in it. It dripped with cheap magic, and not only cheap magic but a crude specific against his own sleep spell.

'A nasty little amulet, this! And come very recently from the Spire if I'm not mistaken. Who gave it to you?'

'It's my own business where I got it!'

'Oh, you're a very bad spy.' He cast a leonine look at the guard that burst off the remains of his bluster. 'By the moon and stars, word gets around quickly in this warren! Is there nothing that happens here that the red hands don't instantly get to hear about?'

It was a monstrous question. The guard gasped and gritted his teeth in fear but still tried to give nothing away.

A blue gleam grew on the tip of the knife in Will's hand, grew into a pentacle, then burst. He let the man go, got up and hardened his eyes at him. 'Does the duke know about you reporting to other masters? Well? Does he?'

'I . . .'

Will stepped dangerously, feigned indecision. 'What will the duke order done with you when I tell him?'

'No! Please . . .'

'Perhaps it would be a mercy if I turned the air in these lungs—' He splayed his fingers and stabbed them, serpent-like at the man's chest '—to glass!'

'Nnnng!' The guard stiffened, his eyes bulged as he clawed at his throat, suddenly terrified that he could no longer draw breath.

'There's fresh air outside,' Will told him. 'Go and get it! Run for your life! Run, before you turn blue!'

As the man fled, Will closed the door and reached up to bolt it. But then he laughed a despairing laugh that was soon replaced by a weary shake of the head – the door bolt was no longer there to be shot. It seemed a gross pettiness that it had been removed, and he pitied the king the loss of this little piece of privacy.

He tossed the pewter token onto the desk, seeing that perhaps the king had read his laugh wrongly. 'I apologize for frightening the man, your grace, but he deserved it. This palace is awash with intrigue, and if you have something to say to me it'll be better said in privacy.'

The king seemed to Will more saddened than he should be by what he had witnessed. He held out a limp hand and took the quill knife back. 'I think you have changed since last we met . . .'

'I've grown up. When last we met I was but a lad.'

'Whereas now, we see, you are educated in the ways of power.'

'I've learned how best to deal with certain difficulties.'

'And in so doing you have lost your innocence.' There was more regret than accusation in the king's voice. Delicate fingertips played with his ring of state. He wore only one ring, his personal seal. 'We pity you.'

Will bowed his head, feeling admonished. 'It's the way of things these days. I regret it, your grace, but if we are to live in the world as it presently is . . .'

'Aye . . . *if*.'

The moment lingered strangely, but then the king's next gesture disposed of the matter and he tried to pass over it. 'Ah, well. You would rather be elsewhere, we suppose, for there is much that needs mending in this Realm, but since you are here in this city we hope you might spare us a moment. As for our own feelings, we greeted Trinovant with a heavy heart. This is no city of ours, however much the churlish folk seem to delight in us. We have no stomach for kinghood, you see. We would much rather our place was filled by another, our sceptre lifted from us, our balm washed off at last. We would that no knee might bend, no lord call us king, no humble suitor press us for favours. For how can poor Hal help the common man when he cannot help himself?' He left a space that seemed like a sigh. 'But still, we *are* king, and born unto it, and no man may take that away. King we must be until we die – that has been our sovereign promise.'

'I understand, your grace.'

'Though . . . there are many these days who say that promises are like piecrusts.'

'Piecrusts, your grace?'

The king gave a wan smile. 'Aye, made to be broken.'

Will bowed his head even lower, feeling for the lonely monarch whose reign had been such a disaster. Hal was not used to making light conversation. He did not have the directness that Will was used to among men of power, nor did he understand the humour of the common crowd. His only ambition was to be left alone to study his papers and to write what he would in peace.

Silence stretched out almost beyond endurance while Hal tucked a wisp of grey hair under his hat. 'Our days are as simple as we can make them. We make a friend of habit. We enjoy nothing better than to sit here at this desk, or to go down with the only trusted servant who remains to us, to search ancient records.' He brightened. 'We are compiling a "Historie", you see. This is our great work, done in dark and dusty places, with the squeak of rats our only music. It is a labour that is, as the Duke of Ebor has told us, "as pointless as counting crows," but we value it. And we would say this to him if we could: he who thoroughly knows the past may come in time to know something of the future. And those who are ignorant of the past are doomed forever to repeat it. Do you not think that is correct?'

Will was losing patience. 'I suppose it must be, if it please your grace.'

The king's expression softened, and he almost smiled. 'But now we want you to tell us something.'

'If I can I will, your grace.'

'Then say all that you know about the Ebor children.'

The request surprised Will and he let his surprise show. 'What sort of thing would you have me say?'

'Whatever you wish. But we would rather you were truthful.'

Will considered. Not only had it been a while since he had lived among the duke's family, there was politics to consider. What was the reason Hal had asked him to speak? And what decisions hung upon his answer? Nevertheless, Will had encountered several of the duke's brood about the palace, and he had picked up bits of news from Willow about the others. And what harm could there be in telling the king bare bones?

'The older children are hardly children any more,' he began slowly. 'The Lady Anne is now twenty-one. She's married to Henry, Lord Exmoor who attended the Great Council that your grace called at Castle Corben. Lord Exmoor fought against the duke at Delamprey. He did not attend the last Great Council, nor is it thought he'll attend the next.' He paused, knowing that Anne's marriage was a failed political ploy, that Exmoor had sided with Henry of Mells, Mad Clifton and the Hogshead, helping the queen to gather forces secretly in the north. But it was hardly the time to broach the matter of the queen's continuing struggle, so he said, 'After the Lady Anne comes Edward. He's now twenty, while the second son, Edmund, is yet seventeen. After them comes—'

'Tell us more about the two sons.'

Will trod carefully. 'Edward is the Ebor heir. You must have seen him many times. He's now much concerned with affairs of state and the maintenance of his father's army, whereas Edmund, having been touched in the past by an illness, has been declining in health. He's the one who limps and has a withered arm.'

'We have noticed the lad. Was it sorcery that struck him down?'

Will had meant to gloss over the matter of Edmund. He had not wanted the king to question him on the matter because he feared mentioning the Dragon Stone, which had been the real reason for Edmund's infirmity. Instead of the intelligent, considerate youth that Will remembered, Edmund had been ruined in body, and, some said, in mind also, though Will had seen no sign of that.

'It is not sorcery, your grace, but an old accident that has not yet come right. After Edmund—'

'Tell me: does Edward behave well towards his brother?'

'Towards Edmund?' The question gave Will pause. 'I would say so, your grace. A little while ago I asked him, "Is your brother still afraid of the dark?" and Edward's reply was short and to the point. He said, "My brother is not afraid of anything."'

'That is well. Go on please . . . after Edmund?'

'After Edmund comes the Lady Elizabeth, who is sixteen. Her marriage to the Earl of Southfolk was arranged long ago, though she has still not seen her prospective husband, and complains loudly of that. She is much taken up with perfume, paint and powder. As for the Lady Margaret, she is fourteen – quiet and no fit company for her sister, who has become somewhat . . . shall we say, flouncing. The Lady Margaret would rather have a book in her hand than a looking glass. Sadly, she is by no means the beauty that was portrayed in the painting recently made of her. The two girls are chalk and cheese, and I shall leave it to your grace to decide which may be which.'

Will's attempt to make the king smile failed. Hal said only, 'Perhaps, if ever the Lady Margaret thinks kindly of her king, she might come and read to us. In the afternoons, when the light begins to fade.'

'Perhaps she will do that, your grace. If her mother will let her.' Will smiled briefly.

'And what of the younger two boys? George and, ah . . .?'

'George and Richard. George is now, let me see . . . eleven years old. He's bluff and about as clever as a doorpost. He's always trying to persuade people to do things for him, and he throws fits of temper when he doesn't get his own way. On one occasion not so long ago, he got amongst his father's wine and had to be dragged out, reeling drunk, on the orders of Tutor Aspall. Sir John Morte took him to a water tub to have his head soused!'

'And the last boy?'

'Richard? Oh, he's sharp and handsome of face. I've sometimes watched him from afar. Despite being a year or so younger he cleverly taunts George, then shuns him when he tires of his sport. He's a lonely child who sets himself apart. He showed my wife where his collar-bone had not set properly after a fall, but his main interest in coming to see us was to look in upon the lodgings of the Wortmaster during his absence. He wanted, I think, only to satisfy his curiosity about what might be there. He has an inquiring mind, you see.'

'But what do you make of his character, Master Willand?'

It seemed an odd question for a king to ask about a lad who was not yet ten years old. Will thought it opened a window on the morbidly tender mind of the monarch. 'Young Richard takes his lessons and his duties seriously. He's at once inquisitive and suspicious, but there's something about him – something I can't quite put my finger on.'

'Try. For us.'

Will blinked. 'It's . . . small things. He stares too long at his own shadow and fears steps that lead downwards. He dislikes dogs – says they always bark at him as he passes. And it's true. It's as if they smell something that raises their hackles.'

'What is it they smell?'

'I don't know, your grace.' Again Will tried hard to put the feeling he had about Richard into the clumsy medium of words. He took a deep breath and said, 'Richard seems to me to be a little boy who has looked into his own future and seen there only a mess of disappointments. I can say no more than that.'

The king deliberated on what he had been told, then he said, in a way that made Will realize the brief audience had come to an end, 'We thank you. We think you have been candid and most patient with our tiresome questions.'

'Your grace.' Despite himself, Will was touched by the remark. He stepped back, and where other men would have bowed he made a wizard's gesture of respectful parting, though he felt like an impostor in doing so. He knew it was not his place to ask uninvited questions of a king, but he thought himself entitled to know the answer to one at least, and so as he reached the door he said, 'Your grace, may I ask . . . why did you want to learn about the duke's family?'

The king looked back at him with sad eyes. 'It is because we believe we might have found a solution to our stalemate. Another Great Council approaches and we must make an important decision, but first we wished to know a little more about those who would be king when we can be king no longer.'

Tonight the draw was strong. The feeling would not go away, so he decided to leave the palace by the water gate and go down towards Southfolk Steps. There boatmen sometimes drew alongside at night hoping to hook late wayfarers who wanted to return into the City after dark. It was dangerous to go out by the tilting yards where the annual jousts were held. At night no one travelled the roads that joined at the Charing unless in the company of armed men. Those wishing to avoid the sightless stare of the Fellowship were forced to creep through dangerous back alleys, for a single unmolested sentinel stood at the crossroads every hour of the day and night, heeding neither heat nor hard weather, but silently serving his masters. That man took note of each item of traffic that passed to or fro and made report of it.

But no trade was headed for the City now. The gates were closed at sundown and not reopened until morning, which hour still seemed a long way off to Will. It was a cold night and dark, and the stars crowded in such multitudes as to form a solid mass that moved with him as he hurried along. No better proof could have been offered for the way in which the old world was still clinging stubbornly to its truths, he thought. And yet it was easy to believe that tonight these stars that tracked his steps were a lot further away than usual.

'Hey, you!'

The rough voice shouted out from behind him. Will spun on his heel to face a familiar figure in studded leather brigandine and an iron kettle hat. He had two palace guards at his back.

'Captain Jackhald,' Will said evenly.

Jackhald approached and grabbed a fistful of Will's jerkin. His words were hissed low so his men heard nothing of what passed. 'Is this how you repay me, Willand?'

Will did not resist. 'Repay you, Jackhald? What do you mean?'

'When I put a man on a door I don't expect him to be suborned and given the terrors by a crow – 'specially after I've stretched out my neck to find that crow and his kin fine lodging.'

Will realized that Jackhald was talking about the guard on King Hal's door. 'Jackhald, he's *reporting.*'

'Of course he's reporting. He's a guard ain't he? It's part of his pay to sell what he sees and hears.'

Will sighed and made a display of his disappointment. 'Oh, not you too? Is everything in the Realm falling into corruption and self-seeking?'

'Earners are earners, and you should know you're poking your sticky beak in where it's not wanted.'

'It's what crows do, Jackhald. We turn over rotting leaves to see what worms there may be sliding about underneath.'

Jackhald let go of his jerkin and walked back towards his underlings. He jabbed a blunt finger. 'I'm watching you, Willand. Remember that, my friend. And don't say you haven't been warned!'

Will straightened his clothing. He turned and headed down past Palace Steps where the royal boats waited. He allowed himself a small smile at Captain Jackhald's performance. It had all been for the benefit of his men, of course, a little demonstration of authority, and Will could almost hear Jackhald embroidering it: 'I told him straight and no mistake: you don't mess with my boys!'

Yes, that's it, Will thought, rubbing his chin. At least I hope so.

A low-lying fog hugged the marshy shores of the river. It had seeped into every ditch and trench along the road like a rising tide, and curled slow, wraith fingers up from the water's edge to drown out the lower stars. The way underfoot was iron hard in Greene's Alley for there was no moon to light the way. No one would track Will tonight, for there was no one about to do the tracking. Not even those chancers who usually lay in wait beside dark roads imagined that tonight was worth the game.

'Nggh!' Will stumbled, stubbing his toe hard. He lifted his foot, waiting for the sudden mind-numbing wave of pain to subside. As the ache cleared he opened his mind and felt the distant response of Chlu's dreams as they began swimming up through deep fathoms of sleep, eager to lock onto his own.

He closed his mind again quickly. 'Go back to your slumbers, my brother,' he whispered into the night, glad that he had succeeded in eluding Chlu's usual watchfulness. 'Sleep on, and I'll be upon you before you know it.'

And then Will sensed the clinking of a chain.

It was not a sound, but a feeling, an image in his mind. There were three boatmen, one asleep in his boat, and two more standing by the wooden jetty, both alert and aware of him. They were armed as boatmen always were, with stout cudgels – nothing more, for anyone rash enough to cause a boatman lethal trouble would have the entire guild to reckon with.

But the chain Will had sensed was not a boat chain . . .

He felt a vivid human presence a moment before the hand reached out for him. He turned, prepared to meet the threat, and the movement put the man behind him off balance.

But no blow was attempted, only a hand placed on his arm, meant to surprise and frighten him perhaps, but no more. He sensed all this in the brief moment of contact, and that was fortunate, because magic had been about to roar out in his defence.

He did not shake the hand off, but said evenly, 'What do you want?'

'Forgive me.' It was a deep, hard voice, and not interested in anyone's forgiveness. 'In the end I grew tired of waiting for you.'

'And now you've come to find me.'

'That—' the clink of a chain came, heavy and metallic, to pierce the night, '–was my hope.'

Will's plans drained away like a river tide. He had learned enough about life to know when humility was needed. 'I'm sorry, Lotan. I should have come sooner.'

'I believe you.' Lotan's voice was a growl, his words insincere. 'Does not one of your most important redes say that a promise delayed is a promise denied?'

'I shall make amends.'

'Amends . . .'

'You don't believe me. Come, let me prove it to you.' Will led Lotan back the way he had come.

'My waiting has been worthwhile.' Lotan seemed to be talking to himself.

'Be warned – I promised you nothing more than that I would try on your behalf. That promise still holds.'

'It is enough.'

Will cringed at the big man's pitiful hope. He tried to soften the blow he half knew must fall when the request was put to Gwydion. 'But you do admit, Lotan, that you gave away your sight of your own free will? And you understand that by the moral rules of magic this must count greatly against you?'

'I understand. But doesn't your magic allow that a man ought to be able to make one honest mistake, especially when that mistake harms no one else? If your magic is truly moral in nature as you believe, then there must still be hope for me. Is that not so?'

'I don't know if magic is that forgiving, though I'd say it should be.'

The big man groaned. 'What I would not give to see again a ray of sunshine on a spider's web, to watch the clouds roll by, to delight in a pretty girl's face.'

They came to the North Turret and Will rapped on the stout wooden door that was set within the great gate. A small window opened high up and to the side. It was lavishly barred and banded in iron and though the light inside was only a candle, it was blindingly bright to Will's eyes. A sharp, suspicious face viewed them.

'Take your hand away from your face and announce yourself.'

'My name is Willand. I'm with his grace the Duke of Ebor's establishment. You should know me, for it was you who opened the door to let me out but a little while ago.'

'Then step up and be recognized.'

A lantern was thrust out on a rod. 'Hmm. What's your business?'

'No business. I live here.'

'Who's that behind you in the shadows?'

'A friend.'

'You can't bring him in. Standing orders.'

'I don't mean to bring him in.'

They waited a leisurely moment while the narrow door opened. Then Will stepped inside and tapped the guard neatly on the forehead. 'But if he chooses to follow me in of his own accord,' he told the unconscious man, 'then I can't really be accused of bringing him in, can I?'

Lotan reeled as if from a physical pain. But then he turned sideways and slotted himself nimbly through the gate. He groped after the stricken guard, put his hands on him and tried unsuccessfully to stand him up. 'Will he live?'

'Lotan, there's nothing wrong with him. He's just decided to sit down for a little rest.'

'And all from the lightest touch? Truly, this is great magic . . .'

'Sleeping on duty – tut, tut – whatever would Captain Jackhald say?'

He led Lotan to the stair and along the passageway. Willow slipped the bolt on their door when she heard Will's special knock, but she was stunned to see the huge hooded form looming behind her husband. She almost dropped the lantern that was in her hand. Will took it from her and gave her arm a reassuring squeeze. 'Say hello to Lotan. Lotan, this is my wife, Willow. He wants our help.'

'I'll fetch Gort,' she said, shocked.

'And Master Gwydion too, if you can find him.'

Will offered Lotan a seat. He took it, his great bulk no less obvious when he sat down. Bethe slumbered in her neat wooden cradle behind his back, undisturbed by the light. Will decided that neither she nor Lotan would appreciate his making empty chatter, but a cup of Gort's dandelion wine might be welcome, all things considered. Before he could pour it, however, Willow returned and ushered both Gort and Gwydion into the room.

The wizard flew into a flurry of magical gestures as soon as he entered.

'He wears the robes of the Black House!' Gort cried. 'Why did you bring him here, Will?'

'Name yourself, Fellow!' Gwydion commanded the unstirring figure.

'I was called by the Fellows Eudas. I was of the Black House—'

'*Was?*'

'Eudas is not my name. My name is, and always has been, Lotan.'

Gwydion's stance was grim and unbending. 'Why did you come here? What do you seek from us? There can be no escape from the Fellowship.'

Again, the deep, patient voice came slowly. 'There is a rede, I think, which says there is always a first time for everything.'

'Do not quote the redes at me, *worm*!'

Will took a pace towards the wizard and tried to mollify him. 'Master Gwydion, please – remember your manners. This man is our guest. He saved my life.'

'Stand aside! It may have looked as if he was helping you—'

'He *did* help me! And when I was in mortal danger.'

'From whom? Others of the Fellowship, no doubt. And now he says he wants a favour. He says he wants to get his sight back. Is that it?'

Will nodded, surprised at the accuracy of the wizard's guess. 'Yes. We need a miracle.'

The wizard's anger boiled over at the word. 'Miracle? *Miracle?* That can never be! His sight was given away of his own free will. And even if it were possible, I would not attempt to restore it.' The wizard's hand moved like lightning and threw back the newcomer's hood. 'You see? There is nothing left to heal.'

Will blinked, appalled at the wizard's behaviour. He said tightly, 'There was a day, Master Gwydion, when you would have tarried longer over a lame horse.'

'It is not a question of time! This is an old trick. I have seen it too often.'

Will turned to Gort. 'And you, Wortmaster? What have you to say? Won't you at least try to help him?'

'That would be a task for Ogdoad magic . . .' Gort's apology faltered as he stepped back and made himself small. 'What he asks is far beyond my humble skills with herbs.'

Willow had edged closer to her daughter's cradle. Her hand was pressed to her mouth. She was looking at Lotan with huge eyes.

Will put his arm across Lotan's shoulders. 'I'm sorry. But I made no promise. It is, in the end, how the wiser part of me supposed it would be: I was wrong to encourage your hopes.' He faced Gwydion unsmilingly, but still directed his words towards his seated guest. 'My . . . *friends* . . . must leave now, but the night is cold and hospitality, at least, is ours to promise freely. You are welcome, Lotan, to stay here with us.'

'I will not have him sleep on the passage floor like a dog and with nothing but that oaken chest to lay his head against,' Willow said. It was mid-morning and she was sewing one of Will's old shirts, into which she had let a number of darts and panels. 'Perhaps Master Gwydion will think more kindly of him once he's out of those dirty rags.'

Lotan had been sent down to the kitchens on a minor errand, largely so they could discuss what might be done about him.

'I doubt Master Gwydion will change his mind whatever Lotan wears.' Will continued cutting onions on a wooden board using Morann's priceless blade. 'And I don't think Lotan will be too eager to go about without his hood.'

Willow put her sewing aside. 'Whatever happens, they're not going to turn him out, and that's that.'

'I'll make sure he's given lodging here even if I have to wring the permissions out of Edward myself.'

She looked at him and he saw a flurry of expressions cross her face. 'Let me see to that, will you?'

'Why?'

'Because I can ask the duchess and it'll be easier than stirring Edward up unnecessarily. I'm sure her grace will say yes if I tell her you want a visitor to stay here over the Ewletide.'

Will looked critically at the onions he had chopped. 'Either I've just discovered a new magical property of Morann's knife, or onions are not as strong on the eyes as once they were.'

'I'm ashamed of Master Gwydion,' Willow said, pre-occupied by the injustice of what she had heard. 'I hate to say it, but just lately he's turning into a cantankerous old man.'

'I've been that since the Slavers first landed!'

Will looked up and saw that Gort had put his head round the door.

'Oh, Wortmaster,' Willow muttered. It was a chilly welcome and meant to be. 'I wasn't talking about you as it happens.'

'I know. Don't be too hard on Master Gywdion, Willow. There's a good lass.'

Will pointed the knife at Gort and it flashed green. 'This time he deserves it. Now I know why I was dithering for so long. What's got into him?'

The Wortmaster sniffed, and eyed the knife with interest. 'You frightened Master Gwydion off when you asked for a miracle.'

'Did I?'

Will watched Gort absently pick up a piece of onion and put it in his mouth. 'It'll have reminded him of a time some years ago, hey? When he went with the king to Verlamion.'

'Oh?' Will asked, despite himself.

'It was a royal visit to the Shrine of the Founder. A man came forward to King Hal with cries, saying that a miracle had been accomplished because of the king's visit. The man said that though he had been born blind, the honour King Hal had done the Fellowship in attending their shrine had caused him to see at last.'

'And what did the king say about that?'

'Sad to say, the king straightway believed the man.' Gort shook his head. 'Friend Hal has always been ready to believe too much without the need for close enquiry, and this the red hands knew very well. It was their plan to persuade the king to make a law so that anyone disrespecting the Fellowship publicly could have their lips cut off.'

'Filthy swine that they are!' Willow said. 'They put the truth under a bushel whenever they can and try to make men fear to speak out against whatever they say. I always wondered where that wicked law came from!'

The Wortmaster waved a querulous hand. 'That's a law that came much later in the king's reign, for at the time I'm speaking of Master Gwydion would not permit such a law to be made.'

'And how did he prevent it?' Will asked.

'By setting the king straight about miracles. He showed that the red hands' so-called miracle was all just an empty ruse. And the miracle man was sent away and the Fellowship put under a smarting embarrassment, I can tell you!'

'How?' Willow asked. 'How did Master Gwydion set the king straight? It seems to me that if a man claimed to have his sight restored, who could argue against him? Surely all he has to do is show that he sees things?'

'Ah, Ogdoad wizards must be cleverer than you, then,' Gort said, and he tried an endearing grin on her. 'For Master Gwydion knew a very good way to prove the man a liar!'

'Well?' she said, still unwilling to let Gort wholly get round her. 'What was it, this clever proof?'

'Master Gwydion asked first: "Did you say you were born blind?" And when the man swore that it was the truth and many Fellows swore it also, then Master Gwydion said, "But you say you can see well now?" And then the man boasted, "As clear as any man!" So Master Gwydion asked him, "Then tell me what colour is the coat that the king wears?" "Oh, that's easy," says the man. "Brown!" "And this coat here?" said Master Gwydion, taking hold of the Chamberlain's coat. "That one is red." And so it went, until the man had correctly named the colours of a dozen different courtier's coats.'

'So?' Willow said. 'How does that make the man a liar? Didn't he get the colours right?'

'He got them far too right,' Gort said, winking at her. 'Because a man who was born blind and just lately given his sight might know the names of all the colours from hearing them talked about, but he couldn't possibly know which was which.'

'Aaah . . .'

'Now that *is* clever,' Will said, laughing. 'Good for Master Gwydion!'

'Then you forgive him?' Gort asked, looking at them from under bushy eyebrows.

Will looked to Willow. She too could see they were being buttered up. 'Not wholly. And we won't have Lotan treated badly, no matter what the man's past mistakes might have been.'

'Maybe the mistake was yours,' Gort said gently, not wanting to jeopardize the fragile peace he had so clearly been sent to establish. 'Did you not think that Master Gwydion would be angered? You compromised him by promising to put a case before him on behalf of one who wished to escape the Fellowship.'

'I thought he would do what was right and take the case on its merits.'

'In a perfect world, perhaps. But many years ago, Master Gwydion fought a bitter battle with the Fellowship, and when that fight was over the terms of the truce were that he would not meddle in their prerogatives – lest they choose once more to meddle in his. It is a treaty that was wrapped in solemn magic, and so has been held to ever since by both parties. It has served the followers of the Old Ways in these latter days, for Master Gwydion has grown feebler while the Fellowship has grown strong.'

Will hung his head. 'Why did he not come here himself?'

'He's down in the kitchens, making sure that Lotan gets well fed.'

'Making sure Lotan's not here to overhear you, you mean.'

Gort grinned. 'Mayhap that too.'

Will pursed his lips and made his decision. 'Well, you can tell Master Gwydion that if he wants to show himself this evening he's most welcome to dine with us and any other company that we might choose to invite to our table.'

CHAPTER TWELVE

THE KING OF PENTACLES

The next time Will saw the cat, Pangur Ban, they were in the White Hall and all was in readiness for the Great Council. The lords had just done with the preliminaries when the creature walked along the main aisle as if he owned the palace and everything in it. And when he climbed up onto the dais to sit in plain sight before the throne and wash his face, Will could not help but smile.

Will stood with Gort and Gwydion. After he and Willow had received the wizard to break bread with them and made a sort of peace with him, Gwydion had accepted Will's decision that Lotan should be allowed to stay at the palace. But his agreement had been grudging and he had put his foot down when Willow had said that the big man should be trusted. In return, Will had insisted on attending the Great Council, despite the wizard's opinion that he should stay away.

A palace usher went forward to gather up the cat, but it bared its teeth and danced away, lifting its tail up straight, then curling it with incredible nonchalance as if to curse the minion and teach him his place.

Murmuring chants passed back and forth across the White Hall, choirs of Fellows leading and then answering.

Will took the cat's presence to be a sign. But if it was, then it was a sign beyond easy reading. Will's spine was tingling, his acute sensitivity to great events surged and roared inside him, despite the seeming calm. The atmosphere as the lords took their places was far from the chaos he had expected. He had worried that the intervening time since the last gathering might have thrown up new alliances and new difficulties, but a stern discipline attended those who now packed the benches. It was as if a quiet sense of purpose had descended over the whole assembly, as if persuasions of various kinds had been exercised, and disruptions of other kinds quashed or muted. And that was just as well because, as Will knew, the future of the world was about to be decided.

The boiling atmosphere must have been of Gwydion's making, but its very artifice oppressed Will. It added to his anxiety as he pressed forward with Gort and the wizard past a break in the benches and slipped into an inconspicuous side aisle. He began to sweat as he watched Gwydion survey the scene with a hawkish eye. Above the throne, the giants' niches gaped emptily. No echo of their stout guardian presence remained, and Will wondered at that. The Stone of Scions was in its place under the throne, though, and he wondered that Gwydion had not had it spirited away lest it shout out that the king was no longer rightful.

But then Will began to shake. He felt as if the blood was being drained from him, for a gigantic thought struck home as he stared up at the places where Magog and Gogmagog once had been.

'Where's the king?'

Gwydion would not interrupt his mutterings but eventually he fell silent and seemed to awake like a man lifting himself out of the delirium of fever. 'What did you say?'

'King Hal – where is he?'

Gwydion's eyelids drooped. 'He has not been called to attend. That is best, for too many kings spoil the troth.'

Despite his little joke, the wizard seemed utterly weary and far from satisfied that he had done enough to ensure a steady passage of events. He had expended great efforts, and Will suddenly saw the wizard as the magical equivalent of a lone mariner who must steer and haul on lines to trim the sails of a stormbound ship, even to the point of exhaustion. Gort too was reacting to the tension in the air, chewing on his thumbnail and looking about as if aware of great flashes and detonations that no one else could see or hear. Worrisome thoughts were obviously running through the Wortmaster's mind, and Will himself could not put out of his head the questions the king had asked him, nor the profound connection he had just made.

'Master Gwydion . . .' he panted. 'Do you remember the verse that once revealed itself on the Dragon Stone?'

But the wizard had already turned away and was once more occupied in vast and difficult matters. 'Not now, Willand. I told you you shouldn't have come.'

'My first in the west shall marry, my second a king shall be. My third upon a bridge lies dead. My fourth far in the east shall wed. My fifth over the seas shall send. My sixth in wine shall meet his end. My seventh, whom none now fears, shall be reviled five hundred years.

'Master Gwydion, all this time I've thought the verse was the Dragon Stone's riddle, clues offered about other battlestones. But now I see the verse for what it is – it's exactly what Edward called it, a prophecy, a prophecy about the house of Ebor . . .'

His voice tailed off.

'Quite so,' Gort muttered, pulling him back. 'It seems to refer to Duke Richard's children. Have you only just realized that?'

'You *knew*?'

'We guessed it,' Gort said. 'But save your thoughts until later, Willand. Master Gwydion must manage what passes now with great care. Do not try to speak to him – he will not hear you for fear of what you might say.'

He screwed his face up. 'What I might say?'

Gort would not explain but only made another silencing gesture. Will threw back his head and stared up into the huge hammer-beam roof. It seemed to him that he was in the belly of some great fish whose ribs enclosed them all. He blinked at the many ancient battle standards that mouldered there, and tried to maintain clarity of mind enough to think through the details of the Dragon Stone's message. The duke's firstborn, Lady Anne, had indeed married in the west – to Lord Exmoor whose lands bordered the Dukedom of Corinow. Lady Elizabeth's marriage was arranged with Lord Southfolk, whose earldom lay in the east. And it was whispered by the Ebor gossips that an optimistic portrait of Lady Margaret had already been sent across the Narrow Seas to be considered by the Duke of Burgund . . .

Will swallowed dryly, feeling the omens drench him. So what of the boys? he thought. Is Edmund to die on a bridge? And George – is he really fated to be ruined by drink? And what of the seventh-born child? Is Richard to be reviled five hundred years? But more than all these, what about the son and heir? Can Edward really become king?

Will roused himself and looked to the armed men who flanked the aisles of the White Hall. He thought of the troops of soldiers that were still camped out on the May Fair Fields, a strength which the Ebors had at their beck. When he started to warn about them, Gort tried again to hush him, but this time Gwydion seized him by the shoulders and answered with desperate assurances.

'Friend Richard may be trusted in this! It is far from his mind to make a shambles of the White Hall!'

'That's your hope.' He felt the magic bewebbing the hall very strongly. It was making him feel ill.

The wizard shook his head. 'This is a parliament house, not a slaughter yard! Richard knows what he must do.'

'But he doesn't care! Not any more. He's been got at!'

'Shhhh . . .'

'Do you see those men? They're the ones who watched their friends' heads roll at Delamprey! Just one drawn knife will set it all off again! It's no use. The army—'

'Please!' Gort seized him. 'You must be quiet, hey?'

He shoved Gort's hand away. 'Well, wouldn't you? If you were shown your dead master's head dripping red at the neck?'

Gwydion directed a furious gaze at Will. The fire of it turned his flesh cold. 'Do not speak prognostications!'

'It's not a prognostication.' The corner of his mouth began to bleed.

Gwydion lanced a bony finger at him. *'Leave me to my task!'*

'This is my affair too!' But his legs had lost their strength and he tottered.

'Wortmaster, deal with him!'

Gort made an anxious face, took Will's weight and pulled him away on his heels, out of the side aisle to a place behind a great gilded iron tomb where an alabaster king of old slept away eternity.

'He slapped me down,' Will said, recovering a little from the faint. A piquant smell made him turn his head. Gort was administering a balm. 'Master Gwydion cast a spell upon me.'

'Forgive him, Willand. He's spent many a night wrapping a great deal of magic about these proceedings.'

'What's happening?'

'You must allow Master Gwydion a little working room. He must attend developments closely.' Gort's whispered appeal softened. 'He's right – you should have stayed away, but since you didn't you must put violent thoughts far from your mind. You mustn't interfere this time.'

'Wortmaster . . .' The ribs of the great fish heaved and threatened overhead. The swelling din of the Fellowship's discordant choir threaded the air. The stink of incense drifted like a miasma. 'He's mad if he thinks I'd jeopardize his work with prognostications . . . We're on the same side.'

Gort's eyebrows lifted. 'You did more than jeopardize his work last time. You ruined everything.'

'*Me?* But . . .' He stopped. What more could he say? In truth, he *had* affected the outcome of the last such gathering. He had shouted out. He had not meant to, but he had. He had been the pebble that had started the landslide, and that was all that mattered in the end.

The balm was working. His mind steadied. But Gort bowled another ball, knowing just how to knock down the rest of his skittles. 'The world becomes whatever we decide it should become – ever hear that before, hey? And some folk's thoughts count more than others in the process. So you see, words *are* prognostications – when they come from you.'

'Then let me try to want what must be,' he muttered, browbeaten and so weak he could hardly struggle upright. 'I can't even think my own thoughts, it seems.'

He pushed the bottle of balm aside, wiped the brightness from his lips and forced himself to his feet. Gwydion was standing with his fist clenched white about Maglin's staff, his eyes rolled up into his head, muttering incantations at tremendous speed. Will, feeling slightly better now and half-chastened, folded his arms and dourly watched the drama unfolding beyond the rail. He began to see more clearly the source of all the magical pressure he had been feeling – after his mistakes at Delamprey he had so wanted to abide by Gwydion's rule. But sticking to wizardly plans for the future meant crushing himself down and setting aside his own imperatives.

He made an effort to discipline himself and exercise patience. When he looked again for Pangur Ban he saw an old woman shuffling forward to stand in a corner not far from the throne dais. His thoughts had begun to drift elsewhere, but the oddness of the figure struck him. It was curious that no one else seemed to have noticed her – certainly not the guards, for they had let her past the screen and into a reserved part of the Hall. She was dressed too plainly to be a person of rank, yet this was no time to allow in a common petitioner. Where had she come from? How had she got in? She stood in the shadows, her back to Will, just as Duke Richard came in, ivory rod in hand, and readied himself to speak.

Mists of smoke layered the still air. Will felt the sickness move in his belly as he tried again and again to penetrate the old woman's disguise. The attempt felt like trying to walk through a wall, a sure sign that he had dug to the bedrock of appearances. Which could only mean that there was no disguise to be penetrated! And yet . . . the woman *sparkled*.

He plucked up courage and shook Gwydion, murmuring, 'Who's that over there?'

The wizard's eyes swam back into focus, then alighted upon the figure. He said, 'I think you know Brighid very well.'

Will looked again. A familiar feeling flowed over him, one that turned suddenly leaden. 'It's Mother Brig? The beggarwoman? She's come all the way from Ludford?'

'Beggarwoman?' Gwydion replied wearily. 'Did she not say in your hearing that her name was Sovereignty? She has come here today to pay one of her visits to King Ludd's city. It is said that the rightful king will not treat her as an old woman, but as a beautiful young maiden. She has come to try the matter.'

Will stared back. 'This is very dangerous.'

'That I understand very well.'

'What if she *speaks*?'

'What indeed . . .'

The duke moved perilously close to the throne. He brandished the white rod as if he was the Lord High Treasurer, saying, 'We bid you welcome, my lords, to the White Hall on this most auspicious of days. We have called you here in conclave to settle the matter of the monarchy to the satisfaction of all . . .'

Empty talk, Will thought. Empty but perhaps worth something if it greased the axle on which the burden of the state might be carried forward. But his thoughts were already feverishly returning to the moment at Ewletide seven years ago when Mother Brig had told Duke Richard what his fate would be.

How the churlish folk of Ludford had gasped when Gwydion had led the duke in, for Duke Richard had been in his nightgown, barefoot and bound, sleepwalking. Mother Brig had brought him before King Ludd himself, and he had declared that she was no crone but a beautiful young girl. And Mother Brig had told the duke that, even so, he would die if once he dared lay a hand upon the enchanted chair – 'in the first fight that follows' – those had been her words. But there was more, for she had also said, 'If you would know the future then look to your shadow upon the wall.'

What the duke had said next had stayed with Will over the years, though he had found it impossible to understand at the time. Richard had said, 'Mine is the right!'

What had he meant by it?

Now Will saw it clearly. A Ewle log always burned with the truest flame. That was why no one dared to look at the shadow such a fire cast upon the wall, for if it was a headless shadow that person was doomed to die before the year

was out. At Mother Brig's invitation, the duke had seen two
shadows dancing on the wall that night, one on the right
with nothing amiss, but also another from seven years hence
– and that one had been headless.

'He's about to seal his fate,' Will hissed urgently.

Gwydion's face remained thunderous. 'This time you
will stay out of it!'

'But we must do something!'

'I already have done something.' And he moved off to
a place of better vantage and concealment across the main
aisle, where he almost disappeared among the shafts and
shadows as a moth vanishes against the mottled bark of a
tree.

Will started after him, but Gort said, 'Leave him to his
tasks. He has much to do.'

And all the while, the business of the Council was
proceeding. The duke was consulting now with the serjeants
over some dubious legal point. Things seemed to have
stalled. Will watched the lawyers crawling over the matter
like flies over rotten meat until the lords grew restive and
blew them off the corpse. Then objections were flung up
from the floor, until it was announced that King Hal would
have to be brought.

Will watched as the duke tried to block the move. He
stood like a tower in the tide, but there was such a swell of
opposition from the benches that to preserve any hope of
support he was forced to relent. And all the while,
Gwydion's grim eye was upon the struggle. Will recognized
in his ungiving stare a power that had the capacity to move
mountains. Strain was etched on cheek and brow, and he
listened as the mariner listens to the tell-tale creak and crack
of spar and line as his vessel founders in stormy waters.

When King Hal appeared he was pale of face and
unsteady. He moved down the main aisle like an old man,
so that it was hard for Will to credit that he was not yet forty

years of age. As he came to the royal enclosure there was no one to lead him forward. He stumbled on the step and put out a hand to stop himself from falling down.

Everyone's eyes were upon the king. Some of the lords who sat on the nearest benches got to their feet, but it was Mother Brig who stepped forward and steadied him. She took his arm, and he smiled at her in a kindly way.

But once Hal was upon the dais the duke would not suffer him to approach the throne. He intercepted him, as if casually, arm outstretched, indulgent. His ivory rod shepherded the king and Hal responded as he had done all his life, obediently, and with all respect to the man of the moment, until the plainly dressed monarch stood forlorn, the very figure of humility.

Will's eruption of feelings got the better of him again as he watched Hal's pathetic form. He felt for the man whose unadorned robes hung from his shoulders, whose black hat looked like nothing so much as a Melston Moberry pie that had been burned in the oven.

Hal did not look at the assembly before him but clasped one hand in the other and gazed at the red and yellow ochre tiles at his feet. And when the question of whether he was king or not was put to him by the serjeants, his mild voice answered, 'My lords, we have reigned over this Realm nigh on forty years. We dare to remind all now present that you have oftentimes before recognized us as your king. You have given your oath to us upon bended knee. Your fathers did likewise to our father. Your grandfathers to our grandfather. And so I ask: which of you will now break his oath?'

It was simply said, a speech delivered quietly and without bombast, but it was as if a thunderbolt had been hurled down.

No one stirred. There was not a sound. Will looked on as Duke Richard seethed with barely suppressed anger.

This was not what he had counted on, and he did not seem to know how to answer.

Once again the duke strayed closer to the throne, until Gwydion's dour eye clamped on him. And then – miraculously – an adjournment was called.

Dukes and earls and knights of the Realm leapt up off their benches, making accusations. Richard was at the centre of these disputes, a hubbub rising over his head.

'What's the matter with him?' a voice demanded at Will's back.

He turned. It was Edward, with a retinue of square-jawed men. They were all of them lesser nobles, Ebor relatives, and all had the right to be here, but they seemed to Will to have formed a knight's guard. Edward seized Will's sleeve. 'Your Crowmaster's put a spell on my father!'

'I don't believe so.'

'Where is he?'

'Why did your father choose to call Hal here?' Will asked, turning the fierceness of the attack. 'That was a stupid mistake, Edward. He's rushing headlong towards his doom.'

'He had to!' Edward's fists clenched and unclenched. He wanted someone to blame. He was hunting for Gwydion, but his eyes were presently upon a different uninvited guest. 'Who's that damned girl? If she hadn't helped the old devil up the step he would've gone sprawling and that would have settled it.'

Thinking fast, Will stepped to the side so that Edward was distracted and Gwydion's already unobvious form was removed entirely from his line of sight. 'You might better ask why your father insists on carrying around that piece of unicorn horn. His touching Hal with it was a pivotal moment, Edward, a turning point. You should tell him he ought not to make so free.'

Edward's attention locked fast on him. 'The rod? What about it?'

'I've explained to you before what meddling with powers can bring. It's as the redes say: "All power corrupteth in proportion, and great power corrupteth greatly."'

Edward scowled, bethought himself a little, but then cast about impatiently. 'I don't want your platitudes. I want Master Gwydion to *do* something for us instead of letting it all go to Hell in a handcart.'

'Magic cannot be used in the way you want. Only restoring the proper balance—'

'Useless man! If there's no spell upon my father's head, then why does he not simply seize the throne? I would if I were him!'

'Yes,' Will said quietly. 'I know you would.'

'It's the wizard's doing. We must find him!' Edward and his guard of cousins moved off to the centre of the storm where their leader struggled. Will looked to Gwydion but could not see him at first against the granite columns. Then his outline appeared, transparent as a wraith in the dusty light until Will's tutored eye began to fill it in.

The wizard was still gazing towards the throne. A blare of trumpets shocked Will's attention back to the proceedings. More angry words were spouted as the lords heckled the serjeants-at-law, but when the duke stepped forward the chaos subsided. A fresh sense of expectation took its place, and was satisfied at last by the announcement that all had been waiting for.

'My lords,' Duke Richard began. 'To the right wise, notable and discrete lords of this present parliament here assembled, and by the king, right trusty and well beloved, for as much as we have granted our . . .'

The preamble to the duke's speech was long and hard to follow, but the meat of it was easier chewing. It was received by some with jubilation, by others with stunned silence. Will could scarcely believe what he had heard. Hal was to remain king, but Ebor to succeed him.

'Well, that's fixed it,' Gort said, shaking his head sadly.

'But this will only fuel the war like the outrage at Delamprey did!' Will cried. 'Is this what Master Gwydion meant to happen?'

'It is not.'

The wizard had approached unseen and looked to Will like a man at the very limit of his strength. He had now the waxen pallor of a corpse and leaned heavily upon his make-do staff. He raised his hand weakly, only to let it fall again. He was almost too cast down by what had happened to speak, but he said, 'Everyone knows that lawyers are knaves who thrive on discord, but I did not know until this day how wedded they had become to foolishness.'

'Master Gwydion, this is the worst possible result!' Will said. 'Such a compromise satisfies nobody. Haven't they any idea how much the queen will be provoked by it? To cut her son from the succession is calculated to enrage her beyond measure. And in three days she'll know exactly what has passed here and use it to rouse up feeling all across Umberland and the north.'

'She will know sooner than that,' the wizard said, his eyes seeming to follow invisible lines of force that criss-crossed the space above their heads.

Will turned to see Lord Warrewyk strutting gleefully in the aisle. His attention had been drawn by Will's words, which were an offence. 'If you dare to speak of Mad Mag now,' Warrewyk said, 'that is no matter! She, who is living on charity across the border in Albanay! It matters little what a penniless *widow* thinks.' He laughed.

Will realized when he heard that deadly word the true danger that had arisen, for there was now in place a terrible incentive – that Duke Richard's way forward would be made clear as soon as Hal was dead.

'Are you thinking what I think you're thinking?' Gort asked.

'I'm thinking about murder, Wortmaster.'

Gort nodded. 'If the power of the lorc were to rise again soon . . .'

Will saw in his mind's eye the serpentine complexities of the situation. The Realm was slithering ever closer to conflict once more. In truth, Duke Richard was not to blame. He had been unable to do other than accept the lords' verdict, while Hal, forlorn and alone, had had little choice. Indeed it should have been clear to all that events were being carried forward by some far greater power, and that they had now developed a momentum all their own.

But it was another event that stabbed Will to the heart with a blade of fear, for the king was being escorted from the White Hall and as he came near he paused at the step. Will watched him take the royal ring from his finger and gave it to Mother Brig. 'For you, my dear,' he said before continuing on. 'You were kind enough to steady an old fool when it seemed he might fall.'

And in both Will's and Edward's hearing Mother Brig made her reply: 'Know this, your grace – Ebor shall over-look Ebor before the year is out!'

CHAPTER FOURTEEN

PROPHECIES, LIBELS AND DREAMS

When Will burst through the door he found Lotan sitting with Willow. The big man had his back to Will but did not have his hood up. Willow's hands were on his face and she was crying.

'Don't be angry, Will,' she said, looking up at him.

He had sensed something was wrong, a feeling that had grown more acute as he had got closer to his lodging. He had taken the final stairs at a run, but had not failed to notice that the chest that Gort had refused to keep in his room was no longer in the passageway.

He heard Lotan say in a faraway voice, 'You are so beautiful . . .' and put his hand to Willow's cheek.

'*What have you done?*' Will heard incredulity and accusation in his own voice. But Willow had only acted out of compassion, and that – surely – was what mattered. Yet the fact that the medicine chest had come from Maskull's chamber – had been of his making – filled Will with dread, and he recalled Master Gwydion's warning him long ago that fine intentions were by no means all there was to magic.

Glass vials and jars of powders and tinctures were

scattered around. Some had pictures, others words, on their labels. Despite the odour of stale magic Will forced himself to pick up one of the lidless vessels and examine it. There was a grey ointment inside, greasy on his fingers, mintily aromatic. He dabbed a little onto the knuckle of his middle finger where a white scar circled the joint. It was the reminder of a cut he had got while sparring with Edward years ago. By a count of seven the scar had started to vanish; by thirteen it had gone.

It was a reckless trial, but necessary. He moved round so that he could see Lotan's face. The big jaw was square now, the cheek whole, and where once two empty sockets had scanned the air, the eyes were restored.

'Gort said it needed Ogdoad magic,' Will said, controlling himself. 'I never supposed Maskull would be the one to provide it.'

His stiffness of demeanour accused her and she said, 'This must be right.'

'Must it?'

'Well, ask Lotan!'

'Why should he know?'

And Willow's face showed that she had never considered that the man at the centre of a magical issue might be the very last person to consult over the question of its ethical standing.

'It's *his* life, Will.'

'And you, Willow? What has this to do with you?'

Lotan stirred. 'I asked her for help, and she was kind enough to give it.'

'She had no right! No right at all. Not without talking to me first. And you – you've betrayed me and abused my hospitality!'

As Lotan turned, the light caught in his eyes and Will saw that they were different colours. One was blue, the other brown.

'I took them,' Lotan said, 'from those who can no longer use them.'

'The right came from Magog and the left from Gogmagog,' Willow said quickly. 'Will, they were going to be *burned*!'

'But they weren't burned. And now they can never be restored. You haven't thought this through.'

'No! And thinking things through doesn't always work. Look at you, Will. You're stuck. You don't know what to do, so you wait and you wait until events move along, and then you respond to them. This is not the Will I know. And you'll have to do better if you're going to be a king.'

He felt the indecision still grinding inside him. Suddenly he seemed like the fool who cannot bring himself to cheer a victory until the basis on which it has been won can be shown to be wholly and completely without blemish. Yet Willow, pragmatic as ever, had simply acted from the heart. She had, by an act of love, cut the impossible knot, and it seemed that her inner lodestone might, after all, have pointed them in the right direction.

'Will, it can't be wrong,' she said, willing him to believe also. 'I'm sure of it.'

If you think that, he wanted to say, then why did you do it behind my back? And why are you begging so hard now for my approval? But the more he considered the more it seemed that she was in the right, and – right or wrong – the deed was irreversibly done.

He wiped his fingers clean, offered the others a hopeful nod. 'I don't know what you've thrown into the air here, and I don't know what Master Gwydion will say when he learns about it. As to whether it was the right thing to do, we shall have to wait and see.'

'What did she mean by it?' Edward asked, the next time Will saw him.

His breath boiled visibly in the December air. Three days had passed since the disastrous agreement between king and duke had been struck. Will found himself cornered in Albanay Yard as the clock struck four. Edward's guard of men closed in. Their usual function was to clear a way for the young Earl of the Marches, to make sure he received the respect he thought was his due.

In his case it's the respect that rats give to a terrier, Will thought.

'I'll ask you again, Will: what did she mean by it?'

Will treated the question as if it was a threat. 'I'll assume you're speaking about Mother Brig. Let me ask you, Edward: what do *you* think she meant by it?'

Even so innocent a question could be a provocation to the duke's son when he was in the wrong mood. Still, Edward seemed minded to keep his temper, although his men reacted in exaggerated fashion with jeers and whistles.

'My friends have decided you're being too familiar.'

'Have they, now? And these new friends of yours – don't they know we're *old* friends, you and I, Edward?'

'I don't think they care about that.'

Will looked around at their eager faces and felt their excitement, but also their ill-concealed fears. 'And how if I bite my thumb at them? Are you sure they won't all fall down like so many nine-pins?'

Edward's voice hardened. 'I'll ask you for the last time: what did the girl mean?'

Will parried the question as squarely as he dared. 'When I ask what *you* think she means, that isn't a question I pose without reason. I must know what you want from me before I can answer you.'

'Damn your word games!'

Edward was not sharp enough to realize the exchange had already given Will all he needed to know. 'I wish I could answer you, but sometimes the world just isn't as simple as we might wish it to be. I can find you any number of fawning false astrologers who'll tell you exactly what you want to hear. It'll cost you no more than a silver penny. But you'll waste your money.'

The toothed wheels inside Edward's head turned like those inside a great water mill, until a heavy hammer was tripped and fell. Neither he nor his men could tell if their victim was being clever with them, but Edward chose to let it pass and instead he took another slant.

'Why do you call her "Mother Brig"?'

'Her name is Brighid.' Will straightened. Edward's retinue had by now boxed him in uncomfortably. 'I told you I'm not to be leaned on, Edward. If you don't call them off, I'll make them all sweat.'

'My friends . . .' A tired gesture of the hand, and they drew back. Another and they were dismissed out of earshot altogether. 'You see? They're just like dogs.'

'Then you should be more careful of the company you keep.'

'What do you expect? These are unsettled times, and if you think my friends are bad, you should see my enemies. Was it a prophecy or not? Tell me. You owe me that much.'

'Owe *you*?' Will inclined his head, pointing up the mismatch of their understandings. 'You're behaving as if you think I know something that might be of use to you. I don't.'

'I hope you do, for your own sake. Or am I supposed to be fooled by that ominous manner you're so much at pains to cultivate?' He drew a disappointed breath. 'Is there anything to you, Willand? Anything at all, underneath all that *mystery*?'

Will put on a deliberately enigmatic smile. 'You must try me and see.'

Edward absorbed the retort easily. 'Truly, I don't see what's the harm in a little good-natured co-operation between boyhood friends . . .'

How like his father he sounded when he adopted a jocular tone. Will decided to lay it out plain. 'You've no idea how we've laboured night and day to keep you and your father in whole skins. But neither of you will be told, because your pride cannot bear advice, and in any case you don't like the solution to this war. But it is the *only* solution in the end.'

Edward rolled his eyes. 'And now I suppose you'll want to lecture me on—'

But Will cut him off. 'There is a far greater force in the land than you allow. Far greater than—' he gestured deprecatingly at the richly carved stone of the palace buildings '—than all *this*. You won't rest until you and all your people are dead, and a great many others who have nothing to do with you and your ambitions.'

Edward grasped his arm, suddenly intense. '"Ebor shall overlook Ebor before the year is out." Gort says you know what it means.'

'Why would Gort have said that?'

'Because I asked him!'

Will wanted to say outright that Edward had laughed off the warning about his father's doom. Why did he think he deserved another chance? But he resisted the temptation. Telling Edward home truths was a dangerous game at the best of times, and Mother Brig's words had disturbed the Earl of the Marches more than he wanted to admit.

'Gort's wrong. I don't know what her utterance means. But Mother Brig is a seer. And whatever she says will come to pass after a fashion.'

'It means that my father will overlook me and give the crown to Edmund, doesn't it?' Edward blurted out.

Will was momentarily thrown. *'What?'* He looked away, hoping it was some kind of joke, but when he turned back he saw that Edward was in complete earnest.

'You asked what I thought. "Ebor shall o'erlook Ebor".

It means he's going to try to put a damned cripple on the throne, doesn't it?'

Will had never heard Edward talk like this about his brother. Something was running badly out of kilter.

'Your suspicions have got the better of you,' he said, wary now of giving more fuel to Edward's trend of mind. But he added, 'And, you know, it feels like a piece of dirty magic has been put on you.'

'So – you think it's *sorcery*?' It was said more out of curiosity than fear.

'That's likely, listening to you speak. A spell-cast to create tension between two brothers. Another to do the same between father and son. Somebody's seeking to open rifts in the house of Ebor. Have you accepted any tokens lately?'

Edward was on that like a cat. 'Tokens? From whom?'

'Anyone. I mean, are you carrying anything unusual about your person? Something that might have been tampered with before being given to you?'

There was the slightest of pauses. 'No. Nothing like that.'

'Are you sure?'

'Yes, I'm sure!'

'In that case there's nothing to worry about.' He stroked his chin in a deliberately judicial way. 'But I would counsel a formal reconciliation even so. A clearing of the air. If you want I'll ask Master Gwydion if he'll arrange it.'

A haunted look came over Edward, and he said, 'So things have come to this, have they? The day has finally arrived when I need permission from a damned crow to meet with my own father!'

Will watched wordlessly as Edward turned about and left, taking his kinsmen with him. There was nothing more that could be said.

Rain blustered against the window panes and threatened to wash out the cold, grey dawn. Will's feathered nest was snug and warm, but something insistent was driving him out of it. Then he heard Willow's voice calling to him from the stair. 'Will! Will, wake up!'

He rolled over, then sat upright. 'What is it?'

'Gort says they've all gone!'

He shook his head, still heavy with sleep. She had got up without waking him, had let him snore on as she sometimes did on mornings when the night before had turned out to be overly convivial.

'Who? Who's gone? What's happening?'

She had come in bringing with her a great draught of cold air. She was bright and breathless with the news. 'The duke. He's gone. Sneaked off this morning. With a big party of men. Gort just told me.'

Anger briefly flared that he had not been awakened sooner. 'Where are my shoes?'

Willow opened the window and studied the foul weather. 'I thought I heard horses in the middle of the night. But it must have been just before dawn. What a day to pick.'

'Gort might have said something.'

'He didn't know. He's only just heard – Will? Hey, wait!'

He ran down the stairs while still securing the ties on his jerkin and pulling his shirt straight. When he reached the middle of Albanay Yard he wondered what he was doing beyond uselessly confirming Willow's words. The duke's personal guards were gone, and when he reached Edward's apartments he found the main doors locked and no guard posted.

He banged a fist on the heavy wood, then waylaid a couple of palace servants. They did not know where the duke had gone, except to say that all the nobles lodging in Albanay Yard had left before sun-up, and the strangest thing – the horses had all had sacking tied over their hooves.

'Yes, I bet they did! They didn't want to wake anyone. What about Edward?'

'My Lord of the Marches departed some time before them.'

'Before? When?'

The servants looked at one another. 'Howbeit . . . some-time after the midnight hour.'

It took Will a little while to get the full story out of them, but it seemed there were murmurings about men breaking camp and soldiers mustering ready to leave the May Fair fields.

'Edward's got a good head start, I shouldn't wonder,' he said, touching a knuckle to his lips, then turning to the servants again. 'And Warrewyk and Sarum? Are they gone too?'

The question was met by an uncomfortable shuffling. Having no silver, Will pushed the difficulty aside. 'Never mind about that. Tell me: is her grace the duchess in her apartments now?'

They brightened and nodded vigorously. 'Yes, sir.'

'And his grace the king?'

Likewise.

'Thank you. You may go.'

Will stood alone in the cold, moist air. *Willow's right about the duke sneaking away,* he thought, and kicked off his shoes. Despite the cold and wet he planted his feet on the flag stones and tried to sense below the slabs for the good earth. Then he cautiously opened his mind and began to feel for Chlu.

Nothing.

That in itself was strange. Chlu could not still be in Trinovant, or anywhere else within a dozen leagues. A coin-cidence, then, that he had chosen to leave on the same night as the duke? Possibly, but very unlikely. For first Edward's host, then that of the Duke of Ebor suddenly to muster and leave within hours of one another – there must have been a plan, and a secret one at that, and Chlu had reacted most swiftly to the departures.

'Out of bed at last, I see,' Gort said, coming up. 'And out of your shoes too. A bit cold for that kind of dance, hey?'

Will frowned. 'Where have they all gone off to in such a wildfire rush, eh, Wortmaster?'

'Wouldn't we both like to know the answer to that? So . . . better try to find out, hey?'

A fresh warning sounded at the back of Will's mind. 'And they all got away without Master Gwydion getting wind of it? That's something.'

'Not so much as you might think, since the sneaking off was done in Master Gwydion's absence.'

'He's not in the palace?'

'He was abroad all last night. He's still not back.'

'Then you'll have to find him. I have something to tell him.'

Gort rumbled. 'Finding him's easier said than done these days.'

Will knew he had heard an undertone of concern. 'What do you mean?'

Gort's vigilance returned. 'Oh, only that if a wizard doesn't want to be found . . .'

'*Doesn't* he want to be found? I should have thought that at a time like this he'd be looking for *us*. Wortmaster, is there something you're not telling me?'

'I'm always not telling you lots of things.' Gort's glance alighted on Will, but then fluttered away again like a butterfly. 'As you say, Willand, I'll try to find him.'

Will nodded. 'And I'll see what I can find out. Let's meet back here at noon. I promise I'll be here. And tell Willow to prepare to travel.'

Gort headed back to the stair and Will went the other way, passing the stacked timbers that had once been Magog and Gogmagog. They were slick with rain now, and water had collected in their empty eye sockets, so their blind gazes seemed full of sky.

When Will reached the main gates he noticed a knot of men and approached them. Edmund was among the shadows under the arches of the gatehouse. He was preparing to leave. Two servants were helping him up onto his horse, and his bodyguard moved to block Will as he came up.

'Edmund! Please, I must speak with you.'

The tragic young earl turned and recognized Will. At first, Will thought he would ignore his plea, but then he motioned him forward, and the guards allowed him to pass.

Edmund's stoop was pronounced, even on horseback. It seemed as if he had lost the power over half his body. He favoured his serviceable left arm and kept the withered right hidden inside a fold of his riding cloak. His mouth closed lop-sidedly so that he drooled. The cold had blotched his face with red, and caused spittle to chap his skin. But Will had always liked Edmund. Lately he had come to admire his stubborn courage, and even his ingenuity. Edmund had taught his favourite horse a whole new set of commands, and had even had his saddle remade according to a pattern of his own devising, so that he could ride without discomfort.

Edmund drawled, 'Wish a safety . . . upon me, Will . . . and upon my father's . . . enterprise.'

At first, Will could not grasp the meaning. Edmund could not easily get his words out. Speaking was so painful a process that it destroyed cadence and emphasis in all that he said. Listening to Edmund required patience.

Will reached up and took the young earl's offered hand in a brief grip. 'I would put a blessing on all your house if I could, Edmund. Where has your father gone?'

Another mumble while Edmund's eyes rolled in their sockets. 'I may . . . not say.'

'Then answer me this: has the Earl of the Marches gone with him?'

Edmund's helplessly roaming eyes slid deliberately away. 'Edward is . . . elsewhere.'

Will could feel the silent consternation that passed among Edmund's guard. Everyone knew that it was dangerous to give any kind of clue to a crow, for by his arts he would work upon it and soon come to know more than he should. Whatever the truth, Will could see clearly enough what must have happened. Edward had tried to square matters with his father without employing Gwydion's help, so it had all gone wrong. There had been hot words, and the bonfire against which Will had cautioned had flared up.

The headstrong fool, Will thought, though part of him wondered if some of the blame was his own for mishandling Edward. He said, 'Edward's gone to the Marchlands to gather forces. He's angry with your father. They argued. That's so, isn't it?'

Edmund became animated. His head jerked this way and that as he brayed, 'In . . . in-vasion!'

'Invasion?' The castle of straw that Will had built in his mind came tumbling down. 'Is that what you're saying?'

'Queen Mag . . . no more . . . in Albanay!'

Will blinked at the harsh sound, then at the news.

'Thank you, Edmund.'

He understood. But how had Queen Mag come to afford an invasion? The penniless widow must have bargained with the Regent of Albanay to raise an army.

Will recalled Mag's extraordinary talents. He now saw how wide of the mark Lord Warrewyk's assumptions had been. To Warrewyk, Mag was no more than the exiled wife of a captured king, a defeated power, a pauper hoping to work her wiles in a faraway court. But Will knew how formidable she would be in her plight, and with Maskull at her side she would be quite impossible to refuse.

Will nodded, suddenly aware of what effect the inflammatory news from Trinovant must already have had all

across the north. The likelihood was that Mag had promised to give away the long-disputed border territory of
Tweedale – 'Berrick and its castle to you, my lord Regent,
as soon as I am queen again.' Yes! And if she had gulled
the Weirds of Albanay too, then . . .

Will felt the ghastly stirrings of the lorc and his stomach
turned over. 'Where's your father headed? Tell me,
Edmund!'

But Edmund's knee trembled against his horse's flank,
and his impatient party began to move off past the North
Turret and into the road.

'Why wouldn't Edmund tell you?' Willow asked as she flung
clothes into a basket.

'Because he'd given his word to his father.'

'It doesn't matter. We're going to find out soon enough.
Half the traders of Trinovant will be alongside the duke's
baggage train by the end of the first day's march.'

'I agree. We can afford a day's delay, but no more. We
can hardly lose them. And if we follow on horseback,
we can hardly fail to catch them.' He rubbed the back of
his hand across his face. 'But to what end? The duke won't
brook any more interference from Master Gwydion, so
what can we do?'

'Doesn't he see that an Ogdoad wizard is the only one
who can save him now?'

'No, he doesn't see that.' Will took his wife's hand. 'And
is it true any more? The world is changing fast and the duke
believes in magic even less than he used to. Where's Lotan?'

'Out in his new finery.'

'Doing what?'

'He says he feels naked without a sword.'

'By the moon and stars! No sooner does he get his flesh
back than he wants to start chopping other people up! Is
there any hope for mankind?'

'Don't blame Lotan. It's our world that's turning grey.'

Will dug his fingers in his hair and swept it back from his face. 'If the world is turning bad, then maybe not believing in magic is the only thing that will save the duke. Maybe he's doing the right thing in adjusting piecemeal to this terrible new world that's coming.'

Hope and strength faded from her face. 'So . . . where does that leave the likes of us?'

'For the moment we're going to have to tail an army.' He began to make for the gates.

The journey was no more than half a league, though the weather was against them. They arrived at the place where the Ebor army had lived for months and found there only the filthy remains of a camp. Skinny dogs and beggars raked over the ground, scavenging whatever they could, but what soldiers left behind, even when in a hurry to leave, was scant reward for those who braved the raw wind and driving rain.

The nearest alehouses were called the Lord Ordlea's Arms and the Hogshead in the Pound, mirthfully renamed, no doubt, to ridicule the enemy in a way that soldiers would appreciate. In the first they found the innkeeper lamenting his loss of trade. In the second they picked up a confirming rumour that the queen's host had already marched south across the border into Umberland with an Albanay army raised in expectation of plunder.

Among its many companies – or so it was said by those whose art it was to spin a tale in exchange for a drink – there lumbered wild-men and ogres from the haunted oak woods of Birnam. Once in Umberland, Queen Mag was said to have been joined by the Lords of the Pierce clan who commanded great numbers of men. And giants had come down from the misty crags of the Mountains of Umber to add their weight to the rampaging mob.

'Giants?' Willow asked, as they came away. 'I don't like the sound of that.'

'That's just Cheap-side chatter,' Will said, looking up and down the dismal winter road as if for a better clue as to where the duke might have gone.

'Surely we'll find them on the Great North Road.' Willow picked her way across a sea of mud. 'They'll be heading for Verlamion, or I'm a fool.'

For a second time Will surveyed the filth and destruction that had been left behind in May Fair Fields. He felt for the power that surged in the land, but the nearest lign passed too far away for his toes to pick up any sensation.

'North . . . maybe you're right, after all,' he said doubtfully.

'Do you think otherwise?'

'Hmm. Don't forget that the armies are being attracted to the next battlestone like flakes of iron to a lodestone. But is that battle necessarily going to be against Queen Mag?'

'What do you mean?'

'Something has been working powerful trouble between Edward and his father during their time at the White Hall. I must find Master Gwydion. You go back to the palace and gather up Lotan. I'll meet you both there at noon. I have a promise to keep.'

But it was not until mid-afternoon that Gort came in, and he brought Gwydion with him. The Wortmaster said he had arranged an urgent gathering, and Will might be surprised at who came to it. In return, Will whispered to Gort that he should brace himself for a bucketful of trouble.

'A rift between father and son, you say?' the wizard remarked, having listened with only slight interest to Will's suspicions.

'There must be some harmful token,' Will said. 'A carrier

of Maskull's mischief still hidden inside the palace walls, something you've missed.'

'That is most unlikely. But what do you say of this *undeniable* curiosity?' Gwydion held up a strange fruit in triumph.

Will was surprised. 'What's that?'

'Something the like of which has never been seen here before. This morning I spoke with a Bristowe sea captain who claims to have set foot upon the isle of Hy Brasil. He brought this and other things back as proof.'

Will turned it over, unhappy at Gwydion's way of leaving aside that which seemed most important and looking instead at trifles. 'Fascinating. But this has no bearing on what I'm trying to tell you.'

'Oh, but you're quite wrong about that,' Gort said excitedly. 'The mariner speaks of many flowers and trees of unknown form.' He took the fruit like a sacred offering. 'Is this not *marvellous*?'

'Wortmaster . . .' Will put a hand briefly to his head then shook it in a gesture of perplexity and frustration.

Gwydion laid an arm across Will's shoulders. 'A whole New World is out there in the Western Deeps, Willand. Whoever thought that our own world would end thus? Certainly not I.'

'Master Gwydion, please listen to me!'

But the wizard still paid him no heed. Today he seemed paler and greyer and somehow less substantial than Will had ever known him, but it was the lack of focus to his thoughts that worried Will most. The wizard drew something from a fold of his robe and laid it on Gort's untidy table. 'You know what this is, Willand.'

It was the white rod that belonged to the duke, the one he carried as if it were a rod of office.

'How did you get that?' Will said, amazed. 'I can't believe the duke left without his unicorn wand.'

'Unicorn? Oh, not so,' Gort muttered, still engrossed in the foreign fruit. 'That's corpse-whale ivory.'

Will looked at the wand again. 'Not unicorn? But I've always thought—'

'Few people now remember unicorns,' Gwydion said. 'Ask whoever you like, most will claim such beasts as that never were. And why? Because there is no longer any proof. Their every trace has vanished.'

'But . . . that *was* a unicorn's horn once.'

'Was it? It looks to me as if it was always a corpse-whale's tooth.'

Will sat down heavily. 'And what, may I ask, is a corpse-whale?'

'A denizen of the deep.' Gwydion sat back and steepled his fingers. 'Called by those in the Far North "narwhal". The he-narwhal has but two teeth in his head. The leftmost grows out twisting widdershins about itself until it is longer than a man is tall.'

Will scoffed. 'Such a fish as that? It's surely ridiculous nonsense!'

'I speak the truth! And it is not a fish, but a creature that breathes the air like you or I. Often a broken end like that one is found on some icy northern beach and brought south, where it is inevitably taken for a unicorn's horn by the credulous.'

'I don't believe that for a moment!'

'You had better.' Gwydion stared at him strangely. 'For it is the only kind of unicorn horn this world shall know soon. And the only kind of truth. That pretty yale you saw – did you ever think that perhaps you had been honoured with the last ever look at such a noble beast?'

'The last ever? You mean—'

Gort cut in. 'Did you not know that a yale was washed up at low tide below Southfolk Steps yesterday?'

'Dead?'

'As a doornail.' Gwydion sighed. 'I would wager a king's ransom that it was the last of its kind.'

'Oh, no . . .'

'This is how far the world has come in just a few short months. Our world is saying goodbye to us. Can't you hear it?'

Will swallowed hard. 'This is like some horrible dream.'

Gwydion snapped his fingers. 'Then you must *wake up!*'

Just then there came a knock at the door that made Will jump like a guilty man. He opened it, and Willow ushered Lotan into the room.

'You see – now our friend has truly escaped the Fellowship,' she said triumphantly.

But the wizard hardly regarded Lotan. He shrugged his shoulders. 'Willow, you have done what you were always going to do. I knew you would do it, for wilfulness is in your nature.'

She braced herself, ready for the confrontation that was to come, but the wizard merely turned away.

'Aren't you angry?' Will asked.

Gwydion sighed deeply, and his voice, when it came, was unruffled. 'The time is past when a show of anger on my part could achieve anything. Willow will have to accept the consequences of her actions when the time comes. And there will be consequences, you can be sure of that.'

The wizard's soft words struck more alarm in them than any loud remonstration could have done. But then there came the sound of footsteps in the passage outside. Heads turned, Lotan's hand tightened on his sword scabbard, and the door flew open.

'Morann!' Will cried, relieved.

'Aye, large as life.'

'And twice as nasty.'

Morann grinned. His hat was gone and a recently healed scar lined his cheek. Wrapped in his travelling cloak of earth colours he looked like a living part of the moorland that he loved. Ever since Will had first known him there had seemed to be an air of adventure about him, but never more so than now.

'Well, don't just stand there with the door open!' Gort cried. 'Bring him in, hey?'

The greetings were elaborate. Everyone clasped one another dearly and much was spoken in the true tongue that passed Will's meagre understanding. For a while it was possible to believe that the heyday of loremasters and wizards had not passed away, but at last Morann's smile faded and he grew serious.

'I come with news concerning events in the north.'

'We already know about it,' Will said. 'Duke Richard's army left this morning.'

'Indeed. But do you know why? The queen is marching upon the brave city of Ebor.'

'Ebor?' Gwydion and Gort exclaimed together.

'She has lately named it as the new capital city of the Realm. She said it will become so once she has captured it, and remain so until Trinovant is retaken.'

'Has it fallen?' Gwydion asked.

'By now Ebor's walls may have been breached, I can't say. And ten thousand pities upon that place if they have, for the queen's host is a fearsome thing indeed, and her anger boundless!'

'That was quick,' Willow said. 'She can only just have heard about her son being dispossessed.'

'The queen's armies were on the move long before that. This is the revenge she has been planning since the day of Delamprey Field.'

Gwydion's hands clenched as if he had reached a grand conclusion. '"Ebor shall overlook Ebor before the year is out" – I think we too must go into the north.'

'For what reason?' Will asked sharply. 'We can't do

anything about the next stone even if we find it, and we surely daren't try to prevent the next battle for fear of dropping the world even faster into Maskull's hands.'

'True,' Morann said. 'We daren't.'

Gwydion dismissed their objections with a wave of his hand. 'This concerns neither stone nor battle, but Maskull himself. I have examined his chamber in detail and it seems to me that I may have found a way forward. Though it could be a dangerous one.'

'The entire Realm is in danger . . .' Morann murmured. 'Maskull has filled the hearts of the noble warriors of Albanay with greed. They're marching through the Northern Shires laying waste to everything in their path. Every hearth and home south of Dunhelm is being torn apart even as we speak. And there's worse – hill trolls are in their midst. Wart-faced ogres and wild-men have come down from the mountains and high moors. They're flocking to the queen's banner.'

'Then the rumours we heard were near the mark . . .' Willow said. She looked to Will, who frowned back equally concerned.

'Hill trolls . . .' Lotan murmured. He had been sitting quietly with his sword laying across his knees, staring into the fire. 'They are not so difficult to kill.'

'I have something for you, Morann,' Will said suddenly. He drew the loremaster into the adjoining room and lowered his voice. 'Master Gwydion's power is hardly recovered yet, and we don't know if it ever will. He's changed since the time he spent in Maskull's fetters. He's in no fit state to take on his old enemy and . . .'

'And?'

'Whatever weapons might have been fashioned out of the harm Maskull tapped from the Delamprey battlestone, Master Gwydion mustn't be tempted to use them.'

'You speak mainly of Master Gwydion, but this is no longer his fight. A crucial moment is at hand, Willand. It's a moment that will decide the future. You must seize it manfully.'

He swallowed. 'I . . . I mean to. Though I wonder if one such as I can ever become a king in a world where there is no magic.'

Morann's eyes gleamed guilelessly. 'There is still magic enough for that. Fae magic is the oldest and will be the last to leave the world. King Arthur will come again. Put aside your fears, Willand. You must not lose faith in yourself.'

Will felt the strength flowing into him from Morann's simple words. He went to the table, lifted up a pouch and began to unwrap the leather thongs. Then he drew out a knife that glinted green. 'Yours, I believe.'

Morann's delight was plain to see. He met Will's eye as he took the blade. It was the knife that had been sharpened on the Whetstone of Tudwal, the blade that Chlu had stolen, the one that had later saved Will's life.

'Aye, that's mine right enough. And I didn't think I'd clap eyes on it again. How did you come by it?'

'I'll tell you that once you've told me how it was taken from you.'

'I think you already have a good idea about that.'

'I think maybe I do.'

Morann scratched at his stubbled chin. 'When I came to Castle Corben all those months ago I told you I'd been asked to go into the Blessed Isle.'

Will nodded. 'And I asked you to put the word about that you'd been sent to kill Duke Richard.'

'And I did as you asked. But that course must have been against Maskull's plans, for when I left you I headed north towards Caster to find a ship, and on the way I was waylaid. Now, no one easily waylays me, but . . .'

'Chlu found a way.'

'He did.' Morann smiled ruefully at the memory, turning the blade over. 'He's a strong one, and he had the advantage on me, you see. And that's because at first I thought he was your good self.'

Will grunted. 'That was a sorry mistake to make.'

'Well, it was dark. And in a certain light he does have the outline of you and the same timbre of voice. There was a slight altercation, you might say. He took my knife from me and then killed me with it. Or so he thought.'

Will laughed. 'You too, eh? That old blade is as worthless as they come. Did it ever cut anything?'

'Oh, now. I won't have that. The magic upon it causes it to cut only when it should. I'm grateful that it chose not to cut me, for that twin of yours plunged it hard into me above a dozen times before he ran off into the night.'

'Then I'm not surprised he thought he'd done for you.'

'Well, I guess that's what he's told his master.'

When they returned to the others, Morann showed everyone the magic blade. 'Do you see how things still come full circle, Master Gwydion? If this is not proof of how magic clings on even now, then I'm the Queen of Elmet – which I'm not. So this old world is not wholly done for just yet!'

'The question,' Gwydion said ominously, 'is how are we to prevent the collision of worlds?'

Morann sat down and put his elbows on the table and waited for Will to speak up, but he did not.

'Well, if no one else wishes to offer a solution,' the wizard said. 'It seems to me that I have no choice but to try to vanquish Maskull once and for all.'

'He's wrought magical weapons with which to destroy you, Master Gwydion,' Willow said. 'I think you ought to be trying to kill him.'

'Aye, it would be a fight to the death,' Morann said. 'Unless anyone can think of a way he may be constrained.'

No sooner were the loremaster's words out than Gwydion reached inside his robes and threw onto the table a piece of metal. It was heavy and maliciously wrought, the large fetter that Will had seen in Maskull's chamber. 'This is, I believe, an original – a first attempt which he then refined into the bracelets used to capture me.'

Will shifted uneasily. 'You said you would never try to use Maskull's weapons against him, no matter how desperate the strait.'

Willow said, 'He won't have to. Master Gwydion need have nothing to do with them, for I'll gladly play the queen's part and put them on Maskull myself – so long as the rest of you promise me that you'll kill him when you catch him!'

Will sat back slowly, seeing just how desperate their strait had become. 'No, Willow. The cost of failure—'

'—is too high,' Gwydion finished. 'Your fiery courage does you much credit, Willow, but yours is not the way.'

Will looked from face to face, relieved. But then his concern hardened. 'Then what? How do we attack Maskull?'

'My friends, you have learned much, but you know little of wizardly matters. No member of the Ogdoad has ever tried to kill another. The very idea is repellent, and no occasion of necessity has ever arisen. There are sound reasons why even Maskull should not have tried, and sounder ones why we of the Ogdoad must not attempt to punish our betrayer with death, no matter what his crime. You see, there is a principle that magic and paradoxes make poor bedfellows.'

'What does that mean?' Will asked. His feelings closed against the argument. But Gwydion's gesture called for a moment of indulgence. 'For a lawmaker to kill a man because he has committed a murder – that is a paradox, do you see? So if a punishment of death were to be visited on that murderer using magic, then a number of unfortunate consequences would result, consequences that would in the end outweigh the justice of the case.'

'But Maskull has no scruples about using magic to kill,' Willow said. 'If anyone deserves—'

Will sliced the air with his hand. 'And *that's* why he's a sorcerer – he has no scruples about using magic to kill. Now, are you saying that we should all descend to sorcery?'

The Wortmaster, who had said nothing until now, broke his silence. 'Of course we must not sink to his level. We do not believe, and have never believed, that an eye is worth any other eye, or that a tooth is worth any other tooth. We believe that eyes and teeth are better sitting in people's heads, hey? Isn't that better sense?'

Lotan growled at that, but otherwise held his peace.

Willow said, 'Then what *are* we to do with Maskull? If Master Gwydion will not try to kill him, and killing him is beyond the powers of anyone but an Ogdoad wizard, what shall we do? It's all very well having high principles, but unless you can stop him doing what he wants by throwing a barrel of kindness over him, then you'd better find another way.'

Morann calmed her. 'We'll just have to try again to send Maskull away somewhere. Somewhere even further away than last time. If there is any such place.'

'Are you joking?' Gort said. 'He escaped from the Realm Below. If that endless maze of darkness could not hold him, I should like to know what manner of place can!'

Gwydion was tired and his hands, lifting momentarily from the carved arms of his chair, revealed a deep frustration. 'Alas! No remedy is simple. Maskull's jealousies have driven him to seek ever more arcane knowledge to use against me. He has wandered far in the world. Long ago he overreached me in the destructive arts. In his search he learned much and took to himself many cunning skills, though most would have been better left undisturbed. He took something of great value from a cave in the east, and many years passed before I found out what it was.'

'Another weapon?' Willow asked.

'In fact it was just the opposite – a protection of sorts. It is said that whomsoever washes in the Spring of

Celamon shall henceforward only ever suffer one day of imprisonment.'

'And did Maskull wash there?' Will asked.

'He has twice boasted to me of it. And I believe him.'

'Well, it couldn't have been a very thorough wash,' Willow said. 'What about the four years of peace that followed the battle at Verlamion? We only enjoyed peace because Maskull was locked up for all that time.'

Will nodded. 'That's right. It was four years that Maskull was exiled in the Realm Below. How does that square with his washing in the Spring of Celamon?'

Gwydion got up and slowly began to pace the room. 'You must be more careful with your use of words – exile is by no means the same as imprisonment. Nor is wandering in a maze the same as being locked up. Maskull was not confined – he was merely elsewhere and lost.'

'Surely this is splitting hairs,' Will objected. 'Mere words.'

'Oh, not so. Not so.' The wizard let his own words sink in, then he said, 'Laws are made of words. Magic is brought into being by them, for they are ideas that have been given expressible form. Words, and the meaning and power of them, are what we all live by.'

Morann touched his shoulder indulgently. 'What Master Gwydion is trying to say is that Maskull could not find a way out, but there *was* a way out.'

The wizard spread his hands. 'That is why I did not try to trap Maskull into any kind of locked prison. I vanished him deeply – to a place so vast and labyrinthine that it should have taken him the rest of the Age to find his way out.'

'That's no use to us now, Master Gwydion,' Willow said.

'Maskull caught one of those poor, shadowy creatures who dwell in the Realm Below,' Will said, remembering the ked. 'He forced it to show him the way out, so his return is no mystery. But where can we put him that's more secure than the Land of Annuin? Perhaps we can sail him to the

Rim of the World and cast him down into the space between sea and sky. Once he tumbles into the Desolate Sea that lies below—'

Gwydion raised his hands like one who has grown tired of fruitless debate. 'And how would you tempt him aboard your ship and keep him there? My friends, we must do the seemingly impossible. We must find Maskull a place of exile where there is no guide to conduct him out again, a place from which there is truly no escape.'

Then out of the silence an unlooked-for comment came. 'I know of such a place . . .'

Gwydion had reached the window. Now he turned and looked at Lotan. 'Did you speak?'

'Yes. I said I know a place from which there would be no escape for Maskull.'

Gwydion showed his impatience. 'Do not concern yourself with things about which you cannot possibly know any—'

'I not only know of such a place,' Lotan said, shoving aside all objections, 'I have been there.'

'You?'

'Yes, me.' The big man's voice became wistful. 'In my youth I sailed with sea rovers across many an ice-cold ocean. I visited the Baerberg, which is the northernmost isle of the whole world.'

'I suppose you will claim to have stepped ashore there,' Gwydion said as if he were interviewing a liar.

'No mariner will willingly land there. But I have seen it as close as any man – from the distance of a bowshot. It is a tall mountain that rises from the sea, and on its frost beaches there are mermen and mermaids who bathe by night in the silvery moonbeams. Their skins are blue and green and their teeth are sharp and they are a handsome and strange folk. They come in great numbers to swarm around any ship that dares to approach their beaches, but there can be no trade with them, for they go bare and lack for nothing, and no one knows their tongue, for they speak a language known only to gulls and skarvens.

'The mountain called Baerberg has a great stone stair that rises up into the sky. I have seen it, though its top is most often wreathed in cloud. A secret is kept by the Sightless Ones that speaks of it. At the top, so they say, there stands a door, and the keyhole in that door awaits a golden key. I do not know what lies beyond the door unless it be only the brightness of the stars. But I will tell you this – the Fellowship believes the legend of the Baerberg, and part of it says that mountain is a place where no magic can be worked.'

All of them stared at Lotan, while he in turn gazed in fascination at the merry flames crackling from the log in the grate.

'Fire is so beautiful,' he said. 'I would have risked everything a thousand times for just one moment such as this.'

The sentiment touched Will's heart, but still he wondered about how Lotan's view of the Baerberg fitted with what he had once been told by Gwydion; that Maskull had visited the Baerberg, that it was there he had opened the door in the sky and first gained knowledge that there was another world. Few men had ever travelled in sight of that far island, and Will found it wonderful that Lotan should be one of them. From the calculating expression on Gwydion's face, however, it seemed that the wizard did not share Will's sentiments. One by one, the company began to stir from their thoughts. Lotan's interruption had served to draw a line under their talk. Willow sensed their mood and said, 'We'd all better get some sleep, for tomorrow looks like being a very long day.'

'Sound advice,' Gwydion said, moving towards the door. 'And since it is poor policy to send you to your dreams with no greater hope in your hearts than this evening has so far provided, let me say to you in parting: I may have the beginnings of a plan in my mind. I shall summon Maskull to a meeting. And if all goes well, it will be a meeting he will wish he had never attended!'

All except Will greeted the wizard's words with nods and gestures of approval and they too began to head for the door. As they stood before it, amazingly, Lotan began to sing.

> 'Patta inca tutna,
> Farel sut sehutma.
> 'Isi arki par charwan,
> Gurna, ganta, gusarnan.
> 'Lamba uscra ra raahan,
> Jarga hura maddana chan.'

'What's that?' Willow asked, surprised at the sudden melody.

'A ragha, or song. It comes from the Tortured Lands, and is a very old form, woven from thoughts of hope and despair.'

Will looked to him perplexed, not knowing why he had burst so unexpectedly into song. 'Well . . . what does it mean?'

'The first part of a ragha is always hopeful. It says that even a broken stone can be made whole. The second part is always despairing. It says that life passes as quickly as sand falls in a – what do you call it?' He made a shape with his hands like the contours of a woman.

'An hour glass,' Willow said, grinning.

'Yes, an hour glass.'

'And the third verse?' Gwydion asked. His presence was becoming more real, swelling suddenly like a fanfare as his interest burgeoned.

'The third and last verse is always the most hopeful. It says something like . . . hmmm . . . that, nevertheless, it is a long road to the cemetery.' Lotan grinned at the wizard. 'I think the song has much truth in it, but I didn't expect to find it written here.'

Will's eyes went wide with the sudden realization of what had prompted Lotan to sing – it was the parchment pinned to the back of the door. Lotan had not only read it, he had sung it out!

The wizard pulled everyone away from the exit and made them sit down again. Then he tore down the parchment on which he had written the inscription from the Delamprey stone and spread it wide on the table.

'Show me the script,' he commanded. 'I want you to tell me everything you can about it.'

PART THREE

ON THE SEVENTH DAY

▫ ▫ ▫

□ □ □

CHAPTER FIFTEEN

THE FAST-FLOWING STREAM

The next morning they waited for their horses in Albanay Yard during the last dark before dawn. The air was very cold and dry, and though rain puddles had collected over the last few days they had now largely drained away. The king's ostler brought out their mounts and baggage horses. Will heard Gwydion and Morann whispering in low tones, and something about the manner in which they huddled made him suspicious. But it was the way they switched to the true tongue as soon as he appeared that irked him.

'I don't care what you're planning,' he told them both as he passed, 'but if I'm going north then Lotan goes too.'

Gwydion looked back stonily. 'Is it your wish to humble me?' he asked quietly. 'Have I not already agreed that, between your wife and I, Willow has by far the greater wisdom? I have merely warned that we should not forget Lotan's oaths to the Fellowship.'

Will stuck his foot in the stirrup and swung himself up into the saddle. 'Oaths like that count for nothing. He was suffering and in misery.'

'That's when the oath works hardest,' Morann said.

'He's helped us once. He deserves to be trusted again.

And Master Gwydion has said himself that without Lotan we wouldn't know where to go.'

Gwydion forced a smile and offered a compromising gesture that Will decided concealed much.

He sees difficulties everywhere, Will thought. But he should remember the rede that says, 'Perfection is the enemy of progress.'

He recalled how bitterly it had pained Willow and himself to kiss their daughter goodbye for the second time. Bethe would stay in the duchess's tender care once more, and though Gwydion had not liked the instant obligation that the favour had put Will under, he had had little choice.

Breath plumed from the horses' nostrils as they passed out through the gatehouse. Will pulled on his gloves, glad to be quit of the suffocations of the palace. Willow rode to his left, darkly cloaked, her face pale and drawn, but she had been adamant that she would not be left behind. He respected her for that decision – more than she knew, for he was quietly aware of the honour it did him, and his spirit blazed up at the depth of love her choice had shown.

After the gates slammed shut the horses walked quietly along by the tilt-yards. This road, which usually reeked of horse dung, now smelled only of clean night air. Damp that had fallen overnight as dew now rimed everything with frost, and the uneven dirt of the road that had been shaped by the previous day's traffic was now unforgiving under the horses' hooves. As the road widened Will noted that they were being followed by a point of light that stood over the City. It was violet and intensely bright, and Will knew it as Rhiannon's Spark, the sky wanderer that often heralded the dawn.

As the roofline fell, he looked to the east and saw the reluctant day gathering. A haze of smoke hung over the sleeping city and he felt a hollowness in his belly, something like hunger or disappointment – a feeling that confirmed

Chlu had left the City. He had gone into the north to prepare himself for the final conflict. Will understood that the bond linking them was strengthening, for he, in his own way, was doing exactly what Chlu had already done.

But the mood now was far from being one of trenchant resolve. They were sneaking, rather than spurring, out of the City. They went on in silence a little way until Lotan showed them a half-hidden lane opening to their left. He suggested they take it, saying it would lead them wide of the Charing and the lone sentinel who always stood at the foot of the spire-like monument.

'And why should we do that?' Gwydion said, turning to Lotan.

'The watcher is there to control the crossroads,' Lotan explained. 'If he steps out into the Charing and blows his horn then the road will be set swarming with Vigilants. We should not go that way.'

'Do you fear they will come for you?' Gwydion asked.

'No. I fear they will know Will for who he is.'

'He's right,' Morann said. 'Best not show our hand unless we're forced to, eh, Master Gwydion? Or they'll have us marked for sure.'

'As you wish.'

It was a reluctant agreement on the wizard's part, but then Will saw the confirming glance that Morann sent Gwydion's way, and he knew that Lotan had been up for some secret test – and had passed it.

They led their horses alongside a tall brick wall, then a little while later they came to a pair of ornate iron gates. Gwydion opened them easily, though they were locked and chained. Then they crossed a plank bridge over a shallow ditch and began to make their way through what Will knew was the royal deer park.

Here leafless oaks grew black from the mist-white ground. It was said that the ghostly figure of Herne the Hunter sometimes appeared among the herd, though his true home was at Wyndsor, many leagues to the west. Will pulled his cloak tighter around him and turned his mind instead to the way Gwydion had become fired up last night. He had leaned over the verse and questioned Lotan rigorously over his knowledge of the Delamprey inscription, then he had run what he heard through the medium of the true tongue.

'And this word means?'

'Break.'

'So this one is "stone"?'

'Yes. That is the root-word.'

'And in this line the roots are "make" and "heal"?'

'Yes. And here – "sand", "fall", "hour", "glass". And here – "long", "road", "awake" and "field".'

'But you said this word undoes what comes after it, so "not awake".'

'No. This and this together means "not sleeping". But here it means a place of burial.'

'A graveyard? Why?'

'Why?' Lotan had made noises like an affronted expert, then he had given a dismissive gesture towards the parchment like a gamer casting down dice or knucklebones. 'Because it is.'

But there had been many more questions about the finer points of grammar and even the poetic form that Lotan had called a ragha, before finally Gwydion had stood up, satisfied, and said,

> 'The stone that was broken,
> Is now healed.
> The shadow falls fast,
> Like sand in a glass.
> And the way is long,
> To the sleepless field.'

The meaning had hardly been very clear, Will thought. But it reminded him of something, and after a while he realized that it rang eerily like the verse he had read on the Harle Stone.

> *'Soon no more the plague pits,*
> *Shall hold the dead of Corde.*
> *A field of statues shall awake,*
> *And death shall walk abroad.'*

That message too had been about illness and graves and awakening. But as Will opened his mind to it a little more he began to recall yet another verse.

> *'King and Queen with Dragon Stone.*
> *Bewitched by the Moon, in Darkness alone.*
> *In Northern Field shall Wake no more.*
> *Son and Father, Killed by War.'*

That one had appeared on the Dragon Stone. The last time Will had read it was moments before the malign power trapped inside had lashed out and overwhelmed Edmund.

The puzzle stayed with Will as they rode up through Isling Forest, where well-to-do young men came to hunt on rest days like these. He saw children wrestling, leaping and playing at ball upon Fensburgh Hill, and much sliding on the frozen ponds of Finchlea. Will wanted to veer off and take a quicker way across the fields, but at the wizard's urging, they stuck to the main road. By the time they reached Whetstone, three leagues north of the City walls the sun was fully up and the road thawing, and Will had begun to taste the particular flavour of the hazel lign. Then at Baronet Hadlea, where they halted to water the horses, he recognized the bitter foulness of the elder lign emerging from a rise. It lay beneath the taste of the hazel and corrupted it, a taint he knew from Delamprey and from Verlamion before that. Will sickened suddenly, and the moment he slid down from his horse he knew this for a place where a battlestone of great power lay.

'What is it?' Willow asked, coming to him while the others looked on anxiously from a distance. 'You're as pale as a cheese.'

'Tell Master Gwydion,' he said, his throat so constricted that his voice seemed strangled. He waved a hand vaguely to the north. 'It's here . . .'

And then he fell down and his head banged hard, and he lay groaning.

'Quickly! Get him off the ground!' Gwydion ordered.

Judging by the look of concern on Willow's face I must be a sight to see, the calm, disembodied part of Will thought. He knew his face must be twisted up like one suffering the racks of a dread disease, but there was a disconnection between his mind and his leaden body, so that it would not do as he told it.

'Come on, Green-gills,' Morann told him gently. 'Let's get you back on your horse.'

Spirit and body joined again with a clap. He retched then vomited as Morann and Lotan lifted him. And they all stood poised, waiting to see if he would slide off his horse again.

'I don't like it here,' he said, spitting untidily as he came to. 'Elder, hazel and yew – all of them flowing into one another. The place stinks of . . . death!'

'I won't tell you what you stink of,' Morann said, his humour stoutly intact, but he was worried. He had never seen Will's talent react so strongly.

Willow handed Will a cloth and he wiped the mud from his face.

'A premonition?' Gort whispered to the wizard, but it was loud enough for Will to catch.

'No!' he cried out to the pair of them. 'Let that not be so!' And the cloth fluttered from his hand, was caught by the wind and flew up into a stark, leafless bush.

As they rode on, the stomach cramps and dizziness began to leave him, but he could not yet marshal his thoughts as he wished. His spine seemed to have turned to gristle and he had difficulty keeping his saddle. They stopped and tied his ankles together, passing a rope along his horse's girth strap. Gort laid healing hands upon him and gave him a draught of something that overpowered his senses and made him wipe his mouth often.

'Have a care. We don't know what he's seeing,' Lotan said, lifting up one of Will's eyelids. 'I think we must try to get him out of harm's way.'

'How can we?' Gwydion demanded harshly. 'How, when we cannot see the ligns that are doing this to him?'

'Don't you know where they run?'

'What business is it of yours what I know?'

For the next hour, Will swam in and out of shallow consciousness, and the horror of the vision that played in his head ebbed and flowed. He seemed now to be enfolded in thick fog, now seeing ghost armies marching out of a misty morning, men-at-arms and knights in harness, banners held on high, swords drawn, chanting as they advanced upon the enemy. And then he saw himself locked in among the men of the first rank of an unsteady rabble, armoured only in a leather coat and an ill-fitting iron bonnet. He had a billhook in his hand, and he was being thrust forward, too fast, by the pressure of men behind him. He was their shield, and the speed with which they forced him towards the enemy was frightening. It was as if they wanted the clash to be done and over as quickly as possible, as if they knew they had no choice but to try their hand against death and wanted to find out if they had won or lost. But Will only wished they would stop. He wanted it all to stop – for everyone to stand still and drop their weapons and shout out, 'I won't do what you tell me!'

But the gap between Will and the men they called the enemy was narrowing with every step. The clash was coming closer and closer, and now he could see the horror in the faces of the enemy. Now their bills and poleaxes were lowered and they began stabbing and chopping furiously and there were screams and he saw flesh cleaved open, steaming obscenely in the cold morning air. Then as he fended off blows, there came a deafening clatter, and his helmet brow was shoved down so that its hard rim split open the bridge of his nose. The lines of men closed, smashed together, and his arms were shoved back, pinned, and the shaft of another man's poleaxe dug into his neck and prayers to Almighty God filled the air around him.

The irresistible pressure at his back had forced him chest to chest with a terrified man whose face was splashed with blood but whose right hand had found enough space in that tightly packed crush to stab him full in the belly with a dirty little knife. Then the pain came, and the under-standing that his body was being ripped open, inch by inch, butchered by a man screaming insanely in his face. There was not even the decency of death to blind him, and nothing he could do but look into the man's eyes and beg him not to tear the wound open any further for fear that his dear guts would spill out on the ground and be trampled into the mud. But the man just screamed into his face . . .

Abruptly, the horror shut off as he felt a blow against his cheek. One blue eye and one brown examined him closely. Then a deep, stolid voice ordered him to be quiet and to listen to the birdsong. It was such a strong voice that he trusted it instantly and was glad to have it tell him what to do in this new nightmare world.

'It is not real,' the voice said. 'The battle you are fighting is not real. Do you understand me?'

Will clapped a hand to the pit of his stomach and his eyes stood out in amazement. He knew there had been a miracle, for somehow the irreversible had been undone. Somehow the clock had been turned back, and he was more grateful than he could say. He never wanted to see horror like that again.

Though the road meandered along the Collen lign, Will knew they were moving away from the fork at Wrotham Common where the ground had so foully betrayed him. All afternoon he fought against the lorc, and he fought alone, for his friends were powerless to aid him.

'It was near the obelisk,' Gort said. 'That's when his pain was at its height.'

'Obelisk?' Willow asked. 'What's that?'

'The grey pillar set back from the road. Did you not see it? Square in form, yet narrowing as it rose. And pointed at the top.'

'Perhaps she means the word, Wortmaster,' Gwydion said. 'We have never heard you use that word before. Where did you learn it?'

Gort scratched at his beard. 'I . . . I've always known it.'

'Have you indeed?'

Will's glance fell upon the wizard as the latter said, 'More than one strange word has been used within my hearing just lately.'

'That doesn't surprise me,' Will joked. But his attempt at levity fell on stony ground. He said, 'You know, when I spoke with Edward he kept using a particular word as a sort of curse. I didn't know what it meant at the time, but I think I do now.'

'What was the word?' Gwydion asked.

'Damned.' Will held his gaze. 'I know it means . . . sent to Hell.'

'Quite so. But where is Hell? Do you know that yet?'

He shook his head wonderingly. 'No. But I think there's

a monster called "Almighty God" who lives there. Where are they coming from, Master Gwydion? These new words, these terrible ideas?'

'Where do you think?'

'From the other world, I suppose. Because we're already changing, fitting in with it.'

'Correct. The closer we approach, the more like it we become. If left alone it will become an inevitable process. Soon there will be no stopping it.'

When next they halted, Will sought his own company, but though he had made it plain that he wished to be left alone for the time being Lotan came and sat close by him. The big man said nothing, being himself deep in thought, but all the while his fingers were playing with a gold coin, spinning it time and again on the flat top of a stool, catching it as it fell, or watching as it spun faster and finally came to a dead stop.

'Where did you get that?' Will asked, abandoning his own thoughts.

Lotan looked up in surprise. 'This is not what you think.'

'Not . . . money?'

'It is not a coin. In the Fellowship we called them "eallub". You see these two holes? That's where the stitch goes. One of these is sewn inside every Fellow's robe on the day he loses his eyes.'

Will took it and examined it with grim fascination. On one side was inscribed a radiant heart and the legend, 'ecipsuA .nretarF.' which he knew meant, 'Under the guidance of the Fellowship.' On the other side was 'satinretarF dA tE bA', meaning, 'From and To the Fellowship.'

'I had no idea that Fellows carried gold pieces about with them.'

'One more secret. And kept for reasons you can easily understand. When a man's eyes are taken, this lessens the pain. That's why you must have it.'

Will's gaze flickered to Lotan's. 'I . . . can't do that.'

But Lotan held it out to him and Will received it reluctantly.

It was a vastly personal possession – how could Lotan give away an item of such significance? And whether Will liked the gesture or not, the token had been made by the Sightless Ones. That fact alone was enough to cause him to think again.

He tried to give it back. 'Lotan, I mustn't.'

'Please. It might help.'

Lotan made no move to take back the button, and as Will weighed it in his palm he wondered how he could avoid giving offence. When he closed his eyes he could feel no magic in the metal. And when he looked at it again, he saw that it was more than just a stamped and worn disc of pure gold – it was a gift, made compassionately, by a friend.

'Well, then I thank you for it.' He smiled and put it in his pouch. 'Best keep it hidden though – I don't think Master Gwydion would understand.'

As they rode on over Dancer's Hill and crossed the Mymms Brook, the road turned north-west. There was no doubt that a large army had come this way, and Lotan surveyed the road knowingly. 'Maybe ten thousand went through here yesterday.'

'Aye, and in two separate passings, one coming after the other.' Morann stared at the ground. 'Edward first, then three hours later his father.'

'How can you tell that?' Lotan asked, amazed.

Morann winked at him. 'I asked the brewster at the inn back there.'

When the light began to die they took themselves far from the road and made camp in a quiet hollow that sheltered them from the west wind. All the land roundabout had been scavenged clean by the troops who had passed through the day before, but they eventually found enough dry kindling to make a small, smoking fire, and soon the smell of bacon fat was in the air.

'I can see the lorc!' Will shouted out, shattering the calm. He was tortured now by the vastness of the power he could sense flowing through the veins of the land.

'Tell us what you see,' the wizard cried, holding him fast.

'It's on fire, Master Gwydion! Five ligns all passing within a league or two! Three go through the Doomstone at Verlamion, three through the monster that I felt back there. And there are two more stones each standing where two ligns cross. The lorc is in full spate! This is the final battle, Master Gwydion! It must be! We're too late!'

He tried again to force his panicking mind shut, but feared now that he was too weak to do it.

'Shhh!' Willow calmed him and gave him fresh milk to drink from a leather bottle. He gulped until it ran down his cheeks and Gort took it away from him. His mouth burned, but the Wortmaster made him wait for an infusion of sweet herbs, and all the while he suffered, feeling that he was trapped, boxed in by a demon forest of holly and hazel, of rowan, yew and elder. Branches were plucking at him, thorns digging in, roots growing through his flesh, until he was eaten alive.

But through all that nightmare vision, a diamond-clear point still shone in his mind, hard and lucid, like the Star of Annuin. That, he knew, was his own fortress of self-possession, an inviolate watcher of the world that never let go, never willingly abandoned him to danger. It warned him that a horrifying experience could tear down a man's mind *whether or not that experience was real* – for the horror certainly was. It told him that he must try one more time to close his mind to the lorc, or risk madness.

'Not too much medicine, now,' Gwydion told Gort. 'He must return to clear-mindedness.'

'He's suffering great pain, Master Gwydion.'

'Then I shall speak softly to him and divert his mind.'

The wizard came to his side and began to speak soothingly as he had done in years gone by, telling a tale that Will's mind easily latched onto.

'A great army once gathered near here, Willand, at the place that is now called Wetamsted. Four thousand chariots mustered upon Nomansland Common as soon as news of the Slaver invasion was heard. Those were the days when Caswalan was king, and it fell to him and his brother Neni to face the might that was come . . .'

Will's thoughts slipped away from the world once more and the picture of ancient days and the swirl of wizardly words was lost in a dark void, until . . .

' . . . and so you see how the power of the lorc saved the Realm in those dark days. There is no question of it, for Iuliu was very great in war, and though brave Neni fell, still Caswalan had the victory. And afterwards, Iuliu took his steel-clad warriors back to their ships, and Caswalan withdrew to his great hall at Ayot and there took a blessing upon the Lulling Stone.'

Slowly Will returned to his right mind, and presently he looked around and asked in a puzzled voice, 'Where are we?'

Gwydion told him, 'In a tent, and camped a league to the east of Verlamion. We have crossed the Colne Brook. I thought it best to take you as far away as possible from the places where we know the ligns run.'

'Where's Morann?'

'He has gone with Lotan to find something out for me.'

'Where?' he asked, alarmed.

'Verlamion.'

'Oh, not to the chapter house?' he cried. 'The shrine's guarded by Sightless Ones. This time they are ready and greatly roused up!'

'Do you think we are *all* insane?' The wizard chuckled.

He subsided. 'Where have they gone, then?'

'Ask them when they return if you must know their precise movements.'

'The stone that was broken,' Will muttered through chapped lips, 'is now *healed*.'

'What are you saying?'

'The Doomstone of Verlamion – it has repaired itself. Such power, such ancient power . . . and back there, the stone Gort called ola . . . olbal—'

'Obelisk.'

'Obelisk – that has a greater power even than the Doomstone.'

Gwydion clicked his tongue. 'Greater? How can that be?'

'Because it also stands on three ligns. That must be the reason. The stones have powers that are in proportion to the strength of the ligns that feed them.'

'But . . . a second doomstone there? That does not fit our pattern.'

'Then our pattern must be wrong!'

'Calmly, Will,' Gort said, attending most solicitously now.

Will nodded at the Wortmaster, acknowledging his own rudeness, yet he remained fervent. 'Don't you see, Master Gwydion? Our world has always been one where things go in the direction that the sum of our beliefs sends them. If we do not believe in the isle of Hy Brasil, then there *is* no Hy Brasil. But once the *idea* of Hy Brasil becomes a reality, and once people begin to believe in the place, then the discovery of the actual Hy Brasil cannot be far off. This is what allows magic to work, what permits us to influence the world by means other than the purely physical. I've come to see how it's all to do with willpower and belief.'

'These things are well known . . .' The wizard nodded, but he said nothing more. And even if he had, Will would not have been deterred from going on because now he could hardly stop himself.

'Yes, that's it! That's why there's no magic in the coming world – because in the coming world if the facts don't fit the ideas, then it's the *ideas* that have to change, because the facts can't. It's a hard world that's coming. A hard world where the facts are fixed . . .'

'There now,' Willow cooed. She tried to soothe his raving, dabbing his brow with a wetted scarf. 'Don't worry, you'll be all better by tomorrow.'

'I'm better now! I've never been saner. Listen to me! I have the answer!'

But no one listened to another word from him, because a twig snapping in the darkness made them all look into the void beyond the reach of the fire. The hairs on the back of Will's neck stood up as Gwydion's hand groped for his staff. Then a shape appeared. A hooded figure in grey and black, immensely sinister, shot bolts of fear into them. It loomed for a moment that swelled unbearably just as a moment of torture swells to seem like an hour. But then the set of Gwydion's arms relaxed and he sat down.

'Welcome back,' he said.

Willow put a hand to the nape of her neck and let out a shuddering breath. Her relief was palpable. She said, 'That wasn't funny.'

Will sank within himself again, struggling to recall the great insight that had just come to him. Instead he could bring to mind only something that Willow had said to him long ago before the battle at Delamprey. He had remarked that some battlestones were near one another while others stood far off, and she had said that there had to be a pattern in the way they were laid out. And later that night he had dreamed there was a way of picturing the whole Realm, as if he was looking down on it from above . . .

'The duke's split his army,' Morann said, throwing back his hood and coming forward.

'Where's Lotan?' Willow asked.

'I'm here.' He emerged silently from the space between the tents.

'We skirted the whole town around,' Morann said. 'Five thousand men are headed into the north under the duke. And five thousand more have gone up the Wartling.'

Will knew that the Wartling was the old Slaver road that ran north-west from Verlamion. Just as he had thought, Edward was repairing to his castle of Ludford, the fortress which had become his the day he had taken the title Earl of the Marches.

'That's Edward's army,' Will said.

Morann blew out his cheeks. 'He should have known better than that!'

'He's angry!'

'Edward?' Willow asked. 'Who with?'

'With his father. He thinks he's about to be dispossessed, passed over in favour of his brother.'

Morann screwed up his face. *'What?'*

'It's become an obsession with him. "Ebor shall over-look Ebor before the year is out" – remember?'

'But now Richard has stopped pursuing his son – if that was what he was doing,' Gwydion said.

Morann shrugged. 'We don't know what either of them intends. Richard may have sent messengers to persuade Edward to halt. Don't you think so?'

Gort said, 'Maybe there's no rift at all, hey? The duke might have sent Edward on ahead and across to the Cambray Marches to raise men. He'll not lack for recruits in the west, especially at Ludford – not after what the royal forces did there a little while ago, with all that burning and looting and murdering and the like.'

'What is certain,' Gwydion said, 'is that Richard and Sarum are making haste into the north together with just five thousand men. That is not nearly enough to meet the host that is coming south under the queen's banner, which if you are right, Morann, numbers thirty thousand and more.'

Morann nodded. 'All the magnates of the north are roused up. And the word is that Warrewyk and Lord Northfolk have been left to secure Trinovant and keep the king, so their strength may not be counted upon by the House of Ebor.'

'What I'd like to know,' Gort burst out, 'is has the duke taken complete leave of his senses?'

Will grunted. 'He took leave of them months ago, or didn't you notice, Wortmaster?'

Gort had unpacked his writing gear, and Will took a couple of quills, a knife, the little bottle of ink and the roll of parchments that had been scratched clean. He called his companions closer. 'Let me show you something. Suppose these lines are the coast of Albion,' he said, outlining the Isles. Once the ink had dried he marked Trinovant and Ebor and all the cities and towns of the Realm he could recall. It was a crude plan, but clear enough.

'What now if I try to mark the ligns? Nine ligns – all straight as arrows. The battlestones all stand upon one lign or another, many on more than one, for where the ligns cross, there always lies a stone. There is our pattern.'

They all stared at the ink lines, seeing nothing significant. Then the wizard said, 'The ligns are laid out haphazardly. There is no pattern.'

But Will was sure there was something in the way the ligns connected that reminded him of something.

They slept soon afterwards, Will fitfully, plagued by vile dreams that harried his mind. Lotan's gold token had not helped ward off the pain in any way, but the kindness of his having offered it nevertheless warmed Will's heart.

Early the next morning they saw Morann quit the camp and ride on ahead. The loremaster did not pause to say where he was going, and neither Gort nor Gwydion would admit they knew. As the rest of them packed up and prepared to leave, Will bit his tongue, though he could not help but press the point once they had passed Wetamsted.

'Morann has business of his own,' was all the wizard would say. 'He did not tell me where he was going.'

'Do you know where I think *we* should go?' Will said.

Gwydion looked askance at him. 'Up the Great North Road, I presume.'

'Or wherever else the duke leads us – or is himself led.'

'Why do you say that?'

'Because the Great North Road runs alongside two ligns at least. Celin and Collen – holly and hazel. They sit side by side just as rowan and yew do, but whereas those ligns run a little north of west from here, holly and hazel run a little west of north. I think Edward was being drawn into the west along the Wartling to Ludford. Whatever his reasons – or whatever he thinks are his reasons – this is surely the lorc's doing. For a certainty, Edward's father rides into the north and to his death.'

The wizard thought about that, then offered a contrary smile. 'So it is along two ligns we must go, eh? Well, that should make for an enjoyable ride. I have no love for Slaver roads, and the Great North Road follows several of them.'

Will knew that the Slavers had built their roads as straight as the land allowed. They had been set in place to cut the Realm into shards and so destroy the power of the lorc, but there had been another, more practical reason – Slaver roads aided the swift deployment of their legions from one stone fortress to another. They were the quickest way to move troops.

'It was always their aim to make the Realm into one great farm,' the wizard said. 'And to turn all the people into either field slaves or tax gatherers.'

Will murmured half to himself, 'I wonder if the duke will go to Foderingham on the way north.'

'Foderingham? I do not think Friend Richard will be calling halts for old times' sake.'

'He might overnight there. It will be his last chance.'

'He will not go near the Dragon Stone, and nor should we.'

'And what if the duke, in his wisdom, decides otherwise?'

Gwydion scowled. 'He will not.'

'He's taken no notice of your other warnings. Nor has he heeded Mother Brig's prophecy.'

'He has become very bone-headed lately.'

'But have you thought about this, Master Gwydion: what if he tries to use the Dragon Stone to coerce you into helping him against the queen?'

'Then he will burn his fingers.'

'It's not his fault,' Will said, unsatisfied. 'If I'm right, his stupid choices have all been made because of the draining away of magic. Or as I suppose we ought now to think of it, the turning of our world into a different one.'

'As the lorc awakens, Willand, so do you it seems.'

'Is that any surprise to you? We've been made by the same fae magic, the lorc and I.'

Will fell silent then as they rode on past Ayot. By Baldock the grey afternoon dipped suddenly into darkness. They were making better time now towards Ivelswade, and Will fancied that the shortness of the day this close to the winter solstice would bother the duke more than it bothered his pursuers.

When they reached the River Ivel they made camp, but Will knew that the roaring torrent he could hear inside his head was no muddy stream but the mighty hazel lign, which lay at least a league to the west.

Once they were settled, the wizard turned to him grimly and said, 'Have I told you about the Castle of Sundials?'

Will nodded. 'You've mentioned it once or twice. Why do you ask?'

'The duke maintains many houses – Foderingham to guard the Great North Road, Wedneslea and Sheriff Urton in the north. The Castle of Sundials stands some half dozen leagues or so to the south and east of Ebor. It belongs to the duke, but is kept by Braye, who is a master of sky lore.'

'Old Father Time?' Will mused, seating himself comfortably in the tent. 'It's said that he has a profound knowledge of the stars and what their movements portend. Gort once told me that his castle is filled with great machines of iron and brass, toothed wheels that measure out time and track the paths of the sun and moon and all the wandering stars.'

'That is so. Braye is an irascible man who ill fits our world. Many years ago his nose was struck off in a sword-fight. Since then he has worn a false one made of silver. He has a favourite rede – "History repeateth." So if you value your good looks, you will not argue with him.'

'And you think the duke is heading there?' Will asked, wondering if Duke Richard had thought of using the Lord Keeper's knowledge of the mysteries of time to somehow wind back the queen's advance. Will thought of the way the duke had tried so often before to wring advantage from magic. 'Surely, if Richard wanted to tamper with the flow of events, he would be better off going to the source at Rucke. If he were to put the needlewomen of Rucke to the sword it would stop everything dead – or so the legend says.'

Gwydion gave him a thoughtful look. 'Legend, you say? Is that what it has become. But there is no need to worry, the idea will not occur to him.'

Will's irritation surfaced. 'I hope you're right.'

'I do not think anything quite so final as an end-game is yet in Friend Richard's mind. He is a soldier, remember, not a philosopher. He wants to win the game, not throw the chessboard over. He will want to garrison the Castle of

Sundials if the queen has taken up residence in the city of Ebor, and he will want to do it for purely strategic reasons.'

Will nodded, happier now. 'That's just as well, for his army is too small to fight a pitched battle against Mag. But from the sound of it, the Castle of Sundials isn't an ideal fortress.'

'As ever the future is taking care of itself.' Gwydion looked up as a heavy patter of rain blew against the canvas and the candle flames that lit the tent shivered. 'As Braye will no doubt tell you himself soon, our todays are little more than yesterday's tomorrows.'

'Yes,' Will said dismally. 'Or tomorrow's yesterdays, depending on how you choose to think about them.'

CHAPTER SIXTEEN

THE SLEEPLESS FIELD

The Castle of Sundials lay some sixty leagues to the north of Trinovant as the crow flies, but Will's party could not travel so straight. After Iverswade they rode on to Buckden and then to Sawtree, and Will felt an increasing sense of fear. The few folk they encountered were watchful, wondering at their muddied horses and suspicious about what errand could have sent them abroad. Skinny dogs barked at them as they passed, and Will saw only empty fields and many a cottage that had been burned or broken. Some villages had been barred against strangers, and what little news there was spoke of bands of roving outlaws preying on whoever dared to use the road.

In the middle of the afternoon a quantity of blood began to pour from Will's nose and, at the same time, his grey mount took a sudden fright and bolted, throwing him to the ground.

Lotan dashed to the place where he fell, gathered him up and rode hard for the best part of half a league until the ill effects began to wear off.

'Indonen . . .' Will gasped as he woke up. 'Tell Master Gwydion. It's the lign of the ash and it's running very strongly.'

'What was it?' the wizard asked as he came up. 'Tell me!'

'A couple of stones,' he said, shaking his head.

'Two? How far?'

'Along Indonen, but before it reaches Delamprey. Where Indonen crosses with Celin and Collen, I should think.'

'Is their time come?'

Will's arm and shoulder had been bruised in the fall. He knew he could have easily broken his neck. As it was, his face and hair were crimson with blood despite Lotan's best efforts at cleaning him up, and he was covered in filth.

'Willand! The stones! Is their time come?'

'I don't know . . .'

'You must open your mind!'

'They all . . . they all seem ready to burst to me.'

Gort closed on the wizard and steered him away. Willow picked Will up and tended his grazes.

'I'm all right.'

'You're not all right. Look at you. You mustn't let him drive you like that!'

'He's been driving me all my life.'

'Then it's time you took control.'

'Let me be, will you?' He pulled his arm away from her angrily, but the pain made him wince. 'Everybody is always telling me what to do!'

Later that day they pushed on harder through the churning mud, sometimes closing on the hazel lign, sometimes drawing further away from it. Always they followed the tracks of the duke's army into the north. At one point the road turned sharply westward and Will saw that it altered course to follow a river, a river which Gwydion said he ought to be able to recognize.

They forded the river at Wann, and Will realized that it must be the Neane, and that to the east lay the Great Deeping Fen. The tales he had heard about the hags and water drakes that inhabited the mires there ran through his thoughts as they made the crossing, and he saw a dark shape flash briefly silver in the shallows and stir up the surface.

'Did you see that?' Gort said, excited. 'It was a big one.'

'If my new eyes do not deceive me,' Lotan said, 'that was a salmon.'

And Will knew, without any doubt, that this was the same fish that had escaped his grasp in the retting pond at Harleston months before, the one that had made itself out of his green talisman and Chlu's red one. Somehow it had got into the Neane and was now heading for the open sea.

What does *that* mean? he wondered, staring as if in a trance at the water.

For the rest of the day, dark thoughts occupied his mind. He could feel the moon and sun ruling him as they always did. The phase of the moon was vital, or more exactly the continually changing angle that the sun made with the moon as it swung about the world. The sky ruled him as it ruled the tides. His mood became feverish, leaving him at times hovering on the edge of awareness. What significance, if any, did the salmon carry? Had the remade creature been drawn to him? Had it perhaps been drawn to Chlu when he had passed through here on his own journey north?

Then the two puzzles came together in his mind in a jarring flash and suddenly both were solved. 'I recognize it, Master Gwydion,' he babbled, his eyes burning. 'Do you remember the fish talisman I used to wear . . . engraved on the fish was a device that showed three triangles set one within another . . . Chlu's red fish had the same mark . . . the pattern is that of the lorc!'

'Shhh . . .' the wizard said.

'You must believe me! I see it clear now!'

'Hush! I believe you, but it is a discovery best kept to yourself. Is Chlu near?'

Fragile as he was, Will nevertheless dared to open his mind a little. It was dangerous so close to the fast-rushing lign, and induced in him profound feelings of vertigo. Nor was there any reward for his efforts, for if Chlu was nearby then Will's mind was not able to reach him.

'No Chlu . . .' he said, drifting again. But this time a warm glow shone in his eyes like a sunset, for the revelation had been tremendous – three triangles, set one within another, and all the battlestones sited at the corners and along the edges of those triangles! It was astonishing, but true.

A dull day turned duller as the mists closed in. Drifting wisps crossed the track and lit Saint Elmo's fires in the distance. All that filled his head was the lulling slush-slush of hooves in mud and the jarring unevenness as the horses picked their way forward.

They had now come further north than Foderingham, and Will's ideas about visiting the castle which had once been his home had blown away like autumn leaves. Gwydion was right, he thought. It's no good thinking about the Dragon Stone. There are so many others still in the ground, it's the least of our worries.

All afternoon they came upon stragglers from the duke's army – a cart with a broken axle, soldiers who had injured themselves while hunting or foraging for food. Gwydion questioned them while Gort laid healing hands upon them. Progress was not as bad as Will had imagined. He was pleased to find that the army was not too far ahead. They were gaining on it. The duke had crossed the Stammer Stream at dawn the day before.

After an arduous afternoon, they overnighted at Burghlea Martin, near Stammerford. There was a mean farmstead there that Gwydion knew which belonged to a pig farmer by the name of John Sisil. He gladly let them stay, fried them thick rashers of bacon, and for his trouble received wizardly blessings. The first was a pentacle chalked by Gwydion on his threshold stone, the second a sign made upon his baby boy's head as the party readied to leave in the moist and misty morning.

'That's a trade in magic,' Willow warned, as they rode away.

'Not so,' the wizard told her.

'Get on with you – it's just as if you'd paid him in coin!'

'How? I agreed nothing with him beforehand. I have taken an interest in his family since before they came from the Earldom of Erewan. They are the sort of people who, when they see a need, will make an offer of help.'

'But he expected a blessing from you from the start. I saw the anticipation of it in his eyes. You protected his child and his cottage in payment for eggs and bacon.'

'You are mistaken.'

'I don't think so. He'd have been disappointed if you'd not given his son some advantage.'

The wizard huffed. 'If that is the case then the blessing will not help him, for that is how blessings work: in strict proportion to need, and somewhat inversely to desire. Mark my words, the Sisils will never amount to much in this world by the measure of some men's standards. They will never be lords or leaders or landowners, but they will cure excellent ham and be loved for it hereabouts for many generations to come, and what is more they will be content with that, which is a blessing indeed.'

As Willow fell silent, Will despaired privately, for he had begun to see how, in the terrible world that was coming, the worth of a man would henceforth be measured in ways that were themselves worthless. He tried to imagine what kind of a world it would be if all reward was to be offered in silver alone, if all other marks of respect were made subordinate to coin. The thought of that kind of world appalled him, and he pledged himself once more to temper his steel and do what he could to avert the dreadful collision that was coming.

But what could be done? They were a pitiful band of beggars, disregarded, ignored now even by their friends, and so, it seemed, doomed to fail. Even his revelation about the pattern of the battlestones seemed worthless, for what good could it do?

'This is the Slaver road called the Emin Strete,' Gwydion said darkly as they passed through Stammerford early the next day. 'It looks to me as if the duke has picked up only a few men on his march. He must have hoped more would flock to him as he went along.'

'They're too wise around these parts to heed such a call,' Will said, but he knew that the song of the lorc would eventually be too powerful even for the strongest of minds.

They had not been riding for even an hour before the birdsong ceased and dark woodland began to crowd in around the road and the world became a green tunnel that made Will deeply uneasy.

A fresh bout of sickness engulfed him, and though he waved Willow away he almost fell from his horse once more.

Willow steadied him. 'Come on, Will! Back the way we came.'

'Again?' Gwydion asked. 'What potions have you been giving him, Wortmaster?'

'Me?' Gort said, indignant. 'It's nothing to do with my healing, I'm sure of that!'

Gwydion grabbed the reins of Will's horse. 'It cannot be a lign! Not here. Surely Collen is still more than a league to the west. Something else must ail him.'

'Perhaps it's the phase of the moon,' Gort suggested. 'You know how susceptible our friend can be to its silvery influence at times, hmmm?'

'We have to find another way through Tickencote Oaks,' Will gasped. 'The forest is alight! The road is blocked!'

'The forest is *alight*?' Gort echoed.

'Blocked?' Gwydion demanded. 'By what?'

'Leave him alone, Master Gwydion!' Willow cried, kicking her horse forward. 'Can't you see he's ill?'

'The . . . stone,' Will murmured.

The wizard fumed. 'But how can there be a stone so far from a lign? It makes no sense!'

But when Will raised his head blood began to well from his eyes like tears, and even the wizard recoiled from the sight of him.

Now Lotan took up the burden and helped to get him off the road, leading him over old rabbit warrens and around the woods. No one saw anything untoward, no fire, no danger. Nothing.

But lights burned in the mists of Will's befuddled brain. He called out to Saint Elmo and asked why he had set the forest blazing. Angels, saints and seraphim swarmed in the air, closing in on him before they froze into a grotesque painted ceiling that cracked like an eggshell and fell down on him. And there, flooded in the excruciating light of the Beyond, the eye-burning brilliance, the undeniable flame. It was terrible, and he knew its name.

He screamed and screamed, for he saw that his end was coming, and this time he understood it as clear as day. He had been born in flame and fire, he had exploded into the world, to live the life of a man, to toil and to love and to know joy and sorrow, but his end was coming, and coming soon. It would not be long now. He would explode out of the world just as he had exploded into it. He would echo away into cold and darkness and be gone from all things and nothing would remain of him but a memory in the minds of those who laboured on . . .

And in Will's own mind there was the running of cool water in river shallows, and a grey salmon surging from sight – grey, yet shimmering green on one side and red on the other. It swam towards the depthless ocean, showing him the way home.

'Well, there it is . . .' Gwydion was saying.

The wizard was shading his eyes, staring at something hundreds of paces away: a pall of smoke over the trees. The smell of burning was in the air, like the thatch of a village that had been put to the sword, like the stink of a sky-blasted oak. Gwydion's robes were scorched, his beard singed. He had been among the flames.

Will groaned. Willow held him, smiled, put a hand to his cheek then looked up at the wizard. 'He's with us again.'

'You were right.' Gwydion knelt over him. 'It was a stone.'

'You went there?' he asked, horrified.

'I have . . . dealt with it.'

'Then it was a guide stone, a minor one.'

The wizard cracked a smile. 'It was a battlestone. But I bound what remained of it.'

'It wasn't on a lign. Not quite,' Will said, levering himself up. 'Where does that leave us?'

Gwydion shook his head. 'Are you forgetting about the battle on Blow Heath? That was fought after we carried a bound battlestone twenty leagues and more north from its burial place. This one was brought here from the hamlet of Empingham. Our example was noted by someone.'

'Who?' Will's question hung in the air.

'Who do you suppose?'

'This can only be Maskull's doing.'

'My conjecture is that he found the stone on the Collen lign, dug it up and carried it eastward a league or so to the road.'

'An ambush for the duke's army?' Willow asked, unsure.

'A trap. Perhaps meant for Friend Richard, perhaps for others.'

'Us,' Will said, getting unsteadily to his feet. 'He must

have used Chlu to find the battlestone. He must know we're following the duke.'

Gwydion turned away. 'If Maskull's firework was meant for either target, it has failed him. It burst too late for Friend Richard and too soon for us. I now have some account of his methods, at least, and perhaps some notion of his limits. He has outreached his skill – he cannot yet make the battle-stones dance exactly in time to his tune.'

Will wiped his lips. 'What did you see in Tickencote Oaks?'

Gwydion would not answer but moved away, saying, as if it pained him, 'There is no virtue in speaking of it now.'

Will looked to Gort, who shook his head. He knew when to let a matter be.

When Will went over to Lotan and thanked him for his timely work, the big man was awkward taking praise. 'I did what I could.'

Will flashed a glance towards the wizard. 'What happened out there? What did he do?'

Lotan shrugged, his look morose, reluctant. He gestured towards Gwydion. 'Your wizard wouldn't let me go near.'

'Then has your gift of sight yielded us nothing at all?'

'I saw . . .' He waited, then waited again until Gwydion had moved away. At last he said, 'I saw agony.'

'Agony?'

Lotan lifted his head and Will saw that his eyes were red now. 'Flaming skeletons were running from the blaze. And your wizard was striking them down with blasts of blue fire. He called what he did "mercy".'

The next day was blustery and rainy. Lotan dourly endured it, but Gwydion said that if any present found the rain hard to bear, then they should consider how they would like it if a really large battle should take place. 'For it is said that hard rains follow upon great battles.'

Will supposed that the wizard was talking in impenetrable riddles, but they seemed nevertheless barbed and aimed at Lotan. He jogged Gwydion's arm, saying, 'Well, I have to say that I don't like the rain either. And if you'd clear it away for us I'm sure we'd all be very much obliged to you – if you still can, that is.'

'Between "can" and "should" there is an important distinction, my friend,' Gwydion told him tartly. He raised an eyebrow and grunted, but then he went on to say that this was where the Emin Strete came closest to the Wette, a great grey-brown gulf that was the domain of the ancient mud-giant, Metaris. It was his habit to rise up from the mussel beds as the silty tides ebbed and scatter the curlews and dunlins from his shoulders. But when the mood took him he liked to drown men by overturning their ships.

'Many an unlucky mariner has Metaris preyed upon,' Gwydion said with grisly relish. 'Whether they were Slaver war-galley or Easterling pirate ship, he made no bones about any of them. Or rather *many* bones, I should say, for he has sucked many a sailorman's rib clean.'

'Does he live still?' Willow asked, casting an uneasy eye eastward.

Gwydion grinned darkly. 'He lies even now in his watery lair, counting the riches that he once obliged King John to leave with him.'

The views opened out and all day Will saw nothing that might be called a hill. He recalled the days he had spent as a child surrounded by hills and the yearning he had felt to know what the world looked like from their tops and what might be on the other side. And then, by turning that idea around in his mind, he understood that boys who grew to manhood in a land of flats and marshes would see the world another way entirely, and that thought pleased him for it was an understanding about life that was new to him.

They passed through Streetton and then came by Woolthorpe where Will saw a great sky-bow overarch the grey northern clouds. Its colours spread vividly and there was much beauty in it, though its significance was not so clear.

At last Gort said it showed where stood a certain garden, and in that garden there grew a tree that bore special apples. 'They hang,' he said, 'only from the uppermost branches. But those fruits never drop of their own accord, Will. They have to be worked for, picked from the highest branches, else they wither where they've grown.'

Will nodded. 'As the rede says, "Hard won is dear loved, but easy come is easy go."'

'Aye, and so it is!'

'Truly?' Willow asked, grimacing at the strange notion of apples that refused to be picked without a great effort. 'Then why do folk bother with them?'

'Ah, because these are no ordinary apples. When baked in a pie they give anyone who eats of them a wonderful quickness of mind! The eater gains the wisdom to see answers, answers to all kinds of questions about the world.'

'Then why don't we go there and learn what *we* must do,' she said.

But Gort grimaced at the suggestion. 'We already know enough about that, I think. And though our world is failing fast, it's no duty of ours to give it any kind of a helping hand in that direction.'

After Woolthorpe the road veered a little eastward into the Flatlands and away from the ligns. The rain abated and a great shaft of sunshine blasted down upon them, making a second sky-bow of nine startling colours.

Will found that he was glad of the respite. But then he realized they were heading towards the city of Linton and he drew less comfort from the weak winter sunlight.

'Is there not a great chapter house there?' he asked Lotan.

'Yes. It's high upon a hill and so sees far.'

The wizard glanced at the big man, sudden to pounce. 'And how do *you* know that?'

'I have never been there, but I have heard tell of it.'

Gwydion's jaw clenched. 'We shall avoid its malign influence just as we have avoided all the others!'

Lotan scowled. 'I have no wish that we should do otherwise.'

They went on until the town of Linton began to appear out of the mist. Will saw that the dwellings were indeed spread at the feet of the chapter house, which sat high up on a mound and looked out over fifty miles of good growing land. The afternoon came on wetter and they took shelter in a barn when the last of the light died.

'Well, there's one thing for sure,' Willow said, stretching and yawning. 'The way is certainly proving long.'

Will turned to her. 'And the shadow has fallen fast. Do you realize that today is Ewle?'

'The shortest day,' Lotan said, watching the rain abate. 'We should have marked Ewle with ceremony. We'll light a fire at least.'

'And set the barn ablaze?' Gwydion said. 'It is dry in here. If you are cold, pack your shirt with straw.'

'Oh, Master Gwydion. There's no cheer in that,' Willow said. 'Let's ask the farmer if we can kindle a small fire in the yard.'

The wizard huffed. 'Fire is a signal, and smoke even more so. Anyway it will rain again soon.'

'Better safe than sorry,' Will said, trying to make peace between them. 'We don't want to attract attention.'

In the damp, gloomy silence that followed, Gort began to sing.

'The shadow falls fast,
Like sand in a glass.
And the way is long,
To the sleepless field.'

Will's mind drifted. He was calmer now and he could order his thoughts more easily. Who had moved the stone off the Collen lign? Was it really Maskull? Or could the Fellowship have done it? Maybe the stone had spooked whoever had tried to carry it off and they had abandoned it. Was it happenstance that it had gone off just as they had come close to it?

Their evening food was unwrapped and taken cold. The company leaned together, their conversation quiet and insignificant as the wind in dried grass. Will noticed the wrinkles and spots of age on the backs of the wizard's hands. Rats squeaked somewhere, making Gort smile.

Will saw Lotan go outside. After a moment, he got up and followed at a distance, like a man with business of his own.

The big man walked away in the grey-dark, stood with his back to Will, and unsheathed his sword with a sudden, deliberate jerk.

Will pressed himself up against the bole of a hollow ash tree. The deep grooves of its bark were damp and hard under his fingers, and tar-black blobs showed where a fungus was eating the tree alive. The smell of rotting wood rose out of the innards of the trunk, reminding him of death, of the wood pile in which Magog and Gogmagog had been dumped.

There was a wind now, rustling the bare branches. Overhead the clouds had opened, moving on missions of their own. There were valleys of stars standing between their bluff faces. And far below them the man with the stolen eyes threw back his head and cast an unblinking gaze up at the sky. He breathed deep, like one marvelling in private at a great spectacle. Then he sheathed his sword and returned again to the barn.

Silently, Will watched him go, feeling ashamed to be spying on a friend, but glad enough that he had witnessed nothing more than a brief spell of wonderment.

The wizard noted Lotan's return, and he let his glance linger long enough for Will to see it.

'You still don't trust him, do you?' Will said when, a short while later, he got Gwydion alone.

'I do not.'

'Why is that?'

'Because I dare not.'

Will snorted. 'You *dare* not? You trusted Anstin the Hermit. Anstin helped you, though he once made spires for the Sightless Ones.'

'Anstin worked on their houses. He was not one of them.'

'So you'll continue to refuse to put your trust in Lotan?'

'Too much hangs on it.' The wizard corrected himself, '*Everything* hangs on it.'

Gwydion's voice had risen, and Will cast the others a glance to check they were not listening. But he need not have worried – Willow and Lotan were laughing as Gort embroidered some unlikely tale.

Will turned back. 'It seems I missed quite a blaze back there.'

'You *see*? – I asked him not to speak of it to you. Yet he did. He is not to be trusted.'

'Perhaps he told me because he counts himself my friend first. And is that any wonder?' Will drew a fast breath. 'He said that men burned like torches.'

'They burned as we all would have burned had you not sensed the stone and stopped us.'

'But Lotan said you killed them.'

The wizard's deadly face showed how much he resented the implication. 'I carried through an act of mercy.'

'Lotan says you murdered them.'

'I did exactly what had to be done. No more, and no less.'

Will felt the moment bite. 'Who were they?'

'That was impossible to tell. Perhaps innocents, perhaps the ones who had fetched the stone for Maskull. Perhaps . . . others.' No more words came, only a wall of wilful reticence.

'Perhaps red hands,' Will said. 'And after it was over, did you wait for the flames to die down around the stone?'

More suspicion flashed in the wizard's eyes. 'Why do you ask that?'

'I want to know if you interrogated the stump!'

'How could I? I did not know if it was yet a stump. I did not know if it had flared off all, or only a fraction, of the malice it contained.'

'So what did you do?'

'When it cooled I bound it and then Gort took it. He hid it somewhere far from the road.'

'Do you think it still contains enough harm to cause a battle?'

Gwydion shifted and wrapped his robe tighter about him. 'That I cannot say. Why? Are you looking for a boon from it?'

Will drew back stiffly. 'Will you tell me whether or not you got its verse?'

'I got nothing. Nor would anything that it gave freely be of any use to us.'

That was evasive. Will knew he was leading the wizard onto dangerous ground, but he could not resist saying, 'The Dragon Stone gave us a message, one that we believed, and still believe.'

'That was then, this is now. I remind you again: the times are *changing*. Everything is changing – even, in the end, the lorc.'

Will stirred as he began to see the sense of what was in the wizard's mind. 'Yes . . . how stupid of me.'

The wizard sucked his teeth. 'Trust me, Willand, in the world that's coming there will be no lorc. Maskull's meddling has pushed the world another step closer to the abyss. The lorc has begun to fail, just as I am failing, just as you are failing, just as the last yale has gone from this world. And what we must ask ourselves is this: is it more likely that the lorc will end with a whimper – or with a bang?'

The next day was drier, but colder and full of the grey that attends a year's end. Duke Richard's army had followed a branch of the Great North Road as it turned westward at Scanton and passed along a stretch known to carriers and carters as Bridge Lane, for on its way it crossed many tributaries of the Umber. Unfortunately for Will the road also strayed across the Collen lign.

He smelled it first like a gust of corruption, then the sickness descended on him as a fit. His limbs began to twitch and then jerk, moving in a way that was beyond his control. His friends galloped him across as quickly as they could, until he began to regain a little colour and revive.

'It's flowing north,' he said, tears reddening his eyes. 'Very strong.'

Soon the character of the road changed, and the appearance of the land itself, for at Boar Tree there was a gate bearing a gilded crest that gave notice to all who travelled this way that they were entering the great Duchy of Ebor.

There was to Will's eyes a glitter to all things beyond the gate, as if a weird's spell rested upon the place, but he could not be certain that it was not an aftershock running through him – that, or some foul glamour caused by the presence of both the Collen and Celin ligns, a power which now ran strongly to either hand.

'Thus we depart the ancient kingdom of Axenholme,' Gwydion said.

'Is this then the Mezentian Gate?' Will asked, vaguely remembering the fame of the place.

'Alas, it is not,' Gwydion said. 'For that is at the port of Memison. That is a far grander gateway than this, a thing of lofty pillars and set with many fine statues. We will not go that way, for ahead of us lie two more leagues to the River Dunne, and there are four more to Castle Pomfret if ever we should go there. We will not do that today, however, but cut westward instead.'

'Shouldn't the way we choose depend on the one that Duke Richard has taken?' Will asked.

'We must go where my intuitions say we should,' the wizard insisted. 'There is no longer any doubt where Friend Richard is bound, and I would rather not go by Pomfret in whose dreadful dungeons Hal the Usurper did starve to death his rightful king!'

Will agreed, but before they came to Duncaistre there was bad news. The old man whom Gwydion questioned knew little enough, but it seemed that the Duke of Mells had fallen upon the advance riders of Duke Richard's army and there had been a skirmish.

'A slaughter, they're calling it. Some dozens of men slain, but more fled, and all from deadly giants.'

'And the queen's army?' Lotan asked.

The old man waved a shaky hand northward. 'There be monsters holding the castle at Pomfret.'

'And may the shame of the Usurper's crime humble them all,' Gwydion muttered.

'We must take special care now,' Lotan said. 'For we do not want to meet Duke Henry's armed bands while we are out in the open.'

The wizard turned on him. 'Is that so? Then you would have us waste more time finding a way around?'

Will gritted his teeth at the wizard's hostility and wondered what purpose he thought it served. They pressed on, and when next the two of them were out of earshot he said to Gwydion, 'Why do you always have to belittle Lotan? What has he done to deserve it?'

The wizard's chin jutted. 'I may ask you: what do you think of the nightmare Willow had last night?'

'What nightmare?'

'She told Gort of it. Did she not tell you?'

That rankled. 'No. And if she didn't, maybe that's because she doesn't want to trouble me with trifles.'

'It was no trifling matter. Her thoughts led her to a speculation that I have long had in my own mind.'

'Which is?'

'Simply this: that Maskull's magic may be allowing him to see all that passes before Lotan's new eyes.'

Will reined in his horse and drew back. He looked daggers at Gwydion, but he made no reply.

Later, as Will followed on alone, the idea plagued him. Of course it was a foolish fancy, no more than a feeling of guilt playing on Willow's sleeping mind. But Gwydion's speculation was like a worm in the apple of his confidence. What if Will's own intuitions about Lotan had been less than sound? What if his judgment had been confused by the new vigour that was rushing through the lorc? What if Maskull really had been apprised of everything they had said and done? What then?

He tried again cautiously to open his mind, to send out feelers towards Chlu, to make contact without himself being detected. But as the door of his consciousness cracked open, the roaring beyond filled his head and made him pull back in confusion.

As they turned across the Celin lign Will's skin started

to itch and then his joints began to creak with pain, and before his horse could go more than a few paces further on, a crippling agony spread through him.

'By the moon and stars . . . help me!'

Again they were forced to rush him onward a hundred paces, carrying him now groaning and slumped across his own packhorse. When they stopped to look at him, his face was patched with leprous red. Gort tore open his shirt and saw the marks on him, like weals raised on a back that has been freshly flogged.

No sooner were the marks revealed than Gort began to pass his hands over the skin. Amazingly, the hurts began to vanish again almost as quickly as they had come, leaving behind only faint echoes of pain.

Afterwards, Will's memory of that moment was unclear, but it seemed to him that the Wortmaster had passed some healing implement over him to draw out the ailment.

'How was it?' Willow asked, pale herself now as he lay in her arms.

'I saw three white leopards sitting under a juniper tree,' he told her faintly. 'Clear as day to me, they were.'

'What was their meaning?'

He looked at the knuckle of his middle finger where a small wound had opened, or reopened, for he had got the original cut from Edward half a dozen years ago.

He laughed hoarsely. 'I don't know about meaning – Death, at a hazard.'

'Death?' Willow said, and with such desolation in her voice that it broke his heart.

He squeezed her hand and lied. 'But maybe not mine, after all. Hmm?'

'And the flow?' Gwydion asked like a splash of cold water. 'What about that?'

'It's worse than before. We're surely approaching the

place where the next battle will be fought . . . The flow is a torrent now. You wouldn't believe it.'

'Me? Why not? Why wouldn't I believe it?'

He shook his head tiredly. 'Master Gwydion, it's just an expression.'

Willow hugged him. She was on the point of tears. 'What are we to do with you? We can't take you near a battlefield if it'll make you ill like this.'

Later that day, they laid up again, erecting their tents inside the remains of a ruined cottage for fear of being seen. Gort gave them all a herbal tonic to drink. It had the kindness of bistort root in it, he said, buckthorn bark and burdock too, and so was good for endurance. Gwydion brought in a pair of burbot from the river. Coneyfish, the Wortmaster said they were known as hereabouts. Their flesh was good to eat and their bones had a magic that made them much prized by Wise Women. The wizard paced and danced and muttered long into the night while Will drew what strength he could from stone-hard ground that had once been a vegetable garden.

It was now that Gwydion decided to tell Will the plan upon which all their hopes depended, though to Will's annoyance he waited until Lotan had excused himself from their company before speaking. His idea, he said, was simply to find the next stone before Maskull did.

'He will come to drink of its malice and we shall be ready for him.'

'Ready?' Will asked. 'I don't see how we're that.'

'As you know, a certain something which was once in the duke's possession fell to me, almost by chance.' He opened his crane bag and drew out something small. 'You remember the corpse-whale wand? I have cut three slivers from it and made these.'

Will took what was offered – three small white pieces of ivory. 'They're arrowheads.'

The wizard nodded. 'I intend to bind them to fletched shafts.'

'I'll shoot them into Maskull, when he comes,' Willow said. 'It's quite simple.'

'No . . .' Will looked quickly from one to the other. 'No! No, Master Gwydion. Tell me you're jesting with me!'

But Willow laid calming hands on him. 'Will, it's already been decided.'

'Willow, it has not been decided! What are you thinking, Master Gwydion? She'd never get near enough to Maskull to hurt him. She—'

The wizard got to his feet and lifted the cloak of shimmering white feathers out of his bag. 'She could get close to him if she were to wear this.'

Willow grasped her husband's sleeve, enthused by the plan. 'Don't you see? A vanishing spell triggered by these arrowheads. We'd send him to the Baerberg and that would be the last we'd see of him because there's no magic there and he'd not be able to get off the island again.'

'Master Gwydion, you're forgetting what you once told me; that Maskull has already been to the Baerberg! If he got off it once he can get off it again.'

The wizard's eyes softened in appeal. 'He went there in a ship, Will. A ship! And it was the same ship that bore him away. He put those mariners under compulsion, for did you not hear what that adventurer said? No mariner goes to the Baerberg willingly. But if Maskull is sent there by magic he'll have no way off. No more than a kitten has a way down when you put it up into a tree.'

'No! You can't do it. Put the cloak away, Master Gwydion. Maskull is no kitten, and I forbid it!'

There was silence. Then Gwydion raised his eyebrows and said, 'Well, then. I trust you have a better idea.'

'Look, Will!' Willow rose and took the cloak. As she

draped her shoulders she began slowly to fade from view, until by a count of seven she had vanished completely.

Will stared uneasily into the space where his wife had been standing. The sight of her turning ash-pale then greying into thin air was not one best calculated to encourage him, yet the wizard's charge that he had no better plan was undeniable.

It was now that Lotan chose to return. He halted by the door like a man stumbling in on a private argument. When they all stared at him, he looked from face to face uncomprehendingly.

'What?'

And when no one offered any reply he pursed his lips in vexation and sat down.

Gort rushed in to fill the silence. 'Did I ever tell you about the day one of the Foderingham cats had her first taste of snow? She tried to jump onto a snowdrift, poor little thing, and got the fright of her life! Up and down she went, springing hither and yon like jack-in-the-box!'

Gwydion got up surreptitiously and left. When he returned, he was with Willow. By this time Lotan and Gort were in more measured conversation and the secret, it seemed, had been preserved.

For his part, Will remained alone with his thoughts. He could see no virtue in angering himself further over what had just passed, so he tried to broaden his thoughts. But disappointment at Gwydion's grand plan had stirred him up and was letting in all kinds of doubts. When he went out to stare into the darkness he could sense the ligns like taints on the wind, rumbles in the bones of his well-planted feet – Celin, lign of the holly to the east now, and further away to the west the birch lign called Bethe. They were converging towards the north, running strongly, and he knew there would be a great battlestone at that point. It was maybe half a dozen leagues away, and that fact gave some relief to his mind. They might be able to ride for a whole day before the sickness descended over him again.

What would it be like this time? Doubtless a fresh terror made manifest in his flesh, some new god-awful affliction for him to bear . . .

There was that little word again! A little word, but a gigantic, dangerous idea. That was the power the Sightless Ones believed in, the one Gwydion had called the Great Lie. Could it be that the Fellowship would turn out to be right in the end? Could it be that the new tomorrow that was coming would belong entirely to them?

It surely seemed that way, for now there could be no grand heroic future such as Gwydion had once promised, no future in which Will was magically transformed into a great king. The very idea seemed absurd now, and he felt ashamed that he had ever allowed himself to believe in it.

When he returned to the others he saw two drooping grey tents and Lotan alone as he preferred, in a hammock that had been slung between the masonry of the cottage and a tree trunk. A cape of waterproofed leather was thrown over him, and his sword lay down beside him. Those extraordinary eyes were closed now, and he seemed to be asleep, but he never truly slept, or if he did, it was so lightly that any hooting owl or any cracking twig his mind could not account for would stir him.

That night Will saw dream visions again, only this time they were not of three white leopards sitting under a juniper tree. This time he saw Lotan. He was alone and stroking the breast of a white dove which he then released into the air.

The next day and the day after, hail storms came, then icy rain with snow mixed in it. High winds tore down the last clinging oak leaves and roared in bare beech branches. When the winds abated, scavenging parties began to appear in the woods, riding with lances at the ready. They missed the hideaway Gwydion had wrapped in spells, but they left Will in no doubt that it was far too dangerous to travel onward for the moment.

The place Gwydion had found for them was a cheerless one, deep among banks of impenetrable brambles. The bushes threw up bare, wintery coils to twice the height of a man, and Will found the wait in their thorny embrace all the more galling because they were now very close to their destination.

When Gwydion went to spy out the land, Will climbed a tree and watched their dismal camp. Presently he saw Gort crouching down over five horn beakers that he had lined up. He poured measures of cordial such as he had given them all along to preserve their strength, but when he had done he looked to left and right then he added a white powder to the last of the beakers.

After Gwydion's return, Gort dispensed the drinks one at a time, and when he came to Will he said, 'Drink it down. All in one, now.'

Will took the beaker, but he would not let Gort take his hand away. 'You drink it down!'

Gort recoiled. 'What? I've drunk mine already.'

'Aye, but this one is different, is it not?' And he roughly opened Gort's purse to find a shard of stone there, one sharp as flint and shaped like a spearhead, yet powdery and half ground away at the base. He held it up angrily in Gort's face. 'What's this?'

Gort looked out from under his bushy brows, anxious lest their tussle be noticed. 'Shhhh! Master Gwydion mustn't know about it.'

'Oh? And why's that?'

'It's from the stump at Tickencote Oaks.'

Will eyes widened. 'You chipped it from the *battlestone*?' He stared at the beaker as if it was a scorpion and made to throw it down, but Gort stopped him.

'Easy now! I didn't so much chip it. A piece sort of came away in my hand when I pushed the rest of it off a bridge.'

'A bridge? Oh, this gets worse!'

'Yes, into a river! Master Gwydion bade me bury the stone somewhere far from the road, but I thought—'

'You thought you knew better than an Ogdoad wizard!'

'I thought I'd tip it into the first hole I came to. Easier, hey? And I kept this little piece, stumps being beneficial and all. You've supped a goodly part of it down already.'

'Gort, what have you done to me?' Will grabbed him by the shirt. 'Master Gwydion said the stone might not have been emptied of all its malice.'

Gort blinked sheepishly. 'Well, it looked to me like it had. I watched it vomiting out all its horrors. And afterwards it had a glow of kindness about it.'

'That's just a part of its deception, you fool!'

Gort drew himself up. 'No, Will. I may be many things, but a fool I am not. There was a benefit of healing there. I felt it. And besides—'

'Besides?'

'Well . . . I passed that shard over you after you crossed the last lign. That's what took the pain and all those welts away. 'Twasn't any skill of mine.'

'You—' Will recalled how the whip weals had rapidly faded away under Gort's hands and how he had felt some instrument at work. 'You did that?'

'I had to find out. And you seemed to be in such agony, Will, it would hardly have left you any worse off if it hadn't worked, hey?'

Will growled, but he let go of the Wortmaster's clothes. 'You . . .'

'You do feel a little better though, don't you?'

'What if I do?'

'Apart from that nasty piggish temper. That's a new thing.'

'Well, I'm sorry if you don't like it.'

He stared at the Wortmaster and saw his true intent. Then he looked at the cordial and the oily colours that moved on its surface. He could not decide whether to drink it or tip it out. Mistrust flared in him again and he dunked the still unhealed wound on the knuckle of his middle finger into the liquid.

Nothing happened for a moment, but then the redness around the cut began to subside as he watched, and he knew that he had given the shard a true test.

Gort poked him in the chest. 'Ah-ha! You see? But it would have worked better with a little faith on your part.'

That shamed Will, and he made his decision. 'Maybe I do owe you an apology, Wortmaster. It looks like your judgment is sounder than that of an Ogdoad wizard after all.'

'Oh, I wonder about that too,' Gort muttered, knowing immediately what Will was implying. He glanced towards the place where Gwydion stood. 'I wonder whether the dregs of malice that're still in him from those bracelets don't have something to do with the way he's been behaving.'

Will nodded. 'Then why don't you poison his brew as well as mine?'

The Wortmaster looked hurt. 'Will, that's not a nice thing to say after making such a pretty apology.'

'I mean it. Why don't you?'

'Because you might need all of what's left. And it's too late to go back for more, heh?'

'Hmm.' Will took the stone chip.

Gort scratched at his beard. 'There. Put it in your pouch. You better keep it now. Take it daily, or at need. Or not at all if you so decide.'

They stayed in hiding, not daring to risk themselves until the dawn of the third day when a freezing fog rolled down from Caldordale. They came out into the mists and struggled onward. When they found the road, they saw that it had been churned to mud, and in among the mess Lotan found a footprint that was much larger than any man's. It was indistinct, and though Gwydion dismissed it with a specious remark, the sight of it made Will uneasy.

But the imminent danger was still from armed riders. Many foraging parties were out roaming the land. That these parties did not notice them Will put down to the subtle art of Gwydion's dancing. Late in the morning they came in sight of the town of Awakenfield. It sat resplendent with flags across the River Caldor, and a bridge of many spans with a strong stone parapet was clearly visible leading to it.

'So this is the "sleepless field",' Will said, looking to Gwydion.

'Indeed it is. But hold hard, for we must not go that way.'

'Not go into the town?' Will looked at the small chapter house that stood by the bridge. It seemed innocent enough. 'Why not?'

'The town would appear to be held by the queen's forces.'

Will looked again. 'I see no one there at all.'

'What do you expect to see? The Weirds of Albanay sitting all in a row?'

The question balked him. 'We were told of wild-men, of wood ogres and hill trolls, were we not? Surely if the queen had occupied the town, then—'

'Look closely at those coloured rags stirring in the breeze. They are the royal colours. A wry welcome – a taunt, set there by a queen to enrage a duke. They say to him, "I have the city of Ebor in my power. I have Awakenfield also." They are there to tempt Friend Richard over the bridge. But I know him. He will have given orders to his men not to approach the bridge, for none of those who presently scour the south bank of the Caldor have yet ventured that way.'

'Then, which way shall we go?'

'To see Richard, of course! And if you would know where Richard has gone, look yonder!'

And there, half a league distant where the wizard pointed, Will saw many towers rising. It was a castle – strong walls, seven bastions, curtained and battlemented. The Castle of Sundials, first sited here on its motte by the Conqueror to control Caldordale and all the lands as far east as Pomfret. And the view from the highest of those roofless towers would be unimpeded across the tracts of cleared land and woods. A land that was now in the deep mid-winter, and with all its yeomen already fled with their stock and in hiding from the queen's host. It would be a hard place for five thousand newcomers to scrape a living.

As they drew nearer, Will saw cavalry horses tethered and attended in the woods nearby. Then he saw that each of the towers of the castle was surmounted by what looked like a great iron siege engine, though he soon realized that these were engines of a different kind.

'The stars!' Gort told him. 'Braye Skymaster watches them all and accounts their movements in a great book. These are his machines for measuring the same.'

And so they were – huge south-pointing quadrants, sighting frames and skeleton spheres of glinting metal, all hinged and hooped and set with pointers, and there were the small figures of men working among them, as if upon some unknown design. Will regarded the activity with mixed feelings, surmising yet again that there must have been a reason beyond military strategy for the duke to have come here.

It seemed that Duke Richard's army had not arrived so long before them. It was partly encamped unhappily beside the castle. Trees had been felled and logs were being dragged in. Many fires tainted the air with woodsmoke, and much activity attended the soldiers' preparations.

Gwydion called upon someone he knew to see to their horses. He gained them entry to the castle quietly and without demur from the guards, but once inside Will found that the castle was not what he had imagined. There were indeed many sundials and time machines set up on pillars or sunk in stone pits, but the castle itself had been built as a fortress of immense strength. The outer curtain wall screened a deadly ditch and, within that, the strong inner keep was set high on a mound, with a barbican the like of which Will had never seen before to guard it. This last seemed wholly impregnable.

Separated from the keep by a drawbridge was a large, crescent-shaped bailey on which now thronged much of the duke's host. Tradesmen had set up amid the bustle, and Will noted the signs of imminent war that he had seen so many times before. Heaps of goose wings showed where fletchers and arrowmakers had been hard at work. Armourer's hearths glowed red. Steam rose where iron was quenched and last-minute repairs made to blade and harness. But Will also saw where Braye's instruments had been broken. Many littered the ground or lay tumbled in the ditches. Several of the intricate devices had been purposely hauled down and smashed, their iron parts hammered into bill-heads and their oaken beams chopped up for firewood to feed the forges. It was as if the Skymaster's machines had spoken strange heresies and had borne the penalty.

It was not long before the wizard and the Wortmaster were noticed. The rumour of their arrival soon reached the ears of Sir Hugh Morte, the aged lord who attended ever at Duke Richard's right hand. Though he was grey-haired and jowly, he was sound in body and had the stature and stance of a warrior.

'Why are you come here, Crowmaster?' he demanded.

Gwydion faced him. 'Ah, Friend Hugh. But this is no way

to greet your lord's helpmeet, one who has travelled a hard road to be at his side during his time of greatest need.'

'Helpmeet, you say? You are a worker of wily words, a spinner of spells. Yet you can think of no better name for yourself than that?'

'What name would you have me use, when I am one who habitually sups with the enemy?'

The knight bared his teeth at that, recognizing the sentiment as one he had expressed himself while outside the wizard's hearing. Will saw that if Gwydion had meant his irony to set the lord's teeth on edge he had succeeded.

'There, Crowmaster, you prove my point! Come now, answer me straightly. Tell me your business then be on your way!'

Gwydion scowled. 'I come to speak with your master.'

Sir Hugh, half-armoured, truculent now, folded his arms and stood four-square in the middle of the drawbridge. 'But my master does not desire to see *you*!'

Gwydion's answering gesture was the barest of bows. 'That, of course, has ever been his choice, but I would hear it from his own mouth.'

'You may not! Nor may you stay among us, so we say fare thee well!'

The wizard was unmoving now. 'May I at least know why I am to be sent away without a kind word?'

'I know not. Nor do I care to know. I am a soldier. I only follow my master's orders.'

'And that you do very well, Friend Hugh, but it is often the soldier's claim when he knows he is in the wrong that his orders are to blame.' The wizard put out an accusing finger. 'But if you love your master, you should tell him this: there are less than two days before the year's end and *he will surely die on one of them*.'

Sir Hugh, instantly wrathful and heedless of the wizard's staff, took a step forward. 'You *dare* to imagine his grace's death? To speak of that is a crime! Did I not say you are no longer welcome here? Now get you gone!'

The lord threw Gwydion back with a mighty shove that almost robbed the wizard of his balance. Poleaxes and glaives bristled as the barbican guard came forward. Will drew himself up, ready to intervene. He knew Sir Hugh of old, knew his opinion of wizardry, knew there could be no arguing with him. Will swore under his breath at the way Gwydion had mishandled things. But then the door of the keep opened and a knot of guards issued out, among them a figure in black and brown who pushed his way to the fore, head bobbing and face twisting.

'Edmund!'

'Twice have I ordered this rabble out!' Sir Hugh shouted, drawing his sword. 'I shall not do so a third time. Guards! Drive them into the ditch!'

Edmund, face colouring, stuttered and spat furiously, but he was overruled.

'No, Sir Edmund! Your father will not have it!'

There was a brief flurry as Edmund's bodyguard drew steel, tore the sword from the old warrior's grip and pinned him.

'Infamy!' Sir Hugh shouted. 'Barbican guard, take them!'

But Edmund's bodyguard cowed the barbican garrison with a bullish display of arms, and Edmund limped past the stricken seneschal to greet the newcomers with courtesy and lead them into the keep.

Furious shouts burst from Sir Hugh, and put the rest of the keep guard in doubt. Will raised his eyes in dread to see the iron-shod teeth of the portcullis hovering as he passed beneath. So similar were the guard liveries of the duke and his sons that a mistake must surely be made soon by one of the archers on the walls. A fight would be triggered, then disaster. But Edmund's men came single-mindedly through the gatehouse as the others looked on, then they clattered noisily up the stone-faced passage towards the Lord Keeper's tower, shouting, 'Clear a way there for Edmund, Earl of Rutteland, or die!'

The earl habitually dragged his left foot, but that hardly impeded him when upon a vital errand, and he led them speedily up the killing ramp to the open doors of the tower. Gort and Gwydion followed close behind. Will steered Willow ahead of him, while Lotan brought up the rear. The big man's sword was held tight to his side, his cloak drawn over its hilt, for he would not surrender it willingly.

Once inside, Will listened carefully to what the duke's son had to tell them. 'Loremaster Braye . . . fled . . . his assistant flogged . . . both sent out of the castle.'

'What?' Gort whispered, horrified. 'Why?'

'Because . . . he would not . . . give my father . . . what . . . he needed.'

'Which was?' Will asked.

Another grimace. 'T-t-time!'

Gwydion shook his head. 'No man could have done that, loremaster or not, for as I have warned, the seer has spoken! Now, Edmund, you must do as I ask and take me to your father.'

'My father is . . . m-mad with anger. He will not . . . see you.'

'The lorc is speaking to his mind, Edmund,' Will said. 'Against his better judgment he's being drawn into battle. That's why we must speak with him, if we can.'

'He will k-k-kill you! And . . . after what I have done . . . he will . . . kill me too.'

Gwydion's thunderous gaze fell upon him. 'It matters not, for the House of Ebor has already fallen.'

'Let the enemy come,' Lotan growled, looking around appreciatively at the thickness of the walls. 'This place will stand, even to the last grain of sorcerer's powder! So long as there are victuals and a sweet well here the—'

'There are no victuals!' Edmund stood firm. 'I told you: Keeper Braye failed my father . . .. he has not bought us time . . . he did not . . . p-provision the castle with all necessaries as he was bid.'

And Will suddenly saw what Edmund had meant. There had been, after all, a plain, matter-of-fact reason for the Lord Keeper's flight. Will felt the world make another dreadful lurch towards the prosaic. 'Not enough food? Is that all there is to it?'

Gort took Edmund's arm. 'Loremaster Braye could not have obtained grain hereabouts for love nor money with the queen's presence already at Ebor, and there was a day when your father would have understood that. Are you sure the Skymaster did nothing else to bring down your father's wrath upon his head?'

'He went mad.'

'Mad?'

'He spoke . . . false prognostications.'

'Of what kind?'

'Perilous . . . pernicious . . . my father would not hear them.'

'Concerning?' Will asked.

'Why . . . about the sky, of course.' Flecks of white foam bubbled at the corners of Edmund's mouth. 'The motions of the red wanderer . . . the star that governs war. When my father asked Braye what would be . . . he said only mad things . . . that he had lately found . . . the true reason for the red star's motions. He claimed that it is another world . . . one far, far away . . . but somewhat like our own. He said he had proved that our own world . . . circles about the sun . . . instead of what is obvious to . . . to every man. He said . . . the red wanderer . . . did not govern the ways of war at all.'

Will stared, dumbfounded. 'And so your father had him thrown out?'

'Braye was . . . in the end . . . mad . . .'

Gort and Gwydion exchanged glances, then the wizard turned to Edmund, his eyes flaming. 'We must persuade your father to tread with greater care, for we have learned much about the way the world is changing that appears to confirm the Skymaster's ideas.'

Edmund stared back queerly, as if a matter had been broached that was far beyond him.

The wizard went on. 'But let us speak rather concerning the strength of the queen's forces. She has come from Albanay with a greater power than you seem to suppose. She has six men in the north to every one loyal to your father.'

Edmund fetched from his purse a little scroll of vellum that looked as if it had been wound tight around someone's finger then angrily crumpled. On it, Will read a message that accused the duke of cowardice and dared him to do battle.

'You see? . . . arrows are found each morning . . . all over the keep . . . my father has them collected . . . and burned.'

'Love letters from Queen Mag,' Gwydion said with heavy sarcasm.

When Will asked after the whereabouts of Edward, Edmund confirmed that he had gone to the Marches to raise men. And it seemed that his young brothers Richard and George were with him. Of Lord Warrewyk there was equally dispiriting news – he had remained in Trinovant to have the keeping of King Hal.

'Then the Ebor force is split three ways!' Will groaned.

'That is not good,' Lotan said heavily.

'Is some attempt going to be made to free the king?' Willow asked, and Will saw that she was now worried beyond reason for Bethe's sake. 'Will, if there should be bloodletting in the palace, and if the duchess becomes caught up in it—'

But there was no chance for Will to reassure her, for now the doors flew open and the duke himself appeared. He was white-faced and red-eyed and he seemed suffused with a weird light. His cold anger was awesome to Will.

'I fight for the crown!'

Edmund's whinny was pitiful as he was roughly pushed aside. 'Father . . . please! Those words . . .'

'Were you not all instructed by my seneschal to go from this place?'

'Father . . .'

'Get out, all of you! Go! The dread hour is at hand!'

Then Gwydion spoke with all the power he yet commanded. 'Richard, hear me!'

'No, Crowmaster, you may not speak here!'

But then the magnate collapsed and the weird light fell from him. He sat down on his own step like one suddenly aware of a weight of tragedy that had settled upon him.

When next he spoke, it was with a sigh. 'No, you may not speak here, Master Gwydion, for you will only try to tell me that I must keep this castle and defend it the same until my son comes with his power of Marchermen. I will not be counselled thus, for my fate is upon me and I must meet it in the manner best fitting. If you have loved me as you say, how now would you have me dishonoured? You never saw me hide from mine enemies like a bird included within a cage, for I am a *man*! I have not kept myself behind walls nor hid my face from any man living. Would you that I did so today for dread of a scolding woman? No, my friend, the great number of mine enemies does not appal my spirits, but rather encourages them, for if I am to die then it will be as the rightful king of this Realm dies, and in no other way.'

This time Gwydion did not seek to argue. He bowed deeply and withdrew without demur. Nor was the reason hard to fathom, for no one could negotiate with insanity.

'I'm leading you to it as fast as I can!'

Gwydion halted. 'I would rather you led us away from it, for we can do nothing about the battle now.'

Will gave the wizard a hard look and dragged him onward. 'Nothing? Nothing except to secure it against Maskull and his helper. By all means feel despair, Master Gwydion, but there's no need to give in to it so readily.'

But though he berated the wizard for his faintness, Will did not know himself what he would do once he had found the Awakenfield stone. They could not drain it in time, not with Gwydion so weakened and Will's talisman gone. And, in any case, they dared not disperse more harm into the middle airs for fear it would tip the balance further and send the world hurtling down a steeper slope towards Maskull's new future.

Will called them into a circle. 'We must stay together. We'll get as close to the stone as we dare, then wait while the battle rages all about. We'll make Maskull think twice about approaching the stone, and set upon him when he tries. And afterwards, if we're able, we'll see what the stump can be made to reveal, and maybe even draw a boon from it to help us.'

'What plague waits in store for us this time?' the Wortmaster asked fearfully.

'If we die, then we'll die fighting,' Will told him. 'But if we live, we'll have denied Maskull his desire. If there's one among us who is not fast in this aim, speak now, for we must enter this final fray together. Lotan once told me that he would not, for shame, die in the company of cowards. We have proved, I hope, that we are worthy company for him. Gort, you are a healer, what better place for you than the thick of battle? Willow, my best beloved, if I am as dear to you as you are to me then know that this matter is my life's burden: it is grained deep in me like the veins that are in marble. So help me if you can. And you, Master Gwydion, your task has been to guard this little world of ours against all the weaknesses and the failings that come to undermine it. Will you not do your final duty now, in this last battle at the year's end? I ask you: have we the strength to fight?'

Lotan produced a grim smile and drew his sword. 'Let them come!'

'They'll not take an Ogdoad wizard, hey, Master Gwydion?' Gort said. He patted Maglin's ancient staff. 'Not with this on our side to make the difference!'

Willow nodded. 'Yes, and open up that crane bag of yours, Master Gwydion. Let's be having that nasty black bangle you keep in there. I'll take charge of that, in case the chance comes.'

'Good!' Will said, seeing them all take heart. 'Now, Master Gwydion, what say you?'

The wizard's eyes were on Will. 'It is a fine thing that when folk act in concert their efforts do not add up, but rather multiply. Only this do I ask: that first we make haste to spy out the lie of the land so that I may get some better notion of how the battle is to proceed.'

Will agreed, though the wizard's words surprised him. After all that Gwydion had said about firing narwhal arrows into Maskull, he seemed oddly reluctant to come to grips with the sorcerer, and that made him suspect that Willow's part was even more dangerous than he had admitted.

They hurried north to intercept the dark waters of the Caldor and then turned along it a short way. As they approached the deserted town of Awakenfield they heard clarion calls and a distant beat of drums that sounded to Will like a death knell. And when he looked into the east, there was a rising mist, or perhaps a stirring along the marshy banks, then hulking shapes moving through the grey.

'Duke Richard's army will be caught like fish in a net here,' Gort said.

'He'll be a deer in a buckstall,' Lotan agreed.

Will nodded, realizing now that the Awakenfield stone could not be in the town, but must lie in the fields between the river and the castle. To find it he would just have to walk the lign itself and chance to his protections.

A rolling thunder began to reverberate from the woods, and Will saw with alarm just how close the queen's forces had already come, for riders were hidden back there.

'The stone is the other way!' Will cried. And they were relieved, for they saw that to have gone further would have taken them into the midst of the Duke of Mells' cavalry.

It was not long before he pointed to a place in a long meadow where it seemed that a giant molehill was being thrown up.

'It's unburying itself!' he said, flinging his arms wide to stop them. 'Quickly! To the trees!'

They took cover in a little brake of birches nearby, and there, as they watched, a grey tooth that was as big as a man thrust up through the turf. It cast a ghastly glow all around, and the air began to turn and twist above it so that it seemed to draw down the leaden clouds above.

Then Willow stiffened, seeing something that captured her whole attention. 'Will, look! Oh!'

'Willow!'

She began to run forward and Will dashed after her. He threw his arm around her waist and brought her down just ten paces short of the stone. And then he saw what she had seen.

'She's here!' Willow said, scrambling to her feet.

It was Bethe, standing by the stone, her little face anxious, holding out her arms as she did when she wanted to be lifted up.

'No!' Will yelled, grappling with Willow. 'It's not her!'

But the semblance cried for its mother and Willow struggled madly to be near her.

'Let me go! Let me *go!*'

'It's the stone!'

And then Gwydion was with them and his staff was thrust towards the apparition and cunning words were in his mouth.

'Begone!' he cried, and there was a flash of blue light. Painful to the eye it was, bright as a lightning stroke, and Will shielded his face from it. But when he looked again, there, stepping out from behind the stone, was a beautiful woman. Her hair was red-gold, she was as slender as a weasel, and dressed in raiment that marked her as one who had lived in an Age that was long dead. She reached out to Gwydion as if to beg his help.

The staff fell from the wizard's grasp and he whispered, 'Gwendolen?'

And Will saw that although Gwydion must have known the semblance for what it was, still he went towards it, for he was captivated by the power of the stone and unable to do otherwise.

This time it was Gort who launched himself upon the wizard and smothered him to the ground. Will picked up the discarded staff and danced out a spell that gushed clouds at the apparition and engulfed it thickly, snuffing out the vision.

They drew back to the brake and held the wizard until he came to his senses. Will hastily stepped out a spell of protection upon the trees, that they might go unregarded by all who would otherwise have seen them. He could feel the magic trailing eerily from his fingertips, the flux being dragged from him by the close presence of the battlestone. He danced out augmenting spells, enveloping their hide with stronger words of concealment and magic that bent straight lines of sight around them. When the spells settled a darkness came upon them and Will knew that he had succeeded in cloaking them.

By now the whirlwind had begun to descend from above, and was already tearing at their clothes. Will stood on the forward edge of the protected area. The very air here tried to drive him back. He wanted to approach the stone, and forced his way against the blast with outstretched arms. But it was useless. He was blinded by hail that drove into his face.

He tried to rally, to attack the stone directly, but with Willow so near he could not press forward for fear that she would try to help him.

'It's no use!' Lotan cried.

'I must try!'

Gort grabbed his arm. 'If it's Chlu and Maskull who're worrying you, I think neither will dare to jeopardize himself out there today!'

And it was clearly so.

The advice shook Will's resolve and he wavered. Almost immediately the sky began to swirl with bruises – yellows and reds and purples. It seemed like a bloody overcast, underlit by an inferno blazing unseen in a pit. Then the ground began to shake with giant footfalls, and he saw moving through the mists the heavy heads of trolls. They were not giants such as Magog and Gogmagog, but half-wild hill dwellers who stood head and shoulders above ordinary men.

Crests of russet hair flowed from their heads, and many wore bracken-red beards. Their gross-featured faces were tattooed blue in terrifying war masks, for it was their habit to raid incessantly. Usually they held to their own fastnesses in the mountains and fought among themselves, or troubled remote castles upon the moors of Umberland where they came to steal sheep and cattle, but when times were hard they could range all down the mountainous spine of the north in worrisome numbers. And now they were in thrall to a terrible power.

Will saw that their presence explained the sounds of rolling thunder, for when warring upon men they wielded knobbed maces, and made a fearsome din by slamming them against their shields, which were as big as cottage doors.

The company stood fast in their little hide. Will watched grimly as the battle erupted. To the north he saw the colours of the men who led the queen's battalions. In red and gold, and on his high horse was the Hogshead. Helmless he was, and in high dudgeon, wholly transformed at last from the neck up into a great, tusked boar, with no lingering trace of humanity about him. His foaming snout gurgled orders, while all those around him did his bidding. His red-clad levies rushed on with billhooks and poleaxes, ready to encircle their enemy, confident they had the numbers and enough advantage to carry the day.

When Will looked to the east he saw the blue and white of the Duke of Mells' footmen teeming forward in vast numbers from the woods. Most of them waved axes and pole-arms, but many were carrying arquebuses, weapons that allowed sorcerer's powder to be burned inside a small cannon and a volley of stones to be shot out into the ranks of the foe. Emerging along with Duke Henry's colours were a forest of others now, those of the northern lords, like Duke Pierce of Umber with his stiff-tailed lion on a field of black and red, and the red and white banner of Duke Richard's son-in-law, Lord Exmoor. And then Will saw with dismay the flags of Jasper of Pendrake and his father, Owain, staunch supporters of King Hal, for reasons of blood.

Will decided he must go forward alone and engage the stone as best he could. It was a plan as suicidal as Duke Richard's, but he knew he must try. Before he could shake off his friends' restraining hands however, the wet ground trembled again. Will turned to see a great piebald charger whinny and rear. Astride it, red-armoured and shimmering

with crimson silk, sat Mad Clifton. Will had not clapped eyes
upon him since the day at Delamprey when the battlestone
had filled him with foolhardy passions and he had sent out
a thunderbolt to unseat the insane lord. Will had brought
down Clifton's airborne steed that day, and the wyvern had
snapped its neck in the fall, but the Mad Baron had lived to
fight again. Here he was now, implacable, drooling for blood,
and hardly able to wait until his enemy's head was properly
in the noose.

Will swore, seeing that he had lost his last chance, for
even with all the magic that remained to him he could not
appear before Clifton's bloodthirsty legion and hope to
reach the stone alive.

Then all hope vanished, for Duke Richard was already
leading his bodyguard from the South Gate of the castle
and his army was wheeling around to meet the threat that
was bearing down upon them. There would be no victory
here for the duke. Even so, he harried his men on, impetu-
ously leading the charge deep into the enemy. And they,
loyal and faithful as the best men are, followed him towards
the jaws that would gobble them up.

The bangs of arquebuses peppered the air with noise.
Sorcerer's powder gave its distinctive taint to the air. Will
saw the blue and yellow Morte banners and the green eagle
of Sarum flanking the duke's own standard. He saw the
Lord Harringdon and his son spurring their chargers on,
and Sarum's second son, Thomas of Norvale, raising up
his sword. And there, visor closed, and wholly encased in
shining armour came . . .

'Edward!'

'He has come!' Gort cried. 'Edward is here!'

'Then there is hope after all,' Lotan growled.

But the spiralling clouds drew themselves tighter around
the battlestone, and snuffed the hope from his words, for
when Will looked again he saw that he had misread the

azure and murrey colours of the banner. This was not the white lion of the Earl of the Marches, but the peacock badge of the Earl of Rutteland. It was brave Edmund who was leading forward the thousand men of his father's rear guard.

The clash when it came was fierce and fearsome. Duke Richard thrust deep into the ranks of the enemy. A wedge of men fighting around him and his standard bearer rode down the enemy ranks. They set about themselves with sword and mace, contending furiously to reach the person of the Duke of Mells. But, just as it seemed the heroic drive would succeed, the man-trap was sprung.

Richard of Ebor's army was caught riding hard down the throat of a monster. From right and left the flank attack came, so that now three armies were bearing down upon one. A wall of Albanay hill-men with their curved blades and round, iron-studded shields shattered the mounted attack. Blue-faced ogres threw down riders and tore saddles from horses. The force that drove the spearhead faltered, and soon the Ebor army was severed in the middle. The forward guard in which the duke fought was surrounded and steadily cut to pieces, while the rear guard was halted before a troll shield-wall.

'They're breaking,' Lotan said as he watched them turn and be put to rout.

Will watched bitterly as Edmund's efforts to rally his men failed. He could not reach his father, but saw him dragged down from his horse by a great tattooed hand to vanish among a morass of wild-men.

'Run for your life!' Will shouted, though he knew Edmund could not hear him. He started forward, his reason now cast to the winds, wanting only to help Edmund get away. But Lotan seized him.

At last, Edmund's bodyguard succeeded in extricating him. They turned his steed's head and sent it galloping away from the enemy. Tears were in Will's eyes, for a dreadful slaughter was being visited upon those among whom he had grown up. Those who had been surrounded fought valiantly but died violently. Duke Richard's colours were snatched down and the shout went up that the duke was dead.

Will knew it beyond question. He stared and stared, hearing only the death rattle of the house of Ebor. It filled his head and left him incapable of feeling anything except horror.

Down on the field the battlestone was still fulminating, gouting black fumes of harm into the air. But the rush and swirl above it was already breaking up, and Will knew that it had almost emptied itself of harm.

After all they had come here to do, neither Maskull nor Chlu had deigned to show themselves. Why not? he wondered. Had they foreseen the trap that lay in wait for them? Or had they *known*?

'Was I right to have brought us here?' he asked the wizard. 'Should we have stayed in plain sight, and behaved as if there was nothing we could do but watch?'

The wizard could find no words of comfort in his heart for Will. From their unregarded little thicket the company looked out like mariners upon a tempest ocean. Men were streaming away from the fight now. The duke's followers had thrown down their weapons and were dashing for their lives. Horses were galloping past as armoured men threw off helm and gauntlet, undoing the straps of their gear as fast as they could, both to unburden themselves and to strew in their wake valuable booty that their pursuers might prefer over murder.

A war standard was thrown down from such a rider, its peacock colours trampled in the mud. Suddenly, a running man burst through the magic that hid them. He fell amazed in their midst like a fish that has leapt into a boat. He gasped and struggled in panic, no doubt thinking himself slain. But then terror seized him and he threw himself to his feet, and he was off in a flash, and running again.

Will smelled the stench of fear on the man, and saw that the concealing spell must already have begun to lose its virtue.

'To the stone!' he yelled, gathering them.

This time Lotan did not try to stop him, but rather followed, and once he moved so did the others. The air was still glittering with motes of pain and every lungful of air tasted foul and prickled the skin with vileness. But the lorc had had its day and the onrush of malice was already lifting into the upper airs.

They gathered at the stump, eyes and teeth aching, just as the last sigh came. It stood, tilted and steaming and withered, and Will thought the last dregs of malice that left it made it seem triumphant and self-satisfied, a rock of adamant in the eye of a dying storm.

CHAPTER SEVENTEEN

MUCKLE GATE

It was a ghastly afternoon. Will stood for what seemed like an age as the queen's horde scattered from the field in pursuit of their vanquished foe. Then he watched Gort and Gwydion circling the stump, impatient to know the verse that it would yield. Willow, with a hastily gathered knife, and Lotan, with his broadsword, looked out for their backs, but the fury of battle had already ebbed.

In the end Will left them all to the stone. He staggered forward unseen, wandering a hundred paces then clambering over a barrier of dead horses and men. He found the place where the bloodletting had been at its greatest. Here the dead lay thickly in an unimaginable litter. The fallen had already been deprived of their costliest possessions – weapons and armour were the prizes, rings and purses, shoes and saddles, lordly treasure left for the taking. A few tardy looters were fighting one another like carrion dogs among the bodies, looking now for lesser gains. They were stripping the dead of their last shreds of modesty, tearing off arming jackets, silken shirts and underlinen, leaving the bloodied corpses to lie naked in the mud.

Those who saw Will snarled at him and pulled back as he passed among them. Perhaps it was shame that made them draw away, for he went unarmed, but there was something about his demeanour that gave them pause. They could see he was not here to do what they were doing. Will paid the scavengers no heed, for his heart was leaden with woe. The death prophecy that had sat upon the head of Duke Richard had now been fulfilled in terrible fashion. In the end it had come to this, despite everything they had tried to do to avert it.

But Will found no sign of the duke's body. He stumbled among the carnage, turning the naked corpses over one by one. There were too many he recognized – Sir John Morte, who had taught him the soldier's art, and who now lay dead because of it. And near the son lay the father – Sir Hugh, who had tried to turn them back from the castle gate. His Bulldog face was no less fierce in death, and Will saw with horror the open wounds that showed he had gone down fighting to the last, trying, it seemed, to reach his slain son.

Will searched silently, breathing the intimate stench of death, numbed by the odiousness of the task. All around him lay ogre-bitten bodies, some headless, others crushed. Here were a dozen more faces known to him, men remembered from Foderingham, Ludford and Trinovant. Over there, trapped under a dead horse and likely one of the last to die, was Thomas, Lord Norvale, the Earl of Warrewyk's brother, and there were others he knew but could not name. Men lay blood-splashed and carelessly entangled with one another, men of high station and low, equal now in death. Yet of the duke's body there was still no sign.

A strange kind of hope sprang up in Will's heart. He wondered if he should pay it heed, for what use was hope that was not listened to?

The truth was simple: there was not much value in butcher's meat. Yet a wounded lord, captured and borne away – such a prize would be worth a lot, for any duchess or countess would surely be prepared to pay a king's ransom to see her beloved again . . .

Battle shock beat through Will as he staggered out of the bloody maze. Neither the duke nor the Earl Sarum had been there, he was sure, and that added weight to his hopes.

He shook his head in an attempt to clear it of the ringing that muted his thoughts. He hoped and trusted that Willow would be safe with Gwydion, but hope and trust were quantities easily twisted by the lorc, and the nearness of the stump would send his feelings awry. He must not forget that.

After a while he was drawn back to the battlestone. His state of mind was dream-like now and the stone's appeal overwhelming. He imagined he would meet the others there, but a fog of unreason blinded him as he approached. It tried to make him uninterested. It invited him to sit down and rest and put his cares aside, but he stayed on his feet and so saw the truth at last. Of course the others were not there. They had retired to some safer remove once the verse had been coaxed from the stump. The pain had reached a climax in Will's head. The worst was over and, as the mists cleared and his mind began to settle, the shape of the battle emerged from fragments of memory.

If the lorc had been working to confuse the duke, it must have been directing the queen's commanders with lucid clarity. Her host had seemed like a vast and unruly mass of men, an army studded here and there with lumbering half-giants which had been partly tamed by Maskull. These creatures had been tempted south to be the queen's hammer, but the laying of so complete an ambush had the stamp of a sorcerer's intervention about it.

Will decided that must have been the reason why Maskull had not come to tap the battlestone. Then he asked himself what would happen when Maskull's power over the queen's forces wore thin, as it surely must now.

The lorc's influence would have bent and buckled what remained of the sorcerer's magic. And now that the lorc was weakening, what corrupted spells were guiding the horde? Where would the magic send them now? What would they do?

The likely answers gave Will little comfort, for ogres were dangerous beasts – dour, lumbering creatures whose only interest ordinarily was to spit and roast stolen mutton up on the moors. That they had had their simple hearts twisted to an unnatural desire for booty did not bode well for the land hereabouts. Would the army withdraw now to Ebor to enjoy its ill-gotten gains, or was there fresher meat at hand?

Will found himself hugging the stone. He wiped the sweat from his face, wondering in particular now about the madness that had sent Duke Richard sallying forth from the Castle of Sundials. To his warrior's eye, the enemy troops must have seemed like a rabble who were breaking every rule of military discipline, a mob that could easily be routed. Nettled into rage and suspicion, and taunted by Queen Mag's enchanted challenges, Richard had refused Gwydion's advice. He had ridden out by the South Gate, swinging his thrice-outnumbered army around to meet what he saw as a morass of farmers and fieldsmen. But other forces had come from the woods and driven down into the open space between castle and town. Duke Henry of Mells, Baron Clifton and Lord Strange had each sent a column cutting into the fray like a spearhead. And the most fearsome of these warriors had been Lord Strange, who sat tall upon his charger, laying about him furiously with a six-flanged mace.

Now, as Will cast about, he saw Gwydion, and, sitting among the dead, one of the great man-like trolls, a trickle of blood drooling from its thick lips. Taller by half a head than Gwydion it was, though it sat on its haunches, groaning like thunder. But still the wizard attended it in the same way he attended any other self-knowing creature, calming and curing, tenderly teasing arrowheads from its flesh. It seemed to Will that all the wizard's old strength and power had returned . . .

'Let's go! They're coming!'

Will turned to see Lotan, out of breath, hulking and grim-faced, bare steel in hand.

'Willand! There are trolls and wild-men hunting down all who have no spell of protection upon them. Come with me!'

'Did Gwydion send you?' he asked dreamily.

'Stop hiding behind that damned stone! It feels good, but it will not help you stay alive.'

Will would not be persuaded, and even when the big man pulled at his arm, he resisted until roughly dragged away. But Lotan was right: he *was* drawing false comfort from the remnant of the battlestone. And now as he looked again he saw that the dying ogre was indeed alone, and no one had bothered with its sufferings.

'Give me a moment,' he said, shaking off the kindly visions.

'We don't have one to spare,' Lotan growled. 'Trust me. I know about these things!'

Will checked himself, then he began to follow Lotan towards the river. Now that he was beyond the stump, fears for Willow bubbled up inside him. In a shambles like this there was no easy way to tell friend from foe, and it mattered little to men whose main concern was to find, then hold onto, the rain of riches that battle had scattered among them. Will was fortunate, for those who saw Lotan showed little desire to contest the sword from his hand. The big man picked up a tabard of russet red that looked much like the faded livery of one of Lord Strange's men, and threw it at Will.

'Put it over you.'

Will and Lotan joined the great flood of men that were pouring northward like a tributary gift sent from the bloody battlefield to the River Caldor. Men streamed towards the little town of Awakenfield, leaving others to take apart the Castle of Sundials, which was an altogether harder nut to crack. The defenceless town lay like a bound hostage, its people helpless now. There was no longer any reason to keep them cowed with promises of safety, so doubtless Maskull had unleashed his dogs upon them by way of payment.

'Take what you will!' was the cry from the parapet as they came to the bridge. 'Have you not earned it this day?'

And there the brazen sorcerer stood, high upon the stone lip of the bridge's main arch. Maskull held only his staff, a glittering rod of iron, careless of the danger, yet secure as a crow on a roof ridge. His beetle-black eyes had not alighted on Will, for triumph was upon him. Now he was exhorting those who had won the fight to set about still fouler work.

'Use the people! Wring them dry then burn their hovels! Did I not promise you a great victory?'

Will felt the compelling rapture infect those who heard it. He himself was caught among that same press of men, running across the bridge into the town. But something made him stop before he reached the end of the bridge, for there he saw another fearsome and familiar figure: Mad Clifton, unmissable in his wyvern-hide armour, sword in hand and aroused to an immense passion.

There at his feet, imploring mercy on bended knees, was the cause of his vengeful ecstasy – Tutor Aspall.

Will's old teacher from Foderingham was older and greyer now, but unmistakable. Will staggered at the sight of him, white-faced and pleading on another man's behalf.

'Mercy!' Tutor Aspall begged. 'Please save him, for he is a duke's son and worth your while! If you must kill, then take me in his stead, for he is but a young man!'

Yet the scholar's well-meant words proved to be a death sentence. A long knife was put at the tutor's throat, and a gleeful shout rang out from Mad Clifton.

Then the other man, until now bent down in the mud, leapt up and threw off his cloak. He dived awkwardly at the dagger blade and wrestled for it.

'Edmund, Earl of Rutteland!' the madman exulted. 'What a prize!'

'No!' Will cried, throwing out his hands and kindling green fire there.

But it was too late and too little. Will's feeble spell-cast burst into splinters against resilient wyvern skin as Clifton bent to slit the strings of the learned man's neck.

Edmund's second lunge saved his tutor's life and the latter fell back, but with a grasping fist Mad Clifton lifted up the unarmed youth and shook him like a rat, saying, 'By God's blood, your father slew mine, and so I will do to you and all your kin!'

Then he stuck the young earl to the heart, deep as his dagger would go, and bade Tutor Aspall bear the earl's mother and brother word of what he had done.

Will felt sympathetic pain lance into his chest as brave Edmund lay frothing blood. There had been no time for Will to act, and the next moment rooted him absolutely, for a purple fire broke over them all, scattering men from the bridge in screaming panic.

The core of the flame searched Will out. It roared and scorched, searing skin and infusing whatever flesh it touched with agony. But the wavering brightness had smitten a knot of men who happened to come between Will and his persecutor. They took the worst of the fire and fell as cinders or ran, hair and coats flaming.

The noisome stench of burning flesh rose up. Will had known that his desperate spell-cast would draw Maskull's eye. He now realized that it had drained him utterly and he must suffer the afterclap as the magic burst back on him. He threw himself down and hugged the road, desperate to draw earth power. But he was on the bed of a bridge and no renewal was possible. He felt the sorcerer's eye mark Lotan and then fall upon him. The purple blast came again, this time well-directed and shaped to kill. But in that moment while Will lay on the ground searching for his last reserves of strength, a perfect peace descended over his mind and he was able to pull together all the unmade strands of his talent and bind them into a whole that was more than its parts.

A green glow sprang out and enveloped him like a beetle's carapace. It batted Maskull's deadly fire aside. Then Lotan roared, charged the bridge parapet like a berserker, and his sword melted as he hewed deeper and deeper into that spewing flame. Sparks fountained from the grinding contact.

It seemed that the fierce fire must soon be turned on the source of such foolhardy daring. But the purple played single-mindedly on Will as he continued desperately to shield himself inside his shell. So it was that Maskull's fixed hatred became his undoing, for though he would not change his plan for a mere swordsman, that swordsman was now so close that he was able to fling a red-hot hilt into the sorcerer's face.

Lotan threw the iron cross with all his might, and with a mercenary soldier's aim. Abruptly, the stream of flame burning down on Will's back broke off. Maskull was caught unprepared, was forced to lift his elbow to fend away the smoking steel. He began to fall and had to twist in order to right himself. He stepped lithely to keep his balance on the narrow stone ledge, and it was then that Will's tardy green bolt struck his knee and lit him up purple and gold. He threw his arms wide, leapt like a tumbler then disappeared, leaving behind only a billow of black smoke.

Will could hardly believe his success.

'You hit him!' Lotan shouted.

'I couldn't have. Not Maskull.'

He reached the parapet at Lotan's side and they both looked over and down into the clear, cold waters of the Caldor.

Smooth brown boulders showed under the rippling flow, but no Maskull.

'Where is he?' Lotan demanded, astonished.

'Vanished . . .'

But there was no time to think the situation through. A crowd of soldiers was pressing towards the southern end of the bridge and Will knew their spell-born urge to cross into the town would be irresistible. Lotan took up a broken poleaxe while Will went to Tutor Aspall who cried out for fear of his life, not knowing who was upon him now.

'Up!' Will shouted, stern-faced and furious. 'Run for your life! You cannot help him now.'

'I . . .'

'Leave the body and do as you're bid! Carry the news of Edmund's death to those who most need to know of it.'

The tutor's short-sighted eyes opened wide and he was caught in two minds, though he shook with fear.

'*Sir . . . who are you?*'

Will gave no answer but thrust the worthy onward, as he knew he must, to save his life. Lotan followed fast, his warrior's brain convinced now of the better part of valour as the queen's army once more began to pour across the bridge in unstoppable numbers.

So it was that the poor yeomen of Awakenfield bore the brunt of Maskull's plan that night. Their doors were burst open and their thatches broken in by wart-faced monsters. Their houses were set alight with them inside, and they died in their hundreds like dogs, seeing all that they had ever owned or loved carried away, for such is the curse of war upon any land.

And while such horror was unfolding in the dusk of the day, Will went out by back ways towards the town midden, and there he shoved the bewildered tutor into a thicket of holly bushes that lay a little way beyond. He stepped a spell out, saying afterwards, 'Stay here, Robert Aspall, till the dark be truly down. Then go by the light of the moon, south, south and south again! Do you hear me?'

Tutor Aspall sank to his knees, terrified by the shadow of Lotan's poleaxe, but more by the wonder-working stranger. He gabbled like a madman. 'I shall do as you say, kind sir. Nor shall you want for reward once report is made of this deed that you have done. Only give me your name so that I may remember you by it.'

Will answered grimly with a rede. 'My name is not important. If it was a kindness I have done, then that is reward in itself. Take news of that bloodsupper's doings as you have promised. Do not fail me in this!'

Then the tutor peered more closely and was amazed.

'*Willand?* Can it be you?'

But they left him without reply or further farewell, and though Will needed to draw fresh strength from the earth, even that need was set aside in their urgency. They went to the north-east, following the flow. Will was already feeling hale and clear-headed. His mind was again turning over the fate of the duke, but the way to find him if he was alive remained unclear. If that was their aim, Lotan said, then they must try to discover what fruits might be found dangling from the grapevine.

In the event, there was a surfeit of rumour to be had from the looters of Awakenfield. Lotan's demands were met with eager but uncertain answers. Some men swore upon their souls that they had seen the duke die on the battle-field. More than one said that a great lord had been taken and was now on his way to Castle Pomfret. A few of them said that an earl had been caught and beheaded by the common soldiery for his crimes.

Whatever the truth of it, Lotan waylaid a number of men and established on pain of death that throughout the battle the queen had kept to the city of Ebor, and that seemed to be the place to which her entire army was repairing.

'What shall we do?' he asked.

'Go there,' Will told him. 'What else?'

A look of concern pained Lotan's features. 'Not to Pomfret, then?'

'Not unless the queen has gone there. If Duke Richard has been taken, she'll want him brought before her. Don't you think?'

The big man continued to look unhappy. 'What about the others?'

'They'll know where to find us.'

'Will they? How?'

Will seemed to ignore the question. 'Maskull's vanishing trick must have taken him back to the place where he set up the spell. I don't know what the trigger was, but my guess is that he made that precaution in the days before the battle in case things went awry for him. That would most likely have been done with the queen's safety in mind. I think he's in Ebor with her now.'

'Slow down. Who's in Ebor? Do you mean Gwydion?'

'No, no – Maskull.' Will realized he would have to explain. 'Look – Queen Mag plays a most important part in Maskull's plan. That's probably why the queen was told to wait seven leagues away in Ebor. So that, if her forces suffered defeat, she could still be ridden off to safety.'

'But they didn't suffer defeat.'

'In the event, no.'

Lotan rumbled, 'I think I see what you're saying, but it doesn't answer my question.'

'Which was?'

'How will the others know to find us in Ebor?'

'Well, obviously Gwydion will go to Ebor because he'll realize that Maskull is there.'

'Obviously.'

'I know him well enough, and he knows me. He'll know how to find us and he'll take care of Willow.'

'Hmmm. The way of wizards is strange. I hope you're right.'

'Don't worry.'

And so they set out upon the journey in the early Ewletide dusk. Though he had never had the good fortune to visit Ebor, Will knew that it was the greatest city of the north. Gwydion had spoken of its long and bloody history, saying that its formidable walls had been built and rebuilt a dozen times. They had first risen up at the command of the Slavers, and the city's many-sided towers had once been a famous sight. Since then, two castles had been built there, one on each side of the River Ouzel, near to where it joined with the River Fosse. A king of old had ordered the Fosse dammed as a defence, and Gwydion said there was a lake there full of fish that made good eating for those who dared to poach them from the Sightless Ones. There was a very large chapter house in Ebor, but all in all, it was the queen of cities, and known as such far and wide. How sad, then, that it must now play host to a real queen, and one so deadly.

Mag's human plague, having ravaged Awakenfield, was now being drawn away from the battlefield by a power greater than either drunkenness or exhaustion. It would soon fall upon Ebor. As Will and Lotan travelled along moonlit lanes the air was dry and still. The cold intensified as the moon rose higher. That silvery disc stared down on Will like a dead man's eye.

Twenty thousand soldiers were making their way north,

some walking in disciplined formations, others in ragged bands, still more raking the countryside in ones and twos, but all would eventually meet the Great North Road.

Will felt for the lign. There were glimmerings in his feet, but nothing like the spirit-destroying power he had felt in the days before the battle. It was the lorc's usual torpor, having just spent its malice on the battle. Will longed to repair to a grassy meadow and plant his feet in the ice-cold dew, to drink a draught of earthly powers, but he could not risk revealing himself, so once more refreshment would have to wait.

As they went on they saw baggage waggons clogging the way at every bridge. Thousands were coming back together into one mindless army. Will was pleased he had taken Lotan's advice and put on the livery of the Hogshead. To be taken for a member of one of the most feared companies in the queen's array gave a measure of protection. But it was not Lord Strange and his men who played most on Will's mind that night; it was Mad Clifton.

Edmund's murder had shocked Will more than he had allowed. Now he felt a gush of guilt that he had not been quicker upon the scene. Nor did it help when Lotan asked how he could have known. A burn of wicked desire stirred at his core as he walked. He pictured in his mind the thrusting of an obliterating bolt through the body of the bloodsupper. He imagined doing him to death with his own hands. And how great was the effort Will had to apply to blot out that pleasurable phantasm. He succeeded, at last, in bringing the savagery in him to heel, and told himself strictly that for a lawmaker to kill a man for murder was a paradox and so against all the laws of magic.

I would for choice burn him down like a scarecrow, but the consequences would in the end outweigh the justice of the case, he told himself, feeling almost at first hand how revenge piled upon revenge in the hearts of wronged men.

And while they walked Lotan felt his pain and said, 'The red knight is no soldier but a tyrant, for the lion is wont to be a furious and unreasonable beast, cruel to them that withstand it. He is no soldier, and unworthy prey for such as you.'

'He is mad, and known to be mad,' Will said shortly. 'And it is all the lorc's doing. What blight the Dragon Stone began was finished up at Awakenfield. Such was Edmund of Rutteland's unhappy lot.'

My third upon a bridge lies dead . . .

Lotan said, 'And it's not finished yet. I can feel it in my bones.'

'Your bones tell true, I think.'

They forded the River Hare at Woodle then joined the Slaver ridge road that ran due north through the ancient kingdom of Elmet. All the way Will was increasingly aware of the birch lign that passed through Awakenfield, and how it seemed to provide a pointer to the tramping army that pushed north and east more or less in company with it. They crossed the lign not long after passing through the ruined hamlet of Bywater, and its influence faded, but after Bramham Cross, where they turned east, they crossed the strong-running power of an entirely different lign.

'Celin!' Will said, stopping dead at the first appearance of it.

'Trouble?' Lotan asked. The sheared-off poleaxe still in his hand rose up.

'No, it's the holly lign.' He looked back over his shoulder.

'So?'

'I was expecting . . .'

'What?'

'I'm getting ahead of myself again.' He faced Lotan squarely. 'I expected the ligns to cross at Ebor, but they cross somewhere else.'

'Do you mean there's another stone where they cross?'

'Yes.' He put out his arms, measuring the angle, then pointing. 'It's that way. Almost due south of us. A couple of leagues, maybe more.'

'And the power's flowing there now?'

'Not as strongly as before. Not a ninth, nor yet a thirteenth, of the power.' He orientated himself and felt for the flows in the earth, scrying towards the south for the magnitude of the stone. 'I might be wrong, but that one seems big. I'd say it was a battlestone as potent as the Dragon Stone or the one that caused the fight at Delamprey.'

Ghostly soldiers flowed past them, their eyes candid with questions as to what he was doing.

'Come,' Lotan whispered. 'Don't spook them. You're one of them now, remember.'

After that they bridged the River Worffe at the little town of Tadpole, and then they crossed the birch lign again. Will's hopes guttered as he dared to consider the face-by-face reading of the Dragon Stone verse that he had read so long ago.

> *King and Queen with Dragon Stone.*
> *Bewitched by the moon, in darkness alone.*
> *In northern field shall wake no more.*
> *Son and father, killed by war.*

Whatever it meant, it seemed eerily apt tonight. And if the Dragon Stone had told true, then there was no hope for Duke Richard.

Now that the heat of the battle had truly cooled in the wash of moonlight, Will could see the day in its full awfulness. So many men he had known and liked were dead of the violence. Thousands had perished. What exact numbers might be placed on the disaster hardly seemed to matter, for the arithmetic of death was a strange count that did not keep the usual proportions. When the heralds reported 'a thousand dead' they hardly described the thousand private tragedies of which they spoke, every death being total to the man concerned and to those who loved him. But what was beyond doubt was that many more men had died today than in any previous fight, and their sum surely betokened further grief.

Distant figures, hooded and walking in lines, caught Will's eye. They were moving against the northward flow. Red hands, thousands of them, stirring from their chapter houses. Every Fellow for three leagues around would be aroused by the whiff of blood. They formed blind, caterpillar queues, preparing to make their pilgrimage to the sleepless field. Over the next week they would gather together what could be found of the local people and oversee the digging of grave pits.

Will felt fatigue growing in his limbs, but there was a greater need oppressing him. He dared to tune his mind to listen out for Chlu and found a shocking presence. Not close, but too furious to tolerate for long, and he quickly closed his mind again. Whatever was happening with Chlu, he was not in a mood of prudence or moderation. Judging from the ache Will felt inside his skull, his twin had directed a seemingly endless supply of malice throughout the battle, spending spells like a drunk spends silver. He had been part of the rout, riding down hapless men for sport as a hunter pursues wild boar, and now his mind was fixed on a more vital quarry. Why he and Maskull had not come to the Awakenfield stone and fallen neatly into their trap was impossible to say. Will's earlier speculations seemed insufficient now – that Maskull had had his hands full with the fight. Could it be that his trials with fae magic were now complete, that he had no further use for the stones or the harm they contained? Was the greater fight already over, and the deed done? Had Maskull already made the checkmating move?

These questions and others vexed Will's mind mightily as the army fell back upon the city. Will was amazed to see that tall bonfires had been heaped up and fired at the news of the queen's victory. The road that led from the south into the Muckle Gate was lined with blazing cressets. The gate itself was formed of two round towers with an arched entry between and a wooden balcony set above from which prestigious visitors could be showered with white rose petals as they halted to ask permission of the City Father to enter.

No such welcome met the unwanted army that now poured into the city. Red shadows blazed across the white walls, and the chanting of troops resounded from Lord Clifton's tower. The curfew bells of the Great Chapter House tolled midnight as Will passed beneath the portcullis fangs of Muckle Gate. The streets were packed with men, drunk now and revelling. The light of a thousand candles blazed from the ancient hall where the Elrondyng, the council of Ebor, usually met. The City Father and his aldermen had had no choice but to open the city to admit the queen, for there were many already within who would have thrown wide the gates for her. Now the city worthies were sitting in dutiful celebration of the victory, fearing for what the night would bring by way of fire and sword to their fortunes. But the sight that made Will's heart sink the furthest was that of the crowd trying to enter the castle.

Will urged Lotan to clear a way, and the big man cut a path to the castle gate. Normally the bailey was barred to all except those who had business with the king's steward. Tonight it was packed tight, so that even knights of middling rank who had arrived late found it difficult to reach the Great Hall. Lotan shouldered his way through like a giant mole and Will followed as if he held higher authority.

He did not dare apply magic here. The taint of Maskull's corruption grew in Will's nostrils as he entered the Great Hall, and he knew he had walked into the gravest jeopardy.

There was the queen, accompanied by her solemn young son and surrounded by the nobles of her party. Tonight she wore crimson velvet trimmed with royal ermine, and her slender figure occupied the High Chair of the city, the one reserved for the sovereign. Not far from her, and all in black, stood Maskull. Will was staggered by the air of expectation about the hall, so thick that it could almost have been sliced and served.

What were they waiting for? His eye danced from person to person. There were many here that he knew – the Hogshead, Lord Exmoor, the Duke of Umberland, even Lord Dudlea and the white-haired Owain of Cambray. Will's blood boiled to see Lord Clifton among them with his smooth-shaved jaw and his insane smile, but where was that prime mover and favourite of the queen, Henry de Bowforde, Duke of Mells? Was not this his greatest hour?

Hot wax spattered down from the candle wheels that hung on chains above, bringing Will back to the moment. Then there were shouts of 'Make way!' and a bodyguard dressed in the blue and white Bowforde livery entered. Will saw the golden portcullis badges glittering on their breasts, saw an aisle open that revealed floor tiles of red and ochre. And down that aisle marched Duke Henry, a fierce expression on his face. He looked to Will like a man damming back a great torrent of feeling, as if this moment was the one that his efforts had been leading him towards for the whole of his life.

Silence descended. Henry walked straight down the aisle and approached the queen to within a sword's length. He carried in his hand a short pike, its top obscured by a sack. It seemed to Will that Henry had conceived some grand surprise for the queen and was about to reveal it. But then Will noticed that a thin red juice ran down the pole and onto Henry's hand, as if a fresh chicken carcass had been spiked there.

And it dawned on him what horror crouched ready to pounce on the scene and devour it.

Henry set the foot of the pike down on the ground, saying, 'Gracious queen, I come tonight bearing gifts.' And he flung off the sack to reveal his first ghastly present. 'Your war is done, my queen! Here is your king's ransom!'

There, atop the pike, was the impaled head of Richard of Ebor.

Will turned away, disgusted by the sight, all his hopes now in ruin. Around him there were shouts of delight and a burst of rejoicing. Will felt like giving out a warning that he who made merry at the death of another today would surely rue it upon the morrow. But he said no such thing, for he knew that if he did it would be Willow who would have to bear the consequences of his bravery.

He knew suddenly that he must get out of the hall or else soon be spotted, for he could not join the celebration nor even seem to. But the gleeful rituals were by no means complete, for now two more heads were brought in on spikes to general approval. The first was the Earl Sarum's, and the other was poor Edmund's.

Then Duke Henry, warming to his grim comedy, produced a paper hat cut in the shape of a crown, and he clapped it on Richard of Ebor's head with much ribaldry, so that the fierce queen and all in the Great Hall laughed to see the mocking respect a 'subject' paid to his 'rightful king'.

'And what shall we say to him who is the other son of this "rightful king"?' Duke Henry asked now turning to the queen's child.

And the six-year-old boy gazed back and announced, as if having been previously schooled to say the line, 'Death to Edward! Off with his head!'

There was laughing applause, which Duke Henry cut off, saying, 'And what shall we do with his head when we have it?'

The prince giggled. 'Stick it on a hook and let the crows pick out its eyes!'

In the uproar of mirthful approval none paid any heed to Will and Lotan as they burrowed their way out of the hall and then out of the castle.

First they sought the darkness of cramped alleys, and Will gnashed his teeth and raged against the cruelty he had witnessed. He knew he must range far into the frozen fields and settle his boiling mind and finally gather his powers. Unless he could do so he would not be able to pledge himself again to peacemaking, for this barbarity had truly struck home with him.

But it was no mean task to get out of the city. The crush of men entering now was twice what it had been, and the gateway was packed tight to the jambs. Again Lotan took the lead and somehow they made their exit to find a great crowd gathered expectantly outside, including many wildmen and trolls who had so far been denied entry into the city. The crackling fires threw an uncertain light up at the gatehouse, and when a roar went up from those around, Will turned to see the queen herself and all her entourage coming out onto the wooden balcony.

The queen stood stern and remorseless. And there too, in his white garb, the queen's son, as innocent as a swan yet already turned to the dread path by those who would see war promoted. And soon the son of the man many thought was the child's true father, the Duke of Mells, came there also, and the Hogshead, and all the others, parading out to stand beneath the place where carpenters had already fixed a bracket with five up-curving hooks on it.

And Will saw the duke's head placed up there, still wreathed in its mocking paper cap, and he recalled the words Richard of Ebor had spoken that very morning: *'I fight for the crown!'* That was what he had said, and how true the sentiment, for now in the end he had got his heart's desire, but not in any way that he would have wanted.

'Now he looks like a king, does he not?' Queen Mag asked, working her oratory upon the crowd. 'Behold the traitor who dared to set his rebel hand upon my Hal's golden throne! The impostor would have sat himself down there in majesty had not so many gallant men denied him. Do you see these five hooks I have ordered to be sharpened? I think Ebor's head should take centre place, flanked to left and right by the traitor, Sarum, and the cripple, Rutteland. We have but three heads to show you this night, but two more shall soon adorn these walls. The far hook awaits the coming of treacherous Warrewyk! And this, above me now, is reserved for the head of Edward of Ebor! He is hereby attainted and made outlaw! Now raise the father up above this town so that Ebor shall overlook Ebor!'

That gloating speech made by the queen was cheered rapturously by the multitude below. As the bonfires blazed higher, trolls and wild-men shouted and stamped, adding their bass voices to the noise. Will looked on, wordless and numb, seeing how vilely the war – and the world – had slumped to a new low. He was sad and sorry, like one of those great, dumb ogres in their midst, who could not understand anything of what passed, but who felt it all keenly.

Will saw that the ogre closest to them was roaring and crying now as competing influences vied inside its slothful brain. Men around it had taken note of its agonies, and they laughed and poked fun at it in a dangerous game, like dogs baiting a bear.

Slow of mind it may be, Will thought, yet it feels both the power of the lorc and Maskull's enchantments, and they are tearing apart what little there is of its rudimentary emotions.

But now, up on the balcony, it was the Duke of Mells' turn to address the soldiery and rouse his men to a new passion, for he told them that their great army would rise up on the morrow and march unstoppably into the south, where all the riches of Trinovant awaited them.

'There lies such bounty as makes this city of Ebor seem like a bare hillside! In Trinovant, treasure is at every hand! Silver apples and golden pears hang down from the trees for the taking! Who among you will come with me to shake those trees and make the treasure fall?'

Whereas the shouts from the crowd had been vengeful when the queen had spoken, now they were shot through with veins of pure greed. Lotan seized Will's shoulder and hissed through gritted teeth, 'His intent to move the army south is something your wizard has to know about. We must find him right away!'

But Will had no time to make a reply, for the nearby ogre, maddened now by its tormenting neighbours, lifted itself suddenly up off its haunches and ran amok, dashing men down as it began to flail its fists.

A space opened up around the commotion, but Will and Lotan stepped bravely forward, the first trying to calm the stricken half-beast, while the second urged the fevered crowd back.

Will raised his hands and began to step dangerously before the enraged creature. For a moment it seemed he would be stamped down, but then it looked as if it had bethought its violence, and though the lone man was now at its mercy it refused its chance to kill and merely swept him aside with an open hand.

Will crashed to the ground, and then keepers and collarmen came, holding up gaudy charms before them. 'Back, Scabbe! Stand down, I say!'

Scabbe did not stand down, but defied them and roared out its anger, but in the end the rebellion petered out, for those amulets were oozing magic that coshed the ogre into submission.

When Will picked himself up and began to dust himself

down worse happened. A not-so-gentle blow fell upon his own head from behind. He sank to his knees, not knowing who had singled him out, or for what reason, but as he knelt he was hit again and this time the blow knocked him cold.

First came the nightmare – pain and bright hues swimming in his head and Chlu riding through the night on a blown horse.

Then, very slowly, he became aware that the resonant sound he could hear was snoring, though he was himself no longer asleep. The pain and the nightmare became real. He found that breathing was hard. Confusion disorientated him. It made no difference, it seemed, if he opened his eyes or not. There was only darkness, a void written over with ghosts of vivid colour like those that came after a heavy blow to the head. And then he began to remember.

The pain swelled as he tried to adjust his position. He realized there was something wrong with his hands which were held up and out somewhere above his head. That was why his chest was stretched, and what made breathing so hard. A surface, hard, damp and gritty, pressed lightly against his back, but when he moved his feet only his heels touched solidity. He was floating in the form of a human letter Y, strung up by his hands against a wall . . .

The sound of laboured breathing was speckled not by the jangle of horse tackle, but by the chittering of rats, and something else – the clink of iron that called a certain person to mind.

'Lotan?' he said.

His voice was dry and weak and went unheeded. He swallowed hard and tried again. This time his call was louder, then the breathing faltered and there was a groan.

'Lotan, is that you?'

He had to repeat the name three times before he got a reply.

'Willand . . . are you hurt?'

'My arms are dead. I can't feel them. I can't move my fingers. How about you?'

'It's either totally dark in here, or I've lost my eyes again.'

Chain rattled and there was the sound of a man sitting up. Will felt Lotan's head against his feet as he recoiled from the contact.

'It's only me.'

'What are you doing up there?'

He would have found the question ripe for retort had not the pain dissuaded him. 'Can you stand up?'

'There's an iron hoop around my neck. And my wrists are bound . . .'

Will heard rusty chains being snapped taut. They sounded sturdy enough to keep a dragonet tethered. 'Sit up and let me rest my feet on your shoulders for a little while.'

Lotan obliged, taking his weight.

'I'm . . . trying to get the blood back into my hands,' Will groaned. He dwelt on advancing the tingling that was the first glimmer of sensation. The pain rose and rose, as torturesome as cramp, but he suffered it in the hope that it would soon reach a peak and begin to fall away. He muttered in the true tongue to help himself through, then when the worst was over he tried to distract his mind with more commonplace words.

'I wonder how long we've been here.'

Lotan's growl was heartfelt. 'I'm more interested in how much longer we'll stay.'

'I know the answer to that.'

'Along with the dungeon master's first name, I hope.'

'There's not a great deal of choice, but I'd rather it was Henry of Mells. I'd prefer him to the queen or Maskull. Wouldn't you?'

'Compared to them even the pig-headed lord would be a welcome host.'

'I know a thing or two about pig-headed lords.' Will tried again to flex his fingers, releasing another torrent of pain. 'Whoever's put us here, we won't have long to wait. My brother . . .'

He stopped himself. Until now he had made no mention of Chlu to Lotan. But now he wondered why he had said nothing before. Perhaps he had been affected by Gwydion's unreasoning suspicion.

Now he explained about Chlu, haltingly but leaving out nothing.

Lotan braced his back more comfortably against the wall. 'So . . . your brother knows you're here, and he's coming to kill you?'

'He's bound to try. My drifting mind saw him on a horse. He's riding here as fast as he can. He was at Awakenfield or somewhere close by when the battle was fought. And if I felt him, then he'll have felt me. He'll know that I'm in pain and confined somewhere in Ebor. There can't be that many dungeons in the city, even a city as big as this.'

'He has a choice of two castles and the guild prison. His guess is as good as ours.' Lotan's words sounded resigned.

'I'm sorry to have got you into this.'

'I'm not worried.'

'You're not?' Will managed an incredulous laugh.

'No. Didn't I tell you? I've always been lucky.'

A great deal of time seemed to pass while they heard no sound other than the squeaking of rats. In the darkness, Will's imagination made a picture of their cell. From the smell he knew the floor was earthen and filthy. From the touch on his back he knew the walls were as thick and damp as only castle foundations could be. And from the way the sounds echoed he knew there were four walls, a barrel-vaulted ceiling and a single door. Beyond that, he surmised, must be a passage and steps and probably another door beyond, for the lack of light was total and they must have been imprisoned for longer than even the longest of winter nights without the least smudge of light reaching them.

Thirst began to afflict Will now. By careful management, the feeling had returned to his hands, though he still suffered much discomfort in hands, arms and chest. Sleep was not possible for either man, and every once in a while Lotan shifted his position, though on the whole he bore the trial of Will's weight with immense patience.

'If your brother really is coming to kill you, I wish he would hurry up,' Lotan said, after another readjustment.

The remark made Will laugh, and the laugh seemed so incongruous in the dank darkness that he found it hard to stop. At last he let out a long sigh, and the gloom settled back on him like crows on a furrowed field.

'I don't know what's keeping Chlu, but whoever's put us here knows who I am. I'm afraid that can only mean we're awaiting Maskull's pleasure.'

'Do you mind explaining to me how you know that?'

'What's the floor made of in here?'

The odd question took Lotan by surprise. 'It's . . . unmade. Hard-packed earth.'

'I thought so. And that's why I've been dangled up here. Once, years ago, I was embraced by the Green Man and I think that changed me so that I could draw power from the earth just as a tree draws what it needs to live. Of all the people here in Ebor only Maskull knows that I have a magical talent and that my capacity to do magic may be thwarted in this way.'

'If you're right then we are both of us done for.'

The matter-of-fact way that Lotan replied made Will smile wryly in the darkness. All along the big man had dismissed his own ordeal with apparent unconcern and Will was grateful for his steady refusal to admit despair. That was an admirable trait, a sign of true courage.

They began to swap tales of many things, of Will's home in the Vale and of Lotan's travelling days. Will spoke of horses and helmets and how to grow green beans and Lotan told of sea-faring in the Far North and drinking ale in a contest to save his life in the mead houses of the Easterlings.

Then Will sang a poem that Gwydion had taught him.

> *'Hearken to this truth I tell you,*
> *Lost, we sailed the stark salt wave.*
>
> *'Dealing days of bitter hardship,*
> *Steering straight, our lives to save.'*

And Lotan joined in.

> *'Strange the seas and mischance many,*
> *So far the fathoms, so deep the swell.*
>
> *'Of frosty, fearsome waters travelled,*
> *No landsman, haven-safe, can tell.*
>
> *'Fast the fogs that gird the Baerberg,*
> *Soon the strand where silver lies.*
>
> *'Looming large the subtle stairway,*
> *Rising rare before our eyes . . .'*

There were many more verses that spoke of a hero's journey to the northernmost edge of the world and his quest to climb a secret stairway and use a golden key to stop the sky spinning and open a door that led into the Brightness beyond.

When the song was over Will ached in the darkness, his blood tingling. He told himself that had he wanted someone to look up to, someone from whom he could learn about what it meant to be a man, and a man worthy of kingship, then there was no one better than Lotan.

But it was too late now. So many of the heroes of Will's youth had been killed or broken. He thought of Sir John Morte, lying dead in the field, of Tutor Aspall, fleeing south in terror. Then there was Duke Richard himself, whose glamour had once touched Will, and of course Gwydion. What would happen to him, now that the magic was leaving in earnest? The process was quickening every day, starting with the leeching away of the little magics of everyday life, then the influences of Wise Women, the wonder-working of loremasters – eventually even the high spells of the Ogdoad would fail, and in the end the power that was the ancient work of the fae.

Suddenly there came sounds from outside that drove all other thoughts from Will's mind. The grinding of old iron bolts and the creak of hinges filled his belly with fear. The moment he had tried to deny had come. He gathered himself to face his tormentor. But when the door was opened a piercing light burst across the room that made him turn his head aside.

Two black shapes moved in the torchlight. A ladder propped against the wall at Will's side and a stocky figure climbed up and leaned across him. Deft fingers began to unscrew the bolts that secured his hands. He groaned at the ache in his chest as he was moved, but then he was lowered to the ground and left to lie there while the shackles on Lotan's neck and wrists were undone.

As soon as Will touched the ground he began to draw surreptitiously upon the power that could be found there.

'I should apologize for the delay,' a sharp voice said, 'but you must understand that I had to wait until the last of the army had left before I came for you.'

Will shielded his eyes from the light of the torch, trying at the same time to identify the dark shape that had spoken.

The voice seemed familiar, but not so familiar that he could place it.

'Where are you taking us?' he croaked.

'To dine with a friend.'

Despite everything, Will felt hope spring alive. 'Who are you?' he asked.

'Do you not recognize me?' the figure said, tilting its head. 'I am John Sefton.'

CHAPTER EIGHTEEN

THE DOOMSTONE OF THE WEST

And so they were released by John Sefton – or Lord Dudlea as Will better knew him. Dudlea had not issued the order to lock them up, or to release them, he said. He was only a go-between.

Dudlea's servant gave them a skin of water. Enough to drink, then more to wash in.

'Trust me,' Dudlea said. 'I haven't forgotten my oath to do the right thing.'

Will grunted. 'If having us thrown in here was the right thing, then I'd hate to see you do wrong.'

'I didn't put you here. That was your friend, and done to protect you. As you'll soon see.'

Lotan growled. 'Have you any idea what it's been like sitting in this stinking hole?'

'What better place than here to keep you safe from the general tumult?'

Will's patience wore thin. 'We are used to looking after ourselves, and we resent interference!'

'I'm sure of that my good crow, but you were about to be recognized and killed.'

'I'm no crow. And if you're playing games with us,

Dudlea, then my hard-done-by friend here will snap your neck like a dry twig!'

But Dudlea was blithe enough to smile. 'Gratitude is powerful enough to make spells from. Your Master Gwydion once told me that. Perhaps that's why you hold it back like a miser.'

'Now, listen to me, Dudlea—'

'Be calm. We're on the same side. And the man whom you're about to meet is your friend – despite having a little too much royal blood in his veins.'

'Royal blood?'

'At least it's not the queen,' Lotan murmured.

'Oh, Mag's long gone.' Dudlea's teeth glittered in the torchlight. 'Although the prince who requests your company is most loyal to Hal's cause.'

'Prince, did you say?'

'Oh, yes. In fact, he's just been given the Army of the West, though I think "Lord Commander" is a title that would sit rather better with me.'

Will and Lotan exchanged questioning glances. Army of the West? What was that? So far as they knew, no such army existed. And who could the queen have appointed to a command like that? Surely no one who might be described as their friend.

Will contained the impulse to make Dudlea tell all. If he was up to no good, then they would know soon enough. They cleaned themselves up as best they could, then were conducted speedily out of Clifton's Tower and hurried towards the Great Hall of Ebor Castle.

The bailey was now in darkness and almost deserted. A cold mist hung over the castle and there was a keen smell of woodsmoke in the air. It tasted like wine to Will. His misgivings began to evaporate – at least they were out of the dungeon, and that was something. Helmeted guards stood in the lee of the two main gateways and several small windows showed lights, but the place was eerily silent compared to the night before. As they emerged from under the keep and went out into the open, a clock struck the hour. Will counted three, which made him wonder how much time they had been forced to waste. What it might mean for the Realm could only be guessed at, for events were now once again moving along rapidly.

'Has Master Gwydion come here?' Will asked as they came to the doors.

Dudlea looked askance. 'If he has then he's not shown himself to me. Are you expecting him?'

Will did not answer, but put his hand on the iron door-ring so that Dudlea could not open it. 'You're sure the whole of the queen's army has left Ebor? The Duke of Mells, Lord Strange and all the others?'

'I tell you they're making their way into the south. The plan is to take Trinovant as soon as may be. Did you not hear my Lord of Mells say as much? Be easy in your mind – if your enemies had not gone do you think I would have dared to let you out?'

'I think if the slightest thing had gone wrong you'd have left us to rot.'

'That's most unfair.' Dudlea's reply was wounded. 'It's not just myself I had to consider. I couldn't risk coming a moment sooner because the sorcerer didn't leave the castle until after midnight, and if he'd discovered you it would've implicated the Lord Commander of the West. All along I've done right by you. If you disbelieve me you may ask my wife and son, who both continue in rude good health.'

'You're truly a reformed character,' Will said dryly, seeing a very different reason why Lady Dudlea might not yet have begun to complain about stiffness. In a world without magic her condition would never deteriorate, no matter how faithless her husband became.

'So it was this Lord Commander of yours who had us locked up?' Lotan asked, seizing on the important point.

'That's what I've been trying to tell you.'

Will shook his head. 'I don't understand. How does this man know me? And how did he know to have me hung from chains?'

'Ah, that was because of me,' Dudlea admitted. 'You see, I told him who you were. And I warned him what you could do.'

'And the chains?'

'That was my idea too. I remembered a moonlit night not so very long ago when your Master Gwydion drew power from the earth and then gave my wife back to me. I watched how his steps and movements cast the power into spells. I didn't want you stepping and gesturing your way to freedom. Not for the moment anyway.'

Will hardened his gaze, relieved that Dudlea had not really appreciated the mechanism whereby a crow gathered his powers. 'You took a foolish gamble with me, John Sefton. Ordinarily it would only have taken a few words of the true tongue to set me free, even from a lock-hole such as that one. And then I would have come for you!'

Lord Dudlea put out a placating hand. 'Oh, I wouldn't have gone so far as to cut out your tongue. But you must understand that I could hardly lodge you in comfort. I needed to cover myself should news of your arrest reach important ears.'

'Maskull's, you mean?' Will said.

'Among others. I needed to make sure that things were *explicable* if he found out about you. As it was, he didn't find out, and he didn't pay that visit to your cell.'

Lotan said, 'If he had, he would have congratulated you on your diligence.'

'Old habits die hard, it seems.' Will rubbed again at his wrists. 'I thought you'd foresworn double dealing. What are you after?'

Dudlea became intense. 'I promised I would do the right thing, and that's what I've been doing. But I don't see how jeopardizing myself would have helped our side.'

'Our side?' Will said, rolling his eyes, but Dudlea seemed to be in complete earnest.

'Yes. Those of us who are working for peace now. The sorcerer had you marked. Your name was on the list of those who were to die after the battle. "The Crowmaster and his helper." That's what it said. I saw it with my own eyes, and then I saw you. I could hardly believe it. I wondered how one so cunning could be so stupid as to come to Ebor and show himself just as Mells was bringing in the heads!'

Will gritted his teeth. 'I didn't realize I was so well known around the queen's court.'

Dudlea's scorn was undisguised. 'Oh, they know about you, all right! Enough to put quite a sum of gold on your head. That's why we have to be so careful.'

Before Will unlatched the door, he looked up and saw the full moon riding high in the south. His deepest feelings had led him to Ebor, but so far nothing had gone right. They could not have been wholly in error, could they?

It's Morann, he told himself silently, thinking back to the time when the loremaster had vouched for him in front of the Duke of Mells. Who else could it be?

He steeled himself, knowing that he had come to an important crossroads. But when he entered the empty hall there was but one figure sitting in shadow in the tall-backed chair. It was not the man he expected.

The other did not get up or make any move, but lounged there, negligently drumming his fingers on the arm-rest of the High Chair of the city.

'Thrones are ten-a-penny these days,' he said as Will approached. 'It seems like everybody wants to be king.'

'All except the real one.'

The figure leaned forward into the light and smiled. 'That's the truth. How goes it, Maceugh?'

That was a welcome Will recognized, an echo from the past. Between the sack of Ludford and the battle at Delamprey he had been obliged to adopt the identity of an emissary of the Blessed Isle and had lodged dangerously with the queen's court. That emissary's name had been Maceugh.

As Will shook the proffered hand he breathed in sharply at so unexpected a turn. 'Jasper of Pendrake . . . Prince of Cambray. Well, well, well. Now it all makes sense.'

'None other.' The red-haired swordsman had once been sent to investigate the truth or otherwise of the Maceugh's identity, but he had found himself liking Will better than his paymaster. He now made an open-handed gesture. 'Who else did you think would have troubled to save your foolish neck?'

'Not you.' Will smiled, though a serious question was on his mind. 'When last we met I was clothed in the flesh of another. How did you know me?'

Jasper laughed. 'Think again. Last year we met another time. It was in the aftermath of the battle at Delamprey. You may not have noticed me for, as I recall, you and Lord Warrewyk were having something of an argument at the time.'

'That's right. I was accusing him of murder.'

'The reason I remember it all so well is that I was in some slight difficulty with the said lord. As it happened, your arrival saved my neck. And "One good turn deserveth another", as I think one of your redes says.'

Will thought back to the beheadings after Delamprey. There had been a row of miserable men waiting, naked and bound, for Lord Warrewyk's axe. Jasper had been one of them, and so too had Lord Dudlea.

Jasper said, 'A man can't really let a favour like that go unrecognized. I asked high and low after you, but I was given no satisfactory answer. Until I met our mutual friend here.'

Will looked to Dudlea. 'Him?'

Dudlea pursed his lips. 'We had something in common, you might say. He asked me and I put the pieces together for him. In the end the conclusion I came to was inescapable. The Crowmaster's apprentice and the Maceugh must have been one and the same person.'

Will nodded. 'A spell of transformation.'

'I'd heard of such things.' Jasper grinned. 'I hope you didn't mind my locking you up. Like all newly persuaded men, my lord of Dudlea can be a little overzealous in the cause at times.'

Will's gaze was unwavering. 'So, what now?'

'Like I said, my lord Dudlea and I found we had views in common. We'd both rather the war stopped.'

'You're not the only one.'

'It's dangerous work, but someone's got to do it, eh?'

'So says Queen Mag's Lord Commander of the Army of the West.' Will said, puncturing Jasper's flippancy. 'How do you square that appointment with your views?'

'You think I should have rejected the honour? I had no choice. And I'll say this to you: what better position could there be to work from? My father, Owain, is in Cambray, raising an army. We'll take it to Ludford and try to flush Edward out.'

'Bring him to battle while the queen takes her hammer and knocks on the gates of Trinovant,' Lotan said, nodding at the soundness of the plan.

'Oh, your friend here thinks like a strategist,' said Jasper. 'There's only Lord Warrewyk who can put armed men between Mag and the White Hall now. And with those half-men in her army she'll sweep him aside like autumn leaves.'

'Edward's almost certainly at Ludford, raising an army of Marchermen,' Will said.

'We know where he is.' Jasper shrugged. 'We need to catch him and bring him to terms. That's why I must ride at first light.'

Will put his face in his hands for a moment, then he looked up and said wearily. 'So – let me get this straight – you're going to draw your armies up and face one another. And then what?'

'We won't sue for peace, but nor will we demand he surrenders to us. If we come to him in sufficient strength . . .' Jasper saw that he was failing to dispel Will's incredulity and was angered. 'What else can we do? I'll offer him a settlement in good faith! He'll understand that now his father's dead the greatest obstacle to peace has been removed.'

Will groaned inside. He wanted to seize Jasper by the shoulders and explain to him that there were mighty doom-stones hidden in the earth, monsters drawing power against the most well-meaning plan. Even as they spoke, the lorc would be undermining every one of Jasper's good intentions, and whatever else was true, things would certainly not go as he hoped.

He stared back at the Cambrayman, and whispered, 'You're a good man. You really are. But you're out of your mind.'

Jasper stood up, outraged. 'What?'

'You cannot ride faster than bad news. And you should keep away from Edward if you value your life.'

'Someone has to try to offer him a way out!'

'What makes you think he wants one? To him you're just one of the bastards who hung his father's head from Ebor's walls and set a paper crown upon it. He'll never forgive you now, Jasper. Not even when your own head has been cut off and trampled in the dirt.'

Before Will left Ebor he asked Lord Dudlea for three horses, a tent and a token of safe passage, and they were granted him. The great city had not been as badly treated as Awakenfield, but it had suffered ransack and ruin. They led the horses gingerly down into the town, and as they went Will began to feel for the ligns. He considered the possibility that he had imagined them among the other spectres that his mind had made from the darkness and pain, but they were real enough. The trace was faint, but his scrying sense had not wholly deserted him and now it confirmed his suspicions – the ligns were the birch and the hazel. It looked as if they crossed like arrows piercing the white heart of the city.

'They cross near the chapter house?' Lotan asked, following the line of sight where Will pointed.

'Right underneath it.'

The news seemed to trouble the big man, though he tried to make small of it. 'Do you really think that's so?'

'I'm sure. The Fellowship must have built their chapter house on the site of an ancient temple, just as they did at Verlamion and a hundred other places. Now you see the reason why your erstwhile brothers are so interested in the lorc.'

Lotan nodded silently.

It was a worrying thought because it meant that the lorc was not yet finished with Ebor. Will looked back along the street. City walls and the castle footings mirrored the earth power, shattering the image and confusing his mind, but as he tuned his talent to it he felt the unmistakable rumblings of power rolling beneath his feet. There was a surprise there too, for it was not flowing into the city, but out of it.

That could only mean that although Ebor itself must one day play host to a battle, that battle would not be the next one.

'What are you waiting for?' he asked Lotan who had hung back. 'It's always the next battle that has to interest us, and that's not going to be here.'

Lotan shrugged. 'If you say so.'

'It's going to be somewhere along the birch lign. That's where the power's flowing. And do you know what lies on the birch lign?'

'What?'

'Ludford. It's where the lign of the birch crosses the lign of the rowan.'

'But did you not tell me you already found a battlestone at Ludford? That you pulled it out like a village Sister pulls out a rotten tooth?'

Will grunted. 'We called it the Blood Stone for good reason . . .'

He recalled the terrible time at Ludford as the town burned and the abandoned castle lay under siege with them still inside it. Gort had made him chew on a piece of heath-pea root, and afterwards his mind had taken leave of his body and floated high into a moon-washed sky. And he had seen the ligns crossing below – straight green channels, glowing across the night. He had seen the power flowing in waves along those channels, being drawn towards a point beyond the southern horizon. Then, if he had but seen it, he had had the triple-triangle pattern of the lorc laid out before his very eyes.

'That was the Doomstone of the West,' he muttered.

'What?'

'Another doomstone. It has to be. We thought there must be one in the Cambray Marches, one that made a trio of stones with the Blood Stone and a lesser stone, a guide stone, sited a couple of leagues to the west of Ludford. Do you remember what happened to me when we came through Baronet Hadlea?' Will began to relive the horror of the vision the Hadlea stone had evoked, a feeling that his mind had separated from his body, a feeling so strange and so strong that he had fainted and vomited on awakening. Now he shook his head to dispel it, saying, 'Three ligns go through the Doomstone at Verlamion. Three go through another at Baronet Hadlea . . .'

' . . . and three go through some place in the Marches.' Lotan finished, his mind calculating, 'And that's where the Doomstone of the West lies.'

'Yes.'

'Is that what makes them doomstones? Because they sit upon three ligns instead of just one or two?'

'I think that's so.'

Lotan nodded thoughtfully. 'And the one that's out in the west? What ligns does that sit on?'

'Heligan, Bethe and Eburos – that is to say: willow, birch and yew.'

'Willow, Bethe and you?' Lotan muttered, meeting Will's gaze. 'It could not be calling to you more personally if it was shouting your name.'

Will felt leaden. Dread crept along his spine, for Lotan had made it sound as if the lorc was making some ghastly joke at his expense. Thoughts of his wife made his stomach clench. He had spent much silent hope on her having gone with Gwydion. It was likely she had, but the uncertainty still undermined him.

As they rode out through the Muckle Gate Will looked up to see the three impaled heads. Throughout the day the crows had been at them, but the ragged faces were abandoned now and frozen by the pale light of the moon. They gazed open-mouthed and vacant-eyed towards the south and west as if pointing the way.

Will headed off against the grain of the country, going

westward by Acorne and Weatherbury-upon-Worffe, and only later turning south through the land of Elmet. They passed several homesteads that had escaped the worst of the devastation. Near Barrick, Will called a halt, saying, 'We must rest, but at daybreak we shall have to go on all the faster.'

It was not only for himself that he sought to break their dark journey. He had seen the way Lotan was swaying in his saddle, but he knew that if he had offered him rest the big man would have refused. There was another reason. They had, so far as Will could tell, recrossed the holly lign and had come to a place of extraordinarily good aspect. It was an opportunity for him to draw sustenance.

He wandered away from Lotan and the horses and found a spot by a dew pond where the land was flat and there were long views all around. There he braced his feet and flung out his arms as the First Men had done a thousand generations before, and quietly and confidently he breathed in the draught that he had longed for.

With the breathing came the bliss. It coursed through his chest, pulling power in through his feet and out through his hands. While the power rumbled and shook under his feet, the flow lit him blue-green. A warmth began to radiate from him. It seemed like heat and light, but it was not. They were only the commonplaces that his mind employed to interpret the power of wellbeing that had entered him.

As soon as he accepted the power, the timeless moment dawned in which the boundaries of the self dissolved and he felt one with the world. When that state began to fade he glimpsed that he had understood once again the secret that lay at the heart of all things, but the understanding was elusive and always just beyond recall, like a book that could be read only in a given room and never removed.

He was soon himself again. Always afterwards there

was a wonderful feeling of floating in which, if he were not careful, he could stagger and fall. It passed quickly, leaving behind a mighty sense of satisfaction. The stars stood out bright overhead now that the moon was sinking low. Their paths held a magical beauty all their own, and Will wondered at what Skymaster Braye was supposed to have said about them. Could it be that in the coming world there would be no influences from the wandering stars?

'What were you doing out there?' Lotan asked.

'What did it look like?'

'Were you casting a spell?'

'No. But it felt as if a spell was being cast over me.'

They found a barn and Will slept with the skittering of hay-loft mice in his ears and the smell of mildew in his nostrils. When he awoke he laid a blessing on the barn, then he roused Lotan and they pressed on through the cold mists of morning, all the time looking out for the patrols that had been posted to secure the district and all the main routes.

'What's the plan to find the others?' Lotan asked when they gave the horses their first breather.

'I have none. Master Gwydion will find us if he needs to.'

'You said that before.'

'This time, if he thinks it's necessary, he'll use his magic.'

'Can't you call to him magically?'

'Not without drawing Chlu also.'

An air of disappointment fell over the big man. 'What about the ritual you did back there?'

'Ritual? You mean the blessing?'

'No, when you were by the pond. Didn't that alert Chlu?'

'Probably not.' Will felt disinclined to explain, but he added, 'Don't worry. I haven't felt any echo of his magic for a while.'

'So he's lost us, you mean?'

Will put Lotan's jitters down to his warrior's training. 'It could mean several things. He could be asleep.'

'Or?'

'Or he's not active. Or maybe he's too far away.'

'And you won't know where he is unless he gives himself away?'

Lotan's questions about the nature of Will's relationship with his twin began to feel intrusive. 'I don't care where he is. What concerns me is where he thinks I am. Don't worry about him. He's drawn to me and I to him, but I have a duty that I must put first.'

Lotan nodded slowly and looked away. The answers seemed not to satisfy the big man, as if he had thought up another strategy that was more to his liking. But if he had, he said nothing of it.

After a space of silence Lotan asked, 'Wouldn't it be better if we tried to join up with the wizard before we looked for the battlestone?'

'I told you: Master Gwydion will find us if he needs to.'

'But surely—'

'Lotan, we're doing the right thing. Trust me.'

'You begin to sound like Lord Dudlea.'

'Trust me!'

'I will, just as soon as I know where we're going.'

Will looked to him in surprise. 'You *know* where we're going.'

'No.'

'To find Edward of course. Where did you think? We must reach him before Jasper does.'

'But you can't stop the battle!'

'Maybe not. But I must bear the bad tidings.' Will felt the mismatch of their understandings keenly. 'Edward has to know.'

Disagreement simmered in Lotan's stare, as if he could

not understand why Will felt his duty towards Edward so strongly. 'And all because you feel it in your bones? You ask a lot of your feelings.'

'It's funny you should say that. Master Gwydion tells me I don't ask nearly enough. Come, we must push on.'

Will began to think about Gwydion then, and the wizard's fading powers. What had caused him to misjudge so much? Like a green leaf, marred by insects and browning at the edges as winter approached, Gwydion had begun to show signs that the seven failings were seeping into him at last. He had half-convinced everyone that Lotan was not to be trusted, and that had been only one of his mistakes. Lotan's aura was not without blemish. Dark shadows lay over him. But there was something wholesome at the heart of the big man that could not be denied. It made Will think that things might have turned out better if the warrior had been with them earlier. But it was easy to dwell on might-have-beens and should-have-dones, and easier still to blame others.

After Wrathford-on-Eye they rode east to avoid Awakenfield. They crossed the Caldor further upstream at Horburgh Bridge, but that was only possible by showing the token of safe passage that Jasper had provided for them. As they climbed up onto higher ground Will saw distant patrols riding hard, and knew that the queen's man-hunters were out looking for those who might have escaped the rout at Awakenfield with Ebor gold in their pouches.

They tracked up into the moors of Elmlea, overnighting at the greystone village of Hepfirth. A full day's hard riding took them into even more beautiful country, across the high bogs of Cinder Clout and past the snowy heads the local people called Crow's Den and Dark Peak. Then down they came through Buckstone Wellwater and into the lands where Will and Gwydion had once found the Plaguestone.

All the while Will tried to keep the Bethe lign on their left-hand side. He could feel its power growing ominously. Memories of the dread battle in which he and Gwydion had been caught at Blow Heath, now only a little way to their west, impressed themselves upon him. The echoes of that horror made Will's skin prickle.

As the light faded again he realized they must have entered the Earldom of Shroppesburgh, or Salop as the county was more often called by the churlish folk. They made camp at Wealdmoor Eiton, pitching their tent in the lee of a small hill. The next day another hard ride took them across the remains of the Slaver road called the Wartling and shortly afterwards they passed east of the Wreaken Rock along a road that took them to the huge arch that spanned the Great River of the West at Stonebridge. The last time Will had come this way he had seen the green power glittering under the waters, and he knew they must be careful, for this was the lign, bared raw to the eye as it arced across the gorge.

Once safely across Severine's Flood a short ride brought them to the village of Mart Woollack, and they went thereafter by Luddsdale with its skeletal orchards, through the bountiful places Will recalled from the ride he had taken with Earl Sarum's victorious army south from Blow Heath to Ludford, though now a sifting of snow had bleached all colour from the land.

As they rode through wintry oak woods, the ever-present lign started to eat at Will's thoughts again and he began to blame and berate himself. He pondered the reasons why he had allowed so much time to elapse between the making of his promise to Lotan and his acting upon it. There had been no hex on him, no outside power of constraint, yet he had shied away from fulfilment. That delay had been down to his own weakness. He should have taken himself in hand sooner and made himself do what he knew must be done. But he had lacked discipline. That was where it had all fallen apart. That was where he had missed his chance to become King Arthur!

And because Will forgot to stand back from himself he did not notice that the lign had begun to haunt him. The world was sinking into twilight, and it all seemed to be his fault. His and his alone. A hot ember of shame burned inside him, and he dwelt on it as he rode. Nor did the lign give him any respite from his doubts about the coming battle.

'Is true courage to do with not feeling fear or despair?' he asked Lotan suddenly. 'Or just not letting others know when you feel that way?'

Lotan took the question with due seriousness. 'Courage is not the same as fearlessness. A piece of wood is fearless, but it is not courageous. What men call courage is often only recklessness, or a need to follow another man's orders. Sometimes what is called courage is only a kind of anger. I have known that sort too.'

'You make it all sound less than heroic.'

Lotan seemed about to let the topic go, but then he said, 'There is a true form of courage. It comes from knowing self-sacrifice. If ever you see that kind, you will never forget it.'

Will waited for more, but nothing more came. Lotan's reticence prickled him, and he realized that they had both fallen into a morose silence, and each was now concerned with his own thoughts.

It's the lorc, he thought, drawing a deep breath. The birch lign is running strongly. And it's very close.

He looked up at the clouds and listened to the sound of the horses' hooves among the fallen leaves, then made a conscious effort to shift his mind onto more elemental matters. But however hard he tried he could not sustain it for long. Instead he began to ruminate on Jasper's doomed efforts. That led to a dour little conversation as he tried to make Lotan understand why he had rebuffed the Lord of Pendrake.

'You don't have to justify yourself to me,' Lotan muttered.

'I'm not justifying myself. I'm trying to tell you something important. Jasper's doing what he can to end the war, but he's not impartial. He's the king's half-brother.'

Lotan grunted. 'Impartial? What is that? There's no one in the Realm for whom loyalty to one side or the other is not important.'

'Exactly. It's a family fight in which the dukes, whose veins are running with royal blood, are most closely concerned. And all the earls support one duke or another. And the lesser lords and landowners are already committed within the earldoms. As for the churlish folk, feudal bonds keep them tied to the land and the lords whom they think will protect them. Everything's locked tight.'

Lotan took the message stonily. 'That is the usual recipe for war.'

'I've begun to realize what purpose the Ogdoad served. Only the wizards were not caught up in the snares of allegiance. Only they could recommend any kind of just remedy. But today they represent the tail end of a dying tradition and now Gwydion and Maskull have fallen to fighting one another.'

'You speak of Maskull as if he once acted justly,' Lotan said, uncertain now.

'He was accustomed to long ago.' Will scratched his head. 'Don't you know that he was once a wizard? He betrayed their calling and went to work for himself. It doesn't matter to him who wins the war, he's only trying to further his own ends these days. That's why he's a sorcerer. He and Master Gwydion have seen wars great and small, hundreds probably. They know the shape of war, the way things always go when conflicts arise, and they understand how long it takes to fix things afterwards. But as Master Gwydion once told me, Ogdoad wizards are not men of power. What they hold is wisdom and what they wield is influence. They could never make kings and lords do what they advised, only make the true path seem like good sense.'

'Just like the Fellowship,' Lotan said.

'Huh! I don't think so!'

'Why do you say that? What's the difference?'

'Well, because the Fellowship doesn't see the true path in anything. It uses bribery and blackmail and it enriches itself obscenely at the expense of the churlish folk, whereas Master Gwydion does none of those things.'

Lotan thought on that for a long moment, then he said, 'Is that truly so? Are his motives and his methods really so pure?'

'Yes, I think they are. A wizard's task is to try to make folk see the truth and the folly of things. Remember, you don't know him at his best. Nowadays he's a long way past his prime.'

'Maybe he's started working for himself too.'

'No. That's just it, you see. Because real magic won't work properly when too much self-interest is present. That's exactly what's wrong with Maskull's way. His magic is sorcery, and try as he might sorcery cannot win in the end. It's dead meat that only turns to stink and corruption.'

Will fell silent, thinking how hollow his hopes must sound in the quiet of the oak grove. He began to think about Willow again and to ask whether his own reasons for choosing to come here with Lotan were not at their root a little less than pure. Perhaps they were not, after all, connected with a desire to interfere with the coming battle. Perhaps he was only doing what other men did, trying to protect what was his.

It was true that the idea to drape Willow in a swan cloak and have her shoot corpse-whale arrows into Maskull had sounded as if it might be possible. Now the thought of it terrified him. It seemed absurd and outrageously dangerous, much more so than when they had been back in the safety of Trinovant. And if Will was honest he would have to admit that Master Gwydion had the knack of making anything seem possible when he so chose . . .

As they came to Ludford's Feather Gate, Will began to worry that Gwydion's weapon of choice in the battle between wizard and sorcerer was indeed a cause for concern – because that weapon was his wife.

PART FOUR

THE END OF ALL THINGS

* * *

CHAPTER NINETEEN

THE IRON TREE

'State your business!'
The demand was called down from a tall gatehouse
that had been barred and barricaded against war.

Iron spikes had been driven into logs dragged across
the road, and a glade of sharpened stakes guarded all
approaches like fearsome teeth. It was frosty in the shadow
of the walls.

'We bring tidings for Castle Ludford concerning Duke
Richard of Ebor.'

'Then go to the Durnhelm Gate, for the town is closed
to all comers!'

The voice was uncompromising. Gone was the simplicity
of belief the townsfolk of Ludford had once enjoyed. At
the time of Will's last visit the people had just been told of
a great victory by their beloved lord whose great ally had
smashed an enemy army. But since that heady and hopeful
day, their lord had deserted them, running for his life into
the Forest of Morte while their houses had burned. Many
of the churls who had cheered the news of Blow Heath had
died before the year was out, and now their lord and his
ally were dead also, though they were yet to learn about it.

News of the calamity had yet to come this far, and Will

tried to take encouragement from that, for it was vital that the matter of his father's death be broached to Edward in exactly the right fashion if the explosion of violence that must follow was to be contained. He could not have come here any quicker, not without killing their horses. The hours they had spent in the dark at Ebor had set them back, but not, it seemed, fatally.

As they skirted the town, Will saw the remains of the earthworks that had been dug long ago to prevent the king's sappers from getting to the foot of the town walls. He led the way over the mounds where the Earl of Warrewyk's gunners had set their great guns, and then he recognized the very place where he had been sitting the day he had realized his salmon talisman was missing.

A ray of sunlight pooled around them. Under his thick woollen jacket Will felt suddenly overwarm. He wiped a sleeve against his forehead, then put a hand against the pit of his stomach and, like a man who has been sickening for a day and sensing for the first time the onset of his illness, he blew out a weary breath.

But what sickness was this? Not one of the body, for sure.

He looked up at the sky, searching for the gibbous moon; the pregnant-bellied phase always complicated his blood. But the influence was not upon him. Nor was it the vacant earth, for the blockages of Ludford were long gone. Echoes there were aplenty, but not even the memory of his madnesses here could explain the feelings that welled up inside him as if from under stones. This was a sickness of mind. As if something unacceptable had come to him, something he was pushing down deep and blocking from the light.

He steeled himself and decided to look within, and in that moment of decision the way became clear. He must follow the pain. Pursue it. It was not fearlessness nor even courage, but some insistent need to know. What he saw was ugly – a revelation he did not want to face.

'What ails you?' Lotan said, regarding him askance.

'Nothing.'

'If you're sick—'

'Leave it!' That was needlessly brusque. 'Just . . . a little queasiness. I'll tell you if it gets worse.'

And in the comradely way that all good warriors must learn, Lotan gave space and easy silence. It was a private matter.

Will suffered, for the revelation was appalling. He could see the red and the green fishes for what they truly were now. The former had gone with Chlu and the latter with himself. They must have been made by Maskull's use of fae magic, made out of a live fish, perhaps as a preliminary to the main spell-working. But the trial had gone awry and the result had been two wizened pieces of stone, one benevolent, the other malicious. Still in the shape of fish, but both turned to stone and as dead as doornails.

Good enough, perhaps, for Maskull to know that he was following the right lines with his work, but not nearly good enough to satisfy his eventual aim. For that to happen those transformed by the magic would have to remain alive . . .

Will shivered as he imagined the sorcerer hanging those little stone fish on cords about the neck of the original child on which he planned to perfect his grand experiment of separation. It may even have been that they were a part of the magic – a starter, so to say, like a burning ember applied to the vent of a great gun to set off its powder charge.

And so Maskull had been able to say in his moment of triumph, 'I made you, I can unmake you just as easily.'

I am not I, Will thought. I am merely half of a whole. And the *other* half . . .

Perhaps it was only the muting power of shock , but there was no outrage or loathing in him. Only an understanding.

And that was good enough. He wondered how he could tell Willow.

I am what I am, he thought, with contradicting false confidence. I am what I've always been, and there's nothing wrong with that. Nothing.

But then the idea that he was so closely bound to Chlu overwhelmed his peace of mind: *can we really be the two halves that make the same man?* The idea was utterly repellent.

As they turned towards the wooded slopes that dropped down to the River Theam, Will rode across the rowan lign and felt a powerful blast tear at him. A few paces away was the grave of the Blood Stone. That sickly hollow was full of memories and the air above it thick with ghosts. It was just a gaping hole, icy and bare of grass, but it was the place where Lord Strange had once pulled a monster from its bed before throwing it down the castle well.

The sickness gradually passed from him and Will noted that the earth flow had gone deeper hereabouts. It was as if, no longer pinned to the surface by a battlestone, it had sagged down into the Realm Below. Instead of breaching the land and being shattered into a thousand fragments against the castle ramparts and the byways of the town, the flow was no longer obstructed. Now its power rushed headlong through underground channels to a place of far greater importance, a place which was no more than a league or two further south.

But was that the only reason that Will could see and feel the power with such clarity now? Or had *he* changed too? Had he grown more into his own power? He hoped so, for there seemed little doubt that the final combat was approaching.

'What now?' Lotan asked.

Will realized that he had unthinkingly brought his mount to a halt. He roused himself. 'If Edward's anywhere, he's up there,' he said, pointing at the castle.

The Durnhelm Gate, when they reached it, was also closed. When he called up, a voice came from behind the battlements.

'What do you want?'

'I have an urgent message for the Duke of Ebor!'

The reply seemed to stump the invisible gateman, then a head appeared and another voice, a woman's, piped up, 'He don't live here no more.'

Then the first voice said, 'What do you want with him?'

Will's knuckles tightened on the reins. 'This is an urgent matter and only for the duke's ears.'

There was hilarity at the hardening of his tone. 'Hark at that! Open the gate, he says. Urgent, if you please!'

'Tell him to push off.'

The woman's face appeared and smiled a gap-toothed smile. 'My man here says you're to push off.'

Will waited, wrathful yet considering, then he shouted, 'Your lord will not thank you for turning us away when we have important news for him!'

A new head appeared wearing a kettle hat. 'Our lord thanks us to keep his town and castle against enemies and ne'er-do-wells like you. Now, be off with you!'

'The message I bear is important. I—'

'Aye, and if you were my lord's messenger you'd have given us the password by now, wouldn't you?'

'We've been riding three days from the north. We know no password.'

'Then turn around and get you gone. Or shall I have my lads stick a couple of arrows in the rump of that nag of yours?'

As Will bit back his anger, Lotan touched his arm and motioned him away.

Will scowled, but complied. 'I don't want to use magic on him. Why does he have to make it so difficult?'

'He's a town gateman. It's not his job to make things

easy for strangers, and we're hardly dressed like nobility. Look at the ground.'

Will saw that the place on which their horses were stamping was heavily churned. He met the big man's knowing look. 'Traffic.'

'And all going one way.'

Will nodded. 'Leaving the town.'

Lotan got down and examined the muddied ground with care. 'The gateman's woman was right, the Duke of Ebor don't live here no more.'

'What can you see?'

'An army passed out of the town this morning.'

Will rubbed at his unshaved chin. 'How many men?'

'A couple of thousand. Maybe more.'

'A couple of thousand?' Will said, pained. 'That won't be nearly enough against a fresh army brought up from Cambray.'

'This may have been only a town levy. A contribution to a greater army camped elsewhere. There are wheel ruts. Provision waggons, and many horses without riders.'

Will deliberated. 'We have a choice. We can follow the flow until we get to the Doomstone of the West, or we can track this trail until we find Edward.'

'You must decide,' Lotan said

'I already have.'

It was a simple decision, for as Will explained, wherever the levy had gone, their final destination was in no doubt – they would eventually be drawn towards the battlestone.

But as Will looked east towards the dark mass of Cullee Hill he knew they would go nowhere much for the moment. The light was already failing and after a short while they were forced to make camp. The horses were quickly seen to, their own bellies were soon filled, and a single candle and a little charcoal brazier were hung up to give their tent warmth and good cheer.

'How do you know where to find the ligns?' Lotan asked once they were settled. 'Can you see them?'

Will had been quiet all day, bound up with the morose business of healing himself. He did not welcome the question. 'See them? Not usually.'

'Then how?'

'It's just a knack I have.'

'But how does it *feel*, what you do?'

'We call it scrying. The first thing you must do is make your mind go blank.'

Lotan looked doubtful. 'How do I do that?'

'Just . . . think of nothing.'

'I can't!'

'Well, think of thinking of nothing. That will have to do.'

The big man stared into space for a long moment, then he shook his head as if a wasp had flown into his ear. 'Oh, this is stupid!'

'It's harder than it seems.'

'For me, it's impossible.'

'That may be true.'

Lotan went into a sulk, but Will could see that his mind was ploughing furrows and it was not long before he spoke again. 'If Edward's not at the castle, where is he?'

'That's a good question. He could be anywhere. He's been scouring the Marches for men since before Ewle.'

'Has he got other, smaller fortresses hereabouts? Towers held by his kinsmen maybe?'

'There's Castle Morte at Wyg Moor and Castle Crofter. And some keeps between here and the Great Dyke of King Offa in the west.' Will looked up from studying the ashy glow of the charcoal. 'But I don't think the news from Awakenfield has reached any of them yet.'

Lotan stirred. 'Why do you say that?'

'Because, now I've had chance to dwell on it, I'm sure they didn't know who I was talking about back there at the Durnhelm Gate when I mentioned the duke. I meant Edward, but it seems to me they thought I was talking about Duke Richard.'

'If they've not heard the news, then why was the town shut up like an oyster?'

'Edward's orders. Precautions. And it'll be his way of creating a sense of urgency. I think he knows there's an army coming, but not why. His spies in Cambray must have told him of its approach.'

Lotan was unconvinced. 'But what about Ebor's men who escaped the disaster at Awakenfield? The fastest of them could have got here yesterday, well ahead of us.'

'Those who fled in time to escape wouldn't know for certain that Richard was dead, only perhaps that the battle had been lost. Those who lingered long enough to confirm his death would probably not have got this far.'

'Some must have.'

'Not necessarily.' Will sat back in the flickering candle-light. 'I believe that only a handful got away.'

'But where have *they* gone?'

'Anywhere and nowhere. Anywhere quickly, at first, but then nowhere they wanted to get to. Not after a rout like that. The few who escaped were hunted men, as we saw. We didn't get far before we had to show our tokens of safe conduct. Any survivor of Awakenfield who still carried with him more than a care for his own life would probably have decided to make for Trinovant.'

Lotan nodded slowly. 'Given the choice, it would make more sense to warn Lord Warrewyk that the ogres of Awakenfield were coming to break down the doors of the capital.'

'Exactly.'

'So what of Lord Pendrake?' Lotan asked after a

moment. 'He must have travelled here by a different route. An armed retinue could not have passed through this country as we have. I think Jasper will join with his army today, if he has not done so already.'

Jasper's no fool, Will thought. He said, 'I agree. His escort would have chosen a more protected route than ours. They would have used the Slaver roads and not been concerned with tracking ligns along the way.'

'Also his men would likely have ridden well-shod coursers – much faster than the three dawdling palfreys he gave to us. His knights would have taken many spare mounts with them to share the burden.'

'Then it's our best guess that he's already joined up with his army. I wonder where they are now. Coming by the road that passes under Hergest Ridge, I expect, unless they're already across the Dyke.'

'If Lord Owain has brought the army out of Cambray, then it can't be far.'

'Let's hope you're wrong. I like to think that Jasper will stand by his word, to come in strength, but to use that strength to work for peace.'

Lotan's grim face showed little hope. 'We should sleep as soon as we can, for we must rise early.'

Will yawned and lay down, the unsettling power of his personal revelation still resounding inside him. 'Whatever happens tomorrow, Lotan, I want you to know that I'm glad chance threw us together. There's no one I'd rather have beside me when danger threatens.'

The big man stared back, and his strange eyes of blue and brown were beyond any reading. He took Will's hand briefly in a strong grip, then turned over and blew out the candle.

The night was deep and the ground iron-hard before the first grey of morning. Biting cold snapped at them as they emerged into the still air. Frost had dusted everything in white and they had to shake out the tent before they could stow it. They packed up in darkness and began riding under a high, waning moon, so that by sun up they had followed the Theam as far as Wolferton Mill.

On the way, Will examined his heart's wound again and saw that squarely facing the truth he had long suspected about himself had been the right thing to do. Every man has the right and duty to know who he is. It's the first step. For every man must love himself – or else how can he love others?

After that he dared to open his mind to the land. The strength of the earth power surprised him. A strange ferocity was attracting the flow south, greedily drinking in all that it could. He tasted the flavours of birch, willow, rowan and yew, but as they went the rowan and the birch diminished while the willow maintained and the yew increased. He corrected their course further and further westward through hillier country, until only the rowan was being left behind while the influence of the others still grew.

Progress was painfully slow. At Park Pale they came past what seemed at first sight to be a windmill with only two sails, but Lotan said that it was a signal tower – one of many that belonged to the Sightless Ones. Though no hooded Fellows could be seen, a lone, unsmiling figure in green leather with a crossbow in his hand looked at them as they passed.

Will watched a low overcast roll in from the west, gloomy and featureless. The day was windless, and it looked for a while that it might snow, but then the blanket of cloud began to thin, though never enough for the sun to break through before it plunged below the hills. As they reached Yarple the light was dying. The promptings of the birch lign had begun to overpower the others. Ahead lay the valley of the River Lugg and the wooded bluffs between which a

Slaver road ran north and south. To the north, Will knew, lay the hamlet of Yatton Mystery and the two ancient forts that Gwydion had once told him about, forts which, of old, had guarded the approaches to Wyg Moor. To the south, Luggvale opened out into flatter country, a land of farms dotted with coppices and coverts and neatly planted orchards. They met no one on the road, and there were signs that the farms had been abandoned.

'It's a pretty land, but I have a bad feeling about this place,' Lotan said, surveying the shuttered cottages.

'You and me both,' Will told him.

'Over there must be the route out of Cambray. And that Slaver road was made to move armies.'

'We're very close now. Look, there's the crossing.'

Will led his horse forward across the stone bridge that carried the Cambray road over the Lugg. The little river was flowing purposefully southwards, swollen with icy water. With a shock Will realized that he had come this way before, though he had approached from a different direction. It had been in the days before his talent had sharpened, when Duke Richard had finally seen enough of the future to move his strength from Foderingham Castle to the remoter fortress at Ludford.

Will cast his mind back to that cold winter's night years ago, when he had walked alone under the haloed moon and the stars of the Ell-wand had ridden above his head. Their pitiless stare had survived the brightness of the moon, striking a pattern that, now he came to think of it, pointed down towards a hill where a single oak grew. He had heard a running stream that night – it must have been the Lugg – and there had been a Slaver journey stone at the crossroads to tell that this place was called Morte's Crossing.

Then, the rotting body of a villain had been enclosed in the gibbet cage here. It was a warning to wrong-doers and a statement for all travellers to read that this was Marcherland and they should mind the power hereabouts.

So it was again. As they came to it, Will saw another dead man. Perhaps a killer or a sheep stealer, he had been exposed to parch and starve, to die in a cage and to rot away. The Conqueror's law said that a man deemed to have relinquished his honour in crime had no need of dignity in death. But it seemed to Will too fierce a code, Marcherland or not.

The closeness of the colliding ligns and the gently swinging cage brought back the horrors of Ebor to Will's mind. He turned his head away, but the fire in his veins was raging now. This new corpse accused him just as the other one had. Perhaps, that night long ago, he had had a premonition without realizing it. Perhaps a warning had been sent back to him from the future. It seemed so. How sad, then, that he had not possessed the skill to see that message for what it was, or to believe the dead man when he had whispered that a disastrous war was coming.

Lotan dismounted and looked at the frozen tracks at the crossroads. 'The carts from Ludford did not roll this way. Nor has an army come out of Cambray yet. Twenty, maybe twenty-five men on long-pacing horses passed westward. Yesterday, by the look of it. They had as many unmounted horses with them. All were well-shod and going at the gallop. Hot-bloods, judging by the stride.'

'Was it Jasper?'

'I would say so.' Lotan's breath steamed in the air, for it was still very cold and now the sun had set there was little warmth to be found in the dying day.

Will got down too. He felt shaky, feverish and uncertain on his feet, but he staggered to the side of the road where there was a wreath of dead leaves lying near a fallen log. He picked up the wreath, brushed the frost from it, and began to riffle through the various brown leaves that had been threaded together.

'What is that?' Lotan asked.

'A loremaster's letter.' Will found what he was looking for, a sprig bound up separately. 'Elder, ash and vine, furze and silver fir – it means Lord Morann has been this way too. But this is old. And apart from the signature I can't read it.'

'Oh, but I can!'

The voice had come from the cage. Will whirled about. The horses shied and bolted. Lotan drew his sword, staring in disbelief at the corpse that now jumped down from the gibbet.

But the spike of fear that drove Will back in terror quickly ran to earth. With the flourish of a mouse-brown cloak a familiar figure was revealed before them. 'I see you want to know how I got here so soon – and I a wizard who is such a long way past his prime.' Gwydion plucked the circlet of leaves from Will's hand and scattered it. 'Tut, tut. That is private correspondence.'

'You need a lesson in manners, old man!' Lotan muttered. He was white-faced and held his sword before him in both hands.

'No, Lotan . . .' Will came between them, then he turned to the wizard. 'You must be more careful who you give shocks to, Master Gwydion. Lotan's instincts are . . . keenly protective.'

'Oh, is that what you like to think?'

'All I know is that he spent one of his swords up to the hilt on the last magician we met.'

The wizard inclined his head. 'You have come up against Maskull?'

'After a manner of speaking. To tell the truth I half thought we'd find you – or him – out here. What were you doing in that grim disguise.'

'Watching the road. Nobody looks at a dead man with any expectations.'

Will told everything that had befallen them since they were parted. He left out nothing of importance save the most important: he could not yet expose the revelation, even though he knew he should. Fortunately, excuses were plentiful: the situation was too urgent, and there was one who deserved to know what Will was even before even an Ogdoad wizard.

Gwydion listened sagely to all that was told to him, then he said, 'As for us, we are much as we were when last you saw us. Though Willow has not for a moment stopped asking after what we thought might have become of you.'

'Is she with Gort?' Will asked anxiously.

'Do you see that tree on the hill yonder?' The wizard pointed into the middle distance where a slight rise was crowned with a large oak of fine form, though leafless and looking like black filigree etched against the sky. 'They are nearby.'

'But we must not linger here,' Will said, blinking. 'There are armies on the move—'

'—and they are coming here,' Gwydion finished for him. 'Of course they are, because there's your Doomstone of the West, my friend.'

'It makes a change for you to be showing me where a battlestone is to be found. Do you mean by the tree?'

'Not *by* the tree. Under it.'

They secured the reins of the horses to a fence post and set off up the slope on foot. 'You had better tell me how you knew where to come.'

'The birds of the forest tell me much about what passes, and who may be found upon the road.'

Lotan growled. 'But you didn't follow us. You were already here.'

The wizard's eyes were hooded. 'We came by a faster way.'

'Yes,' Will said. 'I know all about your shortcuts. But you knew to come here. How?'

'Before we left Trinovant I spoke with Friend Hal. The king's scholarship has always been seen as a harmless pursuit by those who keep him, but it has repaid his efforts well. He has spent many a long hour in the royal libraries, but it was in his scroll cellars, those shelved passages that lie beneath the White Hall, that he found jewels beyond price.'

'Jewels?'

'Writings. Ancient fragments which he would never show to Maskull.'

'But he showed them to you,' Lotan said.

The wizard ignored the impertinence and went on. 'They were fragments of the Black Book of Tara. One detail the writings confirmed was that where two ligns cross there always lies a battlestone. And where three ligns cross there lies one of the great doomstones. There are three of them, as befits the triple triangle pattern that you have already established for the ligns. That is why, if you recall, I made sure we went north along the road that passes through Baronet Hadlea.'

Will took the wizard's words angrily. 'Well, thank you for confiding in me! Couldn't you have spoken sooner?'

'The facts required confirmation. And your discomfort would have been made no less unbearable if you had known about any of this in advance.' The wizard glanced at Lotan and added in a needless aside, 'Besides, how could I confide in you when it was clear to me that you had taken leave of your senses?'

Will turned on him. 'Meaning *what*?'

Gwydion's finger stabbed accusingly at Lotan. 'Meaning that *he* is a Fellow, and once a Fellow always a Fellow!'

'Oh, please, not that again!'

'He belongs body and mind to the Sightless Ones. Ask him!'

Will bit back his riposte. The wizard was not making it easy to confide in him, and it was a *necessary* confidence, one central to their quest. Will turned and strode on, letting those who wanted to come follow or not as they pleased.

Foremost in his thoughts now was Willow's safety and after that her peace of mind. He warned himself that the ligns that crossed nearby were active and stirring up all kinds of powerful discord. He realized that without the tonic cordial that Gort had given him, he would have been unable even to stand up by now. But that was by no means proof against all the defences a battlestone could throw up.

Nor was Willow untouched by the nearby doomstone. When she saw him she did not run to him with outstretched arms but remained where she was, huddled in her travelling cloak. Her eyes were red with crying.

'How could you have just gone off like that?' she asked bitterly. 'How could you? I was so worried.'

He tried to hug her, but she stubbornly refused him, and after a few moments he gave up and went to find the Wortmaster, feeling less than half a man.

'She has a point, Willand. You went off without a word.'

'I had to do what I had to do.'

'She was terribly worried. We all were.'

'Get her off the lign,' he told Gort. 'She'll see things differently from that hillside over there.'

'I will, but first you ought to—'

His temper snapped suddenly, provoked by Gort's very reasonableness. 'Do it now, Wortmaster! Or by the moon and stars I'll take my wife home and let the whole world slide where it will!'

Once Gort had hurried to do as he was bid, Will turned to the wizard, who had moved closer to the old oak. It was a strange place for a tree to flourish, just off the brow of a hill, and – or so it seemed from here – in soil that was broken away from its roots as if a whole warren of coneys had burrowed there.

He struggled with himself then lamely called to the wizard, 'So, what's it to be this time?'

'What is *what* to be?'

'You know what I mean, Master Gwydion. What do you intend to do about Maskull?'

'We shall lie in wait for him, and do what we tried to do at Awakenfield.'

Will laughed bitterly. 'At Awakenfield we waited in vain. Why should Maskull turn up for the fight this time?'

The wizard's chin jutted. 'If he does not, then we shall have the battlefield to ourselves.'

'Which will be of no earthly use to us unless we can find a way to stop the battle. It seems to me that Maskull must have found a way to proceed without tapping any more battlestones.'

The wizard halted him. 'Do you know that, or are you merely guessing?'

'It stands to reason!' Will studied Gwydion's grim face, which seemed as white as any sheep's head that might be found upon the moors. Then he turned away and with a tremendous effort he said, 'You're right. I *am* guessing.'

He looked up the slope again towards the hugely powerful stone. It was no more than twenty paces away now, and the fast falling night was feeding its fearfulness. Whenever he had been at Ludford he had been aware of it as a brooding presence. It had learned the knack of unsettling him. His thoughts had been turned more than once by the dark mind-songs it sang. On one occasion it had almost driven him to murder. Now his heart's wound pulsed and throbbed. He could not speak of it to the wizard. Not here. Not now. Perhaps not ever.

The last thing he wanted was to approach the stone any closer. Still, he knew that neither cowardice nor appeasement would help against malice and he forced himself to step out all but the last few of those remaining twenty paces.

'I must not try to drain it,' Gwydion muttered, 'but still I may be able to do something to make the coming battle less bloody.'

Will mouthed a soundless curse. 'While trying to bias its outcome towards your own ends, of course.'

Gwydion was almost thrown by the sourness of the accusation, but he rode it. 'I mean to interfere with the stone's process if I can, as once I did at Ludford, but this time there is an awkward complication.'

Will looked out across the bleak winter landscape as full night came down. His will to plod on failed. This was as close as he dared come to the baleful emanations, at least until he could make a renewed effort to master himself.

'You've been digging at the roots,' Will said, seeing now that the excavation had been done with sticks and bare hands.

'They are not roots. We cannot remove the battlestone from the ground because it is buried under what looks to be a tree, but which, if you look closer, you will see is not a tree at all.'

Will forced himself to move another step. It required all the courage he had, all the courage needed to plunge a knife into his own heart. When he reached out to touch the trunk he saw his fingers vanish, and as he looked down at himself he saw that his left side had become invisible.

He did not draw his hand away, seeing through the crudeness of the stone's attack.

The tree was as cold and solid as an anvil.

'An iron statue of a tree?' Will breathed the words.

'It cannot be hewn down by axes. If you disbelieve me ask that Fellow you call your friend to try his strength against it. This stone has hidden itself well in a cage of its own making. I wonder how long it took for its remorseless seepings to transform this noble oak into a fiendish protection.'

'No longer than one of its brothers took to send Lord Clifton insane, I'll warrant.'

Gwydion walked sunwise around the trunk, igniting blue flames of magelight at intervals, so the iron tree was lit up weirdly like an enchanter's crown. 'I have tried to melt it with blasts, but though the iron glows first red, then yellow, and at last white, such heat as I can direct upon it does not even scar it.'

Lotan caught them up. 'Why don't we blow it to pieces with sorcerer's powder?'

The wizard scowled, but said nothing. Instead he took Will aside and said, 'Come with me a little way, for I would speak with you alone.' And when they had come down the hill and were out of Lotan's earshot, 'You must give me your word that you will not pass on what I tell you. Not to him.'

Will stiffened. 'Do not offer me divisive secrets, Master Gwydion. We are one company and whatever you say to me I will tell to whomsoever I choose.'

'Then at least promise me that you will choose with care when you do so, for this I *must* tell you: there is no sign of the battlestone having been tampered with, but you are right in your guess that Maskull may no longer have any need to work with the stones directly. He has used the harm he decanted at Delamprey to make not just a weapon, as we have been supposing, but I think now a *means* of making weapons.'

The implications of that idea chased one another rapidly through Will's mind, and he narrowed his eyes. 'You mean he has something that he can make as many weapons from as he wishes? Like a store of harm maybe? But that implies—'

'Quietly!' Gwydion looked vigilantly to where Lotan lingered alone. 'Simply put, it is part of Maskull's attempt to survive the collision of worlds with his personal power intact. I believe he is now ready to use fae magic to pack up a quantity of harm and carry it across, so that after the collision he may more easily become sole master of whatever remains.'

'Where did you learn all this?'

'Shhh! As you know, loremasters have ways of keeping one another informed.'

'The wreath of leaves back at the crossroads – that was your message.'

'Not that, but another like it. Some time ago, Lord Morann, who has been about certain tasks on my behalf, warned that Maskull might have found a way to concentrate the harm which has already been released into the middle airs.'

Will gave a gasp of despair. 'Oh, now *that* would be ironic.'

'Indeed. As yet, Morann cannot be sure of the truth of it, but it appears that Maskull has not properly appreciated that if he sucks up the harm that has been dispersed from the battlestones, then he will begin to steer us away from the collision that he so eagerly anticipates.'

'How refreshing to see him do something that works to our advantage for a change.' Will allowed himself a smile until a sudden, vicious doubt speared him. 'But surely he's not ignorant of the consequences of what he's attempting. He must know something that we don't. Or maybe the rumour Morann heard was a calculated lie left for us to find.'

'Well, in that case, our journey to this place will not have been in vain. We shall be here when the armies clash, so if Maskull does need to tap one more stone, then he will have to attend this place with rather more urgency than he attended Awakenfield, hmmm?'

'Is there really so little time left?'

The wizard regarded him for a moment. 'I see from your

eyes that you already know the answer to that. The days of this world are numbered. Days, I say. Not months or years. According to the Black Book our world is sitting on the very brink of the precipice.'

Will fought his despair. Despite Gort's gritty elixir, and despite their having come a fair distance away from the stone, still a sense of doom was forcing its way through his defences. He made his response deliberately brave. 'Then we'd better get on with the job!'

Gwydion's eyes glittered with a weird light. 'This time, I shall sit by the stone and close my trap on Maskull. And you, Willand – you must bear witness.'

That struck Will as an arch thing to say, a rejection. Fears for Willow's safety burst in his breast. The wizard's plan seemed all at once to be ill-considered and monstrously perilous, and the wizard himself to be wheedling and sly. He fought the feelings of revulsion, telling himself they were false and only the stone's doing. But as he began to wander away, Gwydion seized his cloak and growled, 'Do not speak of this to that Fellow, I warn you!'

'You *warn* me?' Will's anger flared up, but somehow, he stifled it and nodded. 'If you will agree to treat him with the respect he deserves while I'm away, I will say nothing.'

The wizard narrowed his gaze. 'Are you going somewhere?'

Will felt more reluctance rumble through him. 'I . . . have to. I must bring news of the duke's fate to Edward.'

'But you cannot leave us now!'

'Watch me. By first light. By moonlight if there be any. I must.'

'Tell Edward what has happened and you will make the killing here all the worse.'

'He must know that his father and brother are dead. That is his right. And the news should come from me.' He looked to the half-hidden stone and back, and said with undue curtness, 'Don't worry, I won't interfere with your plans.'

'You do not even know where Edward is!'

'I shall find him.'

Their stares met – fire on fire – but then the wizard accepted Will's decision with a sigh. 'I am sure you will. Edward is encamped a league and a half beyond Yatton Mystery. Go north up the Slaver road and his tents will come into view. Be careful that the archers he posts as pickets do not mistake you for a Cambrayman. And fair fortune go with you.'

□ □ □

CHAPTER TWENTY

THREE SUNS

A lone man riding a horse in the misty dawn posed no threat to the great army of a Marcher lord, and Will was allowed to enter all the way into Edward's camp before being halted.

There was an assembly of ten thousand men gathered in the crook of the Lugg valley. In addition, perhaps half as many again were moving down from Wyg Moor. Already, bands of archers were being deployed, going in all likelihood to the wooded slopes above Morte's Crossing ready to ambush the Cambray army. The enemy were marching in the slender hope they could catch Edward in one of his lesser castles. There, holed-up and helpless, Jasper imagined, Edward might be brought to terms.

But it was a ludicrous hope, and one destined to be dashed. A general muster seemed to be in progress as Will sought permission to approach Edward's tent enclosure. The wait was agonizing as he went over again what he would have to say. Edward had always idolized his father, and might now blame himself for having left the duke on bad terms. Whether that had been so or not, Edward had certainly believed an erroneous interpretation of Mother Brig's prophecy that 'Ebor shall o'erlook Ebor'. He had, at the last, spoken ill of his brother. And it was wholly possible that Edward, on learning of the tragedy, might convince himself that the rift between son and father had been to blame for it.

Now that Will had put distance between himself and the Doomstone of the West his head was clearer. He tried thinking as Gwydion was accustomed to think. The wizard was an old hand at statecraft, hugely careful about what he said to whom and for what reason. He could put himself in another's position with great accuracy and was adept at predicting what one so addressed would think when given a piece of news. But Will could only wonder what Edward would do when he heard the bitter truth. Would he storm and rage? Would he freeze? Would he break down? Or did he have enough spring steel in his spirit to lay aside the news until after the battle and so do his duty towards those whom he led? Will found it impossible to know the answer, but he knew with certainty that Edward should learn what had happened without delay, and the news would come better from him than from anyone else in the world.

He turned his mind to Willow. After he had taken himself aside and drawn power from the earth, they had hugged one another close in the darkness, but he had found her truly fearful about losing him. He had not told her about his revelation. It was not the right time. Premonitions were not for him alone, she had said. And though he had told her it was only the stone that was making her terrors rise up like that, he had not been wholly convincing. She had always been able to see right through him. She knew that the end-time was coming, and that he was not certain that he could survive it.

'I wish you didn't have to go,' she had said as he prepared to mount up.

He hardened his gaze. 'I must do this.'

'Well . . . if I don't see you before the battle begins,' she said, eyes filling, 'know that I'll stand by Master Gwydion and do just as he asks.'

'That's what worries me. I'd much rather you went to Ludford and banged on the door until they gave you shelter.'

She had hugged him tight. 'That's not for me, Will, and you know it.'

'Come, come!' Gort had said, handing Will the reins. 'Dark the dawn when day is nigh! Hustle your horse and don't say die, hey!'

Will looked up now at the milky pale sky. The dark of dawn had become a morning of low mists and high, spiritous clouds that spoke of turmoil in the upper airs. As the sun rose, its wan rays drove ice from the ground, turning wherever it struck into a cold and volatile dew. A sea of tents filled Luggvale, and threads of woodsmoke rose up from innumerable camp fires into the still air.

Numbers of horsemen were pouring down the valley now, thundering across the slopes and massing on the plain. Will saw his chance passing and insisted time and again to the stern-faced guards who kept the noblemen's enclosure that he had brought vital news. News of a battle lately fought at a place in the north, and that Edward *must* receive him.

But he was kept waiting.

What excuse could there be? The vigil that all knights made on the eve of battle should have been done with long ago. The meeting with Edward's lieutenants must be over too. Even the ritual donning of his steel suit could not be taking so long . . .

At last Will could bear it no longer. He knew that he must act. If the problem needed magic then so be it.

Of the three well-armed guards, the two younger were at the gate. An older guard of greater girth stood a dozen paces away. All of them were helmeted in sallets with visors raised across their brows. That would make it tricky.

Will drew power unobtrusively, muttered as if to himself, and tried not to seem strange as he wheeled and stepped out the points of a pentacle. After a while the two nearer guards began to sweat in the sunshine. Their faces turned red. They moved their weight uncomfortably from one foot to the other. Before Will could count to seventy-seven, the chief guard loosened his chin strap and walked towards the others, blowing.

'It's a warm one for this time of year.'

As soon as they saw their chief take off his helmet the others unbuckled theirs. Will gathered himself again, speedily danced out a jelly-knee spell, knocked off the guards' caps and touched their foreheads – one, two, three! They fell among one another in a faint, poleaxes clattering.

Before they had hit the ground Will was halfway to the largest and richest of the tents. The inside was opulently equipped with folding chairs, rugs, a writing desk and two large chests. But no Edward.

Will cursed. He must move quickly if he was to escape. He turned back to the exit, looked about, then stepped outside. As soon as he was in the sunshine he began shouting for help and calling attention to the sleeping men. When the rest of the guard came he pointed to the tent. 'There he goes! There, the villain!'

'Hold him,' said one with a taller crest on his helmet than the others.

Five of the seven newly-arrived guards made for their lord's tent, fearing some theft was being attempted. Will played the indignant witness with the sixth man but was forced to take a chance by breaking away from the last. The guard tried to hold him, but Will stepped back, wrapped himself in his cloak and melted away.

He was furious with himself for bearing all the delays yet still having to resort to magic, but at least he had escaped arrest. As he went he heard the flare of trumpets, and he halted, wondering what to do for the best. All around, men were breaking ranks and running towards the sound. Will resisted being swept along, but then he too broke into a run, knowing now that he was not the cause, and that only one man could have this effect on the army.

His suspicions were confirmed, for out of the woods galloped a line of huge battle chargers, flying all the standards loyal to the House of Ebor. Men in blued or mirror-bright steel glided through the cheering troops. Wherever Edward had been, he had returned.

Will knew he must fight his way to the front before the soldiers packed in too solidly. In moments they would make it impossible for him to get any closer without the spells he so wanted to avoid. The troops were gathering before Edward in expectation of a rousing speech. They wanted words from their lord, words to boil up their blood, words to put fire in their bellies. Edward, so avidly modelled on his father, would not disappoint them.

There was now no alternative for Will but to thrust himself forward immediately. He broke through into the open path of the cantering warriors, and began to writhe in a serpentine dance that made the lead horses shy. His mouse-brown cloak whirled and threw off a green light. As that light touched upon nearby trees it caused them to bud and burst into leaf. Those who saw it crouched in amazement, struck dumb now as skylarks took up their silence and ten thousand daffodils surged from sleep across the water meadow.

Will raised his arms and called out momentously, 'Edward of Ebor, hearken unto me!'

And Edward did hearken. He tried to urge his horse forward, but it would not go. At a signal all but the earl's squire fell back, but this man came and took off his lord's long spurs so that Edward could dismount and move to within a sword's length of the strange enchanter who had burst springtime from the lea.

Will felt a powerful bond with Edward, a bond that was more than an echo of old friendship. In that moment it seemed blood-powerful, almost like kinship. He bowed his head, and when he raised it there were tears in his eyes. 'Friend Edward, I come with sad tidings concerning your father and brother.'

But Edward was ready for him. 'It is the false messenger!' he cried. 'Let it speak, for that is the only way we shall have done with it.'

Edward's voice was steel hard, his glance deadly, like a man making just so much time for an essential matter he has been neglecting but which now has to be cleared up. Will saw the dreadful darkness in that face and supposed that at any moment he might be seized and an order given that he be beheaded as a liar and a traitor.

Edward shouted to the sky, as if to some hidden magician, 'Let it speak now, or I shall pass on!'

Will took his strange reception with incredulity, hardly understanding the manner that had come over Edward. 'There has . . . there has been a bloody battle by the Castle of Sundials,' he began. Then he went on to tell the story of the Awakenfield disaster as briefly and compassionately as he could, relaying all that had happened of which he had sure knowledge. He told of the death in battle of the duke, and the murder of Edmund, but as he came to speak of the way in which the queen had made her decoration for the city's gate, Edward's strange pent-up expression exploded into impatience.

He addressed the air a second time. 'Hear me, sorcerer! I have heard enough from this *thing*! Whatever it may be, let it speak no more on the matter of my family, or I will cleave it in two parts!'

Will was staggered by the madness that seemed to have overcome the warrior. 'Please listen to me, Edward, your father is dead—'

'Begone, I say, meddlesome spirit! Trouble my days no more!' He tilted his face again to the sky. 'I will have no more of this. Do you hear me, sorcerer?'

And with that he cast over Will a black powder poured out from the heel of his gauntlet, a powder that blinded and choked and threw Will to his knees. And while Will groaned and staggered, the new Duke of Ebor mounted up and led his people onward at the trot.

Will's face burned as if it had been smitten with hot ashes. He rolled and gasped, then found his feet and ran like a madman. And perhaps it was only that insane dash that saved him from being trampled into the grass by Edward's haughty escort, for they were used to despising that which their master despised. And perhaps it was only the presence of the escort that saved Will, for they screened him from the malice of the common soldiers.

He ran like a lunatic across the boggy ground, making for the river. He threw himself into the icy water to thrash like so much dirty laundry against the river stones in hopes of washing that acrid powder away.

'You're no King Arthur!' he cried, cursing himself. 'You're no Master Gwydion! Just a half-man set to flight by a handful of sorcerer's powder! What hope is there now?'

His impotence turned to rage and his rage to violence as he struggled to the banks of the Lugg and tore up fistfuls of cool grass and slammed his toes into the muddy earth. There he lay, caring little for the world, until the cheers and shouts in the distance prickled him more than the slowly subsiding pain in his eyes. He walked across the green, seeing now the withered yellow blooms as they sagged and browned on their stalks. They had been ripped from their bulbs by ill-devised magic and drooped, dying in their thousands. Humbled and hurt, slimed with mud, a pauper in his weeds, he went to sit in the branches of a tree, to see what wonders might come next.

But if there was magic in the air now it was none of
Will's making, for the young duke was giving an oration to
his army, and Will saw that seated on a horse to Edward's
left was his youngest brother, Richard, and to his right his
other brother, George. They were boys still. Young boys.
Too young for battle. Yet they were armoured, and being
shown off to the army as encouragement.

Will dripped and shivered, defeated. He fumed blackly,
thinking out what had just come to pass. The battlestone
was working hard on Edward now, but this matter had the
whiff of another kind of sorcery about it. Even now it was
hard to say if Edward truly understood what had been told
to him. Had a spell been cast upon his comprehension? He
behaved like a man who had already been told some twisted
version of the truth, a man who had already made up his
mind what to believe . . .

And then there was the powder. What knight rode to his
destiny with a glove full of sorcerer's powder? It was as if
Edward had been forewarned to expect a magical intervention. As if he had been counselled about what to do, and
given the counter-measure.

Will squeezed the sourness from his eyes. There had
been weak magic in the powder, a slapdash formulation
that had largely run to ground by the time it had been
hurled in his face. A spell of blinding and burning, but
incompetently made. He took a crumb of comfort from
the fact that, by comparison, his own efforts had not been
so crude. But still he had failed, for here he was up a tree
and catching cold, while the man of the moment was
bewitching the crowd.

Will's teeth chattered as he tried to tune his ear to
Edward's words. When he looked skyward, it was in amazement, for where there had been one sun, shining low down
in the south, now there were three!

Three suns blazing? How could that be? It was a trick

of the moist air, nothing more, a phenomenon of sunlight penetrating the mists. It could not be otherwise for there was no feel of glamour about it, though the men who gawped at it were ready to believe too quickly in omens.

Will tilted his head, shaded his eyes, and almost fell from his perch. Great consternation spread among the soldiers below. Many knelt and clasped their hands together or stared at one another in vast dismay. But when the hubbub died down, Edward's voice carried clearer and he told the assembled thousands that this was indeed a sign that had been foretold. A sign from Almighty God, a wonder carried down from Heaven, a sign of the glorious afterlife now being enjoyed by the previous Duke of Ebor.

A bell tolled dully in Will's heart, for now he saw just how deeply the whisperings of the Sightless Ones had polluted Edward's spirit. He was repeating the dangerous vision that was laid out in the Great Lie.

'Dazzle mine eyes!' Edward cried, looking now to the brilliant light. 'Three suns in a clear-shining sky! Three suns that are to signify the three remaining sons of Ebor! See, my brothers! These that are yet boys – they are not afraid to die, for they see how the pearly sky brings forth for us our omen of victory!'

And now all who watched the three suns saw the flanking lights glow the brighter, then fade.

'See how three suns become one again! We will not fail you, our father! We shall fight for you, and if we win yours shall be the glory! And if we die we shall live again along-side you in Heaven!'

And with those rapturous words, and many another, did Edward, Duke of Ebor, set the blaze then stoke up the roaring fire of his army. He exhorted the men of his battalions to pass southward down the Slaver road, to carry arms between the heights that in the time of the Brean kings had fortresses set upon their crests like crowns. Those hills frowned down upon the narrow way through Yatton Mystery, and though not a man who travelled that old Slaver road knew if he would live to see the sun go down again, not a man cared.

With a heavy heart, Will watched the army march away, watched the last of them, set boiling by oratory, leave the muster field and head joyfully towards their fate, convinced by a mere refraction of the light.

Words, words, simple words. Was that all it took to turn the minds of men? Magic of a new sort that encouraged them to drop the most obvious of truths and set their hearts upon the most self-serving of notions? So it seemed to Will. Those words were far more than they seemed, and he knew it. They were like trigger spells, set to trip the catch of a furnace door that held back a flaming desire to *believe*.

'You all deserve to die!' he shouted after them, shaking his fist. 'Lambs! Calves! Has not one of you even half a mind to question? Must you believe in every sly and designing fancy that is fed to you? I hate your stupidity more than you will ever know, do you hear me?'

He began to climb down from his tree, still muttering and railing against the battlestone's victory over the common herd. He shouted into the face of a woman who stared at him in surprise. 'They do not care for hard truth, only soft lies that they think will help them better! But they are being led away from the true path and no mistake! What's the matter with all of you? Have you no wills of your own?'

But the woman hurried off in alarm and no one else would listen to a lunatic. Will's anger at the foolishness of others began to be tempered by an anger that was directed at himself. He had meant to warn Edward not to engage the enemy, but instead to let Gwydion broker a peace. He had meant to say that this enemy was in fact a reasonable man, Jasper of Pendrake, a man horrified by what had already happened, a man convinced that the war had gone on long enough. But in the event he had said nothing.

Will sat down in the trampled field and laughed in despair. He had meant to do so much, but in all things he had failed. There was no one to hear him now, save the old men, women and boys whose job it was to dismantle the camp and make ready the baggage train. If Will were to mount up on his palfrey now and ride as fast as the patient plodder would go, he could not possibly reach the stone until battle had been joined. The long way around these wooded hills allowed of no alternative. He would have to tag onto the tail of Edward's host as it passed like sand through the waist of an hourglass. He would have to hope that time enough remained while the army took position to slip through to the iron tree.

There was magic, but no spell he knew would help – and there were drawbacks.

But why break his neck to reach the battlestone? To blunder into things again and probably get himself cut to pieces? Or worse, to mess up Gwydion's complicated plan and get his wife killed? Half-man! the stone had taunted him. Half-man! Half-man indeed!

All desire drained from him. He looked up into the milky sky and felt the warmth of the sun playing upon his face. He closed his eyes. The tang of woodsmoke was on the air. He heard the reedy voices of children running about among the tents. And he knew that the stone had struck to the very marrow of his bones. All it takes to make a ship founder is for the steersman to take his hand off the tiller, he told himself. No matter how hard it seems, and how weary and hopeless I am, *I have to try one more time.*

CHAPTER TWENTY-ONE

THE SECOND DUEL

When Will had calmed himself he went to an open space to draw power again from the earth. He knew he must replenish what he had wasted, but there was an uneasy reluctance in the ground. Maybe he was too close to the Heligan lign. Or more likely the fault was with him, for he had asked aid of the earth four times in as many days, and that was something he had never done before.

Where his feet sunk into the sodden turf the water welled warm. When he came to his senses, he knelt down to touch the muddy pools with his fingers. They steamed gently and confirmed what his toes had already told him – that a battle was almost upon them. And now, as he walked back towards the camp he felt a prickle of warning.

Hundreds of waggons were lined up – the Ebor baggage train, waiting to receive tentage. Win or lose today, Edward's army would not rest here tonight.

As he came by the tail of a waggon drawn up where his horse had been tethered he heard laughter. It was not unlike his own laugh, but mocking. And when he turned, he saw himself looking back.

'Step closer to the mirror, little brother.'

Fear gripped him and suddenly everything fell into place. 'It had to be you.'

'Or . . .' again that cruel grin and a pointing finger, ' . . . you.'

The sulphur sourness of misspent magic flared in Will's mouth and nose. Then, with a twist and a flourish of mouse-brown, the cloak and the fair braided hair were gone. A black-clad figure was eyeing him instead, and in its hand was a small bird-hunter's crossbow.

Will stared at his twin. 'You spoke with Edward. He thought you were me.'

'It was not a difficult disguise to put on.'

'What did you tell him?'

'Can't you guess? To beware the one who would come to him moments before the fight. "He will be dressed in my flesh," said I. "A demon messenger sent by the sorcerer, Maskull. A copy of me, albeit a good one. But no more than smoke and mirrors. He will tell you lies, Friend Edward. Don't listen to him."'

'But you told him all the lies already.' Will's blood boiled as he realized how he had been robbed of the chance to bring the terrible truth to Edward.

Chlu laughed. 'Of course, I told him all about his father's valiant fight, and how victory was snatched from him by the perfidy of his enemies. I explained how Duke Richard with his dying breath implored me to bring the news to his beloved son so that he might be avenged. "Do not rest, my son, until they are all dead. Every last one of them. Then I shall lie easy in my grave." Oh, he's ready for the fight now.'

'You even gave him the sorcerer's powder for his glove.'

'To banish the demon. Did it sting your eyes?' Chlu laughed, but then the laugh caught in his throat and he said, 'But it's really down to *me* to banish you, isn't it?'

Chlu raised the crossbow, and in the same moment Will reached behind him and slid a tent pole out of the cart, launching it across his shoulder like a spear in a single movement at Chlu's head. It seemed that the pole made contact, for Chlu raised a hand to ward it off, but it was too late – the crossbow had already shot.

The bolt caught Will's splayed left hand and nailed it momentarily to his chin. He pulled it away in horror, but as soon as he clasped the fingers of his right hand around the bolt head, he was hit by a stunning red beam. He heard himself howl. It felt as if he had been kicked in the jaw by a horse then thrown against a wall. He fought unconsciousness, knowing that if he gave in to it he was a dead man, but an indescribable feeling of dislocation overcame him, and he found himself sprawling upon grass, staring up at a sky that was suddenly all dense cloud and threatening rain.

What had happened? Panic fear drenched him. He suddenly thought that he had been carried somehow into that other world, the one that he feared. What if it was so?

But no, he had felt this strange sensation before.

When?

He jumped up, ready for the fight, heart pounding, muscles tensed, then he stumbled to his knees again. Chlu was gone. The entire camp was gone. Everything was *different*.

His eyesight was swimming, so he shook his head to clear it. When he looked around he saw dry winter grasses shivering, rabbit droppings and sheep-cropped turf, bushes of wind-torn gorse – wherever this was it was high up. A mossy hillside, cold and windy, and an angry sky that was very different from the one he had left behind.

He's vanished me, he thought. The beam – he's landed a vanishing spell on me. But where's it taken me to? And how?

Anger surged through him, prompted by his own weakness and the irony of having been caught by the very same trap that had been proposed for Maskull. I should have been on guard against such an attack, he thought. But at least I'm not on the Baerberg . . .

He felt disconnected from the world, and when he looked down at his hands they struck him as strange. There was no pain in his wounded hand, and hardly any blood yet, just a ragged hole in the web of skin between finger and thumb. He touched his jawbone. Instead of a bloody hole there was a dimple that felt as if it had been closed up by heat. He had been lucky. But wait – he looked again at his outstretched hands. He had the strongest feeling that they were on his wrists the wrong way round. And what was worse, he could not remember if his thumbs should be on the inside or the out.

What's happened? he thought, a grotesque fear surging up inside him. What's he done to me?

But there was a more pressing matter. Cursing, he jammed the shaft of the bolt into a joint in the rock and, with a grimace, leaned on it. The shaft snapped, and he was able to pull it out through the wound.

'By the moon and stars . . .'

The dart's head was a chip of heavy, black stone. He looked at it, then at the dark ledges that protruded from the ground nearby. So that was it! There was no mystery about what had happened – this had been the trigger for the vanishing spell.

A new suspicion made him look to the south. It was hard to tell, but it seemed from the shafts of light that played over the patchwork of farms and woods that the sun was lower and further east than it had been moments ago.

'Change place, change time,' he reminded himself. 'Gywdion said that time could go backwards, but can it do that after a vanishing spell? If it can, that gives me more time!'

He looked at his hands again, still unable to recall which way round they should be. He closed his eyes, but that only made it worse. It was maddening.

'You're just knocked a little silly,' he told himself. 'You'll be alright in a moment or two.'

The ground was astonishing here, like a miniature forest. Gort would have delighted in it, for it was springy as a mattress, green with mosses and spotted with pale lichens. The sky was huge with a glory bursting through the clouds, sending beams of sunlight down over the earth.

As he scrambled over the summit he saw what looked like the skeleton of a building. It stood a little below on the shoulder of the hill. Beyond it, long views stretched east and south and west over what must have been three or four earldoms. The curious building was only a shell, but it was not a ruin: four sturdy posts supported a pitched roof of wooden shingles. It was not meant to be a barn because it was open on all four sides, and there was nothing stored inside except some sheaves of damp and rotting straw and a great lattice of timbers stacked higher than a man into which old tree branches and dried gorse bushes had been packed. When Will approached he saw that the ground was shadowed black like that around a charcoal burner's mound.

Nearby, and unseen at first, was a stone-built hovel, no more than a windowless den set hard against the stone outcrop from which it seemed to have grown. Pale smoke trailed from a chimney, and when Will pushed open the door he found signs that the place had been recently occupied. No one was at home, but it was warm inside and untidy and it smelled unexpectedly of tar. In its way, the place was homely, a welcome relief from the bleakness outside. Wyrmstone glowed on the hearth, and lumps of it were stacked ready nearby. There were cooking pots and rude furniture pushed against the walls – a table and benches where two or three men might sit down together. There was even a sleeping place covered with sheepskins. In the opposite corner was the bucket that accounted for the tarry smell. A wooden handle was sticking out of it.

Blood dripped from Will's hand. He fumbled in his pouch and found the tiny shard of stone, scraped the last of it away with his knife and sprinkled the grit into both sides of the wound. Then he found a dirty rag and began to bind up the crook of his thumb. As he did so, the realization of where he had come to struck him like a hammer blow.

'Of course . . .'

He went outside again. That roof was what had thrown him. The whole structure had been designed to burn. It had to be ready to fire at any time, and how else could the weather be kept off the kindling but by a roof? As for the bales, the light of a fire would be visible by night, but by day a beacon would need to throw up quantities of thick smoke . . .

This must be Cullee Hill, he thought. And the watchers – wherever they are – must be Edward's men!

He turned into the teeth of the wind and went to overlook the western prospect. But he was puzzled to find there was no Ludford down on the plain to confirm his guess, no Cambray mountains beyond.

The watchers must have a look-out, he decided, probably a hut on the eastern side and a little down from the summit where there would be shelter from rain and the prevailing wind. They would want to look towards Trinovant and to the chain of beacons that relayed by prior arrangement great decisions made at the White Hall.

He drew his cloak tighter about him. Prevailing wind? That should be a westerly. But surely this wind was coming out of the east . . .

He shook his head again, trying once more to shake off the oddness of his thoughts. Blood had soaked the rag wrapping his right hand and pain had begun to throb there. His jaw was burning too, but the discomfort was muted and he could feel the magic of Gort's grit already beginning to work in all his flesh.

When he rounded the ridge he saw distant mountains rising in limitless shades of blue, and down on the colour-less winter plain below, a castle and a town . . .

'That can't be!' he cried, staring, looking back over his shoulder and staring again. 'Ludford?'

But Ludford was to the west of Cullee Hill, not east of it. Even so, there could be no doubting what lay below. He could make out the distinctive roofs of the castle and the square mass of the keep. He looked at his hands again, and slowly it began to dawn on him why his mind was so befuddled.

East was west, and west was east, reversed like the letters he had once read in a lady's looking-glass.

But how could that be? And where had he come to?

'Bad magic!' he cried. 'Rough and badly wrought! By all that's best and beautiful, what is this place?'

As he scrambled back across the ridge he realized he was not alone. He caught a flash of crimson light above him, then he sensed movement on the crest. When he stepped back, he saw his twin appear out of thin air.

Chlu was facing in the other direction, but Will could see that his hand was bound up where the metal spur of the tent pole had speared him. And when Chlu turned to look about himself, Will saw that there was blood on his chin. Chlu cast something aside, and Will knew it was another piece of blackstone from the summit, the trigger he had used for the vanishing spell he had laid on himself.

Will dived down like a hunted animal, wondering what else of the destructive arts Maskull had taught to this most superficial of scholars. He brought himself up sharp. Whatever else was true, the rules had changed now, it seemed. Chlu's previous attacks had been furious, but they had not been magical. Something – fear perhaps – had prevented him from using magic against his twin. It was almost as though Maskull had issued a warning against it. But if he had, why?

Will clung to the turf, dug his fingers into the stony soil, his mind still in shock and rushing over the possibilities.

And why has he brought me here? he thought. If he was going to ambush me with a vanishing spell, why not tip the bolt with the claw of a wyrm from far Xanadu? Or better still a sea shell? Why not send me to the bottom of the Western Deeps?

His eyes locked on the black form. Chlu came to a halt and threw back his head. He was still some paces from the beacon, but the flames that came screaming from his hands lit the structure and consumed it with fire. Chlu delighted like a mad ogre, blasting the waiting timbers with brilliant orange, releasing flames in which demonic shapes twisted and tumbled before expiring in black billows.

Chlu staggered back. So great was the pressure of the fire streams that he ejected, he had to brace his feet against the force. So intense was the heat, that he was soon forced to break off, shielding his face as he retreated.

The beacon blazed up strongly, as if the fire had been set in a hearth and blown bright by a blacksmith's bellows. As Will watched, two of the roof posts charred through and the roof collapsed, sending a great column of smoke and sparks skyward. Flames leapt five or six times the height of a man into the air. Then, his task done, Chlu turned and began to walk straight towards his twin.

The sheep that had been patiently munching the miserly hill pasture startled and scattered. Will managed to scramble down the bank. The slope ended abruptly below him where the rocky outcrop dropped onto a flat ledge. The fall was no more than the height of a man, down onto a track. Beyond that the hillside rolled gently away again. He took one last look back, then jumped.

The fire's meant for Edward, he thought. A signal to start the battle. And now Chlu's work is done, he's coming for me.

Once under the overhanging wall Will pressed himself hard against the rock. He opened his mind and tried to maintain the icy concentration needed to draw strength from the mountain. Here the power was fresh as an upland stream, cool and nourishing to his spirit in that it was unsullied by the criss-crossing ligns that passed on the plain below, but it was also thin and threadbare, a meal of light and air. Even so, he drank, grateful for even a short measure of bliss and the encouragement that came with it.

Above him Chlu was only ten paces away now. Will stepped out from the wall of rock and raised his hands as if to fling fire at his twin.

'No further!'

Chlu put his hands on his hips and looked down. His brazen manner was what fools mistook for confidence, but wise men recognized as vainglory. 'Ah, there you are, little brother.'

'Stay where you are!'

'Or what? You'll speak my name and destroy me?' Again that cruel smile. 'And yourself too, I suppose?'

'Never doubt that I'd do it, Llyw.'

Will pronounced the name with precision, but his twin ridiculed him. 'My true name won't help you this time – even if you knew how to say it. Lord Maskull has told me what would happen if you tried. A spell so made would break back on you, and you would die too!'

'Fear won't stop me when the time comes.'

The Dark Child looked at him strangely as if he had formulated an idea beyond comprehension. 'You say that now, but in the event . . .'

The wind howled, carrying Chlu's words away. He danced back from the outcrop. It must have been an illusion, but he seemed to spin, faster and faster, until he had drilled himself down into the earth. Then the whole mass of rock below tore away and began to rumble down. It drove Will before it like some fearsome siege engine breaking open a castle wall. A weight of stones and soil cascaded onto him, but he raised a shield of green light that turned the danger as it fell upon him.

Chlu rode the landslide of earth rubble forward, bursting fire from the gorse bushes below as he came. The ground shuddered with detonations.

Will found his feet, danced again and clapped his hands above his head. The clouds above turned slate grey.

Then – nothing.

'No more clever tricks?' Chlu pouted. 'Are you out of arrows, little brother? No matter. You'll have no need of them where you're going. Don't you realize yet that you've been doomed by your master's scheme?'

'What do you mean?'

'The trap Gwydion Stormcrow devised to send Lord Maskull to the Baerberg seems to have caught a far less able magician – you! Now I've got you where I want you.'

Will whispered and clapped his hands again, harder now. He tore off the rag that bound the swollen ball of his thumb and clapped a third time. The clouds boiled, sickly, dark and heavy-bellied, but still no dousing rain came as Will had wanted. His appeal to the clouds had failed.

Chlu laughed, stood tall and raised up his hands like vipers' heads. Without thinking, Will countered. Twin thunderbolts flew in opposition. They burst against one another in green and red. Where the flames met midway between them, a great disc of fire spiralled out. The heat from it seared Will's face. He roared in reply until he could roar no more, and just as his fire gave out, so did Chlu's.

Smoke rose from Will's singed cloak. His hands had turned soot-black. He dived behind a burning bush, once more taking cover. Then, delayed by its fall from the middle airs, the rain he had summoned came down. It had met the wind on its way and had become dense and driving. It did what Will had meant it to do, which was to put out the fires and quench the combat.

Fighting fire with fire is foolish, he reminded himself. Always use water . . .

For a while, the rain blinded both of them with its intensity. But the deluge was short-lived, and as Will found fresh cover, red beams began to hunt him out. They tore up the hill all around. And there was rage behind those deadly rays – unsubtle, impatient, ill-directed rage.

But if Chlu lacked magical style, he made up for it with raw power. What Maskull had taught him was deadly enough. The beams were powerful, sufficient to burst steam from wet moss and send the sheep bolting. Will went to ground, but he gasped as the lethal light flashed ever nearer to the place where he had chosen to hide.

He'll hunt me out, he thought. In the end he'll find me. He can do no other, for until he does away with me I'll remain a threat to him.

His heart hammered against his ribs. He could feel it beating against the *right* side of his breastbone . . .

He had enough self-possession to realize what must have happened. The slapdash magic of the vanishing spell had left them both turned about. Something in the spell had been wrongly cast. Chlu had managed to mix up left and right.

As he crabbed round the slope, he began to see how that faulty magic had worked on him. He understood now why he had felt disorientated – this was not some strange looking-glass world he had come to. The reason things seemed to be the wrong way round was because he himself had been changed. Not only had his body been reversed, but also his brain and all its workings, so it was the outside world that looked wrong.

And Chlu? he wondered. Surely he had been affected in the same way too.

Another red beam slashed, burning a path through a patch of bracken, flashing across his aching eyes. Will danced away and summoned fork lightning suddenly from the angry sky. He struck it at Chlu, who leapt aside, and in revenge sent twin fire balls to blast the knoll behind which Will had fled.

And so the deadly dance continued, repeating the pattern time and again. Will hid, but Chlu found him. Will fought Chlu off and attacked, then it was Chlu's turn to run. The fight ranged the summit of Cullee Hill, filling the air with deafening bursts as they hurled flame at one another's heads and called down hail and vapours in turn from the air. But it was happening now as it had happened on the Spire: every blow drew a parry, every counterblow was anticipated. Neither could gain the advantage, and in the end both tired and were forced to withdraw to gather strength for a new effort.

Will's body trembled with fatigue as he came down from the top of the hill. He felt drunk with effort. His eyes popped with phantom lights where a scarlet beam had momentarily caught his vision. He was drained. Neither could he any longer draw power enough for great magic, and so soon they would have to start on a fray of fists and fury.

By now the beacon had all but burned itself out, and Will realized that if he was seeing east as west, then time must have jumped forward rather than back. It was no longer morning but afternoon. The sun was setting, not rising, and the battle at Morte's Crossing must therefore already have started. It might even have finished. He teetered on the fragile edge of laughter, seeing suddenly that all his efforts had come to naught. And if that's so, then I have nothing better to do than finish my own business up here, he thought.

He felt that his only protection would be to kill Chlu, despite what that meant. How could he do that? It would require less courage to hack off his own arm. It was hopeless. He dragged himself away, fighting off the weakness that was closing in on him. But the magic would no longer come. He was weak. Nor could he draw further refreshment in this high place until it was itself replenished, for the power here was as thin as the wind.

He cursed his flesh and told himself he should have been better prepared. He could easily have nipped the problem in the bud if he had come to his decision sooner. If only he had had the ruthlessness to believe that getting in the first blow was the right thing to do, then he could have blasted Chlu while his back was turned, while he was busy lighting the beacon.

But it was nonsense. It would not have worked. Because something would have prevented it. Something always did.

What was the point of even trying? He knew now, as certainly as anyone could know anything, that his goal could not be achieved. Whatever the magic that ruled the un-natural link between them, it would tolerate neither a victory nor a defeat.

That much had become obvious, though he had not understood it before. The question was, would Chlu come to the same realization?

Will stumbled and almost fell. He was broken, but he still had the strength to get down off Cullee Hill even if that meant crawling away while Chlu crawled after. Will told himself that he may have been half-blinded, but he could still see that hindsight offered a clear but danger-ously distorted view. 'Put your faith in yourself and the unalterable truths of the world,' he muttered. 'Listen to no lies and you won't go far wrong.'

Gwydion had once told him that. But with the world changing so fast, what could be regarded as an unalterable truth now?

He wiped the black from his hands, saw how the wound under his thumb had knit into a livid scar. So great had

the flux of magic been that it had knotted the broken flesh.
He laughed wryly, knowing that Chlu, wherever he was,
would be doing much the same.

However can I beat such an opponent? he wondered.
Maybe it's not possible. And if that's so, then isn't that my
protection? Maybe I should show myself, walk towards him.
If I did, wouldn't that force him to do the same?

As he pushed his way through the bushes, the gorse jags
scratched at him. Gorse, he thought. The only plant that
has thorns on its thorns. I should shove Chlu into one of
these patches and he'd never get out. I must come down
off this bare mountain. My proper place is with Willow and
the others . . .

But then he saw he had made a mistake in coming this
way, for ahead lay an unexpected interruption in the hill.
When he came to the brink he saw that a great hole, flat-
bottomed, steep-walled and shaped like a horseshoe, had
been quarried out of the living rock. He wasted no time
trying to scale it or even to look down into it, for its walls
were sheer. He made his way as quickly as he could along
the rim until he came to the bottom. The walls rose up
impressively to left and right, but ahead was a sight that
was altogether more astonishing.

It was a work of long ago, a monument of heroic size,
and made perhaps by the servants of giants who had ruled
in an Age when greater magic was in the world. The fear
that suddenly welled in Will's guts was that the figure that
commanded this great throne room was yet alive. But the
giant who sat in the chair was unmoving and made of cold
stone. A king of the Second Age of the world, he seemed. A
monarch from a time when only giants and dragons had
made the Isles of Albion their home. But there was something about this relic that spoke more of men than monsters.

'The Giant's Chair,' he breathed, recalling now the other
name that was used for Cullee Hill. 'So that's why . . .'

But this giant was unlike Magog or Gogmagog. Nor was he kin to the ogres and moorland trolls of the north. Not even Alba bore him much resemblance. Years of wind and weathering had worn his features down, rusted his iron crown into dark streaks that stained his noble face. But the passage of time had not taken away the smallest part of this great king's majesty. The giant-king *possessed* the throne on which he sat.

Will approached until the legs of the statue rose like columns to either side of him. They made an entrance, a black square opening into the base of the throne. What massive doors had once graced this tomb Will could not imagine, for there were only holes where the hinges had been torn away. This was a resting place long ago robbed of its hoard. One clue yet remained – above the lintel, in reversed ogham, carved deep and reading in the language of stones, the single word:

RUHTRA

But there was no time to stand and stare, for ahead, already waiting for him in the shadows, was Chlu. In his hand was a large stone.

CHAPTER TWENTY-TWO

THE STONE THAT WAS HEALED

W ill, fearless now, came and stood in the entrance of the tomb before his other half. He looked silently at the face that had so often disturbed his sleep and terrified his dreams. Not so now. Pale and grey that face seemed, and lacking in life. Will saw fascination there too, and knew that Chlu also saw otherness mirrored. It was like looking at all that oneself was not. This was the way they connected.

'We're not brothers,' Will said.

'We never were.' Chlu stared at him pitilessly. His fingers closed around the stone like a claw, turning it into a club. 'For all that you wanted to believe it.'

'No longer. Betrayal runs too deep in you for any trust that I might want to hazard.'

Chlu's power had thinned, left him a shadow of what he had been. He raised his hand to dash Will's brains from his head. But it was fruitless and Will knew it.

'You're fading,' he said matter-of-factly.

'Fool! It's you who is fading.' But then Chlu gazed at himself, aghast. 'What's happening? What have you done?'

Will watched his counterpart shred into the air. 'Whatever it is, you've done it, not I . . .'

But then his voice was lost like a wolf's whine rolling high on a wailing wind. Chlu dissolved into dust as he watched, and the world lost its colour, and then its form melted away entirely, so that for a moment Will's spirit seemed to go to the place it had gone that time long ago when he had been disembodied for a while and trapped inside an elder tree. All he knew was a sense of self. There was no sight, no sound, no taste, no smell, no feeling. There was no up nor down, no left nor right – only his thoughts, confirming his own existence, carrying him through a tunnel of space and time.

And then suddenly he was ten feet above the ground and falling down into a meadow. The impact jarred his ankles and shoved his knees up under his chin so that his head was thrown back painfully as he fell.

He leapt up, shaking his vision clear and pressed a hand to the back of his neck. He felt as if he had been spat out by a dragon. His mind reeled off balance for a moment, but then new thoughts coalesced in his head.

There was more danger here!

He braced himself to take another hit. But no, it seemed not to be coming after all. Only a meadow of crushed grass and brown daffodils . . .

This was the same field he had vanished from. It had to be. But why did it look so different? There were no tents here now. Only the pits of old camp fires and waggon ruts in the clay. But it was definitely the same field and, better still, everything was the right way round!

What about the wound? his inner voice demanded.

He looked groggily at his hands, at the knot of ill-healed flesh. *Was that his left hand?* He made a scribbling motion in the air, knowing that this hand must be his right one, the one he used to dip the quill. Yes! That felt very good. And so did his heart, which was beating in the left side of his chest . . .

He exulted.

I've come back, he thought. Chlu's vanishing spell was impermanent. The magic has fallen apart and we've reverted!

But how much time had passed? And what about the battle?

The power he had felt running through the land was entirely gone now. He looked around, haunted by the sense of imminent danger. Where was Chlu? A delay had attended his twin's arrival on Cullee Hill, so maybe another delay would attend his reappearance here. It was a good bet that Chlu would also return to the place where he had started.

With a bit of luck he'll fall and break his neck, Will thought. But I guess that's too much to hope for.

The idea of waylaying Chlu as he fell defenceless out of the air tempted him, and he looked around for something he could use as a bludgeon. But if his speculations about victory and defeat were correct, a weapon would solve nothing. Something unknown would intercept his killing intent, just as it intercepted Chlu's.

As his head cleared he abandoned the idea of murder. Going to find Willow and the others seemed by far the better course.

I'll find her, he thought. I'll find her and I'll tell her about what I am . . .

He saw that his horse had been taken. It must have become part of the Ebor baggage train, in which case there was nothing for it but to set out on foot. He ran towards a hole in the nearby hedge and clambered through. It made sense to get out of the open field, and even better sense to find the road. He had a few moments in hand, but it would not take Chlu long to make his appearance and he would quickly work out where his twin had gone.

Will checked the sky and saw that some of the cloud he had thickened to assist him on Cullee Hill had drifted south. The sun was now westering, dipping behind the mountains of Cambray, sending long, cold shadows across the valley. It was already late afternoon and the short day would soon be snuffed out.

He found the road and ran south along it, following the hoof marks and wheel ruts. Edward must have won, he reasoned, for if he had been beaten, then his remnant would have routed northward, in an attempt to fall back upon Wyg Moor and Ludford.

The thought should not have encouraged him, but it did. An impartial spirit was hard to maintain when Edward's mother had Bethe in her care, but the image of Jasper and his men being cut to pieces in an ambush did much to restore his sense of balance.

He crossed the Lugg by the little stone bridge at Yatton Mystery, then ran for half a league further across flat land, pushing on until his ribs ached and his second wind came. Then he began to see the bodies.

A scattering of white-faced corpses lounged carelessly across the meadows to his right. More slept in heaps where they had been tidied to the side of the road to get the carts through. These dead were whole, with heads and limbs attached to their trunks and no gross butchery evident. They had been killed by high-shot arrows entering them through shoulder or breast – most had bloody mouths and chins where they had coughed up their lives in small pools of blood. The killing arrows remained skewered in the flesh; only those that had missed their mark and stuck in the cold clay had been gathered up to be used in reply. Will looked out ahead and the pattern of the battle began to resolve itself.

Already in the gathering gloom the Sightless Ones were appearing. It was their right to possess the killing ground after a battle. At the first rumour of armies marching this way they had spread the alarm abroad. They had allowed certain local families to hide in the walled grounds of their chapter houses. But a price had been put upon their asylum, and now these favoured farmers were being herded out to dig the grave pits.

Will saw how the Fellows drove away the Wise Women who came wishing to tend the field. He hurried on, heeding no call but the terror of what might have happened to Willow.

I'd know if anything had befallen her, he thought. Surely, I'd know. But maybe I *do* know. Maybe that's what this terror is. By the moon and stars, you must stay calm!

He knew he must set aside his fears and read the field with a knowing eye, for it was important to work out how the tide of battle had ebbed and flowed. It seemed that Jasper's men had come up from the south, and Edward's battalions had fallen upon them by the banks of the Lugg. Archers on Edward's right had come from concealment to punish Jasper's advancing vanguard. Then Edward's left had outflanked them and swept their enemies back down the river.

When Will reached the bridge at Morte's Crossing he found a flooded road and gangs of fieldsmen up to their knees in the icy water. Hooded figures stood by, scanning the air, as if they knew a stranger had come among them. The Lugg had swilled back where hundreds of bodies clogged the stream. The dead were packed tight under the bridge, locked together by the force of the water.

Will hurried onward. There was no way to count the cost of what had happened, but it was clear that many thousands had died, far more than had perished at Awakenfield. Once more, the latest battle fought seemed also to have been the bloodiest. Here the rout had run south-eastwards along the meandering Lugg. Its path was marked by much blood, and a great swathe of hacked and harrowed bodies – light Cambray bill-carriers, mounted lancers, heavy mercenary swordsmen, green-clad archers – all had come to grief here. Some of the wounded were still alive, barely so, as their spirits clung to cold and mutilated flesh. They were beyond Will's capacity to aid – he had been too drained by his own fight to assist anyone – and those wounded that yet lived were too far gone now to be helped by any healing that Will might have delivered.

But, horrible though the death-strewn aftermath of battle was, as Will ran on he came to an even worse place. This field stank of bloody murder and gleeful revenge, for here, in a grassy lea by some scrubby hawthorn bushes, captured men had been collected together to have their heads stricken off. Scraps of torn linen and woollen cloth told who they were. Not great men these. Not men of name and high renown. Only esquires and men of middling worth, men whose deaths hardly seemed worth the trouble.

A couple of dozen headless bodies were all that remained of them, for their heads had been tossed into the river, and half a dozen had fetched up on a little shingle bank where a pack of roaming, masterless dogs had found them.

Will shouted and ran at the animals to drive them off. In his outrage and disgust he cursed and cast stones at them, but in the end his anger frothed over into impotent rage and he wept. He had to bring himself up sharp by reminding himself that these were dumb, feral creatures, animals not motivated by any delight in malice. They had been hurt and left hungry by men, and they would feed on men's flesh without scruple. But what made Will shiver and sent him hurrying onward was the thought that it was not the dogs who had descended into the depths of depravity here.

The darkness was falling fast now. He looked hopelessly for Jasper's colours, some sign of his fate, but he found nothing. And then he saw the iron oak atop its hill. The ground below it had been blasted and abandoned by the living who had left a scatter of dead men all about. There was no longer any sense of roaring power here, no malice swirling from its lair. Only a hole where a withered stump should have remained.

But it was not there. Someone had poked a poleaxe through the cage of roots and wrestled the shrunken stump of the great Doomstone of the West out of its long captivity. It was gone, and judging by the marks in the ground, it had been taken away in a two-wheeled cart.

And so, as the inky blackness of night put to flight all the sorrowful sights of a sour day, Will debated with himself what would be for the best. Should he stay here until first light? Or should he try to find the others without delay?

They should not be hard to find, for they must have gone with Edward's victorious army. And they should not be hard to catch, for armies did not move as swiftly as a man travelling alone. The moon offered him advice as well as the chance of a little light. A half moon, it was, and sinking slowly in the south, but it was sufficient and as it showed itself in fissures between the clouds, Will decided there was nothing to be gained from waiting.

No sooner was his choice made than he was glad of it, for he wanted now to be rid of the smell of death and leave this place. That, he knew, would take him many hours. And he was right, for he made slow progress in the unforgiving night. Caltraps had been sprinkled liberally around parts of the field – iron barbs, these were, devices that presented one of their four spikes uppermost whichever way they fell. They were meant to pierce horses' hooves and so break a charge of cavalry, but they would just as soon hobble a man finding his way in the dark.

Wind roared in the tall beeches as Will followed the river, hurrying down past a burned-out farmhouse at Kinsland. Then he turned east for two leagues, heading for the place they called 'the Leen'. It was a place of interlaced streams, and Will's feet found molehills all along the way. He recalled how one of the Wortmaster's rhymes had spoken of the Earldom of Heare, saying, 'mud, molehills and mistletoe', and it was true, for here the soil was a rich brown, and moles were many, and green globes of mistletoe hung in the winter trees like an ancient blessing.

Will found the going easier with the wind at his back, and soon he saw a huddle of dark buildings that could only be the little town of Leenstone. Will approached warily, for there were gangs of men abroad, still looking for fleeing soldiers. But the town seemed untouched by the fight, and Will knew that that was probably because of the wealth of the towered chapter house that brooded near the town, and the eminence of its Elder.

Both Edward and Jasper would have been the target of many petitioners before the battle. And among the petitioners would have been Fellows from each of the chapter houses scattered throughout the earldoms of Salop and Heare. All would have wanted to secure a charter of safety, a parchment they hoped would afford them protection against pillage.

Deals done and soldiers paid, Will thought. How much gold has changed hands? How many victual waggons were filled up by the sale of paper promises signed and sealed with the devices of Ebor or Pendrake?

There was an irony here that made Will shake his head, for the Fellowship habitually sold the worthless and the intangible to others. In the end, even they would have to admit that the possession of a great army trumped all other kinds of power – even that generated by their cellars full of gold.

And a great army had certainly been at work at Morte's Crossing. Edward's coolly competent generalship had directed the violence with masterful aplomb. He had managed the rout with perfectly controlled vengeance. Will pictured in his mind the later stages of the killing: defeated troops streaming away south and east across the Earldom of Heare, wanting to flee back into Cambray but being driven remorselessly through a land they did not know.

Ebor horsemen hunting them with long lances, striking hundreds down to be finished off by footmen following in eager bands. The simple soldier used savagery in victory to get what he wanted. He did it just as the prince used promises made beforehand.

Will dropped down and crawled in the frozen meadow mud, feeling with his fingers for the horses' prints, determining their speed and direction. Jasper's baggage train had probably been seized intact, and sent to join up with Edward's own. Will felt crushing desperation when he thought of how this war had grown stealthily upon the Realm, bursting at last like a plague-filled pustule. And the one who had been meant to stop it – at least if prophecy was to be believed – had utterly failed.

It seemed to be the saddest truth that the more one learned about the world the less there was to like about men. As Gwydion had once taught him, there was no evil in the natural world; nothing was evil except that men made it so. How, then, to stop from falling into a grotesque dislike of all things that men did? Will fixed his mind on his friends and reminded himself that there was more kindness in men than there was harm. That had to be grasped and resolutely borne in mind.

As the midnight hour approached, Will thought he had come far enough from the battlefield and from the ligns to refresh himself once more. Here, surely, he could rely on untainted earth power. But it was no good. There was still a lingering echo of fear in the land, and twice more he came across cold corpses. One wretch was dead in a ditch, but it was the second that struck Will with a bolt of panic fear, for the body sat upright in the main road, open-eyed, though stiff and naked and drenched in congealed blood.

Will howled at the sight, his flight fired at first by fear, but then by despair or something like it. He stumbled on, haunted by the hooting of owls, until his feet hurt and his lungs felt as if they were bursting. Then he tripped and fell, and he lay on his back in the empty road, feeling ready to melt down into the earth.

The moon was nearly gone now, setting in the west, and here he was, alone and half mad and fleeing from dead men in the dark. But then he thought of Lotan's nature, indomitable and steady like a bear, and he took courage.

He had travelled fully two leagues since the bridge, and maybe two more along a road to the south would bring him to the ancient city of Erewan. Edward had good reason to enter Erewan, for it was a populous place friendly to the Ebor cause and there was food and drink to be found. It also had a large brownstone chapter house, the main counting house of the earldom, where Ebor promises could be redeemed in coin. Edward's army must have gone there. And so Gwydion must have taken Willow and Gort there. And so therefore, that's where he would go.

Will told himself that he could easily reach Erewan before first light, but long ago the Conqueror's heirs had girded the city with walls, and the gates would not be opened until sunrise. The best course now was to rest. He found a place of good aspect and planted his feet, opening his mind and allowing cool power to flow into him. Afterwards, as he slowly returned to his thoughts, they seemed somehow less burdensome.

It was not long before Will came to walls that were dark and stark against the purple calm of an eastern sky. It was a freezing morning, and Ayne Gate already had many supplicants. Poor men and women waited, coughing and shuffling, beside the stock pens. Some carried loads on their backs, others sat on creaking carts. There was a knot of straggler soldiers, grim after a night of drink and wrong-doing. Their auras were ragged and brown and Will could smell shame about them, for there was blood on their hands. On the far side of the gatehouse there were four or five

Fellows, cloak-wrapped and waiting silently in the shadows. Will wondered why they were not at the Nickel Gate, which led more directly to the great counting house and the Elder's palace which took pride of place along the banks of the River Whye.

At last there came the noise of the gate-bars being slid out of their irons. The gates were swung open. Four gatemen and a sergeant each in plumed hats watched the motley host shuffle into the city. Some gruff greetings passed, but they stopped no one. These men also seemed to have had a hard night, and Will saw that this was no ordinary morning. A duke and his victorious army had come to town.

The Ayne was lined on each side with carts. Every inn and tavern billet, every house and stable, would be packed with snoring soldiers. When Will reached the Butcher Market he saw a grand house with liveried guards standing sentry. The house was thrice-gabled and set with costly leaded lights and the plaster panels between its sturdy oak timbers were lime-washed white and embossed with symbols of prosperity. The city's wealthiest merchant, it seemed, had taken the opportunity to put himself at the victor's service.

'Will!'

He turned as a grey shadow dashed from the roadside and clung to him. He enfolded his wife in his arms and closed his eyes, knowing before even the blur of her cloak had registered who she was.

'I knew you'd be all right,' Willow said, sounding more relieved than convinced. 'I knew you would. All of this can't be for nothing. Can it?'

He hung onto her wordlessly for what seemed like an age, wondering how to untie his tongue. At last he managed, 'I only got to the battlefield after the fight. I can't deny that I was worried about you.' He stared at her. 'I . . .'

There were tears in her eyes. 'Chlu?'

He nodded. 'We fought. I couldn't tame him.'

'But you knew to come here. You knew that.'

'Oh, yes. I knew.' He kissed her and waited for the emotion to flush through him and run to ground. 'How long have you waited here?'

'All night. I couldn't sleep.'

'I should have told you . . .' he blethered. 'I've seen the truth. I know what I am. I should have told you sooner. I'm not what you think.'

'I know what you are,' she said, looking him in the eye as if she had already worked out what he was going to say. 'Do you think I'd be here if I didn't?'

'But you don't understand. I'm not a man. I'm not whole, just an aspect. I'm what happens when magic splits a man.'

'Will.' She said it very deliberately. 'It doesn't matter. None of that matters to me.'

'But it does to me . . . I—'

'Will – *it doesn't matter*. Not now. Not ever. You are what you are. And whatever you are, I love you.'

'Look at you!' he said, fighting back the tears. There was pure love in her eyes, and he saw how worried she must have been. 'You're perishing cold! You waited all night for me? Even when the gates were shut?'

She squeezed him. 'I knew you'd come. You're my man.'

'Well, whatever I am, I don't suppose you know where a breakfast may be had? I could eat a horse.'

As they hurried to their lodgings, Willow poured out the story of what had happened. 'Master Gwydion did what he could with that cold-hearted stone, but there was no stopping it. I don't know what kind of malice the fae filled it with, but it felt like revenge to me. Every man out there under the Ebor banner was screaming for blood. And every one of them went to their work with a will.'

'Did Maskull turn up?'

She darkened. 'No. The whole plan was a wash-out. And after I got all fired up again to do my best against him.'

'You'd better thank the stars above that he didn't come. Though I didn't think he would.'

She showed her surprise. 'Didn't you?'

He told her what had happened on Cullee Hill, then added, 'So you see, with Chlu using the very same trick that we were planning to pull on Maskull, I couldn't help thinking that something had gone very seriously wrong along the way.'

'So you already know . . .' She stopped and began to feel at the seams of his clothes.

'Know what? What are you doing?'

'Looking for that Fellowship button. The one that knave Lotan gave to you.'

He stared at her. 'Knave? What do you mean?'

'Oh, you'll soon see how he's betrayed us,' she said with uncommon disgust. 'Where is it?'

'Here.' Will produced the golden disc from his pouch. She took it and dropped it in the scrip of the nearest beggar, whose look of astonishment was quickly followed by his rapid withdrawal.

'That's got rid of that!'

He took her wrist. 'Do you mind explaining?'

'Oh, Will, I know you won't want to believe it any more than I did, but that so-called friend of ours – well, he's turned out to be a bad one after all.'

'Lotan? I don't believe it . . .'

'You'd better. And after all we did for him. Master Gwydion really was right about him all along.'

Will was incredulous. 'But what happened?' Suddenly something smelled of rotten dealings. Gwydion. Despite his promise to treat Lotan with respect, had he forced him out?

'You'd better tell me what's what before we go any further.'

'When you didn't come back and the battle was just about to start up, Lotan went to Master Gwydion and admitted everything. He told him how he had been working for the Fellowship all along.'

'Lotan said *that*?' He blinked in shock. It was almost too much to take in.

'I was there, Will. I heard him with my own ears. He said how he'd been sent to track you, how he'd wormed his way into our company. Then he threw himself on Master Gwydion's mercy.'

Will blew out a long breath. 'He said all that of his own accord?'

'That and more. He's been reporting all our doings right back to the Sightless Ones.'

'But I can't believe it.'

'And Lotan was reporting to Maskull too.' Willow's eyes flickered. 'He told us that Maskull and the red hands have common cause now. The sorcerer's secretly in league with them.'

'What did Master Gwydion do to him?'

'Nothing. He just sent him away.'

'What?'

Willow sighed. 'I know. It's not the punishment I wanted to mete out to him, I can tell you.'

Will was dazed, but more by disappointment than any other emotion. He said slowly, 'You know, part of me found it hard to believe that Lotan could have survived when he attacked Maskull on Awakenfield bridge with only a sword in his hand. Master Gwydion warned me that Maskull's magic might be letting him see all that passed before Lotan's new eyes – I didn't want that to be true, and so I wouldn't listen. But it was true after all.'

'It's all my fault,' Willow said, shame-faced. 'You were angry with me for using Maskull's medicines to restore Lotan's sight. It was Lotan who suggested it. He played on my pity, and he was working for Maskull and the red hands all the time. He was sending messages back to the Spire as regular as clockwork. He even gave you that golden button so his masters could track you.'

'But I felt no red hand magic on that gold. It was clean, or I'd never have taken it.'

'Master Gwydion says it's very unusual gold, taken long ago from one of the Hallows and hoarded by the Sightless Ones as a special treasure. Nothing sticks to it. You wouldn't have known a thing.'

Will put his face in his hands and let out a long breath. 'Oh, Lotan,' he said finally. 'How could you?'

As they came to an alley, Willow turned up it, but Will stopped dead. His mind was whirling. Lotan, a traitor? Could it be that he was so fine a liar? Or was this how a wizard failed, collapsing into suspicion and deceit and plotting against true friends? Surely there was more to this than met the eye.

'Willow, did you actually hear Lotan make his admission?'

'I told you. I saw the whole thing. I was as close to him then as I am to you now.'

It felt like the death of a friend. 'But did he . . . did the admission seem to be made of his own accord? Or did Master Gwydion have to badger it out of him?'

'I know it's hard to accept, but that's the way it was.' She looked anxious as she tried to drag him onward. 'Come on, Will, this is no place to linger.'

The tower of the counting house rose above the thatches on the far side of the Butcher Market. It had no tall spire, but four small spines and each of them was topped with a vane that was, even now, whirling out messages to unseen watchers in each of the four directions. Here where the road forked, overseeing the market, the Sightless Ones had erected one of their stone monuments. This one was six-sided, a series of steps that rose up to a central pillar. Around that pillar many a votive candle burned, and at its foot a woman knelt. She was weeping, mad with grief. Then Will saw the object of her torment. On top, spiked so it could not fall, was a head, white-haired and bearded. It had once belonged to Owain of Cambray.

'By the moon and stars!'

Willow took his arm. 'Come on, Will. Don't look at it.'

'Oh, Willow, my darling girl,' he muttered, turning. 'When will this ever end?'

'Ten noble prisoners were beheaded. One after the other,' Gwydion told him as they prepared to eat. 'And last of all was Jasper of Pendrake's father. Until they tore the shirt from his back he never lost faith that his son would ransom him.'

'Those gentler days are gone,' Willow said flatly.

'But Jasper escaped?' Will asked, grateful for a small crumb of hope, though he could hardly keep the reproach from his voice.

'He was not taken.'

'Couldn't you have stopped that despicable act of revenge at least?'

'I cannot change the minds of those who choose not to hear me. It presently seems to Edward the most fitting thing in the world to strike off the heads of captured opponents. And you must admit that his reasoning is impeccable: a father's head for a father's head. What arithmetic could be simpler than that?'

Will closed his eyes. 'And that's the way it carries on and on. What fools men are!'

'Have you only just realized that?' Willow said.

The wizard got up and left them, darkly preoccupied.

Will sat down with Gort and Willow and, as he wolfed some bread and cheese, he reflected on what the others told him. Edward would not see the wizard: he had issued orders that the 'conjuror' be shot at if he should try to make any approach.

'Don't blame Master Gwydion, Will,' Gort said. 'It's this changing world. They don't listen to him any more. None of them do.'

A sudden clanking noise out in the Butcher Market drew their attention, and then Gwydion reappeared, standing at the open door. He beckoned to Will. 'Edward is preparing to leave. But first there is something he feels he must do.'

The clanking came again. It was the sound of hammers and chisels breaking a block.

'What's going on?' Will asked, coming out to see.

Ebor troops were massing in the square, ready to leave the city. Edward sat proud on his great charger, surrounded by his captains. And there, under the sightless gaze of Owain of Cambray, two masons were shattering a friable grey stone with hammer blows upon a bolster. Will knew at once that it was the stump of the Morte's Crossing doomstone. It was being chipped away, and the resulting pieces handed out as luckstone charms to the men.

'They'll love him for this,' Gort said.

'They already love him,' replied Will.

'Where are they going?' Willow asked.

Gwydion did not answer, and so she looked to Will.

'There were three doomstones,' he said, staring into space. 'Or have you forgotten?'

'To Baronet Hadlea, then?' She said it fearfully, and he saw that she was recalling with dread his sickness the morning they had left Trinovant. Going back there would not be a pleasant prospect.

'There's no doubt the flow in the lorc is strengthening again. And it's directed a little south of eastward.'

'Along the yew lign?' Gwydion asked.

'It seems so.'

'Well, that makes sense.'

Will knew what the wizard meant. Edward would have to ride for Trinovant if he wanted to intercept Queen Mag's monstrous army. It must by now have accomplished most of its journey.

'Lord Warrewyk's holding Trinovant,' Will said. 'But he has fewer men under his banner than Edward. To stand any chance of opposing the queen's thrust against the capital, Edward will need to link up with Warrewyk. No doubt messengers have already been sent to Trinovant with orders to that effect.'

'Come!' Gwydion said, eyeing the soldiers who were now flooding into the Butcher Market. 'Let us see if we cannot steal a march on them all!'

Will reached the stables just in time to prevent their horses being commandeered. They left Erewan together and travelled with all speed, taking a back way to the Byster Gate. Once outside the walls they swung down onto the track that would take them eastward.

Gwydion told them, 'This old Slaver road leads to Caer Gloustre, and from there another road goes on to Cirne.'

Will nodded. 'Edward is going to have to take his army across the Great River, and my guess is that he'll do it by way of Gloustre Bridge. How far is it from Cirne to Trinovant?'

Gwydion's eyes flickered as if he was recalling some ancient piece of information. 'It is thirty leagues eastward to the White Hall as the crow flies.'

'And the crow will have to fly like the wind, if we're to have half a chance,' Willow said.

Will saw in his mind the three-sided journey he had made. By the time they reached Trinovant again, he would have travelled completely around the great triple triangle that made up the lorc. The first leg had taken them north up the hazel and holly ligns. On the second he had followed the birch to the south and west. Now the third journey would bring him back along rowan and yew to the very place where he had started. The irony of it was not lost on him.

It's all been a wild goose chase, he thought. How many men have died since last I saw Trinovant? And how many more will have to die before the lorc is sated?

Will sank into a dark mood. To travel along the ligns again was not a prospect that delighted him for, with so many stones gone, the third of the great doomstones was now pulling earth power without hindrance. The elixir Gort had made for him was all gone, so crossing the ligns would be torturesome. But it was no good dwelling on drawbacks, and in any case a more immediate question was nagging at his mind. As soon as he was able to pull away discreetly from Willow and Gort, he came up alongside Gwydion and asked the question straight out.

'Why did you have to drive Lotan away?'

'Hmmm? What did you say?'

'Lotan – you drove him away. You couldn't help yourself, could you? As soon as my back was turned, you made him out to be a villain. You put him under some compulsion, had him condemn himself out of his own mouth. Tell me why you did it, for I know it wasn't pride alone.'

The wizard took the accusation as if he had been expecting it, though the insult stung him. 'Lotan admitted his deceptions freely, Willand. And the only reason you are saying otherwise is because power is flowing in the lign—'

'Oh, no! Don't give me that. You made him do it. You cast a spell over him.'

'That is not true.'

Will's jaw clenched. 'So, on the one hand, you're asking me to believe that he's a Fellow through and through, a hard-bitten spy who's been plotting our destruction. While on the other, you say he just ups and throws it all over? Why? That's a very sudden change of heart for one so committed to our downfall, isn't it?'

The wizard returned a patient look. 'I am not asking you to believe anything. But if you would know how it happened

I will tell you plainly. Before the battle at Morte's Crossing began Lotan's spirit was greatly unsettled. He looked ever and again to the north, hoping for your return. He knew you were to be ambushed by Chlu. That was my surmise at the time, for I saw it in his demeanour. He had made a promise to his masters—' He held up a hand to forestall Will's next objection. '—but you and he have been through much together, and I think that in the end he came to like you too much.'

'He suffered a crisis of conscience because he *liked* me?' Will said incredulously. 'Is that what you're saying?'

'That is exactly it.' He watched Will's resolve waver. 'You see, no man may serve two masters. And some men discover too late that the only master worth serving is their own true heart.'

Will saw that he had no choice but to swallow what was a very bitter pill. 'Then Lotan really did betray us . . .'

'If you wish. But I should prefer to think of it otherwise.'

'Otherwise? What otherwise can there possibly be?'

'That in the end he stopped betraying us.' The wizard smiled regretfully. 'We should rejoice in any withdrawal from wrongdoing, be it ever so late in the day, don't you think?'

'And that's why you let him go?'

'That is why I let him go.'

The doubts that Will had had to voice had flown like birds. The wizard was telling the truth, but Will still found the betrayal hard to digest, or to forgive. He found it hard to ask more, but he needed to know. 'What did Lotan say to you?'

'He told me he had been selected for his mission personally by Grand High Warden Isnar, who knew that pity would be the key.'

Will let out another long breath. 'But surely he could have killed me as I slept. He could have murdered me at any time.'

'He could have. But his orders were not to murder you. Nothing so crude. The Fellowship have been informed that you are to play a crucial part in an attempt to block the union of the worlds. Lotan has been trying to discover whether or not your survival works in the Fellowship's favour. Had he determined that it would not, then perhaps he might have tried to kill you. I cannot say.'

Will pressed his eyes shut as a fresh pang of anxiety flowed through him – so much seemed to be expected of him, yet he could not see how he could even begin to accomplish anything so immense in what little time remained. He forced himself to ask, 'How does the Fellowship know that I'm to play this crucial part? Who informed them?'

'Maskull. He has joined with them, offered them a favoured place in the world to come.'

'But doesn't that jeopardize the absolute power he seeks? Why would he do that?'

'In return for their help now. He cannot reach you on his own. He knows that time is fast slipping away, and that the Fellowship possesses what he does not – a ready-made web, thousands of followers at their beck and call. After hearing what Maskull proposed, the Fellowship sent Lotan to entrap you, to gain your trust then put the golden mark upon you so Isnar could track you.'

'But Maskull already knew how to find me. He controls Chlu.'

'Perhaps. But not for much longer. The day will dawn quite soon when Maskull is no longer able to trust Chlu to act for him. It may already have dawned.'

'I don't understand.'

'Then you have not thought about it enough. As the other world approaches, so magic has been draining fast from us. As my powers have been enfeebled, so too have

Maskull's. Virtually all that will remain in the latter days of this world is the very oldest magic – that which the fae left behind.'

Will looked far ahead to where the road forked. 'You mean the magic which is in Chlu? And in me?'

'Quite so.' The wizard paused, as if to leave time for his words to sink in. 'And – let us not forget – the lorc.'

Will shook his head. 'But Maskull must have sent Chlu to kill me up there on Cullee Hill, mustn't he? Yes, he must have been behind the attack, because Chlu delighted in the irony of it. He told me he had used the very same method that you had devised to send Maskull to the Baerberg. Chlu must have got that knowledge from Maskull, and Maskull must have got it from Isnar . . .'

' . . . and Isnar from Lotan.' Gwydion drew a careful breath, seeming to feel his way forward with care. 'And Lotan from you. And you from – me.'

Will looked up, suddenly rattled. 'You never had any intention of using the Baerberg trap on him, did you?'

'Of course not. You were quite right – it would never have worked against Maskull. But as a probe to discover who was talking to whom, it has worked wonderfully well. After all, Lotan told us all that he had been to the Baerberg, so what better peg to hang the plan upon?'

'Oh, Master Gwydion,' Will breathed. 'Your magic may be abating, but not your cunning.'

The wizard took the remark phlegmatically. 'Tell me, was it the same this time as it was on the Spire?'

'Yes. Stalemate.'

'That is the precise word I hoped you would use. Chlu is committed to your destruction, but whatever he attempts against you does not succeed. And if Maskull did not recognize that before your combat, then he must have recognized it by now.'

Will nodded, thinking that he must now tell the wizard

what he had understood about himself. 'I think there is a reason that neither of us wins or loses in single combat . . .'

But Gwydion's thoughts had already gone off along another path. He muttered to himself, 'So far, Maskull has been able to control Chlu by manipulating his desire to save himself when the worlds collide, but now—'

Will said, 'You think Chlu may have come to realize that's impossible?'

'*Impossible?*' the wizard said uneasily, alighting upon the word. 'Why should you say that?'

'Because it seems to me to be a fact.' Will spoke quietly. 'Have you not considered what must be? What always must be when the opposites of fae magic are brought together?'

The wizard looked up as Will brought his hands together, reminding them both of the green talisman and the red that had become a leaping fish.

Will looked away. 'Chlu will not survive the collision. He cannot.'

A shrug of acceptance. 'That much is a matter of prophecy . . .'

Will stared into the distance, feeling a fresh surge of disquiet. 'And if it's impossible for Chlu to survive the collision, that must mean it's impossible for me, too. Isn't that right, Master Gwydion? Is that something you know to be true? Do I have to die to bring about the end-time?'

The wizard did not answer. Perhaps he thought it best to say nothing more. Perhaps he thought there was no need.

They rode eastward all morning, pushing the horses as much as they dared. They met no carts coming westward, and Will knew the traffic had all been turned around. Sutlers and victuallers were riding ahead of Edward's army, scouring the land to seek out stores of fodder and grain, including any goods already upon the road.

Although the scouring showed Edward's intentions, Gwydion was still at pains to ask all foot travellers whom he met what news there might be. The answers he received added to Will's worries. Before they had reached Gloustre Bridge, his disquiet had grown out of all proportion, and as the bridge came into view he understood the reason. He could feel the ash lign. It came slashing across the land, roaring out of the south-west, echoing with memories of death, for Cordewan, or more exactly the College of Delamprey, had been sited on the ash lign.

When Will closed his eyes he began to see monstrous sights. His thoughts darkened and his mind settled on the impossibility of saving the world from disaster. But then Willow rode up alongside to help him. She had been watching him, and had seen his increasing distress.

'Don't worry,' she said, offering him something in her closed hand. 'I thought I'd take a leaf out of Gort's book. It ought to help you across that lign.'

He took the chip of stone and made a face that showed his respect for her forethought. In return she raised an eyebrow that said: well, why not?

'It was a bit of a scramble pushing in among all those soldiers, but it was worth it.'

He felt his spirits soar. 'Oh, that was kindly done!'

'We all do what we can for you, you know. All of us.'

By the end of the second day, they had climbed over the Wolds. They heard fearful rumours on the road. It was said that the soldiers of Queen Mag's avenging army had been promised as much plunder as they could gather. South of the River Trennet, all towns where the ravaging horde had passed had been declared fair game. They had been ransacked and the land laid waste upon a front seven leagues wide. The queen's descent upon Trinovant had been relentless, but it had been slow.

'He should have shut her up,' Gwydion said with satisfaction. 'Rash promises lose wars. How often have we seen it?'

'You mean Maskull should have shut the queen up?' Will asked, only half understanding.

'Of course! He should have foreseen what would happen when his looters had got as much as their stolen horses could carry!'

'They'd turn for home,' Willow said.

'Exactly. And wouldn't you?'

'I wouldn't steal other folk's belongings in the first place.'

'Ha! I know that, my dear. But these men have fought hard battles on nothing more than promises. They think what they've stolen is theirs by right of conquest. And now they are going away home to enjoy it.'

'How many have deserted?' Will asked.

'It may be an exaggeration, but some say as much as half the queen's strength is gone.'

'Fifteen thousand? That's still enough to take Trinovant by storm,' Gort said. 'If those lolloping creatures are still with the army. Wall-bestriders, they are.'

'Aye,' Willow said. 'If.'

'That's not likely,' Will told her.

Gwydion looked at him. 'Why do you say that?'

'Because if the world is changing into one that doesn't have unicorns or yales or giants, then maybe the ogres will be melting away too.'

'Or shrinking down into ugly little men,' Willow said.

'More than likely,' Will muttered. 'And no longer big enough to climb over a city wall.'

As the third day dawned, the weather was cold and bright and the frosty woods rang with the song of robins. But Will felt other changes in the land. They had been crossing the Earldom of Ockhamsforth, and their path ran along the yew and rowan ligns. For sanity's sake they kept always a

league or two south of the nearest, which was the yew, yet
it was the rowan that Will could feel more easily.

Gwydion was angered when Will spoke up about it. 'But
surely it is the yew lign that passes through Baronet Hadlea!'
he said. 'The yew, not the rowan!'

'I'm only telling you what I can feel.'

'But what you can feel makes no sense!'

'That's where the flow is! Do you want me to apologize
for finding it? Well, do you, Soothsayer?'

The wizard scowled. 'You mock me at your peril, lad!'

'Oh, threats . . .' Will said slightingly. 'And what will *you*
do?'

'It must mean the next battlestone is on the rowan lign,'
Gort piped up, breaking in on the dispute. 'Don't you think
so, friends? Seems that way to me.'

Will grunted. 'Yes it does, Wortmaster. That's what
Master Gwydion can't accept. He's looking for a far neater
answer – a great battle to end all battles, one prompted by
the greatest doomstone of them all, and one that's won by
a shining hero. But it's not going to be like that!'

The wizard said no more, only urged his horse on and
rode ahead.

'He deserves more respect,' Willow muttered. 'You
shouldn't speak to him like that.'

'Well . . . he asks for it sometimes.'

She let it go and reached up to an overhanging bough,
saying with false brightness, 'Oh, look at the buds, Will.
The trees know that spring's coming soon. They can feel
the days are getting longer. I do like the spring!'

And he thought, but did not say, it's a spring I'll never see.

Gwydion dropped back to speak privately with Willow,
and Will could see from their circumspection that they were
talking about him.

'I know what you're saying!' he burst out at last. 'I'm
not stupid, you know!'

But Gwydion's smile was genuine enough, and his touch on Will's arm was meant to reassure. 'I was just telling Willow about what we found down in the valley yonder.'

'Valley? Where?'

The wizard directed his gaze towards a hill and the dip beyond, in which a hamlet crouched. 'That's Fossewyke upon the Eyne Brook. And over there once stood Little Slaughter.'

That gave Will pause for thought. He drew in upon himself and felt the perilous closeness of the yew lign. He now saw that they must be approaching the ancient stone circle called the Giant's Ring, passing by the Vale, the place he had been accustomed all his life to call home.

This final journey has great significance for Chlu and me, he thought. If he's following us, then we're both coming by way of our childhood haunts. We're being forced, each in our own different ways, to say goodbye to all that we've ever known.

He could feel his sensitivity to the lorc increasing by the hour. Eburos, the yew, dragged at him. Caorthan, the rowan, suffocated. Together they made him feel ill and old and tired to the point of exhaustion. He was losing his spark in a war of increasing frenzy, a world whirling faster and faster towards the moment of its own doom. So what possible hope was there that he could be the Arthur of prophecy? Like a stark revelation, he felt the inescapable unity of his own being and the very idea of the violation of it filled him with terror.

When he closed his eyes all he saw in his mind was a spinning disc. Was it a bronze coin or a golden button? It whirled with increasing speed, falling ever faster under its own weight, yet skating on its rim and resisting the fall. The rising, ringing sound that it made filled his head, made him want to cry out – but then dead silence.

Doomsday.

*   *   *

Will awoke to utter comfort. Like an earache that vanishes in the night the flow in the lorc had left behind it a kind of blessed relief, a yawning stillness, a hole filled with unutterable wellbeing. Though they were no more than half a league off the Eburos lign he could not taste more than the slightest hint of it on the air, and the taint of the Caorthan lign had gone away completely.

Will did not mention the change at first, fearing that it was something in him, some complication in his faculties, that had caused him to lose the scent. As they readied themselves to press on Willow, eagle-eyed as ever, asked why he had not taken any powder from the stone chip she had given him.

He handed her the remains of it. 'I don't think I'd better have any.'

'Will,' she said, brooking no nonsense, 'you know what'll happen if you don't! You'll start bleeding and foaming at the mouth like a mad dog.'

He lowered his voice. 'I'm not having it today because *the flow's stopped.*'

She whispered her astonishment. 'Wha–?'

He put his mouth close to her ear. 'There's nothing there. It's gone.'

'But – but that means that the stone must have emptied itself!'

He stared back at her. 'I can't think of any other explanation.'

'We must tell Master Gwydion.'

He nodded. 'I suppose we must.'

The day began bitingly cold, and there were flurries of snow as they passed through the Wychwoode. They saw with sorry hearts the deep cuts that had been made in the forest. Great tracts of wood had been cleared and sold to pay for war. Where once unicorns had run, now there were stumps and the smoking mounds of charcoal burners. They saw in the distance Lord Strange's tower, the place where Will had been schooled in reading and writing. It was in ruin, its roofs broken and its moat dried up. Its erstwhile master had moved on to greater rewards.

The closer they approached to Trinovant, the fewer people they saw on the roads, the worse the news they heard and the more frightened the voices. Gwydion led them through the village of Windover and they mounted up the scarp that carried the ancient path of the Ridge Way along its crest. There they saw a column of armed riders upon the road. These were neither sutlers nor scourers, but men of war, grim and beweaponed, wearing a red livery that Will recognized with a shrinking heart.

Gwydion bade everyone stay hidden while he rode down alone to speak with the men. The wizard was recognized and he seemed to be accepted in friendship, but his words were brief before he beckoned Will and the others down.

Will looked the riders over critically. There were two dozen of them, well-armoured, mud-spattered, wary and weary. Their leader was a nobleman of minor rank, and Will saw that he wore his gorget tight to his throat, and though his sallet visor was up he looked like a man ready at any moment to flee or fight for his life. He was a little way from the others, conversing in low tones with the wizard when Will joined them.

'After the fray at Awakenfield, tidings were brought to my lord of Warrewyk, and he, then sole keeper of Trinovant and the king, mustered his soldiers and his friends.'

'And the lords Northfolk and Falconburgh, were they come to the fight too?'

'Lord Northfolk was there. And Lord Falconburgh marched out of Kennet with a great company of archers and bill-men, looking to revenge himself for the death of his brother, Lord Sarum. There were more men with them, mercenaries of Burgund and Callas. Very well appointed my lord of Warrewyk thought himself when he marched to Verlamion to intercept the queen. Yet in the end she had three men for every two that he commanded.'

'Verlamion?' the wizard repeated, and flashed a glance at Will. 'Was that where the fight took place?'

'My lord did as seemed best to him, yet he spread his forces too thin – a curtain a league wide and more he tried to draw across the queen's path, from Verlamion and all along the Sand Ridge.'

'The attack began in Verlamion,' Will said faintly but with certainty. 'Near to the chapter house.'

The horseman turned, suddenly suspicious. 'You are very well informed. Whence come you?'

'It was . . . merely a guess.'

Gwydion gestured like one disregarding a lunatic. 'Pay him no heed, sir. He is one who often speaks without prior thought. He thinks himself a warrior and has *fancies* about such things. Now—'

'But he is quite right. Lord Strange did set upon my lord's left flank close by the great Verlamion chapter house. The Hogshead's men were made to pay dearly by our archers, but in the end the last of them were hunted out and thrown down from the curfew tower . . .'

They heard the story of how the queen's forces had journeyed through the night to come hard upon Verlamion. To make some semblance of right authority over his actions in opposing the queen, Warrewyk had caused King Hal to be dragged out of his library under the palace of White Hall and had forced him to ride out at the head of Warrewyk's own troops, the embodiment of legitimate authority.

So, Will thought, I was right about the rowan lign. The Doomstone of Verlamion has indeed repaired itself. It's had its way in the end.

'They cut us off and overwhelmed us one by one,' the rider said, glowering at the memory of it. 'My men and I narrowly escaped by another way. But we have heard that my lord withdrew his people in good order to the number of five thousand. I ride westward now in hopes of finding them.'

'Has Friend Warrewyk not fallen back upon Trinovant, then?' Gwydion asked with alarm.

'No, sir, he has not. For he seeks to join up first with the Earl of the Marches – I beg his pardon – with the new Duke of Ebor, who it's said has delivered a powerful stroke of revenge in the west.'

'But . . . the king? What of him?'

'Alas, King Hal is no longer with us.'

'The king is *dead*?' Will said, unable to stop himself.

'I did not say that. But we have had no word of the knights who stood guard upon him, and we fear for them.'

'We must ride on to Verlamion then,' Will said, looking to Gwydion.

The knight grimaced and directed his answer to the wizard. 'That you must not, Crowmaster. Not unless you wish to meet with the queen, for she is mistress of that town now – what little there may be left of it. Even the chapter house has been breached for the sake of its gold and many of the Fellowship lie dead round about its shrine.'

'It was not gold that drew the queen's soldiers into the chapter house,' Will said, brushing off the wizard's attempt to intervene again. 'Tell me, does the Hogshead go helmet-less into battle these days?'

'Lord Strange is famous for riding into the fray bare-headed,' the rider said, answering him shortly. 'That is well known.'

'But why is he called the Hogshead? Do you know that?'

The rider looked perplexed by the fervent questions of

this mad beggarman. 'It is because his personal banner bears that device.'

'Is it not then he has the head of a boar?' The rider tried to turn away, but Will persisted. 'And was there not rumour of a stone? A magic stone, such as those that have appeared after other battles?'

The rider looked at Will with new eyes, then said to Gwydion, 'Is your ragged friend a simpleton or a seer, Crowmaster? There has been talk among the captives of a victory stone, one that has fallen to the queen. But . . . I may not speak of it.'

'Why not?' Gwydion said.

'Orders have been given that no man of my lord's company may do so, lest loose words undermine the resolve of our army.'

'Do not dwell upon the stone,' Will said. 'For Edward of Ebor has a like one which he has given out in pieces to his army. Neither will affect the outcome of the next battle.'

Will saw the still-smoking Doomstone in his mind's eye, a mottled black and grey slab with a part-healed wound across its middle. He could not see the queen distributing it among her followers. Nor could he see Maskull taking too much of a liking to it.

Gwydion said to the rider, 'If you wish to see your lord again you must do one of two things: either ride down to Windover and thence make your way towards the Wolds. Edward of Ebor is presently approaching the town of Chipping-by-the-Wold. Your master will seek to meet with him there. Or, if you would save yourself many fruitless leagues, you may ride with us to Trinovant for that now must be our goal. Be assured it is the place to which Friend Edward will march his men in due course.'

The rider's face revealed only doggedness. 'I thank you for your offer, Crowmaster. But, though we would gladly have your protection on the road, we must, I fear, do as duty bids us and ride westward.'

The wizard nodded approvingly. 'That is well said. We thank you for what you have told us. Fare thee well!'

'Farewell to you also, Crowmaster. And for myself I'll say that I should welcome a return to the days when lordly counsel was governed by sage advice.' The rider gave an order and his column cantered away down the scarp.

'You were right about the Caorthan lign,' the wizard said as soon as the riders had gone. 'I was wrong. I should not have doubted you.'

Will made no direct reply, he only asked, 'Do you still wish to make for Trinovant?'

The wizard nodded. 'Unless you can see how we might steal the remains of the Verlamion Doomstone, which seems now to be in Maskull's possession.'

Will stiffened. 'I was thinking that we might try ourselves against a greater menace – the one that lies undisturbed at Baronet Hadlea.'

Willow looked horrified. 'Do you feel that's where the power's running now?'

'No. The lorc is quiet,' Will admitted. 'But surely we ought to go to Baronet Hadlea ahead of Maskull? He may have reasons to try to tap the stone.'

'What do you say to that, Master Gwydion?' Gort asked expectantly.

The wizard put a hand to his chin and stroked his beard. 'We do not know what Maskull requires. We do not know if he was present at Verlamion, or if he has tapped that stone.'

'But we do know what the queen will do if she is still under Maskull's influence,' Willow said. 'She will march on Trinovant with all speed.'

Gwydion looked to the east. 'Yet, I think at the same time as she threatens to besiege the City, she will send ahead to the Lord Mayor and his Aldermen and offer them easier terms.'

Willow asked, 'Do you mean she'll offer to forget their disloyalty if only they'll open their gates to their rightful king?'

'Something like that.'

'But after what she did at Ebor only a fool would take her word that she'd not harm the City!'

'Ah, well. That is the price she must now pay for her rashness.'

They all looked to Will, waiting for a decision.

He looked at them each in turn, then he said, 'We'll go to Trinovant.'

◙ ◙ ◙

CHAPTER TWENTY-THREE

EDWARD

Will's choice proved to be popular. The wizard had
thought to go to Trinovant anyway, and Gort agreed
with him. As for Willow, her thoughts had been turning to
her daughter.

They rode as fast as they could due south by woodland paths, through the great beech woods of Hugh's Den,
and came before long to a bend of the Iesis, which some
called Thamesis. At the village of Martlow they stopped
at an inn run by two brothers where Gwydion asked to
have redeemed a long-outstanding favour. And so it was
that they left their horses and took a small boat with two
sweeps, which they pulled in turn while Willow steered
them, following all the twists and turns of the river for
seven leagues.

The Iesis was swollen with winter water, and flowing
swiftly. They passed many a river village before Will saw
the great round tower of the royal castle of Wyndsor. On
they went, but now the rowing grew harder, as if the river
itself was conspiring against them. And when they next
changed about, Will saw that the river's flow was ponding
back, swelling water up the muddy banks. No longer was
the Iesis helping them, but rather hindering. Gwydion said

they had come so far down they were in a tidal reach, and that no good would come of rowing for a while.

As they waited, they ate. And as they ate, Willow asked, 'How did you know about Verlamion, Will?'

'Because it's on the rowan lign. When we passed it on our way north I felt the stone. I knew then that the Doomstone had repaired itself.'

'But how did you know about Lord Strange going without his helmet into battle?'

'Because it stands to reason.' Will turned to face her. 'If magic is leaving the world then the Hogshead must be losing his piggish looks. That boar helm of his will no longer fit, and he hasn't had time to have a new one made.'

'I'm sure he'll think himself well rewarded for his choices. As if his return to handsomeness has been his own doing, despite not having taken the hard way that Master Gwydion prescribed!'

'That's the sort of world we're heading into,' Will said bitterly. 'One where there's no closed circle of right and responsibility. No justice. No truth. No substance. Only *appearances*, and false ones at that. I'd rather die than go there.'

'Oh, don't say that, Will!'

'Why not?' he said, meeting her eye. 'It's the truth. And we all have to die sometime.'

Now the river paid them back for their patience. Flow turned to ebb and they rowed more swiftly than ever past the deer chases of Rychmond, past the great water wheel and its booming trip-hammers at Hammersmyth, and as darkness fell they pulled past the wintry meadows of Fool Ham, Wand Ward and the Churl's Seat. Ahead of them now loomed the City.

Gwydion said that years ago two giant chains had been forged and slung across the river. They were hauled up from the riverbed to deny large ships entry to the City during time of war. but the White Hall was upstream of the City walls, and no one would seek to stop their own little boat landing at the Palace Steps so late at night.

He was wrong.

The palace was in turmoil. Its walls were manned by anxious men, archers in Falconburgh's blue and white livery. No royal boats were drawn up, and when their own approached, a dozen longbows were drawn.

Will stood up unsteadily and cupped his hands to his mouth. 'Tell the Duchess Cicely we are here with news of her sons!'

Moments later, the water gate opened. Men in Ebor tabards came down to the Palace Steps, carrying lanterns. But then they laid their lamps on the ground and began to push the boat off with their halberds.

Will began to argue, but then he saw the reason for the refusal; for lingering by the arched doorway were three figures in golden robes and tall hats. They had brought their own agents, men in belted black, wearing studded brigandines and heavy leather boots. They carried cudgels, and long pointed knives hung sheathed at their belts.

'We have our orders! You must go!' the men of the White Hall guard warned. Will noted their looks of concern as they saw the woman in the boat.

'Stop!' one of the Sightless Ones called, hurrying forward. 'Arrest them!'

'Do not let them land,' the captain of the guard told his men. 'They'll kill them all!'

With a start, Will recognized the guard as his old friend Jackhald. 'Jackhald! It's Willand! Give me a hand up, I say!'

But Jackhald had already seen who was in the boat. 'No, Master Willand, you must not set foot on these steps! These Fellows mean to do you harm!'

'It's them who have no business here! Just take my hand and we'll root them out!'

Will began to struggle across the gap, but in the entrance, behind the Elders, a figure swathed in black appeared, a child held in its arms.

Will saw the figure and froze.

'Bethe!' Willow cried.

The six Lamb Hythe guards who had come forward drawing their weapons were almost upon them now.

'Oh, Hell! I knew it'd come to this,' Jackhald muttered, and drew his hanger.

His three men turned and readied their own pole weapons, but before they could clash, Will sprang onto the muddy landing step. He danced up a ball of flame and cast it like a man bowling down skittles. Before it could reach its target the fireball flared orange and threw off a stab of heat that blinded and stung the guards' faces.

'Sorcery!' a voice called out. 'He's the One! Take him!'

But there was no taking of Will, or of anyone, for the guards hesitated, and so were lost.

A voice more commanding than all the others boomed out, 'What is this *disgraceful* show, Warden?'

Will looked at the figure in black afresh. A woman of great self-possession threw back her widow's hood, her pale, lined face adamant in the flickering lantern light.

'Warden, you will call off your men instantly, or, by the moon and stars, I will have you shot through from the towers. All of you, stay where you are! Lay down your arms, do you hear me?'

And up above, a row of archers, bowstrings drawn to their lips, backed the Duchess Cicely's words with the threat of death.

Not a man moved. Willow was the only one to pay the order no heed. She rushed forward and took her daughter in her arms, and as the duchess relinquished the child and turned to usher the new arrivals inside, she gave a meaningful nod to Jackhald and indicated the Fellows. 'Put them in the boat, Captain,' she said. 'And if it should sink on the way back to Lamb Hythe let them swim home.'

They had gathered in the duchess's private apartments, where they were provided with food and wine and the warmth of a blazing fire while their own quarters were prepared.

Will saw with what strength the duchess was bearing the loss of her husband and the uncertain chances of her son's cause. He mightily approved the way she had announced her intention to prise, as far as she could, the dead hand of the Fellowship off the levers of power.

'Lady, you seem less worried than I might have supposed in such a strait,' Will said.

'I've known my share of difficulties, Master Willand.' She used the honorific courteously, to recognize his reputed mastery of the magical arts rather than to remark on his comparative youth. 'You should know that I am no stranger to running a fortress. Even one which has been under siege.'

Gwydion spoke up. 'But never before, I think, have you been in such personal peril.'

The duchess's face hardened. 'That harpy who calls herself queen would appear to be at an advantage. That I will grant you. She has won a victory at Verlamion and is little more than a day's march away from here. But if she thinks that our great capital can now be hers for the asking, she should think again. The good folk of Trinovant have been outraged at the news that has come from Ebor. That my husband's head was so cruelly used as a decoration for that city's walls is as unbearable to them as it is to me. The people will rise up and defend their own walls against a like desecration.'

Gwydion said dourly, 'You should not be so certain of that, Friend Cicely.'

Will saw how that answer did nothing to undermine the duchess's determination. 'Master Gwydion, this palace is

walled and well provisioned enough to keep the queen at
bay for several days at least.'

'Do not forget, however, the extent to which the city of
Trinovant has overflowed its walls.'

'And what of that?' the duchess asked.

The wizard gestured eastward. 'Despite the many
statutes drawn up against the building of hovels without
the City walls, fully half the people of Trinovant now live
there and are thus defenceless. Do not count on their loyalty,
for many voices will be for reaching an accommodation
with Mag. And more so still when a thousand wood ogres
and moorland trolls come down to overtower your walls.'

'A thousand of them, you say . . .?' The duchess put a
hand to her lips.

'Mag's army will get into the City if she orders it. And
if the City falls in flame she will be sitting at this very fireside tomorrow evening.'

'My son is coming, and swiftly,' the duchess said stubbornly.

'Lady, your son may not come swiftly enough.'

As the company went to their rest Will lingered with the
duchess. 'Please forgive him,' he said. 'Our friend sees everything through a dark glass these days. His great life's quest
is nearing its end. He feels the final chapter is coming, and
he fears that all his hopes will have been in vain.'

Another measure of the duchess's strength visibly left
her. 'Is he right?' she asked.

'No one can yet say. But I'm sure things are not as bleak
as Master Gwydion paints them.'

She suddenly took Will's hand in hers. 'Thank you. When
I look at your little girl I cannot believe the world is fated
to sink into a mire of evil. I have borne sons and daughters of my own, more than you know, for not all of them
lived to speak their first word. Two of my babies died. So
it has been a comfort to me in my times of difficulty to be

with a young child again. Your Bethe has been like a grand-daughter to me.'

Will embraced the duchess and dried her tears and said, 'Don't worry. I'm sure things will work out well in the end. We will all do what we can, and it will be enough.'

When Will reached their quarters, he found the wizard pacing in an agitated manner.

'Why did you counsel Duchess Cicely so?' Will asked. 'You caused her to doubt and to fear, when you know the truth is not nearly so dangerous. A thousand ogres and trolls? A dozen, maybe, and those shrinking fast.'

'Oh, Willand, don't you see? It was my intention to steer her towards greater diligence. Just as it has been yours, no doubt, to reassure her that all is quite well – which, I may say, it most definitely is not!'

'Do you know something that I don't, then?' he asked.

The wizard uttered a short laugh. 'Ha! I know many things that you do not.' His expression hardened. 'Willand, she must send her officers into the City to disburse a great many bribes and counterpromises. I have said before that Queen Mag was in debt to many a Trinovant merchant. Most of these guildsmen are also Aldermen. They have the Lord Mayor's ear. What if she whispers that all debts will be settled just as soon as the gates are opened to her, hmm? What then?'

'A powerful incentive that would be to some,' Will conceded.

'And as we know, a city wall is only as strong as the honesty of the gatemen who guard it. The Duchess Cicely must move tonight – tonight, do you see? Before it is too late!'

'And do what?'

'Why, stir up the people! Rouse them with large tales of what horrors await if the Lord Mayor dares to receive Queen Mag or speaks with her deputation. The merchants' greed must be offset by the common folk's fear. I myself shall go out there, even at this hour, to tavern and tower, for the lies that must be spread are urgent!'

'Lies?' Will said, staggered. 'But we must hold the truth above all things, mustn't we? Or has that idea gone by the board too?'

'Lies!' The wizard's stare was uncompromising. 'Indeed, lies! There is no more honest a name for what must be given out. You see, the truth is not always an advisor's best ally, as you seem childishly to suppose. Folk of every degree are full of vain fancies and self-deceptions. They must be managed.'

'But how can we ever put matters in good order in the world if we fail to carry the truth with us?' Will said fiercely. 'Are we to embrace untruths? Are we to take up whatever seems convenient to us at the time? Isn't this the way of the new world? The way that we should refuse? And if not the truth, then what have we been fighting for all this while?'

The wizard looked haggard. 'I do not advocate lies in and of themselves, Willand, but if you are asking me whether benefits can ever come of untruths or mistaken beliefs, then I must tell you that they certainly can. And if you are asking: does truth matter in the end? then my answer is: not so much as *you* may suppose. I remember a man back in the old days, a Slaver he was, though he fancied himself to be a Great Healer. He was thought quite mad, though, having once been a soldier and seen too much of death. He told me he had been drawn to healing by one fact and one alone, which was that he had noticed that whenever he looked carefully into the eye of another he found a tiny version of himself looking back. This, he said, showed there was some-thing of himself in every other person, and so other persons, no matter who they were, were worthy of his respect and sympathy.'

Will grunted. 'A strange conclusion that. For by such

reasoning he would have to keep respect and sympathy for cats and dogs and pools of still water.'

'Quite so. Did I not say he was considered mad?' Gwydion's face lit with a bittersweet smile. 'Though if it be madness to keep respect for cats and dogs and pools of still water, that is a kind of madness of which I can easily approve.'

Will scowled. 'Now you're making fun of me.'

'Only showing you the error of your thoughts. My point was that our self-appointed Great Healer did comfort many folk in his time. So – are we to condemn him for his works?'

'Not for his works, surely,' Will muttered. 'But his ideas were still nonsense.'

'Looked at squarely, perhaps,' Gwydion answered, fussing now with a lantern. 'But it is not given to many men to look squarely at truth, for truth is as bright and shining as the sun. It may not be viewed directly by ordinary mortals without damage. Now think on that.'

'But I'm not an ordinary mortal,' Will said, feeling the ground slipping away from under him. 'I'm just an aspect, one half of an original that was split asunder by fae magic.'

'That is a realization I supposed you would arrive at eventually,' the wizard said with great deliberateness.

'How long have you known it?'

'"Known" is too strong. "Suspected" would be more apt.'

Will tried to focus his thoughts on something other than himself. 'So, what's to be done?'

'The main question is this: if we are to take the middle path, then whose instincts shall we follow? When your hunger for the truth simply mirrors Chlu's ravenous taste for lies? If Chlu is determined to prove the villain, are you, then, determined otherwise? Do you want to spread a little unsolicited kindness about? Consider this question well, and make your choice! Come out with me if you dare and we'll wake the sleeping people of Trinovant up to what they must be told – for their own good, and also yours.'

Will nodded slowly. 'I'll go with you, and if parts of the truth can effect the looked-for change, I shall speak those parts too. But I will go no further.'

'Then we will work together. But first we have another task: I must know if Maskull has been here in our absence. Come!'

Will followed him down echoing passages, crossing by dark diagonals from wing to wing of the palace. He could not guess where they were going until the lantern was thrust at him and he saw the wizard draw from a fold in his robes a great iron key.

When they came to Maskull's turret Will saw that the lock was broken and the door unhinged.

Gwydion gasped with frustration. 'I knew it!'

'He's been here,' Will said, mastering the obvious. 'But how? With his magic failing?'

'His and mine both! Every fetter and magical lock that I placed upon this cell has failed me.'

Will felt the shreds of magic hanging limp from the walls, rotting away like forgotten treasures.

'We must find if he has – oh! It is worse than I feared!' exclaimed Gwydion.

'What?'

'The window!'

Will raised the lantern and tried to peer past its glare into the space beyond.

'It's gone!'

Will looked into the gloom and he searched for an opening onto the world to come. But all he found was a blank stone wall.

The following day was long and wearying. It passed in expectation of doom while the seeds of fear that Gwydion had planted overnight began to thrust up a myriad grey shoots in every corner of the City.

Will had gone out to meet Gort, but he had decided to set off early and take stock of the City first. He disliked the rumours he heard as he went about the streets. In the Cheap the morning traders had nothing better to do than talk of what might befall, their breath steaming, their arms folded and feet stamping. Yesterday there had been a rush to buy, but now the stalls were bare, and all the stock pens empty. Trinovant was not a city that had taken the trouble to prepare for a siege, and now its people were beginning to rue the oversight.

The market ways seemed strange without their familiar sounds. The lowing of cattle, the bleating of sheep and the honking of geese would normally have added to the hubbub, but now there was no hubbub at all. And where the granite gutters of the shambles habitually ran with blood, where mendicant Fellows jostled to dip their bowls into the gory flow, today there was an eerie quiet.

Only outside the Guild Hall and the Lord Mayor's mansion were there crowds and those were threadbare. Folk with big decisions hanging heavy upon them stood in knots, speculating on what might be. Elsewhere life was so thin on the ground that Will wondered whether a great number might not have already left the City. Certainly, if folk were hiding in their houses they were doing so behind locked doors and barred shutters.

Perhaps they felt naked now their gate guardians had died. A sudden plague had laid the last of the silvery dragonets low during the time of Will's absence, and the City did not seem the same without them. But there were other defenders now.

In one or two of the wider thoroughfares Will saw small companies of men and boys, so-called trained bands, standing in rows with rusty iron hats jammed down over felt caps.

Red, blue or white ribbons were tied around their arms to signify what parts of the wall they were to man. They practised ham-fisted movements with sickle and scythe. Butchers and bakers and candlestick makers, listening to college manciples and white-bearded franklins tell them how best to bring down a charging horseman or hamstring a northern ogre.

That the City's fate was down to defenders such as these appalled Will, and he shuddered to think what would happen if just one squadron of the Duke of Umberland's veteran horsemen ever got among them.

Of Gwydion, Will saw nothing that morning. He knew the wizard would be out and about, acting at the fulcrum of events. At one and the same time he would be a moving force and a counterpoint to Maskull's efforts. Both magicians were down to their last glimmer of influence, but both were still in the fight, and all was still to be won or lost. Will supposed there would have been some hard negotiations between the queen's lieutenants and the officers of the city. That was work for which Gwydion had invited no aid, perhaps for fear that his delicate strokes might be upset by Will's blundering.

In that, you're no different to Duke Richard, Will thought grimly. You don't want meddlers messing with your plan. Well – you've nothing to fear from this quarter. I just hope your burgesses and aldermen are up to their task.

Will had not known what to make of the blank wall they had found in Maskull's tower.

'Maybe it's just healed up,' he had offered. 'I mean, if our world's been turning into the world beyond the window, what point would there be in having a window at all?'

'Healed up, you fool? He's taken it away with him!' the wizard had cried, impatient of Will's sluggardly thoughts. 'What I fail to understand is *why*?'

But that would have to remain Gwydion's problem, for Will had concerns of his own. He knew he should busy himself with an examination of the lorc, but within the City there was neither rhyme nor reason to what he felt. All the walls and the nearness of so much masonry interfered with the flow of power, and that was before he even began to consider the brooding presence of the Spire.

Even so, he could hardly fail to notice the tension that made his head hurt. The great bow of the Realm was drawn to snapping point. And he could feel the flow growing once more, drifting northward this time. It tasted bitter and sharp – like holly. And this was a fresh conundrum, for Verlamion was on the holly lign, while the nearest lign to the City was the hazel, on which the Baronet Hadlea doomstone also stood. Yet that lign was quiet, which could only mean that the lorc was orienting itself according to a different intent. It was not doing what he had expected, but rather gathering power for a final battle which would be fought in a place none of them had yet foreseen.

It seemed that relief from all the anxious waiting was going to come at noon, when Will noticed hundreds of men clattering through the streets towards the northern walls, as if in response to an alarum.

Eldersgate! Will thought. That's where they're going. And with such haste that the queen's army must be hard upon us!

He set off at a trot to see for himself, but soon discovered that he had been wrong-footed. Will suspected that money had changed hands and secret orders been given. Foreriders and heralds came to Luddsgate and were received by the gatemen. At a signal the doors were thrown wide and in came the first heavily armoured mounted columns. Will, running westward, saw them thundering towards him along the Wartling. Knowing well the better part of valour, he threw himself into an alleyway, trying all the while to make out the devices that flew at their lance tips.

First the white lion, then the black bull, then the boar and the bear . . . crimson banners and long battle standards, azure over murrey, grounds scattered with the white rose. All doubts fled from his mind. The sons of Ebor were here. Edward had come, and the City was his!

The next important news that Will learned was that King Hal was not dead.

Around the City the manner of his capture was now common knowledge. It was not a pretty story. On the day that Lord Warrewyk had been soundly thrashed on the ridge beyond Verlamion, Sir Thomas Cyrel and Lord Bonavelle had been the king's keepers. They had seen Warrewyk's defeat looming but they had elected to stay with poor Hal to protect him from harm, for though Warrewyk had used Hal to persuade everyone of their unity of cause as the army had ridden from the City, still he had not dared to risk the king's life in battle. Instead Hal had been held in a tent a full league distant from the battlefield. But after the battle the secret had come out and the queen's people had found the king counting his beads. Both Warrewyk's knightly minders had been dragged before the queen and her young son, and lengthily humiliated. At last the men had been forced to their knees and beheaded by order of the boy. King Hal, horror-stricken and babbling, had been returned to the care of his loving wife.

Will did not know what credence to give the tale, for in time of crisis there was no shortage of folk willing to thrill their neighbours with colourful talk. But the portrayal of the king seemed to Will to be the important detail. Certainly the common folk of Trinovant no longer cared what happened to their sovereign, for in time of peace scholarly Hal could be approved and even loved, but he was no hero, and so in time of war he did not afford them the protection they thought was their due. Thus, in his meekness, Hal had failed them.

Besides, the churls had worries of their own. Will saw them creeping from their cellars and lofts now, summoned by an age-old sound. The bronze bells of all the curfew towers had been set a-ringing. A multitude began to gather in the Cheap. Then Lord Falconburgh paraded ten thousand Ebor troops through the Poultery and up Corn Hill, so that the heart of the City was packed with townsfolk, all of them hemmed in by his soldiery, and the mood was one of awe and great expectation.

Will found the Wortmaster waiting for him by an iron rail outside the Guild Hall.

'Wshhht!' Gort beckoned. 'I've just come from Master Gwydion. He says the queen's force is in tatters. It's falling back into the north.'

Will's heart leapt. 'Then she's failed!'

'Oh, but she's not finished! She's only falling back to gather fresh strength.'

'No, Wortmaster.' He gripped the other's arm. 'She's missed her chance. She'll never win now. Remember the rede that says, "He who hesitates is lost"? It applies to queens too.'

Gort looked around. 'Well . . . the City is now safe at least.'

'And that's a relief. How did Master Gwydion manage things?'

'The crux came this morning, just after nine of the clock. Our friend managed a little simple magic on the heads of the Aldermen. He could not prevent them from agreeing to meet with the queen's people, but he did persuade them to insist on the time and place of the meeting.'

That threw Will. 'So?'

'He told them not to wait there like so many scarecrows! He said, "Go out and see Queen Mag in all her glory. See the king too if she will allow it. *But see their strength for yourselves before you bargain with them!*" That's what Master

Gwydion advised. He speaks the language of merchants very well when he has a mind to, hey?'

Will nodded and a smile escaped him as he began to grasp the wizard's wile in its fullness. 'Oh, indeed he does.'

'Well – the Aldermen saw no ogres, did they, hey? They saw no trolls either! Only five thousand or so hungry, wretched men yet remaining, and all camped in a muddy field and wishing they were back home in the north where they rightly belong. And there was old Hal, counting his beads like a madman – he said nothing, but wet himself with fear to be brought out of his tent. The queen has plenty enough warriors with her to call an army, but hardly enough to equal what the honest burghers of Trinovant had been fearing all night long. You should have seen their faces, Willand. And the change in their manners! What new resolve came to them, I can't tell you!'

Will looked northward, to the patch of blue sky that showed between rags of grey. He felt the ancient power rumbling through the land. 'He has to follow them,' he muttered.

Gort turned, eyes wide at the odd paleness that had overtaken his friend. 'Hmm? What's that you say?'

'Edward. If Mag's gone into the north, then he has to follow her and finish the job. He must harry her all the way to Ebor and beyond. No hesitations. Edward must go, and he must go with all speed before she has chance to catch her breath!'

Gort rubbed his face and squinted. 'Aye, he must, if the old redes have meaning any more.'

As they watched, a deputy Grand High Warden of the Sightless Ones, whom Will knew to be a younger brother of Earl Warrewyk, threw wide the upper-floor windows of the Guild Hall then stepped out onto the balcony. Lord Falconburgh came forward too, and with him Warrewyk, then lastly Edward. But it was Warrewyk who began to address the mob of churls who were gathered down below.

'Let me tell to you, good people, a tale of Hal the idiot king, and Mag a proud, insulting queen who caused her husband to lose his reason!'

And at that the soldiers raised their pikes and jeered.

'Nor may this scandal be allowed to run on. A strong right hand must pluck the diadem from faint Hal's head and wring the awful sceptre from him who durst not wield it! Tell me, good people, is that not so?'

Now the people gave voice to their wrath, shouting that it was Hal's fault, and his alone, that they had been brought to so lowly a condition.

'But in this troubled time what's to be done? Are we to throw away our coats of steel and hide ourselves in holes? Or shall we beat upon the helmets of our foes and put these proud birds to flight? Tell me your mind, good people! If for the former course, then hang your head in shame and call yourself unworthy coward, for never was fair fight won by faint heart. But if you are for the latter course then shout, "Aye!" and fill your fists with iron and prepare to come with us!'

Will saw the faces looking up with rapt attention, and his gaze strayed to Edward, who yet hung back and said nothing to those that he would woo, but looked on watchfully.

Now Warrewyk showed Edward to the crowd. 'Do you see this hero who stands before you in brightest gear of war? This great soldier whose victory in the west has saved you? Edward is his name. Edward, late Earl of the Marches, whose title was untimely changed to that of Duke of Ebor by the foul murder of his father! The next degree is the royal throne, for rightful king is he, by virtue of his blood and the law that governs kings. Mighty sovereign and monarch of this Realm is he, come at last to reclaim that which is his from a line of vile usurpers. King – aye! How fine that word sounds, how fine it feels to say it. King he has been proclaimed in every burgh through which he has passed while riding to your aid . . .'

And Will felt the excitement buzz through the crowd and he heard the people begin to shout that they had found a true saviour, and those who called out encouraged the others until there was hardly a man who had not given vent to his opinion.

Will saw what new kind of magic was being worked upon the crowd, for this high talk acted upon the people's feelings and swayed them in spite of themselves. But Lord Warrewyk was not done, for seizing the next lull he whipped the crowd to an even greater ferment, and as they gaped and goggled at him, he went on to make this demand:

'So say you now – will you have this Edward as your king? Will you? And if you will, then tell him so, that he may know you love him! And he who does not throw up his cap for joy should for the fault make forfeit of his head!'

The answering call that began among the soldiers was shouted out the louder by the people: 'Edward! Edward! Edward the king!'

And off the caps did fly, and there was not a head in all the crowd that was not bared to show the love of him who would be king.

As the drums struck up, Will saw how Edward made the people wait. At last he came forth among them upon a white horse and there was cheering and the people followed him in procession all the way to Luddsgate and beyond.

As for Will and Gort, they went another way, fighting first against the press of bodies and then down to the wharves. There they took a four-oared boat and reached the White Hall ahead of the rest. They found the whole palace had become a hive of activity, but in the White Hall itself the wizard stood alone before the empty throne, deep in thought. The staff of Maglin glittered faintly in his hand.

'Master Gwydion, they're coming,' Gort said, rousing him. 'You cannot stay. They mean to have their celebration!'

Gwydion drew breath and turned placidly. 'Then let us retire, for they will do what they will do.'

'Aren't you going to stay and watch?' Will asked.

'There was a time when I might have wanted to. But not today. Stay if you wish. But I shall not, for another duty calls me.'

The wizard left with Gort, but Will decided he must witness another stage in the making of a king. As the distant drums beat louder, he went up into the dusty gallery where he had sat once before. The sight of the niches that had held Magog and Gogmagog made him think of Lotan and his betrayal. The moment sat like acid on his belly for a long while, but then there was a mounting commotion outside as those of the crowd that were permitted came into Albanay Yard and Will shook off his soured memories.

The sound of drums broke in on the hall, rattling the coloured glass in the tall windows. Then noblemen and soldiers burst open the giant doors and began spilling down the main aisle. They filled all the stalls, standing upon benches and crowding forward in a mass. But none dared breach the cordon of scarlet rope that separated the throne from the rest of the hall. The gilding on the golden seat seemed to Will's eyes basely muted now, but those who came were halted by the glamour of it. They turned in hope to see the man who had the courage to sit that enchanted chair without fear.

Edward did not disappoint them. Tall and fair and grim-faced, he strode to the fore. Will knew he must be recalling that ill-timed moment when his father had mounted those same marble steps, when the outburst from the Stone of Scions had shown Richard to be a pretender.

But Edward did not show any shadow of reluctance. Fired by the passion of the day, and possessed of a bloody defiance that his father had never known, he swept to the throne and without hesitation took his place upon it.

The enchanted chair bore him uncomplainingly, and so the deed was done.

The hall erupted with cheers. Edward's chief nobles came to flank him. His heralds had been sent on a special errand, and now they appeared with the Elders of the Fellowship all in train, bringing with them a treasure beyond all counting. A huge, iron-bound chest was opened to reveal the sacred symbols of sovereignty. Not quite the Hallows these, but four pieces of golden regalia that represented them. In place of wizardly wand and ancient blade were uncovered the sceptre and the grand sword of state. And now, standing for cup and pentacle, were taken out from wrappings of white samite the golden ampulla and the royal crown.

Some strange memory stirred in Will, a recollection that made the glitter desert those modern baubles, for he could see in his mind's eye the Hallows as they really were, resting together in glory and lighting up their vault in the Realm Below – the Sword of Might, called Branstock, the Staff of Justice that had once belonged to the first phantarch, the Cauldron of Plenty, and lastly, the brilliant Star of Annuin . . .

And in that moment Will suddenly saw that what was being enacted below was more than just the installing of a nobleman as supreme leader. Here, for sure, was a son who was seizing the chance to revenge himself upon the killers of his father, but it was more than that, more even than the undoing of the usurper's line. This was a necessary setting to rights, a moment of inevitability, when something clicked into place in the mechanism that drove the world. Will felt that change, and though he did not understand it, yet it was as if the world had been waiting for it to happen.

Down below, the rightful king was claiming his own. There was no stopping the momentous rolling on of events. Grand Warden Isnar, as ever an astute political mover, addressed the assembled lords, judiciously declaring Hal to be an oath-breaker, and so to have forfeited all right to the throne. Then Edward himself spoke, telling how his claim was just under the law, and that any who opposed his will should speak up now or forever hold their peace.

In the vast silence that followed, no one dared to gainsay Edward's claim. He promised them all that he would be the strong king that the Realm had so long wanted – the king his own father had wished to be. Then he told them without equivocation that he would brook neither interference nor opposition to his will. He would rule *and his word would be law*.

Now Gwydion came into the hall, and those who saw him fell back before him, for he escorted on his arm a veiled lady of uncertain years, and only when he reached the foot of the marble steps did the wizard choose to speak.

'Friend Edward,' he said, his voice low yet touched with the boldness of olden days. 'I bring to you one who would give a blessing.'

Edward came forward and put out a hand to cast aside the veil. And there was a gasp, for where he and his gathered lords had expected to see the dowager duchess, they saw something else. To all who watched she was only a crone. Yet Edward's eye was differently deceived and lingered on the beggarwoman as if under an enchantment.

'Who are you?' he demanded of the young woman.

'You know that,' she replied demurely. 'My name is Sovereignty. Love me well, Edward, for I am the consort of kings.'

Up in his crow's nest, Will saw the beautiful face that

was revealed and a great confusion overcame him so that he nearly cried out loud.

Gwydion raised his staff and said, 'Know, Edward, that the time for vengeance is over, that a king must be compassionate towards his enemies.'

And Edward walked back a pace or two as he considered. He put his fingers to his mouth fleetingly, and just as fleetingly disposed of the advice. 'I promise you this: I shall not rest, Crowmaster. Not while a single one of my enemies lives.'

CHAPTER TWENTY-FOUR

A BROKEN LAND

In the days that followed, Edward's army swelled to forty thousand fighting men and the gloom that had settled over Gwydion grew deeper. Hammer rang on anvil throughout the City as each soldier was armed and prepared for the long march into the north.

Will looked at his wife and child, hardly daring to face the reason he had asked them to come up here to be with him on the northern walls. Meanwhile, he half-listened to Gwydion's grim estimates of Queen Mag's renewed strength. She had retired with her captive husband to the city of Ebor and the levies of lords still loyal to Hal's banner had also gathered in that city. Reports now had their number at twenty thousand. Added to that, fresh war bands were coming down from Albanay daily, men drawn by tales of rich pickings. Their number was maybe ten thousand. And lastly, according to Edward's spies, the Duke of Umberland had scoured his border domain and come to Queen Mag's aid with another ten thousand, along with a host of border reivers who owed no man allegiance, save their own kinsmen. It seemed that by the time the opponents clashed, the contending armies would be of equal size, and that, Will knew, was no coincidence.

'Edward is almost ready to depart,' Gwydion said, watching the stream of men pouring out to their muster places across Clerk's Well Fields. 'Armies such as these are quite beyond the imagination of the human mind. If all the men now under arms in the Realm were ordered to stand shoulder to shoulder, then the rank would stretch for more than ten leagues! The man at one end would have to march for a whole day without resting before he could meet with the man at the other. Such numbers of warriors, equally divided and determined against one another, must not be allowed to meet.'

'The stone that's calling them sits upon the holly lign,' Will cautioned. 'But we don't yet know where.'

'That lign runs all the way up into Albanay, you told me,' Willow said.

'So I believe, but the battle won't be that far away. It must be fought south of Ebor – but how far south we cannot say. With fair fortune we might reach the stone a day or two before Edward arrives. But a cart on winter roads . . .' As Will's words trailed off, he shrugged.

'And what happens when Lord Warrewyk's foreriders catch up with us and want to take our horses away?' Willow asked when the wizard moved out of earshot. 'What shall we do then?'

Will pursed his lips, knowing she had given him his chance to draw the fatal knife and stab her to the heart. 'You've heard Master Gwydion. He says that this time it will be too dangerous for you to come along.'

'Huh!' She rolled her eyes. 'As if all the other times were not!'

He saw that her reaction was born of fear. She knew him too well, knew what he was about to do, despite what was being said. 'Willow . . .'

'So you and he go with the warriors, and I must stay among the wet-nurses and child-minders? I never agreed to *that*.'

'Please . . . don't make the parting more difficult than it needs to be.' His eyes pleaded with her. 'We must think of Bethe. What would she do without her mother?'

'What will she do without her father?'

That was like cold water dashed in his face. 'If she can't have both of us, she ought at least to have one of us.'

She checked herself and looked away, knowing that he could afford to brook no argument this time. Harsh words spoken now would not persuade, they would only ruin their parting. She said miserably, 'I thought we'd had all this out once before.'

'Yes . . . but now it's different.' He looked at his wife lovingly, feeling no trace of self-pity, no fear, no anger – only regret that, for him, the end-time had come.

'Oh, Will . . .'

'Darling Willow,' he said, taking her in his arms. 'You must let me go.'

He felt the wave of dread pass through her, because at last he had put it into words. She began to protest but he put a finger to her lips, showing her that his mind was made up.

'I have to do this,' he told her. 'You know I do. It's not my duty – it's my fate. I cannot foreswear my nature. This is what I am, and what I've always been.'

'Then you must go. And with my blessing!' she said, trembling.

'Brave girl.' He held her tight as she cried. Then he knelt to pick up his daughter and hug her close to him also. 'Stick close by Gort and Lady Cicely.'

It was all he could think to say. He saw how fiercely she desired to help him, and he wished there was some way it could be done. But there was not. As he walked away he felt the desolation breaking Willow's heart. He felt the child's bewilderment too, then heard the shrieks as Bethe began howling for her daddy. His world dissolved before his eyes, no matter how hard he blinked away the tears. But he kept on walking, knowing that if he turned now all would be lost.

And even when he heard Willow shout, 'I love you, Willand!' he did not hesitate. The moment of separation had come and gone. He had used the knife and left his darling girl to bleed to death upon the City ramparts.

Now there was only the task ahead.

The journey up country would be cold and wet, but the cart had two strong horses and only two wheels to get stuck in the mud. The first day was the worst for Will. He had been increasingly worried by the vigorous movements of power in the land, and so Gwydion decided they should leave the City by its easternmost portal. After Aldermansgate they detoured a little way to the east so they would have to cross as few ligns as possible.

But first there was a test. The great fortress of the White Tower sat on the hazel lign. The powerful doomstone at Baronet Hadlea also sat upon that lign, and it was barely more than three leagues to the north. While inside the City, the ramparts had shielded Will, but as they came through Poore Jury and then crossed the Eastmoat, Will began to hear the head of Bran singing to him. It put him into an odd state of mind.

'Thirteen ravens shall be his guard,' he muttered in the language of stones. 'And Bran himself makes the fourteenth! Twice seven – how neat! Powerful magic, that, Master Merlyn . . .'

'Arthur?'

'Hmmm?' Will said, roused suddenly to his true surroundings.

Gwydion had taken him by the upper arm and was peering at him closely. 'We are across it now, I think.'

'Did I . . . fall asleep?'

'You felt no pain, then?'

'Pain?' At that word the crushing despair he felt at having said goodbye to Willow came over him again. 'Pain enough, but not from the lign.'

Gwydion grinned and patted Will's knee. 'Good. Then I think we have our talisman.'

Will knew he was referring to their load, the treasure that lay in the back of the cart. It was a clever stroke, one suggested some time ago by Loremaster Morann. It was their last and only hope.

That day they crossed the elder, yew and rowan ligns, all within three leagues of Baronet Hadlea, and how the green lanes burned. There was no pain, but Will fell again into a free-running state of mind and saw three great rivers of fire flowing into the north. Their names were Mulart, Eburos and Caorthan.

As night fell and they sought a hiding place, Gwydion tried to encourage Will by reminding him that the worst was now behind them and they would not have to cross any more ligns – save perhaps the hazel – all the way to Ebor.

Each day that followed, a raw east wind blew in phantom flakes of snow. Will watched them vanish as they touched the damp ground and his thoughts turned ever and again to melancholy questions surrounding the impermanence of life. They rode on without fuss or fanfare through a land that had been stripped bare, eating what they had brought with them, and stayed for the most part under the covers of the cart or in lodgings of their own devising.

Sometimes hail rattled down around them, but at other times the wind scoured the sky to blue and the increasing sun warmed them with moments of welcome encouragement. But the warmth was short-lived, and down came the rain again. They found the farmstead at Burghlea Martin deserted and Gwydion's friend the pig farmer gone. Part

of his roof was scorched where an attempt had been made
to fire the thatch.

'So the blessing you laid upon John Sisil's house failed
after all,' Will said lugubriously. He turned as he stepped
out the points of the chalk pentacle that could still be faintly
seen on the cottage's threshold stone.

Gwydion looked around at the cleared field, which was
still a stinking and sow-rutted morass. 'A pig-man can
always hide his stock in the woods. It would take more than
a ravening army to do down Friend Sisil. Living so close
to the Great North Road he has learned that a host that
comes by once is likely to come by again.'

When Gwydion bent to kindle a fire he found to his
dismay that it would not catch. It was nothing to do with
the dankness. Flame would not even flare up in his hands.
It was pathetic to watch him whisper and gesture time and
again to no effect. Finally he stood up and dusted his palms
off against one another, saying, 'Well, I must be more tired
than I thought.'

But Will's powers had remained relatively unaffected by
the universal decline. Now he had come away from the cart
he felt the malice running in the earth and it undermined
him like never before. 'The people can't hide in the woods
forever,' he said.

'I think they will survive.' Gwydion crossed the pentacle
with a wave of his hand. He reached up into the eaves and
worked loose a smooth piece of grey stone. Will saw that
it was an elf-bolt, a charm hidden under the part-scorched
rafters, and meant to ward off fire. 'There is still a blessing
on the baby's head. And this old thing seems to have done
its work too. A fine roof, this. It would have been a crime
if it had fallen.'

'Coincidence,' Will said, looking around the dank,
unlived-in cottage with its broken door.

'Coincidence? Is that what you think?'

'How could it be anything else? There's to be no magic in the coming world. No protections. No charms.'

'Quite so. But fortunately we are not there yet.'

Will's spirits slumped even lower. 'I don't know how you can justify optimism at a time like this.'

'My optimism requires no justification. It is the understanding that virtue is sufficient in itself. And anyway, what is the alternative, hmmm?'

'Gwydion, what shall I do?' he breathed. 'I can't be Arthur. I can't!'

'Do not despair, Willand. It is always darkest before the dawn . . .'

Will's fists balled. He was so sick of hearing the wizard quote the redes at him, redes that these days sounded like no more than worn-out bywords, sayings devoid of all wisdom or power. He put his face in his hands and squeezed fingers into his eye sockets until the pressure hurt, then he whispered, 'The future of the whole world depends on me and I don't know what I'm supposed to do!'

'No one knows how the seers' prophecies will play out in the end. I cannot say how the knots of fortune will untangle themselves—'

'Then what good are you to me?' he said, looking hard at the wizard. 'Do you even know what day it is?'

'Not your birthday . . . is it?' Gwydion said, wide-eyed.

'No. It's what the Sightless Ones call the Twelfth Calend of April.'

'The spring equinox.' Gwydion's chin jutted. 'Well? I knew that.'

'Then why didn't you mention it to me earlier?'

'Should I have?'

Will turned away angrily. 'You would have done if you'd remembered. And now you can't even kindle fire in your hands. You really are just an old man who's fading away, do you realize that?'

'And you are a child who refuses properly to grow up!'

Will put his hand to his chin suddenly and looked around, suspecting now the reason for his sudden gush of spite. To his eyes the world beyond the woods was all in flame.

'It's the flow in the holly lign . . . a wave. A great wave!'

A bolt of power flared as it passed up into the north country. Lightning flashed and thunder rolled out across the land. It made him cower down and shield his face from the sky.

The wizard lifted him up, no longer minded to fence silly insults. 'You can feel it? See it? Even here? When the lign must be two or three leagues to the west?'

The rain came on harder. Will met the wizard's eye. 'I . . . I've walked too far away from the cart. That's what it is.'

Gwydion helped him back a little way. Then he gestured with his arms and seemed to pace the distance out in his mind as if making some calculation. 'The power of protection might fall off not as the square, nor even as the cube, of the distance from the lign . . .' He said it like a doctor observing with detachment as some deadly contagion consumed a sick man. 'Fascinating for all that, though, this new world . . .'

'Since we're not going to get our hock of ham tonight,' Will said wearily, 'I think we'd better press on with your stump as fast as we can.'

That was a remark that had something of a barb to it, the remnant of an argument they had had as soon as Gwydion had announced what they should do.

'I'll ride on ahead,' Will had suggested.

'It would be better if we went together,' Gwydion had told him, lowering his eyes. 'I will need your help on the journey north, for we must take with us the stump of an old battlestone, one that I think must have governed the battle that brave Neni fought against the Slavers. I cannot move the thing on my own.'

But Will had known that was a lie. Even without his powers of great magic, he thought, Gwydion could take that stone the length of the Realm and back without my help. I know what's really bothering him. He thinks that if I ride on ahead I'll get myself into trouble. He doesn't think I can be trusted . . .

Now, as he climbed up onto the back of the cart, Will found that he could not even fathom the reasoning he had used to question his friend's motives. How could I have ridden on ahead, he asked himself wonderingly, when my protection is here? It's only the phases of the moon that are conspiring against me now.

The wizard looked in on him. 'We cannot risk losing you, my friend. For while you live there is hope.'

He reached among the jumble of fodder sacks and travellers' belongings and pulled aside the blanket that covered their precious load. There sat the unassuming block of stone that was at the centre of Gwydion's plan. It was quite small – two hand spans long, by one-and-a-half wide, and one deep – a plain sandstone block about the size and shape of a village money chest. Set into the top were two iron staples that bore carrying rings and grooves so that the rings might lie flat. Will sat down on it as if it was a cushion, and when he did his courage burgeoned.

The wizard smiled as he saw the comfort that the Stone of Scions – the magical stone that was wont to counter-balance the throne of the Realm – was conferring upon Will. 'We have had our suspicions about its true nature for a long time, Morann and I. And yet now, looking at you, I am quite certain we were wrong.'

'Wrong?' Will stared. 'What do you mean?'

'This is not merely the stump of some long-abandoned battlestone, as we supposed.'

Will looked up. 'Then what?'

'The Stone of Scions is a *sister-stone.*'

Will felt waves of kindness flowing through him as he called to mind the notion that lay behind the battlestones – that all things were vessels containing equal measures of kindness and harm. But the battlestones had been made from pairs of ordinary stones by separating all harm into one and all kindness into the other. The stones with a double measure of harm had been deployed in the Realm, being set up on the lorc as a defence against invasion. But the double-kind sister-stones had been hidden in barrows in the Blessed Isle. There they had slumbered forgotten, infusing that fair land with their own mystic power.

Or most of them had.

Will felt silent encouragement flood him. He said, 'You once told me that according to the Black Book there are three ways to deal with the power of a battlestone. We can drain the harm from it magically. We can bind it in magic and store it safely, or—'

Gwydion took up the point. 'Or the third way, and by far the best, is to stand it beside its original sister-stone and let the harm and kindness flow back into balance again. If I am right, and the Stone of Scions *is* a sister-stone that has found its way into the Realm, then we have at least a small chance that it might match the stone that is causing the coming battle.'

Will shook his head. 'One chance in forty, or thereabouts? That's not a gamble I'd ordinarily care to make.'

'These are not ordinary times. And we do not know what happens when a sister-stone is brought near a battlestone which is not its original partner.'

Will disliked the sound of that even more. 'What do you think happens?'

Gwydion lifted his shoulders. 'Maybe there occurs a similar exchange of spirit that largely restores the balance . . .'

'And maybe there'll be a gigantic disaster.'

Gwydion deliberated, then said, 'But there will be a gigantic disaster if we do nothing. So we might as well try something.'

The horses' hooves squelched through the mire as they approached the road. After a moment Will said, 'Master Gwydion, did you take the Stone of Scions from under the throne before Edward had had a chance to sit on it?'

The wizard arched an eyebrow. 'Willand, what a nasty, suspicious mind you have.'

'Just a stab in the dark.' The urge to smile crept over him. 'A king may only be declared in the presence of the stone, isn't that right? So, does that mean Edward isn't really king?'

'You should have asked him what he thought of Brig if you wanted to know that,' Gwydion said evenly. 'But if you think you know what he saw, bear in mind that strange anomalies are thrown up when Ages change.'

'Anomalies?' Will muttered. 'I think Edward saw Sovereignty. I think she pointed his way.'

The wizard's eyes remained fixed on the middle distance. 'Whatever the case, Edward believes he is king, and those around him believe he is king, and that is what seems to matter most these days. But I think you know who is really king. And I would still be prepared to wager that you will yet find a way to become Arthur.'

The rest of the journey passed without surprises. Will counted off the leagues and tried to disregard the wanton destruction he saw. So far he had recognized many places through which they had travelled on their last fruitless foray into the north. Now, though, because of the danger and the ruinous state of the roads, Gwydion said they would henceforth be obliged to go by less frequented ways.

At half a dozen road-bars and bridges they submitted

to search. They gave answer to armed keepers that their strange burden was no more than an innocent counterweight, which in some sense was true. But that did not excuse them from paying their toll, and as usual Gwydion had neglected to bring any coin. Once or twice they were allowed to cross despite their lack of silver, which good fortune Will put down to the stone. But at other times they were turned away by unmovable curmudgeons, and in those cases they went the long way around or found a willing ferryman who still remembered what men like Gwydion had been.

At the Lyttleburgh crossing of the mighty Trennet they found that the bridge had been seized by a band of outlaws. These men were determined to extort what they could while their rule held, and Will finally lost patience. He climbed down from the cart to plead with them, was ridiculed for his pains, and ended up dashing their stubbornness away with the flat of his hand.

'Well, that has ruined it and no mistake!' Gwydion told him frostily as they rumbled past the slumbering men followed by dozens of other hapless travellers who now saw their opportunity.

'Ruined what?'

'You know very well what. That was a magical gesture. You've just told Chlu exactly where we are.'

'Good. Let him know.'

But as Will's anger cooled, he saw that he had indeed been foolish. He wondered if some part of him might not have secretly angled to provoke just such a result. The fast ground they made along the road that led from the bridge made him feel good, but as their wheels bogged and their pace slowed again, Will felt his sanguine determination running into the mud.

Riding hour after hour across these rain swept levels made Will feel grotesquely exposed. The cold spring wearied him, and he noticed how this year the world seemed reluctant to rise from the grips of winter. He felt a remorseless damp-cold seeping into his bones as they steered their cart along waterlogged lanes. As they crossed Axenholme by ancient ways, picking their path towards the Umber's wintery marshes, a cold east wind swept Warping Moor and drove hard against the mists of Old Ghoul.

All the villages hereabouts were either shuttered or ruined. There were few people abroad, either in the fields or upon the road, and where they were to be seen they lingered only until they saw that they had been spotted. Once or twice, Will saw children. He thought of his daughter and how she had cried to see him go. Then he imagined Willow, miserable among the gossiping wet-nurses and child-minders. He was forced to bite back hard on his feelings and sometimes it was too much. He longed to lie flat upon the comforting stone, but he endured, taking the reins while the wizard kept a wary eye on him.

The day they entered the Duchy of Ebor a watery sun flooded the land with oblique light, adding a dull sheen to what lay beyond the famous Mezentian Gate. Will noted with sadness how the great archway was crumbling, with its lintelpiece fallen and its four huge stone pillars flaking away. All the kingly statues had been torn down and even the crests and the legend carved upon it had been cut away. Will saw that the gate had no place in the world that was to come.

They were drawing towards the Collen and Celin ligns again, and whenever Will wandered far from the cart he tasted hints of hazel and even birch, but always these flavours were massively overpowered by the spiky green bitterness of holly. In the distance he could make out twelve grey bastions, the towers of Drack's Ford, and he knew that to the west and across the ligns lay the ill-starred Castle of Pomfret, which for so long had guarded the crossing of the River Eye like a miser.

'Onward,' he told Gwydion, and the wizard flapped the traces and clicked his tongue at the horses without bothering to voice his doubts that maybe they had already come too far.

Will, keenly aware that the flow was still rushing headlong into the north, tried to square his feelings with his understanding of the warrior's mind. Surely Henry of Mells, or Jasper, or Lord Strange would have thought to garrison the big river crossings. These mighty tributaries that drained half the Realm all emptied into the Umber. Each was a natural defence, and the bridges across them vital to anyone contemplating an attack upon Ebor. Even Mad Clifton must be able to see the importance of preventing their seizure by an army that was only a day or two's march away.

'The bridges will be down,' he murmured.

'Maybe.'

They took a ferry at Cowdell, which was a league to the east of where the holly lign ran. They stayed south of the Ouzel, and instead of crossing it at Saltby and heading for Ebor, they kept away from the Great North Road and ended up on a track that wandered through the marshy ings where the Ouzel met with the Worffe.

'It's . . . that way,' Will insisted. He jumped down and turned westward. All day he had been trying to remember the lie of the ligns that he had crossed while in Lotan's company. Those days seemed half a lifetime ago now, though bare weeks had passed. Still, every time he was reminded of the big man's betrayal, Will's blood grew hot, and now he could see why: to have been so deceived was bad enough, but what had hurt most was Lotan's cowardice, for he had chosen to make his confession at second hand, to Gwydion in Will's absence.

Master Gwydion did right to send you away, he thought. And I do right to erase all memory of the friendship I thought we had.

'Are you sure it's that way?' the wizard asked, detecting the uncertainty in Will's manner.

'If we go much further we'll be in Ebor itself.'

'True. But can you actually *feel* the battlestone?'

Will turned his ill-temper on the wizard. 'I can hardly feel anything else! The ligns are roaring rivers of fire! I fear to cross them! Can't you see that?'

But he was not telling the whole truth. He could now see in his mind's eye how the deadly flow was surging up the hazel lign and into the city of Ebor. There it was being directed south-westward by the Ebor stone, and sent a little way down the linking birch lign. There, where birch and holly crossed, *there* was the battlestone!

All this was clear enough, but there was something else that nagged at Will's mind. Twice before that day he had seen black flashes over to his left, voids on the edge of his vision. They could not possibly have been anything other than Chlu exercising his magic.

Now Will fulsomely regretted his own impatience at the crossing of the Trennet. But there was nothing for it other than to press on, and in any case a more urgent and inescapable trial faced him, for there was still one more lign to cross.

'We've made a mistake,' he said, suddenly consumed by panic. 'We should have crossed the hazel lign further south. I can't do it here. It's too strong.'

'We cannot turn around now.'

Just before Ozen-in-Elmet they found a messenger galloping a lathered horse eastward. He bore Lord Falconburgh's badge and knew the wizard by sight. Questioned by Gwydion, he said there had lately been a bloody skirmish at Fordingbridge upon the River Eye and that he was riding with all speed to apprise Lord Northfolk of the tidings.

'A body of our men under Lord Waters came up from

the south in hopes to take the crossing before the bridge might be broken down,' the messenger told them. 'But they rode into a trap laid by Butcher Clifton. It was a—'

'Mad Clifton?' Will asked.

'The same, though we call him "Butcher" since his foul deed upon Awakenfield Bridge. Yesterday he fell upon my lord Waters and slew him also. Most of our men at the Fordingbridge died, but some few got away and ran to the king who is presently at Pomfret along with Lord Warrewyk—'

'Edward is at Pomfret already, you say?' the wizard cut in.

'Why, yes, Crowmaster . . .'

'Go on,' Will told the messenger.

'At Pomfret they told the tale of their misfortune, and straightway the king launched my lord Falconburgh upon the enemy with main force.'

'And was Clifton bested?' Gwydion asked.

'Better yet, Crowmaster. My lord put the Butcher in his grave. Hacked to pieces, he was, and so Edmund of Rutteland's death has been avenged!'

Despite himself, Will felt a burn of satisfaction to know that Clifton was dead. He saw clearly how justice did not taste like justice unless it also tasted of fairness, and fairness could never be without a seasoning of due recompense to the wronged. It was good to know that Mad Clifton was no more, Will reflected. But how different things would have been if the bolt of magic he himself had cast upon the madman at Delamprey Field had slain him and not just his steed. Edmund, at least, would have lived.

'Is the whole army across the river?' the wizard asked.

'Not when I took my leave. The enemy hold the far bank, but the king is determined to force a way, even at risk to himself.'

'A great fight is brewing,' Will said ominously. 'This is only a foretaste of it.'

Gwydion looked to the west as the messenger prepared to leave them. 'So soon the armies have come within range of one another. If Edward succeeds in sending his army across the Eye, we have not so long as I had thought – or hoped. Thank you, courier, and fare you well!'

They came to the hamlet of Ryther as the daylight died. The cart halted on the road out of town and Gwydion tightened the horses' harnesses and put everything in readiness for the dash they could no longer avoid.

'Must we do it now?' Will asked, his courage quailing.

'If you would cross the lign at all. We cannot afford to wait for the moon to increase and diminish. And as for the sun, this is the best angle we shall have today.'

It was true, of course, but the omens were tremendously against them. Will's skin prickled. He could not take his eyes off the hazel lign which was blazing beyond the last of the cottages. It looked to him like a huge wall of fire, and he thought that if they plunged into it they would never come out again. Even so, he mustered his defiance and climbed down to speak to the horses, whispering spells of fortitude upon their heads.

At a word from the wizard Will got into the back of the cart and straddled the stone.

'Are you ready?' Gwydion asked.

Will nodded, his assent barely audible as he struggled to close his mind tight. This was the moment he had been dreading.

'Do it!'

The wizard clicked his tongue and urged the horses first into a walk, then into a canter, then finally to their best speed. The track was uneven, and the waggon began bouncing and crashing over tufts and tussocks as it sped towards the lign.

Will feared that the axle must crack. He turned his mind

away from that weakling thought, as if even to dwell upon it might tempt disaster. He was thrown about, but he hung onto the iron rings of the stone and pressed his head hard to it, all the while muttering a spell in the true tongue to keep the pressure of the lign from bursting his head open.

But still the visions came at him. Like circling demons they tore at his mind. Although he had no direct contact with the ground, the raw power of the flow here connected sharply with his thoughts. As he stared he saw the cart become enmeshed in furnace heat. All around him the wood was blasted as if held in the jet of air that issues from a blacksmith's bellows. The canvas cover blackened, then was burned to the hoops, revealing a boiling sky of yellow flame. Pain and horror assailed him. He saw his feet flare incandescent and his legs burn like sticks in a bonfire until the Stone of Scions smoked under his cheek, the wheels gave way and the bed of the cart collapsed and disintegrated, and he began falling into an abysmal deep among red-hot cinders . . .

'I am in Hell!' he cried. 'Hell!'

He screamed and screamed until the firebursts in his brain passed away, and then – mercifully – came death.

But it was not quite death, because he could feel the stone feeding him. Not with counter-visions of sunshine and spring flowers, but with a memory equally horrific in its way. Once, to save his life, Gwydion had convinced him that he was bleeding to death, and he had lain in the back of a cart not unlike this one. And when the illusion designed to mislead others had been lifted and he had found himself unhurt the relief he had felt at that moment had been better by far than any boon he might have had, even of the king himself.

I'm thinking, he told himself, grasping the only real truth a man can possess. I'm thinking, so I can't be dead. And while I live, there's hope . . .

The next thing he knew the wizard was slapping his cheeks to bring him round and trying to force some fierce draught down his throat.

'We have crossed the lign and left it far behind,' Gwydion said, judiciously lifting each of Will's eyelids in turn. 'I think you will live, for a while at least.'

'I wish Gort were here,' he croaked at last, his mouth burning. 'At least he doesn't force a man to drink potions made from bats' droppings.'

Both of them knew that sometimes a vision inspired by terror, be it real or imagined, would refuse to let go of a man's mind, and he would be lost to sanity. But not today. The wizard heard the humour in Will's words and knew that his spirit had come through the ordeal intact.

'Actually, Gort does use bats' droppings in some of his potions,' Gwydion said loftily. 'But quite rarely, I assure you. And only when it is absolutely necessary.'

The wizard produced a sprig of hawthorn on which white blossom had sprouted and gave it to Will. The tiny flowers delighted him and he murmured, 'Who could lose hope in the spring?'

When Will dared to let go of the stone, he said, 'So much for your idea that the Stone of Scions would look after me. I nearly lost my grip.'

'You are alive, are you not? And in your right mind?'

'Just about.'

'Well, then. The stone has made all the difference.'

Will took the point grudgingly. 'The flow's too strong for it here. The lorc is putting everything into one last effort.'

'Raw malice is running fast in the channels of the lorc,' Gwydion explained, unperturbed. 'But what kindness there is in the Stone of Scions is bound tight, just as the malice of a battlestone is kept within its bounds until the moment of release. However there is always seepage, as we have found. I confess, I had hoped that the kindness might leak a little more easily than it has.'

Will spat and wiped the sweat from his face. 'I'm alive, as you say. But I won't cross another lign. Not willingly.'

'Let us hope you will not have to.'

He met Gwydion's eye, knowing he must now make an important admission. 'Chlu is close by. I can feel him.'

That jolted the wizard, though he tried not to show it. 'Is he alone?'

Will spread his hands. 'How should I know?'

'How far away is he?'

'A league. Maybe.' He gestured vaguely towards the south. 'Now that we're between hazel and holly it's hard to tell.'

'We should go south.'

Will's brow furrowed. 'Why should we make it easy for him?'

'It does not surprise me that Chlu is here. You must meet with him one last time. It will be better if the initiative is with you from the beginning.'

Will thought back to the inconclusive combats on the Spire and on Cullee Hill. He wondered if there was anything in prophecy that made a third meeting inevitable, but he did not ask. It seemed more sensible to spend his thoughts second guessing what new ploy Chlu might try on him in the final battle.

'You speak of Chlu,' Will said after a while, 'but I suspect you're more interested in who's in his company.'

'Quite right. I must establish Maskull's whereabouts. And I must do it as soon as I can. We have little time.'

That night, rather than stopping to rest, they went on through the deepening darkness, watching the bloated moon push its way above the eastern horizon. Before midnight they came to the village of Fenton. It had been stripped of all its men and abandoned by its other inhabitants. Will knew that if they had listened to their Wise Woman, they would be hiding like animals in the wild woods until the soldiers went away. But if the Fellowship was strong hereabouts they might have been herded into one of the walled precincts that adjoined a chapter house. Whatever their fate, they had left an eerie feeling of loss behind them.

The cart pulled into a yard hedged in by a field of tree stumps – an orchard hewn down for firewood. The ground was littered with twigs that snapped under the cartwheels. At the wizard's request, Will dared to open his mind a little. Fire dragons writhed in the sky, but there were black bubbles in the glare, and he gasped, 'Chlu! He's over there . . .'

'How far now?'

'Half a league.'

'Which way?'

Will made an effort to be more precise. 'West. Over there.'

The wizard stroked his beard. 'Not far away in that direction lies Scarthingwell 337. It is a signal tower maintained by the Fellowship. I should go there to discover what I can.'

'Be careful.'

'Always. Wait here. If I fail to return by dawn, drive the cart towards the battlestone and do what must be done.'

'I will.'

It was grim advice. As Gwydion walked off into the gloom, Will fought the urge to huddle close to the Stone of Scions. He wondered if this was the way the world was supposed to end. He understood very well the reason Gwydion had gone alone – he could hardly approach Chlu himself without alerting him, but the wizard might just pass unseen. Still, Gwydion's departure did little to set Will's mind at ease.

As the moon rose higher in the south the sister-stone eased his fears, prompting the thought that Gwydion would not have left him without saying a proper goodbye if he had had serious doubts about coming back. Even when the hours stretched out and the moon began to slide down into the south-west, Will's faith did not fail him. Eventually, stiff and cold, he got down from the cart and began to walk around the abandoned village. The sense of loss was palpable here. There had been deaths and violent acts done against the innocent.

Always darkest before the dawn . . .

The thought-echo trailed away as movement caught his eye. A fox, grinning in the darkness. It stared at him with an insolent look, then loped off. A cold breeze sighed in the trees and raised the hairs on Will's neck. He found it easy to imagine all manner of enemies lurking in the shadows.

Go back to the cart, he told himself silently. But just as he turned he saw a darker shape slide into the blackness of a doorway, and he knew that he was not alone.

How long had he been watched? His blood froze in his veins. It's only Gwydion, he told himself. Who else could it be?

The impulse to call out the wizard's name was strong, but he resisted. What if it was *not* Gwydion?

A pang of impatience assailed him, but he forced himself to control it. He rounded a corner then crept out of sight, moving quickly to a new vantage point that covered the cart and also the door of the hovel where he had seen the dark shape vanish. There he waited, his heart thumping and his restraint draining by degrees. He did not want to give away his position, but something held him back from investigating. He wondered how far his decisions were falling prey to the influence of the ligns. Whenever he had strayed far from the stone he had had to struggle against the flow, and it was not possible to tell what part of his courage was falsely inspired and what part stemmed from his own strength.

Against his better judgement he decided to wait and keep an eye on the cart. Time passed. His bones started to ache and his curiosity began to embroider the darkness. If it was not Gwydion, then who else could it be? One of the folk who had lived here? Their Wise Woman perhaps?

Maybe.

Then he began to worry about what might have happened to Gwydion . . .

By now the moon had sunk into low cloud and the first smudges of grey were lighting the eastern sky. He wanted to open his mind a fraction. That risked showing himself to Chlu, but he needed to feel out the figure in the hovel, to establish malign intent or the absence of it.

Once again he went against his urges and decided to think the matter through one more time. Who was inside the hovel? It could not be Chlu, for Chlu's presence would have left him in no doubt. But what if it was Maskull? A grim smile crept across his face as he watched the doorway. If it was, then the sorcerer had made a huge miscalculation . . .

Without magic, Maskull was vulnerable. He could be surprised and captured, maybe even killed. This was Will's big chance, and the look on Gwydion's face when he returned would be almost too wonderful!

He had almost readied himself to make a dash for the doorway, when a noise off to his left made him turn. It was a small stone, tossed his way by Gwydion. The wizard's left hand was raised, his right held Maglin's staff. His look was urgent and silently questioning.

Will pressed a finger to his lips and then pointed to the hovel. The wizard's gestures said: do nothing, say nothing. Then Gwydion put his head back and made an unearthly noise. They waited motionless for a few moments, then Gwydion made the noise again, a high, edgy bark, and waited patiently until the vixen came to him.

He bent to stroke her head, then she trotted away and

put her snout into the doorway that Will had been watching. After a moment's sniffing, she returned to Gwydion who stroked her head again and sent her away with his thanks. As he set off towards the doorway, he motioned Will to follow. 'She said the man who was hiding here last night was frightened. Foxes smell fear very keenly. He left by the back way shortly after he arrived.'

Will relaxed, feeling more than a little foolish to have been overawed by a phantom and wasted a fine chance.

'It's good to see you haven't lost your touch with animals.'

'Sadly, that is not magic. Merely long experience with the wild world.'

Will walked about the hovel. He could not detect the faintest whiff of corrupt magic, but his opinion was unwavering. 'It was Maskull, wasn't it?'

'Who else?'

'What was he doing here?'

'Chlu sent him to kill you.'

'Kill me? Are you joking?'

'I found them at the signal tower and heard them quarrelling about it. You will be gratified to know that Maskull was against the idea.'

Will grunted with sour amusement. 'That's a change, Chlu sending his master upon a mission.'

'Maskull is no longer Chlu's master. I listened long enough to discover that. The betrayer is now himself betrayed. Maskull walks in weeds, a shadow of his former self, in fouler odour at Queen Mag's court than am I in the halls of the House of Ebor. Apparently, there has been a marked decline in the queen's looks just lately.'

'Ha!' Will cried with sudden realization. 'He's been maintaining her with his magic which doesn't work any more so she's thrown him out!'

'Indeed she has. She is no longer quite the beauty she was. She blames him for all her other reverses too.'

Will laughed. 'It was in my mind to kick Maskull's feet out from under him just now.'

'I thought you had more sense than that.'

'What? When he's defenceless? I could have trussed him up and hung him from the rafters for you.'

'Maskull looks like an old rag, for ragged he goes now and in thrall to his young creation. What a crushing end to one who had such lofty ambitions . . . but he carries a long knife and he would have put it through you as if you were a mince pie had you decided to tangle with him.'

'I think I can look after myself.'

'You would have come off worse against Maskull. He has perfected his crafts over many a long century, and though he has lost his magic, he has not been left wholly bereft of venom. If he had thought he could surprise you last night, then he would have done so. And you would be dead now. As soon as he realized he had been spotted, he made himself scarce.'

Will picked up a note of regret in the wizard's voice and he understood the ambivalence of Gwydion's mood. They had both expected blood and thunder at the downfall of so gigantic an adversary, but Maskull taking orders and creeping away silently with his mission unfulfilled? This really was the world turned upside down.

Truly, Will thought, running a finger round his collar, today marks the end of an Age and this can be no other than the eve of the last battle.

'What excuse do you think he'll spin to Chlu for having failed to kill me?'

'He will think of something plausible. He always does.'

'I think he knows he can't kill me. He tried on Awakenfield Bridge, but it's not my fate to be killed by him.'

'A dangerous assumption at the best of times. If you knew what your fate was we would have no more trouble.'

The wizard returned to the cart, but before he looked in the back he asked, 'What about the stone?'

'Maskull didn't go near the cart.'

'Perhaps not, but one of the reasons Chlu sent him here was to find out what was coming their way. Chlu feels the Stone of Scions just as you feel the battlestones. That is the main reason he did not care to leave the comfort of the holly lign himself. He took refuge in a signal tower that stands upon it. He lured out, then murdered, the signaller, and all night long he has enjoyed his own company while his pet sorcerer did his bidding.'

Drawing closer to the stone made Will feel suddenly better. He turned, his mind comprehending a strange symmetry in the night's events, but objecting even so, for the two stories were different – one involved a sorcerer sent out under compulsion to spy, the other concerned a wizard who went to collect information, willingly risking himself to help a comrade.

'Shall we go after them? Now, when they least expect it?'

Gwydion looked at him unreadably. 'That is for you to decide.'

Will drew a deep draught of morning air and put an arm around the wizard's shoulders. 'I will decide, but your advice is dear to me, Master Gwydion. Tell me what you think we should do.'

'It seems to me that as well as our common goal we each have our own tasks to accomplish. My guess is that Maskull has returned to Chlu with some tall tale of his night's heroic doings—'

Will climbed up onto the cart. 'A spider lying to a hornet.'

'Indeed.' The wizard's sudden lightness of mood was good to see. 'But you can be sure that Maskull is far from finished, not while his window on the new world is still open.'

'Ah, yes, the window . . .' Will had forgotten about that. 'Is it still open? Surely it must have faded away and been lost to him by now, along with all his other magic.'

'Not the window, for that was accomplished through fae magic. Maskull needed to use his own magic and, we may suppose, some of the power tapped from one of the battle-stones, to gain access to fae spells. But the magic of the window itself, once made, is as durable as you are.'

'So Maskull can work no more fae magic, but whatever he's created already, having used that magic, will linger longest. Right up until the moment when the worlds collide?'

'I believe so. And so it must be, for that window is now Maskull's only protection from Chlu's magic.'

'Why?'

'Because Maskull has convinced Chlu that he must jump through the window. Chlu certainly seems to believe that it is the only way he will be able to enter the world to come.'

Will stared into the east, where the sunrise was painting the sky with blood. 'You mean, you think Maskull hasn't told Chlu that the other world is arriving here anyway?'

'What would it serve him to tell Chlu the truth? No doubt he has presented Chlu with some complication or another, the half-story that manipulates him best. Whatever else he may have been led to believe, Chlu is certainly acting as if he requires the window to gain access to the other world. But here is something to consider: do *we* know for certain that the other world is going to arrive? Hmmm?'

'Well . . . that's what we've been working to prevent.'

'Correct. Remember that Chlu hopes for the other world, just as we fear it. For him, that world offers the chance of endless dominance, the overlordship his heart yearns for. We can suppose that Maskull has filled Chlu's mind with brilliant visions of how it will be in that world to come, the world that will be his if only he can crush the final obstacle before the last moment arrives.'

'Us.'

'You.' The wizard pointed a finger at him. 'No one knows for certain what will happen in that final moment. Remember that in this world a preponderance of belief is what tips the scales of reality. It is how extraordinary outcomes can be made, how, ultimately, all magic is done.'

Will frowned, grasping the implications. 'I think I see . . .'

'Believe harder, Will. That is my counsel to you. You seem not to think it likely, but you may yet become Arthur, and we may yet win the day. And what would Chlu do then?'

Gwydion's reasoning was flawless as ever, but Will could not drive away the suspicion that he had been somehow outmanoeuvred. He scratched his head. 'So what do you think Maskull's done with the window?'

The wizard smiled. 'Fortunately I do not have to guess about that. When Chlu sent him away from the signal tower, I followed him. I knew where he would go. It was the first opportunity he had had to check the window.'

'He led you to it?' Will asked, astonished.

'He wanted to see if it was still safe. I knew he would do it, for I have known him a very long time and we were not always adversaries. The window is a bolt-hole, in case his plans go awry. For himself if not for Chlu.'

'Didn't he have any idea that you were following him?'

'None at all. He was too busy making sure that Chlu had remained at the signal tower. He was very careful about that, but the magical protections upon which he once relied to warn him of my presence are gone, whereas my own natural stealth was there to serve me as usual. In the event, I tracked him quite easily to his goal. I saw him open the window when the moon was high. He stood in the draught and looked in on a red sunrise while snowflakes from the other world blew out around him. Then he closed it again and left.'

'What did you do?'

'I waited until he had gone. Then I approached the window myself. It is a strange thing to look into the other world. I saw grey daylight. Their time is presently running a few hours ahead of ours.'

'Or perhaps behind,' Will said.

Gwydion smiled indulgently, and lifted the reins. 'Fortunately, I looked for the position of the moon. They are still some hours ahead of us, although they are slowing down. Do you remember when first you poked your head into the other world? Back then they were months ahead of us. I suspect that the moment when their time coincides with ours will be the moment of collision.

'Well? Shall we go and do what must be done?'

□ □ □

CHAPTER TWENTY-FIVE

WHITE SNOW, RED RIVER

All along the western horizon now the land was burning like a cremation. As they drove the cart towards the battlestone, Will saw a towering column of flame jet abruptly into the sky, and the lign suddenly calmed itself. He understood that the stone was replete, that it had supped its fill and was now preparing to vomit out its harm over the surrounding fields of death.

The hamlet of Sackstone huddled by a small stream, surrounded by strips of worked land. All around it, vast columns of footmen, three or four thousand strong, were assembling. They had come up from the south and were forming into three great fighting battalions. This was Edward's army – it had forced the crossing of the Eye and advanced up to Sackstone overnight. There were woods beyond the hamlet to the north-west and a road that ran along the meandering waters, but to the north-east a great shield of open land bulged gently for half a league so that whatever enemy deployments there might be on the far side, they were hidden and would remain so almost until the armies clashed. The simmering holly lign ran right over the bulge, slicing it in two.

'That's the battlefield,' Will said, pointing towards a lone oak that stood out on the skyline.

'Another iron tree,' Gwydion muttered.

'I don't think so. I can see it moving in the breeze.'

As they neared the lign, Will's skin began to prickle. It was a cold morning with only a little wind coming in gusts down from the north and a spattering of rain in the air, but Will sweated like a man with the plague. He could feel the fire still burning in his face and he trembled at the memory of what he had gone through when they had crossed the hazel lign. But he gritted his teeth, choosing to stay alongside Gwydion this time, determined not to seek the touch of the Stone of Scions before he was driven to it. The fire of the lign had died down, but Will knew that his sickness would only grow worse as they approached the battlestone.

A rider in Lord Warrewyk's colours confronted them as they tried to pass along a lane crowded with soldiers. He looked hard at Will's white face and staring eyes.

'What's to do with him?' the rider demanded of Gwydion. 'Is he sick?'

'Sick enough. He knows he is to die today.'

The rider laughed. 'You'll both die if you go up there, for the enemy is that way.'

'More will die if we do not. Let us through, for the king's sake!'

The soldiers ahead of them parted to let them go on. Hollow looks were on all their faces. They were uncaring, men who had made a long, forced march and who had seen their first fighting the night before in the marshes on the north bank of the Eye. They were shaken and fearful, and the quiet of the grave had settled over them. They wanted the coming fight over with as soon as possible, and the big question answered once and for all – *will I die today?*

Will understood what they did not, that it was only the battlestone that was holding them here. If not for its enmeshing power they would be rebelling against the men-at-arms who harried them onward – wouldn't they?

Will urged the cart forward, but then the rider came up alongside them again and blocked their way with a drawn sword. 'The king's sake, you say? But which king is that?'

'The rightful king,' Will whispered.

'And what is his name?'

'Edward,' Gwydion said, seeing the danger. 'Edward of the House of Ebor, and long may he reign!'

The rider looked at them doubtfully, but he put up his sword all the same. Then, as they began to pass he slapped a hand on Will's chest and said, 'How is it that you do not know what all the rest of the army knows – that King Edward was shot last night at the Fordingbridge?'

'Shot?' Gwydion said, shocked. 'Is he *dead*?'

'The arrow is yet in him. The wound is said to be mortal, though a clever healer attends him.'

'Then why do you still come here to fight?' Will asked, meeting the rider's eye.

The rider turned aside and spat. 'Because my lord of Warrewyk says we must!'

The wizard took the reins from Will's hands. 'We fight to put a twelve-year-old boy on the throne! Young Richard of Ebor! Is that not so? And much glory to your lord for that.'

It was a two-edged remark, but as the cart ran on, the rider did not pursue it. After all, what did it matter if two fools took their cart out into no man's land? Every enemy arrow the cart attracted was one fewer to fall on his own head and the heads of his men. But the fools were right about one thing – many would die today.

Gwydion slewed the cart into the meadow and it began to move slowly up the incline. The short-cropped grass told them this had been a sheep meadow, but there were no sheep here now. And then Will saw in the distance something that might have been a ewe, but that it was unmoving.

It stood a little way from the oak, but directly on the smouldering lign. It was, without any doubt, the battlestone.

They had to approach it, but when the cart came within a bowshot of the lign, Will began to find it hard to breathe. One hand clutched his throat, the other motioned Gwydion to keep going.

'Hyah!' the wizard cried, urging greater effort from the horses. But while they were still a hundred paces from the stone, foam began to bubble from Will's mouth and he knew he was in danger of slipping into unconsciousness.

Unbidden, Gwydion turned the cart aside and ran the horses away again, this time towards the lone oak tree that stood fifty paces to the east. Here, on the very top of the shield, it seemed they were alone. To their south lay Edward's army, to their north lay the hamlet of Towstone and the queen's forces.

Will drew his breath in gulps, railing at the wizard that they must not turn away but go on. He fell into the back of the cart, eyes rolling, lungs filling, drawing breath only after tremendous efforts.

'Do not try to speak!'

'We must . . .' He hammered his fists against the Stone of Scions, trying to draw strength from it.

When at last his breath came more easily he lay gasping, but he knew he must relinquish his grip on the stone and urge Gwydion to another effort, and this time make him go through with it whatever happened.

'I tell you, we must approach the stone!'

'I was wrong!' The wizard grasped his shoulder. 'Did you not see the battlestone? It is much bigger than the Stone of Scions. It is not even the same kind of stone. Ours cannot be the sister-stone that I had hoped it might be.'

'But we agreed – even if it's not the sister-stone – still we must lay them together—'

'Not yet!'

Will tried to muster his remaining strength, furious at the wizard's caution. When Gwydion jumped down from the cart Will took it into his mind to turn the horses around and drive them up to the stone himself. But the wizard was calling to him to follow.

'Look! See what I have here!'

Will decided to hear Gwydion out one more time. He staggered towards the tree. Here the grass was thin and his feet skidded in the mud under the oak's skeletal spread. No hint of spring had yet swelled the tree's buds, but there was something strange about it, something that made him think again of the iron oak that had entombed the Doomstone of the West. It had certainly been tampered with, for there was a faint smell of magic still lingering about it.

Then Will saw the wizard's robes moving, though there was now no wind. And he heard the soughing of a constant breeze, a sound he recognized. He saw two open shutters banging against the bark, and Gwydion staring into a square hole between.

With a shock Will suddenly understood what he was looking at: the window that Maskull had so painstakingly removed from his secret workshop in Trinovant had been installed on the living trunk of the oak tree.

Beyond the window, the other world was in turmoil. There was screaming and shouting and the unmistakable din of battle. Dead men were there in great numbers, round about the tree and as far as he could see. There were horses whinnying and galloping, many riderless. Snow was falling and men charged forward, their weapons comported for the fight, thousands rushing on, yet all in slow motion, as if in a dream.

But it was no dream. The gust that came from the

window was tainted with death, and they had to dodge arrows as the battle surged against the far side of the window. After a while the deadly action seemed abruptly to move on, leaving them behind.

'Behold!' Gwydion cried. 'The tide of battle has passed. The queen's forces are in rout!'

But Will's sympathies were with the world he knew and loved, and which was moving inexorably towards the grey reality beyond the window, a place where no magic coloured the lives of men and a grey God ruled on high.

He began to whisper and to step out his magic. Then he forced the shutters closed, laid hands upon the frame of the window and muttered a formula in the language of stones that enabled it to be pulled free from the living flesh of the oak.

A spillage of fae magic shuddered the tree. It burst fresh young shoots from the branches. The grass under Will's feet thrived as he lifted the window and made instantly for the cart.

'What are you doing?' the wizard shouted after him.

'I've solved the riddle!'

Will climbed up onto the seat of the cart and turned it around. Gwydion ran after it, but Will urged the horses into a gallop and the wizard began to fall behind.

As soon as the stone felt his approach it directed its paralysing power at him. Again he could not draw breath, as if his windpipe had narrowed to a straw. The stone was still fifty paces away when the cart began to falter. The horses came to a standstill, then they began to buck and kick in their harness. Will felt their pain. He leapt down as, instinctively, they began to run the cart away from the battlestone.

With them went the Stone of Scions, but Will had the window in his hands. He opened it and lifted it above his head, then dropped it down over himself.

An extraordinary sensation flooded his body, neither pain nor pleasure, but a sense of disconnectedness. He felt confusion, as if for a moment he had lost the power of thought. Then came a terrific thump in his back as someone ran into him and sent him sprawling on the ground. He cradled his head instinctively and gasped for breath, but when no further blow came he looked up to see a lone figure pelting away from him, scrambling over ill-defined obstacles. He was surrounded by hundreds of dead bodies, their limbs flung out or folded under them, their attitudes seemingly abandoned or unconcerned, for comfort was beyond them.

Will's breath came easily now, but his heart almost stopped beating as he stared at the bloody aftermath of battle and tried to collect his scattered wits. The grey world was grey no longer, but red and white. An icy wind was blowing from the south. There had been freak weather here, a snowstorm, and the dead men who littered the field had been blanketed. Frozen arms and arrow shafts sprang through the drifts like black daffodils. He stared around, trying to orientate himself, but he could see no lone oak tree in this world. Then, with the force of a hammer blow, came the realization that his gamble had paid off. *He could breathe now because there was no battlestone in this world.*

He picked the window off the ground, recalling the sudden flash of insight that had come to him in his own world. Fifty more paces that way was all it would take . . .

Or was it *that* way?

But of course! He already had the answer in his hands.

The window was tugging at him as it swallowed a rush of air. He lifted it up, braced his arms on each side of the frame and looked through. The shutters were waving wildly as air gusted between worlds. The red glow had turned to blue. On the far side he could see the cart, overturned now and the horses furiously struggling to get up. Gwydion was dashing up the slope towards the cart as fast as he could, shouting madly.

Will ignored him. He swung the window and saw the battlestone. Then he ran towards it, keeping it centred in the frame. Ten paces, twenty paces, thirty . . . stepping over bodies, printing footfalls on the white spaces of paradoxical purity. Already the snow was melting, but in this cold world day was passing into night and with the fall of darkness the horrors would multiply.

But at least Will could breathe now and the terrible oppression of the battlestone had vanished. With the pain went his fear. The final steps were momentous, giant strides, for now he was filled with the certainty of victory. The battlestone was slender, no bigger than he was himself, and in it shimmered a hideous form ready to do in Will's world what had already been achieved in this one.

'Not today!' he shouted, lifting the window. Then he pushed it down over the battlestone just as a cooper pushes a hoop down over a barrel. Except that this hoop was big enough to pass all the way down to the ground. The stone appeared through the frame. But in this world it was merely an innocuous block of grey limestone, its back coated with green moss and yellow lichen, that stood mute among the corpses. Will rammed his shoulder against it – once, twice, three times – so at the final heave it easily gave up the shallow socket of earth which had held it upright throughout the Ages. It gave like a rotten tooth, fell wholly into the snow of the new world and lamely broke in two.

The window lay beside it, a square patch of green and wormy soil. Air susurrated, the blue flame burned like magelight, then, astonishingly, the frame lifted itself up from the ground and fell again, progressively revealing from head to toe a wizard's robes.

'They are coming!' Gwydion cried, jumping through and discarding the frame. 'Run!'

'I'll not run now!' Will shouted. No matter what had frightened the wizard, he would face it.

But Gwydion grabbed him and his expression brooked no further argument. 'Run! Do as I say!'

Will shook him off and they ran, hurdling snowy mounds, treading over dead flesh. How urgent must the danger be, how gigantic the horror, if it's forced Gwydion to escape into this place? Will wondered. He turned and saw the window rise up for a third time behind them. A thunder-bolt blasted through, narrowly missing Will's head. The deadly fireball arced high over the battlefield, but it exploded in a harmless burst of red light, unable to exist in a world devoid of magic.

'It's Chlu!' Will shouted.

Two more bolts of fire swept past them as they ran, leaving smoke trails and lighting the ghastly field. They too burst in lurid red, but again harmlessly. Will and the wizard splashed through icy meltwater and a little way down the slope to the west, hiding from the summit by using the lie of the land.

'Where are you going?' Will shouted frantically. 'Master Gwydion, they can't hurt us!'

'Look!'

As soon as they dropped below the sightline Gwydion drew Will to a halt and pointed down the slope. Their way was blocked. For the first time they saw the full horror of what had happened here. The little stream that drained the west side of the battlefield was a swollen torrent from which the death cries of thousands of men were rising. A seething morass of soldiers were locked in a continuing struggle, a grey chaos, like insects contending furiously with one another. But they were men, dying horribly and in great numbers.

Will could see what had happened. The queen's army had been outflanked on its left, rolled up by the arrival of a reserve battalion coming in late and unexpectedly from the south-east – Lord Northfolk's army. And once the queen's left began to crumble, panic must have swept through her ranks and her whole army had disintegrated. It had fled the only way it could – to its right – which was onto the slope that dropped down towards the stream. Men had abandoned their weapons, skidded and tumbled down into the wash of icy water. They were packing the fast-flowing stream and trampling one another underfoot as they sought to escape all at once into the flooded pastures beyond.

Will saw drowning men attempting to pull themselves up, but only dragging others to their doom. He saw men threshing in a mile-long quagmire of blood. He saw merciless attacks launched upon the heads of the dying. The whole stream was now running red.

'The queen's army is being annihilated!' Will gasped. 'What now?'

The wizard stared back up the slope and he gritted his teeth with grim satisfaction. 'Good!' he said. 'They are coming through the window.'

Two tiny black figures had appeared on the shoulder of the hill. Even outlined against the sky there was no mistaking them.

'What are they doing?' Will asked.

'Ha ha! Maskull thinks that the only way to prevent the advent of Arthur now is to take the Dark Child with him into this world!' Gwydion said. 'We've won, my friend!'

'Won? But how?'

'To thwart me, Maskull has had to make good his promise to Chlu. Now I understand my destiny. I am to counter Maskull here. We shall stand in opposition in this new world, just as once we aided one another in the old.'

'You're not going to stay *here*?' Will cried, aghast.

'If Maskull stays, then so must I, for this is truly a world of good and evil.' He threw wide his hands, begging Will to understand his sacrifice. 'I cannot abandon a whole world to him, can I?'

'But surely—'

The wizard shook his head. 'Our spirits are both locked within Philosopher's Stones back in the old world. If Maskull stays here he will have one part of his heart's desire, which is to live forever. I must stay too, for he must never rule in this world!'

'Master Gwydion, you can't!'

But the wizard's face grew grimmer and he stood back a pace. 'My days in the old world are over. My destiny is clear, Willand. Promise me you will do what is necessary to fulfil your own. Lure Chlu back. I will make sure Maskull does not follow. Now, go! We both have work to do!'

With that, Gwydion began to pick his way back up the death-strewn slope. Will could do nothing but watch him go. When he tried to open his mind, he found he had forgotten how to do it. And so he took an axe from the hand of a dead man and made straight for Chlu, roaring out his pain as if the wizard's decision had been his twin's fault.

Chlu raised two hands and tried to step out the magic required to send a thunderbolt spinning into Will's guts as he approached. But Will came on undaunted. Only at the third attempt did Chlu realize that something was wrong. He saw that his magic had failed him, and instead looked to the corpses at his feet for protection, finding among them a war-hammer.

When Maskull pulled a lance from the ground and tried to rush to Chlu's defence, Gwydion moved to intercept him, locking staff against lance in an adamant struggle to force the other to the ground.

From the corner of his eye, Will saw that wizard and sorcerer fought with liquid movements that deceived the eye, whirling and spinning, their magic gone but their mastery of the fighting arts undiminished. Their combat flowed back and forth, but Gwydion was forcing his adversary away, leaving Chlu and Will to face one another alone.

The clash came. Chlu's skull showed beneath his skin: black hair, black lips, eyes burning red in a white face. Laughing.

Will swung his axe at the death's head, but Chlu raised his hammer and their weapons rang together, locking, crook to crook. Will kicked Chlu's leg away, and as he staggered, drove him back, but the jarring wrench of falling tore the axe handle from Will's grip, leaving Chlu sprawling in the snow. Will was first on his feet but now he was weaponless.

Chlu took up the axe hungrily and cast the hammer far away behind him. He hefted the axe and swept it testingly at Will's head. Will spat and clenched his teeth, for in the blink of an eye the advantage had turned greatly in Chlu's favour.

Will readied himself as the attack came roaring at him. It was poorly controlled, a lunge followed through too violently, so that Will was able to duck under the swing and ram his shoulder into Chlu's stomach, lifting him, and dumping him over onto his back. But the ground was slippery and they went down together. Will's left hand closed on Chlu's wrist, pinning the axe, while he slammed blow after blow into his face.

Blood from Chlu's burst nose coloured the snow around them, more gurgled in Chlu's throat as he screamed out defiance. His outstretched fingers tore at Will's eyes, forcing him to turn. Chlu bucked to free himself, and as Will was thrown off he twisted back. A battle-sharpened axe slashed at Will's chest. It sliced open his jerkin just as he regained his feet. He felt the cold and saw the wound, a cut across his side, white-edged and bleeding.

But there was more than shock in his response. The idea came to him at the speed of thought that the tit-for-tat link that had connected him with Chlu in their own world did not work here. No prophecy lay upon either of them in this place, no natural law governed their movements so they were unprotected. Chlu's bloody face and the wound to his own ribs had served notice that the strike and counterstrike he had expected would not happen this time. And the lessons he had learned in all those armoured fights against Edward in the combat yard of Foderingham were not forgotten. Now it was time to seize the advantage.

Hope goaded him to attack. He rushed at Chlu, lunging forward to take hold of his axe-arm. It was a dangerous move for a weaponless man. With the axe, Chlu's reach was already longer than his own, but the weight of it made his movements slower.

Now the Dark Child slipped his grip to the very end of the axe handle before he swung. It was a cunning trick which gave him an extra three finger-widths of reach. It could have been the margin that let the blade bite this time. But Will saw the move coming. He swayed back as the swipe came. Even so he felt the wind of the axe as it shaved his brow.

Will was aware of shapes moving towards them. It flashed through his mind that looters were coming to strip the bodies. There was movement near them, soldiers being drawn to their fight—

Then Chlu struggled and lashed out. Will tried to avoid the blow, but it concussed him. He had been caught under the chin with the back of the axe haft. The contact jarred against his jaw, blasted bright colours through his head and threw him off balance. His head rang and, seeing the next blow coming, he staggered back half a pace. But that was a deadlier mistake, for his heels came up hard against a corpse that lay behind him and he fell backwards over it.

He froze as he grasped that he was now wholly at Chlu's mercy. There was no time to feel terror, for Chlu stepped forward to finish him without delay. He lifted the axe and brought it down with all his strength.

What flashed between them, Will could not tell. A great shape, bearlike, screaming, lunging in from his right. But he knew that whatever it was carried away the danger. It had also taken the blow and saved his life.

Blood splattered him and he stared into the face of a head now cloven where axe had split bone. Will gasped as the Dark Child toppled forward, almost falling on top of him, and in his place there appeared an impossible figure. It was Willow. In her hand was the hammer Chlu had relinquished. She had swung it at Chlu's head and laid him low with it.

Will struggled out from under the dead weight that had saved him and drenched him in crimson. The body groaned and rolled as he scrambled up, but he could not shake off so easily the terrifying sight of the wound that had split the face wide open. That blow had been meant for him, that wound had been meant for his own face. The dead man was barely recognizable, but his eyes were open to the sky, one blue and one brown.

'Will!' She was beside him, fingers on his face. He clutched her, saw her mouthing words that made no sense. How had she got here? What was happening?

'Will! Listen to me!'

His mind found the truth impossible to accept, but Willow's voice confirmed it.

'He begged to come with us. He said he couldn't live with himself otherwise!'

'*Lotan?*' It was his own voice.

'He needed to apologize to you himself, Will. He needed your forgiveness. He begged us.'

Will began to shake.

The great body jerked down as steaming blood guttered from it. Lotan was as dead as any man could be.

'We gave him another chance.'

'Oh, Willow . . .'

She grasped her husband, and he held onto her, feeling as if he would shake apart. Shock blotted everything from his mind. He shut his eyes and found he could not open them. She was crying his name, trying to shout some sense into him, but the world was taking a while to reconfigure itself.

'What about him?' she demanded, her face distorted. 'Listen to me, Will!'

He took hold of himself, braved the new world. He took a dagger from his wife's hand. Death was all around, but he forced himself to focus on the body she was showing him. Chlu's bloody head lolled as she grabbed a handful of hair and lifted it back. Breath gasped from his open mouth.

'Do what you must do!' Willow told him. 'Do it now!'

It sounded like an accusation, as if he had negligently over-looked something vital. And it was true. He had Chlu at his mercy and there was nothing else left to do to win, nothing else except slit his throat. But he could not murder an un-conscious man, not even the Dark Child. He could not do it.

'No . . .' he muttered. 'No, no.'

Willow stared at him helplessly, then started away. 'I'll fetch Morann.'

Morann? That made no sense either. Where had they all come from? What had happened on the other side of the window? Blood gouted from his side, filled his hand. At least Willow had not seen that. Confusion settled over his mind again like a fog. It enraged him. Nor would it clear no matter how he tried to penetrate it. They must have travelled north after him, maybe by a different route, but only hours behind.

'Wait!' he called after her.

But she went on heedlessly up the slope.

He stood up, grabbed Chlu by the wrists and began to pull, knowing only that he had to take Chlu back into his own world. At first the body slid easily over the icy slush, but it was a dead weight and hard to drag uphill. He pulled it ten paces before he lost his footing, then he saw that he would have to lift it. With a tremendous effort he sat Chlu up and hauled one arm over his shoulder, bending until Chlu's feet were off the ground, but then his knees gave and he crashed down in a puddle of mud and gore. Pain gripped him. The wound in his side was deeper than he had thought. He had torn through some membrane beneath his ribs. It would probably not kill him, but it had made it impossible to shift Chlu further.

Will started to get up again, but by now Willow had come back, and the window was in her hands, floating towards him through the air. She stepped over him and shoved it over Chlu. Will felt the rush of air tugging them back towards their own world. Then a more powerful heave came against the body and Will realized that it must be Morann pulling from the other side.

He got to his feet to help but could not straighten himself. Blood had made his side and thigh sodden. With a sudden change in sound Chlu's legs vanished and Will looked through the window to glimpse an oak tree and Morann manfully dragging a body across green grass.

'Now you!' Will said, taking the frame from his wife.

'You first.'

'Willow, do as I ask.'

She began to argue, but he insisted. She braced herself, flashed a glance at him, then dived head-first back into her own world.

Will held the frame in his hands for a moment and looked over his shoulder to see if he could see the wizard, but there was no sign of him.

'To hell with this world!' he shouted. 'They don't deserve to have you, Master Gwydion! And they're not going to have you!'

He started to carry the frame down the slope, but after a few paces it jerked from his hands and flew up into the air. The next thing he knew, it had crashed down over him and he was being pulled by the arms into warmer air.

The pain made him grimace and groan.

'Oh, no you don't, my friend!' Morann said, struggling to close the flapping shutters. 'You have work to do on this side!'

'Gwydion's through there!'

But Morann pushed him back. 'And that's where he has to stay. With Maskull.'

'No!'

Morann flung the window high so it caught in the branches of the oak and hung there out of reach.

Will felt light-headed. *'What are you doing?'*

Willow was staring with horror at the wound in his side. 'Oh, Will, look at you!'

He tried to brush away her ministering hands.

'Don't you see how it must be, Will? You have your own task. We haven't come all this way to see you fail. Your entire life has been leading to this moment. You owe it to yourself and to the rest of us to do your best. Succeed or fail, that's all we ask.'

That brought him more to his senses. He remembered Gwydion's parting words, and grief had its way with him.

Morann said softly, 'The last time I saw Master Gwydion he told me that I might have my work cut out with you when the end-time came. He said he'd been feeling for a long time that a sacrifice might be called for, maybe on his part, one that you might not want to understand. But it's what he wants. It's what must be. He told me that, Will. He said, "make sure he accepts it the way it must be".'

Three horses stood together under the tree. The pack-mare stamped her feet and champed her bit, and one of the others whinnied. The little birds sang, and all was as a morning should be, except for the distant sound of guns and the glitter of soldiery that frosted the south with steel. There was not much time.

Willow took the dagger and ripped open a bundle. She tore a shirt apart and bound it tightly about Will's middle to staunch the bleeding. He winced as he raised his arms, but dismissed it with, 'I'm all right.'

'You're not all right, you fool!'

'Look at them!' Morann pointed to where Edward's battalions stood ready. 'You saw what happened on the other side. I could smell the bodies from here. That's what happens when Ages end, Will. Worlds collide! There's a time of calamity and men need a hero to carry them past it.'

Will breathed heavily and spat. 'I thought he was dead.'

'Who?'

'Edward. The hero. The king. We heard he'd been mortally wounded. By an arrow at Fordingbridge.'

'It's true enough that Edward's sun is clouded. But he's lying at Castle Pomfret where Gort is tending to him. It's lucky Gort came north with us, for Edward was grievously wounded, but he'll not die now.'

'Or command a battle either. The battlestone is dead. I pushed it into a world where there's no magic.'

'A world much like this one now, eh?' Willow said. 'We don't need magic any more to drive us to war. We've learned how to do that without any help from the fae.'

Morann stabbed a finger into the south. 'Open your eyes and see, Will. It's the Earl Warrewyk who's keeping the battalions in readiness now. He'll lead them to death and glory, Edward or no Edward. No more than an hour ago I saw him leap down from his warhorse. He ran his sword straight through the beast's neck. Aye, then he kissed the blooded hilt out there in front of his whole army. He told them, "Let him fly that will, for surely I will tarry here this day. The coming fight shall be to the death, and any man who means to fly must fly now, or once battle be joined he shall be cut down by his own!" It was hard to take, Will, but you see how it is. There's no shilly-shallying with that man.'

'Then there's to be a battle anyway, battlestone or not?' Will laughed until it hurt. 'The lorc has succeeded after all.'

'Not yet. Look what I brought you! Gort asked for it, and Edward sent it with his blessings.'

Morann went to the packhorse and took down another dirty canvas bundle. When he emptied it onto the grass, armour clattered out. It was Edward's war-gear.

Will laughed shortly. 'He always said he'd see me in the weeds of war. But I must disappoint him. And you.'

'Are you sure about that?'

Will's thoughts juddered back to the world beyond the window, the struggling mass of drowning men, the stream running red with their blood. Could he allow that to happen here? Could he prevent it? He eyed the lines of men who were appearing in the south. Many thousands, many tens of thousands, had come to this impasse. 'Lord Warrewyk will get them all killed, won't he?'

'Aye, he will. Every brave man-jack of them There's so little magic in the world that we can hardly hope for miracles now.'

Will took a proffered gauntlet, looked at it for a moment and threw it down. Willow was kneeling by Chlu, watching for signs that the Dark Child might awaken.

Morann told her, 'I think it's time you explained the real reason we came here.'

Willow looked up at Will. 'We all four of us came north with the army. Me, Morann, Gort and Lotan. We had to find you, to tell you what we'd learned in your absence. The day Edward left Trinovant the Duchess Cicely broke down and told me an important secret.'

'Lady Cicely?' Will asked, unable to see the connection, but suddenly fearing for his daughter. 'Bethe? Has she been harmed?'

Willow was shaking her head, trying to make him understand. 'Bethe's with the Lady Cicely. She's well.'

He blinked back the surge of anxiety. 'Then what's the duchess got to do with anything?'

'Will, listen to me. You have to know this. She once told me she'd had babies that died in childbirth—'

He shook his head, impatient now. Many died in infancy.

'She thought she'd lost two children. One daughter was stillborn, and years before that she gave birth to twins and was told that the first of them had died. But in a letter the duke wrote on the eve of his death he told her different.'

He blinked at Willow, still unable to see what she was driving at.

'Master Gwydion was not the only guide the House of Ebor relied on down the years. When Duke Richard's looked-for firstborn turned out to be twin boys, it was Maskull who came to him first and killed the joy. He whispered that all the duke's hopes for the future of the House of Ebor and for the Realm would be dashed if he refused pragmatic advice.'

'What advice?'

'Maskull said that if Richard succeeded in putting himself on the throne there would be war in the next generation. Inevitable war.'

'He made a threat, you mean?'

'He did not put it that way,' Morann put in. 'He said it was mere expediency. A matter of foresight.'

'*Twins*, Will! You see what that means, don't you? Because who, in the future, would be able to say for certain which child was which? Which boy was firstborn? Which man would be the rightful king? There'd be dispute, and then there'd be strife. Royal brother would fight against royal brother. And after that would come the taking of sides – the Realm split right down the middle. Maskull made it sound as terrible as only Maskull could. And so he convinced Duke Richard of the calamity that was to come. And that allowed the sorcerer to offer him a way out.'

'Which was?'

'Maskull took away one of the children to be cared for elsewhere, while the other child was left to enjoy the privilege of being his father's heir.'

'Edward . . .' Will groaned. 'And all of this was in the letter that Duke Richard wrote on the eve of the battle at Awakenfield?'

Morann nodded. 'Friend Richard wasn't ignoring Mother Brig's prophecy when he rode north. He knew he was going to die. Can you imagine the guilt he must have felt, having kept a secret like that from his wife all these years? And all because he thought there was some chance that one day he might sit upon the throne.'

'Edward was one twin,' Will said, looking up. 'But . . .'

Willow took his hand. 'The other was going to be called Arthur. He was taken away by Maskull. Now do you see?'

Will felt the moment descend over him like cold rain. He gasped, then put his face in his hands.

Morann began to examine Chlu's nose and to wipe away the blood that bubbled at his nostrils. 'Only Maskull didn't take the baby away to be looked after, did he? As Master Gwydion came close to finding out, the very reason Maskull hatched this plot in the first place was to gain control of the true heir. That's why he stole the first-born. And from that child he made you – and this nasty piece of work here.'

They looked down at Chlu wordlessly for a moment.

'What's to be done?' Willow asked.

When Will made no reply, Morann said, 'It's time you despatched him.'

Will took the dagger but he continued to stare at Chlu. He knew now exactly what he must do. 'Not so, Morann. He's nothing evil. He's simply my counterpart. And it's not combat and cruelty that heals the world. It's love.'

His eyes were filling with tears. A great fear was in him. He could feel the end-time roaring in upon him. He kissed Willow and clasped Morann's hand, knowing that the next time he saw them he would be a different man.

There was little time left to compose himself. Chlu had already begun to groan and struggle weakly from his stupor. Now the battlestone was gone, Will felt the diminishing magic of the world more poignantly than ever. He drew scant refreshment from the earth and when a little power was with him he bade the others lift Chlu into his embrace where he whispered a spell of transformation in the true tongue. The spell ended with the word 'Llyw.'

There was a blinding flash of light. For a long time he fell, fell through the world, fell from the spaces between the stars, all the way down into the abysmal deeps. The fall was never-ending, a fall from grace. But then the change came and the blinding light blasted him back into the world, and when he came to, they were looking at him with open mouths and faces filled with wonder.

Strangely, he seemed to feel no different, but it was impossible to judge since there was no single experience in his past with which to compare his present self-hood. The spell he had used was one intended to liberate the spirits of those who were dying in pain.

He tried to sit up, but he could not lift himself. He felt as though his head and his limbs had been encased in steel.

There were tears in Willow's eyes as she confirmed that

both Will and Chlu were gone and the conflation of character had taken place. Then she and Morann began to help him to his feet and he saw the reason he had felt himself enclosed in steel. He shone silver from head to toe, for they had arrayed him in Edward's raiment of war.

'Why do you weep?' he asked Willow.

'For the loss of my husband,' she said, avoiding the boldness of his eye. 'This is all so strange.'

'Look at me,' he said. 'I am here.'

'Are you?' she whispered. 'But if you are, you are no longer my Willand. You are Arthur.'

'And all the better for that, I think.' He smiled. 'We lived in disguise once before. We shall grow used to the change.'

She raised her eyes to his. 'But this is no longer a disguise. This is you! You are changed!'

'All men change with time.' He took her hands. 'I think – I hope – that in time you will get used to me.'

She managed to return his smile. 'I hope so too.'

'We have a child,' he said. 'What shall we tell her?'

'The truth, of course!'

He shrugged. 'The truth, then. If you prefer it.'

As he turned he saw Morann looking kindly upon them and he slapped his friend heartily on the shoulder and laughed. 'There, Morann! You shall be my witness. She will have me, she says, new man or no!'

'I shall be more than a witness,' Morann said. 'I shall play the archmage, for look what Master Gwydion has left with us.'

The loremaster drew out from a fold of his robes the ancient crane bag that had been made from the skin of Aiofe long ago. And from the bag he lifted a cloak of shimmering white feathers.

'The swan cloak of King Leir!' Arthur cried, his eyes gleaming with desire. 'Put it on me, for I must wear the White Mantle if I am to show the world that I am king!'

'Then step up here onto this little stone,' Morann said, 'and test yourself against its music.'

And when Arthur looked down he saw that the Stone of Scions lay between the cart ruts that scarred the soil beneath the oak. He stood upon it and Lord Morann, loremaster and archmage for a day, laid the swan cloak about his shoulders and Willow put a hand to her eyes to wipe away her tears.

There was no more time to spend in ceremony, for the drums were beating and two great hosts were on the move. They came forward and spread themselves out in their fighting battalions. Soon the archers among them would be ordered forward and a deadly exchange would begin.

'Come!' Arthur cried, seizing his sallet helm and raising up the royal standard. 'My friends, to the horses! We must seek a parlay.'

'And what if they will not wear it?' Morann said, following him.

'They will wear it,' Arthur said and smiled.

'But for us to go alone? Without hostages? What if we fall to treachery?'

'Lord Morann, faint heart never won fair fight. We know a man among them who we can speak to on friendly terms.'

And so they galloped forward, and soon they were seen and two of Mag's heralds came out to ask what they were about here, between the armies. Not long after these heralds returned to their lines a party of men came out – the Duke of Mells with a retinue of six armed nobles.

Henry of Mells stared in consternation. He murmured fiercely to the man to his left, who was Jasper of Pendrake, 'But you said he had taken a mortal arrow . . .'

'I swear I heard it was so!' one of the other nobles affirmed.

'He is defenceless,' a third said. 'Let us take him now!'

'No!' Jasper said, grasping the man's arm. 'This is a parlay, and my word is given.'

'He killed your father,' Duke Henry reminded him.

'And you killed his.'

Looks sharp as daggers drawn were passed. But then, from the south, came a contending party, also riding under a flag of truce, and headed by Earl Warrewyk. When he saw King Edward he too was astonished.

'Your grace! But . . . but I thought—'

Arthur spoke up. 'Ah, you thought Edward was abed because of an arrow. Well . . . I have surprised everyone, have I not? Come, let us talk, for together we must accomplish an act of mercy and statesmanship, or rue the lost chance for evermore.'

'What is this game you've set afoot, Lord Morann?' Warrewyk demanded, angered by Arthur's answer and even more furious that Edward had turned away from him. 'Statesmanship? What more is there to say? My . . . my liege – have you forgotten that we are here to let our armies speak for us?'

At that remark the Duke of Mells spat fire in return. 'Nor did we come here to sing and dance to you – as soon you shall see! But this is some mischief, some sorcery! My eyes deceive me!'

'My lord,' Arthur told him soothingly. 'There is nothing wrong with your eyes. Do you not both see *and* hear Edward before you? Well, then, you must believe what you see and hear, for if I am not Edward then I must be his twin.'

But the Duke of Mells gathered himself quickly and said, 'It is no matter to me who has charge of the enemy. Whether I speak to Edward or to Warrewyk, my answer will ever be the same.'

Then Arthur spread his hands and amazed them all by nodding. 'That was well said, for which man of honour standing in Henry of Mells' shoes would say a single word different? He is right. He is right to say so.'

They looked to one another with great suspicion, for they were unused to the slightest ground being given freely between Henry of Mells and Edward of Ebor. But Arthur was not finished. He grew both grave and sad. 'Yes, well said indeed, my lord, but now let us all think hard on the matter of fathers, for it is a thorny matter: my father was killed in war. And here stands Jasper of Pendrake, a good man now likewise bereft. And you, my lord of Warrewyk who always bridles to set things right, you are fatherless now too. And you, my Lord of Mells, you who among us lost his father first and so has had longest to taste the bitterness of it. All of us, orphaned by shaft or blade! And which man standing now with our assembled armies has not lost someone dear to him, some person who was most worthy of life? I tell you: if these things be true, then the time for killing is over.'

'Not while you dare to call yourself king,' Duke Henry said, unswayed. 'And what of King Hal in all this fine oratory? You have not yet answered for your treason against him.'

Arthur laughed a great, wholesome laugh. 'Ah, yes, treason. There are numberless treasons loose in the Realm, treasons of every shape and size, I think. And there are almost as many men who have presumed to speak for the king as he has subjects. So, shall we go to Hal and ask him what his heart truly desires? Whatever he says he shall have it with my blessing – that is my promise – whatever it may be.'

Mouths fell open at that, but then Arthur continued.

'Or if we dare speak of Hal's wife . . .' he said delicately. 'Shall we address her latest hopes and fears, for I have heard that she has begun to *change* of late. It's said that she was for a long time under a malign influence, but now that is gone away with the changing of the moon. What think you of that, Friend Henry? Is it true? Has she changed?'

At that, Duke Henry's eyes blazed, for Edward had gone straight to the heart of a great secret. Henry had seen how the failing of Maskull's magic had caused the queen's looks to fade, and with them her ambitions too. Since the withering of her face she wanted only to hide herself away.

Arthur said, 'Lord Warrewyk, consider this idea: I would have a Great Council called today whereat all the nobility of the Realm shall break bread together under this oak tree. All shall sit at this table and we shall discuss what must be done to bring health and happiness to this land . . .'

'We will not sup with traitors,' Duke Henry said sternly.

'Nor we with usurpers!' Lord Warrewyk returned, his face dark with suspicion.

'Well, how then if I make this promise to you?' Arthur said, standing fast between them. 'I will repeat this pledge to all who wish to hear it: that if the nobility here gathered for war will once agree to sit at my table then Edward shall not be king of this Realm for a single day afterwards.'

They stared at him, and all their expectations were shaken to the ground. Arthur talked, and despite themselves the others listened, as two very different worlds began to move apart again. Prophecy had been fulfilled. A piece of new magic had come into play – Arthur himself – and like oil and water, the magicless world and the still-magical one could not tolerate each other. Once the ancient King had been incarnated, his world could no longer be swallowed.

Then the arguments began, and charge followed blame, and claim and counterclaim were hotly levelled, but the subtle steersman, who was not above a little chicanery himself, turned his ship slowly and by degrees, and all the quarrelling crew began to head towards home while hardly knowing they did so. And Arthur began to see how it would be. Talk would replace the spilling of blood. Magic was already beginning to return to the Realm – they could feel his authority.

At his request the noble parties gave their word that no hasty move would be made by either side to precipitate the battle today. They rode out to north and south and began to stand down their armies. Arthur knew that tomorrow a fresh accommodation would be reached, and a week from now he would be wholly in charge of the contending parties. A month from now they would all recognize him as their king, and year on year, the magic would continue to increase. There would be a new Age of peace while he lived.

'Well,' he said to himself as he watched the noblemen go to their soldiers. 'It looks to me as if this war is over.'

EPILOGUE

Standing a little way apart from the diplomacy, Willow had watched great Arthur walk up and down and tell those who would soon become his knights and servants all that he had in mind for the increase of his people once a settlement was in place. And although she knew she would never see her darling Willand again, still she was vastly proud of all that he had done and all he had become. And when the great lords rode away from the parlay on their warhorses Arthur came to her, mightily pleased with himself, and she felt embarrassed at the strangeness of their first kiss. It seemed almost to be a betrayal, yet not quite, for though this man looked so much like Edward, still there was Willand in his movements and in the glint of his eyes.

At last, Arthur turned to Lord Morann and winked confidentially. 'I think she will have me.'

'That's good. But you must give her time.'

'I shall.' Arthur put armoured hands on armoured hips. 'And what will Edward say, I wonder, when he sees my face and learns from me that I have stolen his kingdom out from under him?'

'Before he rises from his sick-bed he will have listened to his mother and read his father's last letter. Edward will support you, Arthur, for if he can't have a father to look up to, the next best thing is an elder brother.'

'Elder by only a few moments.'

'Aye, a few moments, but also a thousand years.'

Arthur laughed and raised his arms and they began to take off his armour. Where Will had been wounded there was only now a pink scar. Willow let go a tear at the sight of it, and Arthur raised her up, saying, 'I'm here. My darling, I'm with you still.'

The moment ripened, as slowly, silently they came to see that in some way Willand was not gone from them forever, for he was in Arthur and in Bethe too.

'I'll miss Master Gwydion though,' Morann said bleakly.

'We all shall,' Willow said, wiping her face.

'But as for the lorc,' Arthur said, rousing them, 'there's better news. For now we have surer knowledge of the pattern on which all the battlestones lie. I shall put all the resources of my Realm into rooting out the danger that remains. Then, as magic returns to the world, I shall have the stones lifted and bound and—'

'Oh, I don't think so,' Morann said smilingly. 'We shan't be having to worry about any of that.' And he took from a fold within his robe the magic crane-skin bag, the one that had belonged to Manannan Mac Lir and to Lugh, then to Cumhal and to Fionn, and latterly to the last phantarch, Gywdion Crowmaster.

'Ah, yes! The crane bag,' Arthur said, his eyes gleaming. 'And what have you in there? Something for me?'

'A thing beyond price.' Morann drew out a simple rolled parchment done up in ribbon. He handed it to Arthur.

'What is it?'

'A gift from King Hal. It was found in his cell at the White Hall, and meant for Master Gwydion, but you may as well have it. Do you recall Hal's strange habits, his dedication to study, his days and nights spent in river-dank cellars among that chaos of rolls and scrolls that lies under the palace? This is his copy of the last lost fragments of a very ancient work – they call it the Black Book of Tara.'

Arthur gazed upon the scroll with wonder. 'The Black Book?'

'Do you remember it?' Willow said. 'Master Gwydion spoke to me of it several times.'

'Yes,' Arthur said. 'Indeed I do! Let me see it!'

He undid the ribbon and opened it. Morann smiled and brought out a bottle from the crane bag. 'It contains a plan of the lorc. And it tells of the places in the Blessed Isle where all the sister-stones may be found, stones that will finally undo the work of the fae. Now I think that calls for a little celebration. Don't you?'

Author's Historical Note

The three books of the Language of Stones cycle are mythic history, and their setting is mythic too, but that does not mean that the setting is not rooted firmly in the real. There is not space here to list all points of interest, but those readers who wish to follow up the place names mentioned in the text will be rewarded for their detective work, since none of them are purely made up.

Geoffrey of Monmouth, the twelfth century monk who virtually single-handedly created the story of Arthur, also wrote about the great city of New Troy, or Troy Novant. Actually the name derives not from Troy, but from the Celtic people called the Trinovantes. They lived, of course, in the lands upon which my own city of London was eventually to rise.

Students of the history of London will recognize much in the detail of my imagined city of Trinovant, for its plan, streets and approaches are intact, an approximation, in fact, to the English capital as it was in the fifteenth century, just as the Realm approximates to the England of that time. There really was a many-gated wall around London and a royal palace once stood at Whitehall. The marshes of Lamb's Hythe eventually became Lambeth, and a great Gothic spire did once rise above the city, but fell long before Spenser wrote of his faerie queene. The Victorians placed cast-iron guardian dragons at the entry points of the City, and they still stand, supporting their red-and-white shields on which the red sword is depicted.

From London, the Great North Road ran through England by various ways up to Newcastle upon Tyne and beyond. Anyone travelling along the present A1 goes for much of the way along the Great North Road. By the fifteenth century a trade in coal, hewn on Tyneside, was running in the opposite direction, except that the real wyrmstone went by sea.

Lincolnshire is the county in which Stamford, (rather than Stammerford), stands. The town lies to the east of old Rutland, England's smallest county, now, alas, mostly submerged beneath a lake. The real 'Duke Richard' was Richard of York. His second son was given the title Earl of Rutland. The Cecil family, owners of Burleigh House, did rather better for themselves in this world than their counterparts in Will's.

Richard of York's unsuccessful quest to become king led to the bloody battles of Wakefield and Towton, (both in Yorkshire, and the latter in the ancient kingdom called Elmet.) These battles were separated by the battle at Mortimer's Cross (Shakespeare's battle of three suns) at which the meteorological phenomenon known as a parhelion occurred. It was at this battle that the future king Edward IV defeated the Lancastrians under Jasper Tudor.

It is a curious fact, and one which led to the first ideas for the trilogy, that if the dozen or so biggest Wars of the Roses battle sites are plotted on a map of England and Bosworth Field is included – since it can be seen as the battle which finished that terrible war – then three concentric triangles can be drawn through all but a couple of them. I extended the lines of these triangles to create the system of ligns called in the books 'the lorc'.